D1436477

WE SAW THE SEA
and
DOWN THE HATCH

Also by

JOHN WINTON

★

WE JOINED THE NAVY

WE SAW THE SEA

and

DOWN THE HATCH

*

JOHN WINTON

THE COMPANION BOOK CLUB
LONDON

We Saw the Sea © *copyright 1960 by John Winton*
Down the Hatch © *copyright 1961 by John Winton*

Made and printed in Great Britain
for The Companion Book Club (Odhams Press Ltd.)
by Odhams (Watford) Limited
Watford, Herts
S.1062.V.QR.

CONTENTS

★

WE SAW THE SEA

★ I ★

THE corridor was long and damp and painted a dark brown; it smelled of disinfectant and, in places, of cats. The high windows in one wall were grimy and the tiled floors were battered and chipped. Walking along, Michael Hobbes thought of a Crimean hospital before the advent of Florence Nightingale. The doors were painted an even darker brown and were numbered, according to a notice by the stairs, from 37 to 61. Michael was reassured that he was on the right floor, despite the hall porter's ambiguous instructions. He was looking for Room 51.

The room next to Room 50 was unmarked, but Michael knocked confidently. He could hear no answer. Slowly he opened the door.

The room was dark except for a single unshaded light bulb burning over a table covered with a green baize cloth. A pair of empty red rubber gloves lay on the table, their fingers and thumbs touching, as though they were in the act of strangling a phantom throat. The room was silent, menacing, like the lair of a savage beast which had only just left and would presently return.

Michael shut the door and tried the next room. It was clearly marked—"ROOM 51 KNOCK ONCE AND WAIT IF NO ANSWER DON'T BOTHER." Michael knocked once and waited. Just as he was deciding not to bother, he heard a voice calling from inside.

"How many *more* times do I have to say 'Come *in*'?" the voice demanded irritably.

Michael went into the room. By the window, a short red-faced man with ginger hair was putting on his overcoat. He slewed round, his overcoat still hanging from his shoulders, and glared at Michael.

"Well?"

"My name is Lieutenant Hobbes, sir, I . . . ."

"I suppose you've come about your next appointment?"

"Yes, sir."

"Hah. Well sit down then, sit down Godblas*tit*."

The ginger-haired man put on his overcoat fully, wound a scarf round his neck, placed a hat on his head, and sat down opposite Michael.

Michael glanced round the office. There was nothing in the room except the desk, with a chair on either side, and a large filing cabinet in one corner. On the desk a placard read, in gothic printing—"Commander J. P. Leanover, R.N., General Dogsbody and Chief Bottle Washer for any Civil Servant who opens his Fool Mouth." Another placard at the other end read—"Beer Is Best." Between the two placards lay a pair of leather gloves, one blank sheet of paper and four trays marked "Aye Aye," "No No," "Passing," and "Waiting—too Difficult." Three of the trays were empty but the fourth, "Waiting—Too Difficult," contained a copy of *The Times*, open at the crossword.

"What did you say your name was?"

"Hobbes, sir."

Commander Leanover took out a ballpoint pen. Slowly and carefully, as though unused to writing, he printed "Holmes" on the blank sheet of paper.

"Just finished Greenwich haven't you?"

"That was some time ago, sir . . ."

"Enjoy it?"

"Very much, sir."

"Nonsense. Only queers and alcoholics enjoy Greenwich. What sort of ship d'you want?"

"I'd like to go to a des . . ."

"Like to go to a carrier, eh?"

"No, sir. I'd rather go to a des . . ."

"Battleship? We haven't got any, anyway." Commander Leanover chuckled. "Come on then, what sort of ship d'you want?"

"I was rather hoping it would be a . . ."

"Like to go to a cruiser?"

"I'd prefertogotoadestroyersir," Michael gabbled.

"Hah." Commander Leanover printed "Not Cruiser— Destroyer" on the sheet of paper.

"I heard *Carousel* was just commissioning, sir . . ."

10

"Never you mind about her. She's commissioned already and anyway we only send people there who're halfway round the bend to start with. Completes the process. Still, you don't want a cruiser, do you?"

"No, sir."

Commander Leanover printed *Carousel* and then, as an afterthought, firmly crossed out "cruiser." As he did so, a telephone on the floor, behind the desk where Michael had not noticed it, began to ring. Commander Leanover shot out a foot and the telephone skidded along the bare boards to the limit of its lead. By a miracle the receiver remained on the rest and the telephone continued to ring.

"Godblastit," Commander Leanover muttered. He pulled the telephone towards him by its lead and growled into it.

"Speak up! Yes. Speaking. Mr Smith-Smythe, if you will tell one of your assistants to bring his small pointed head up to my office this afternoon I'll give him a whole filing cabinet *full* of correspondence."

Commander Leanover jammed the telephone down and kicked it back to the limit of the lead. Then he stared unbelievingly at Michael.

"What did you say your name was?"

"Hobbes, sir. H-O-B-B . . ."

"All right all right. No need to spell it. I've got it."

Commander Leanover crossed out "Holmes" and wrote "Hogg." He leaned back and gazed at Michael triumphantly.

"Tell you what Hogg, if there's a chance of a destroyer in the next few days I'll give you first shot at it. How's that?"

"That's fine, sir! Thank you very much! But my name . . ."

"Good, first come first served. Now what was your name again. Just to make sure I've got it right."

"Hobbes, sir."

"Of course."

Painstakingly, with his tongue between his teeth, Commander Leanover wrote.

"*Right*, Hobbes. That's all. We always try to give people what they want. I wish you the very best of luck."

"Thank you very much, sir."

"Don't thank me. We're only here to help chaps like you. Not like the civil servants. Do you know what a civil servant had the bareface gall to tell *me* the other day?"

"No, sir?"

"He said 'Of course, you know, we always look upon the Navy as just the "ships and men" side of the Admiralty.' The sauce! B-loody pen-pusher!"

Commander Leanover stood up and held out his hand. "We're always glad to see people from sea here. Reminds us that there is a purpose in life. Don't disturb them in the torture chamber next door as you go. They're making out the new pay code in there."

Michael shook hands with Commander Leanover and found his way back through the corridors, down the stairs and out into the bright Westminster sunshine.

Commander Leanover looked at the sheet of paper which now, through a mass of deletions, read—"Hobbes not destroyer—*Carousel*," slipped it into his top drawer, and took out a pair of binoculars which he slung round his neck, settled his hat on his head, drew on his gloves, turned the notice on his door round to "TOO LATE" and sauntered leisurely towards lunch. At his table he tried to remember. What in hell was that keen young man's name again. Hooper? Holland? Surely not Hotchkiss? Never mind, it was all on the sheet of paper. Commander Leanover happily ordered cottage pie and thanked God for the gift of a methodical mind.

Glowing like a successful diplomat, Michael walked up Victoria Street to Westminster. At Parliament Square he turned into Storey's Gate and so into St James's Park.

The trees had already begun to strip themselves for the winter. The bare grey bones of buildings stood up through the thinning branches and the paths in the park were piled with leaves where the keepers had swept them. It was the time of year when the starlings whirled earlier every evening in Trafalgar Square beneath a cherry red glow in the sky and the frost tingle in the mornings brought a stiffening of the spirit and a bracing of the muscles to resist the coming winter.

Michael walked along beside the lake, up to the Mall

and through Green Park. There were telephone booths at Hyde Park Corner.

"May I speak to Miss Mary Bendix, please?"

"Michael darling, it *is* me!"

"Oh hullo. How are you?"

"Don't you know my voice after all this time?"

"Well, I always want to make sure. Did you know you could walk from Westminster to Kensington Palace in parks all the way? That's miles."

"Darling Michael, that's not an original thought."

"It is for me. People are always telling me London is all houses and it's not true."

"Was that what you telephoned me for?"

"Not really. I was going to ask you, would you like to come and have lunch with me?"

"Oh Michael, I *did* tell you, I'm having lunch with a girl friend today. I'm *sure* I told you. She's going to South Africa next week for a year and I promised I'd have lunch with her before she went."

"Oh, all right."

"But I expect it'll be all right for you to come when we've finished. It's that place in Conduit Street I told you about, where all the girls go for lunch. Do you want to come?"

"Good God no."

"I'll see you tonight then?"

"What's happening tonight?"

"Darling, don't sound so *suspicious*! It's Sonia's party. You remember, the girl I used to share a flat with."

"Oh God yes, I remember her. Tall girl with black hair and come-to-bed eyes always saying 'since Daddy got his title.'"

"Miaouw."

"Well, it *is* what she's always saying."

"I know, but it's catty to mention it."

"Are you sure you can't have lunch with me?"

"Quite sure, darling. I promised her."

"Oh well, I'll see you tonight then."

"Yes."

"Mary?"

13

"Yes."

"I love you."

"I love you too, Michael. Aren't we lucky? See you tonight."

The party was in a five-storeyed house in Earls Court which had been split into several small flats. Sonia's flat was on the top floor but Michael and Mary could hear the sounds of the party as they came up the stairs.

"What's this party for, anyway?" Michael asked.

"It's a house-warming party. Sonia gives one every time she gets a new flat. And she normally has to get a new flat after every house-warming party so she moves around a bit."

"I wonder if one bottle will be enough?"

They had to force their way through the room. Michael could see nobody he knew. A gramophone was humming unintelligibly in one corner. Next to it, a couple were swaying backwards and forwards, their arms clasped about each other's necks. On a sofa along one wall another couple were sitting, their faces invisible. There was no sign of Sonia.

"Shall we bother to say hullo to Sonia?" Michael asked.

"She's in the bathroom with a Royal Fusilier if you want her," a tall young man said, over his shoulder. "Well, if it isn't Mary! And you've brought your tame admirer with you."

"Oh, don't be so unpleasant, Stephen," Mary said.

It was the first time Michael had seen Stephen since the party, almost six years before, when he first met Mary. Stephen was even bigger and more self-assured than Michael remembered him. He was wearing a brocade waistcoat embroidered with chrysanthemums; it seemed to Michael that chrysanthemums were Stephen's trademark, what George Dewberry would have called his leitmotiv.

"We're supposed to congratulate Stephen, Michael," Mary said.

"Whatever for?"

Stephen laughed the laugh which so infuriated Michael. "I've just been made *Naval* Correspondent."

"Not of the 'Daily Disaster'?"

"S'right. The word came down from Mount Sinai that

14

we shall have a Naval Correspondent again. The question was, who? There was some talk about getting a retired N.O. for the job, but they're always awkward. They insist on the *details* always being right and they're ashamed to look their old chums in the face. I said I'd done my National Service in the Navy so they gave me the job."

"Perhaps now you're a correspondent you'd like to know something about the Navy . . ."

"Don't fuss yourself, old man. The last one had the job for twenty years and never set foot in a ship in his life. He used to do the chess paragraph. That kept him occupied except on Navy Days or when some Admiral appeared in court when he put in a bit of overtime."

"Are you in the Navy?" asked the girl who had been talking to Stephen.

"Anne, my dear!" said Stephen as though he had forgotten all about her, "I quite forgot! You haven't met Michael and Mary. The biggest thing since Romeo and Juliet! It's taken them a hell of a long time but they're there now. Anne, this is Mary and the chap with the Players Please expression who looks as if he'd like to assault me is Michael. Michael does spend his off moments in the Navy. It's a living."

Anne was a very pretty girl with dark wavy hair, deep blue eyes and a short turned-up nose. She looked innocent and eager to please. Michael wondered where she had met Stephen.

"My brother was in the Navy," Anne said.

"Oh?" Michael was not surprised. Everyone he met had a brother or a cousin or a friend in the Navy; or else a sister, cousin or friend in the Wrens. It was always strange that Michael had never met them; their name was Smith and they were based at Portsmouth.

"Was he doing his National Service in the Navy?" Michael asked politely.

"Oh no, he was going to make it his career. Only he was drowned when he was a cadet."

"What was your brother's name?" Michael asked slowly, with a terrible inkling.

"Ted Maconochie. Did you know him?"

"He was in my term."

"*Was* he. Then you know what happened?"

"Honestly, Anne . . ."

"Michael *please*! We had a telegram from the Admiralty and the Captain of the ship wrote to Daddy and then we had a sweet letter from someone called Lieutenant Commander Badger and then nothing more."

"Oh, I remember this," Stephen said. "We had a picture of the capsized boat on the middle page and . . ."

"*Shut up* Stephen!" Mary said fiercely.

Michael was surprised to discover that he was still able, after so long a time, to be shocked by the memory of Ted Maconochie's death. He remembered now the dark sky, the waves crashing in their faces, Paul Vincent counting the heads, Tom Bowles's face, and the Australian Cartwright staying underwater longer than any of them and coming up without Maconochie. He described for Anne her brother's death.

". . . The boat just capsized and he didn't come up with the rest of us," he ended lamely. He was horrified to see the tears in Anne's eyes.

"He was so keen on the Navy," Anne said. "He was going to do so well. When his *Uniform* came . . . I thought Mummy was going to die of pride."

"Yes, well. . . ." Matters were now beyond Michael's control. He thrust his hand through his hair and looked distractedly round the room. The couple by the gramophone had broken away from each other.

"Excuse me," Michael said. "I think there's someone over there I know."

"Michael!" Mary put her hand on his arm. "You're not going?"

"Be back in a minute."

Michael pushed through to the gramophone.

"Hullo Paul."

"*Michael!* You old son of a gun! How are you? How's the great romance going? It's good to see you again, Mike."

Paul Vincent was older and more handsome. His hair was greying and he had lines by his mouth and at the corners of his eyes. He was the only man present not wearing a lounge suit. He wore a red sweater, grey slacks and a black scarf. He reminded Michael of the leader of a French underground resistance cell.

"Never mind anything just now, Paul. You see that girl over there talking to Mary? She's Ted Maconochie's sister and I'm in trouble talking about that damn boat."

"She's very good-looking."

"For God's sake, Paul, come and help me out."

Recognizing an emergency, Paul dropped his partner and crossed the room with Michael.

"Anne, I'd like you to meet a good friend of mine, Paul Vincent. He's also in the Navy and he was, in fact, in that boat too. He plays cricket for the Navy as well and . . . um Paul, this is Anne."

Accelerating swiftly from Michael's rather clumsy start, Paul took charge. He changed the subject and quickly changed Anne's tears to smiles.

"Thank God for that," Michael breathed. "Trust him to notice her perfume. I wish I had half his finesse."

Mary brushed a lock of hair from Michael's forehead. "Never mind darling. I love you just as you are. You couldn't help that just now. It was very bad luck. And at least Paul's got rid of Stephen."

Paul appeared beside them carrying a couple of drinks.

"My!" he said, "Fancy old Ted having a sister. I would have thought she would have been some little horror who accused respectable men in court of having raped her and had crushes on the games mistress."

"I had a crush on my games mistress," Mary said. "I was absolutely sponk on her."

"You were *what*?"

"*Sponk!*"

"Oh, did you have that word at your school too, Mary?"

"Yes!"

Mary and Anne together fell into a fit of giggling.

"You'd better have this drink, Mike," Paul said. "The distaff side appear to be getting their intoxication by mutual support. Now tell me, what have you been doing with yourself since I last saw you?"

"Nothing wildly exciting. I thought of being a submariner

but they were over-subscribed so I went as Pilot of *Octopus* doing Portland running for a year. Then I went to a coastal minesweeper and now I'm waiting for a new job. I hope to do a long 'N' course sometime."

"And what about all the others? I've been tucked away so long learning about engineering that I've got completely out of touch. I haven't seen a CW. List for two years."

"Tom Bowles and Ike Smith are both pilots. Tom's at Lee and I think Ike's just gone out to the Med. Raymond Ball's a submariner in Australia. Freddie Spink is somebody's assistant secretary in Hong Kong and George Dewberry is in Japan. What he's doing there I can't imagine. Colin Stacforth is Flags to C.-in-C. Rockall and Malin Approaches and Pete Cleghorn is Pilot in *Vertigo*. He's engaged now."

"Not to that barmaid?"

"You heard about that? No, some admiral's offspring, I heard."

"That's more like Pete. Incidentally, this is something I *do* know hot from the press. Have you heard about The Bodger?"

"No? What about him?"

"Passed over!"

"*What!*"

"It's a fact. Someone told me it was the report he got from *Barsetshire* that did it."

"But I thought he was the blue-eyed boy there!"

"So he was, but you remember what a mad-house that ship was. The Bodger was getting on a stinker until one day about a year after we left when old Gregson suddenly announced that he wanted all cadets to be taught how to breed red setters as part of their syllabus."

"Name of a *name*!"

"Precisely. The Bodger gave a merry laugh and then suddenly realized that the Old Man was deadly serious. It was just after a mess dinner, The Bodger had just listened to Dickie Gilpin sounding off about the Yellow Peril, he had a few grogs under his belt, so The Bodger ups and tells old Gregson that he had no objection whatsoever to cadets being taught how to breed red setters, he wondered nobody had thought of it before, they could breed red setters, white setters and sky blue pink setters for all he cared but until the appropriate B.R.s arrived he was going to stick to the syllabus as laid down."

"Cor, the Old Man wouldn't like that."

"Man, that's the understatement of the year. Gregson retired in a huff and when he came to write up The Bodger's confidential report he not only underlined it in red he wrote the whole damn lot in red ink. So that was that. *There* was a Caesar, when comes such another? I saw in the C.W. List yesterday that he's been appointed Resident Naval Officer in Nassau."

"Well, that should suit The Bodger."

"Not that Nassau. The one in the Cook Islands. In the South Pacific."

"God."

"It's rugged luck all right. You know, Mike, the more I look at it the more I'm convinced that to succeed in the Service you've got to humour madmen. Now if The Bodger had said 'Certainly sir, and as you're our only expert at the moment on breeding red setters, would you mind giving the first lectures until the official books arrive and the rest of us get into the routine?' or words to that effect, the old boy would have been tickled pink and instead of being passed over The Bodger would probably be a Captain himself by now."

"By the way," Michael said, "did you see that our old friend Dickie Gilpin got promoted to Captain?"

"Yes, and from what I hear he's all set to go through for Fleet Board for Admiral, and heaven help anyone who stands in his way. All set to be First Sea Lord when the time comes. They already call him The Dauphin up at the Admiralty, I gather. My name is Richard St Clair Gilpin, what's *your* hobby, just about describes him."

"Someone told me he got married recently."

"Yes, guess who to? Seamus Dogpit's daughter. You remember Seamus, the old buffer at the Interview. Dickie never misses a trick."

"Something tells me we're being a bit catty. As bad as women in fact."

"Have you two quite finished talking shop?" Mary asked.

"Quite finished, my dear Mary," Paul said, "and as this is a deadly party, I can't think what's happened to Sonia since she teamed up with that fellow in the Fusiliers, her parties always used to be good for at least one rape and a couple of unnatural offences to speak of nothing better, she's quite gone to the dogs, I think we'll all say our tender good-byes and hop round to the Grenadier for a pint with the proletariat. Coming, Anne?"

"But Paul, I came with Stephen."

"So?"

"I can't just go aff and leave him."

"Why ever not? That's what boy-friends are for. No self-respecting girl ever expects to be taken away from a party by the man who brought her. No girl except Mary, that is. You *are* self-respecting, aren't you, Mary? She always comes with Michael and wherever they go they sit and make eyes at each other and tell each other it's too good to last and a very good line it is too. Breaks the shock when it comes."

Paul took Anne firmly by the hand and forced his way over to the door. Michael and Mary caught him up as he was saying his tender good-byes.

"*Dear* Sonia," he was saying, "if you must live in sin with the brutal and licentious Fusiliery you might at least preserve the decencies and make him take his shaving soap out of your wash-cabinet. Of course I looked. I always look. Good-bye all."

"Is he always like this?" Anne asked Michael.

"Never mind, he's not serious."

"Oh, I don't mind."

Michael groaned.

"Come on," Paul said. "Stop dithering and we might have time for what my old friend Raymond Ball used to call a little bit of *je ne sais quoi.*"

"What's that, Paul?" Anne asked.

"Never you mind. Ask and it shall be given unto you, seek and ye shall find."

Michael groaned again.

20

2

INSIDE the Admiralty, big wheels moved, small wheels spun and tiny wheels made tea. The mighty organism gave a shiver and a heave and belched forth a buff envelope which dropped through the Hobbes's front door and expired on the door mat.

The envelope contained a loose folder of papers which gave Michael Hobbes some diverting reading.

The first sheet informed Michael that he should already have been inoculated, vaccinated or otherwise safeguarded against cholera, typhoid, typhus, yellow fever, tetanus and dysentery. The reverse side of the sheet listed times and places in Newcastle where injections were given. Across the bottom of the page a rubber stamp asked of Michael: "Has your baby been immunized?"

Next was a memo from A.D. of A.M.R.O.B. (C) to Ass. P. Sec. CINC EASTMED STRIKLANTNORD. It was hand-written in green ink and enquired—"What time does Mugsy usually get back from lunch?"

The third and fourth sheets were cuttings from *The Sporting Times* giving the runners, jockeys and ante-post prices at Bogside, Lingfield and Pontefract.

The contents of the folder were completed by a copy of the Highway Code, an F.A. Cup Final programme, a packet of Jescot Jim dahlia seeds and a coloured picture of St Stephen the Martyr being stoned.

The whole collection of papers gave the impression that it had been compiled by a civil servant about to go on holiday who had thought it an excellent opportunity to clear out his trays.

The last and smallest piece of paper, which had been left behind when Michael tipped out the rest, informed Michael that he was appointed Lieutenant, Royal Navy, to H.M.S. *Carousel*, additional for passage and vice Rowlands, to join H.M.T. *Astrakhan* in uniform at Southampton catching the boat train leaving Waterloo at noon. He was to acknowledge receipt of these instructions *forthwith* to the Director of Movements, Admiralty, and to the

Commanding Officer, H.M.S. *Carousel*, taking care to furnish his address.

Michael rang up Mary.

"Hullo, is that you?" Michael sometimes wished he was more fluent at starting telephone conversations.

"Yes, it's me, darling, how are you?"

"I'm fine, how are you?"

"You don't sound fine. Has something happened?"

"My thing from the Admiralty has come."

"Oh Michael. What is it?"

"It's *Carousel*. A cruiser. At least, I suppose you could call it a cruiser."

"Where is she? In the Home Fleet?"

"No, she's gone out to the Far East."

"The Far East! *Michael!*"

"I know. . . ."

"When do you have to go?"

"Now don't get all worked up about it. . . ."

"*When*, Michael?"

"The seventeenth. A week on Friday."

"A *week*!"

"Yes. Honestly Mary, there's no need to get all steamed up just because. . . ."

Michael at last hung up quickly, knowing that Mary was about to burst into tears. He felt vaguely piqued by her attitude; anyone would think he was going on a suicide mission of no return instead of taking up a perfectly normal appointment in a perfectly normal ship which happened to be at the other end of nowhere. Michael went away to look up Hong Kong in the atlas.

Paul Vincent received his appointment by the afternoon post. His had no gay portfolio attachments but consisted of a single sheet of paper: Paul was appointed Lieutenant (E), Royal Navy, to H.M.S. *Carousel*, additional for passage and vice Cardew. The appointment was written in stern handwriting, with hard vicious strokes of the pen, as though it had been written by a civil servant just returned from holiday.

Paul read the appointment watched by his mother and Cedric, her stockbroker. Mrs Vincent was not pleased when she was told.

"Far East!" she said. "They must be mad! The Van Baxters will be furious. I promised them we would all be at Sandra's wedding. I'm going to give Seamus a ring and tell him not to be such an idiot! What was the name of the ship that *stupid* man at the Admiralty promised you, darling? Now, I wonder what Seamus's number is? I used to know them all. . . ."

"Mother," Paul said firmly, "you'll telephone your boy-friends at the Admiralty over my dead body."

"And over mine," said Cedric heartily.

"Cedric!"

"I'm sorry Louise, but for once I entirely agree with your son. It would be most bad policy to approach anyone at the Admiralty over this. It would smack of nepotism, and rightly so. In any case, it will do Paul a power of good to serve in the Far East. Put the fear of God into the Chinks too, I've no doubt."

Paul wanted to tell Anne the news immediately but there were disadvantages to telephoning her. She had only just passed her secretarial examinations and worked in a room full of girls under the supervision of a lady called Mrs Grant. Mrs Grant watched over her girls as zealously as though they were inmates of a Turkish seraglio and she allowed no private telephone calls during working hours and *certainly* none from young men. While Mrs Grant knew of no case where a seduction had actually taken place over the telephone she knew of many where the telephone had been the means to the end; she was determined that hers would be one typists' pool at least which would not feature in the Sunday newspapers.

On second thoughts, Paul considered that it was worth trying. This was a special occasion, after all.

Paul dialled and waited. The telephone was answered by a Wagnerian voice which could only belong to Mrs Grant.

"The RossCommon-Rogers Copying Agency," boomed The Voice, as though it were announcing the twilight of the gods.

"Is that Mrs Grant speaking?"

"It is."

"Mrs Grant, how nice to have the opportunity of

23

speaking to you! I've heard so much about you. . . ."

"Young man, what do you want?"

"Well, I really wanted to speak to Miss Maconochie. . . ."

"Certainly not!"

"Please let me explain, Mrs Grant. This is her brother speaking and I have something to tell her which is extremely delicate and private. There's been some trouble. . . ."

"I *see*," said Mrs Grant, in an ominous voice.

"Oh no, it's nothing like that, I can assure you. . . ."

"Like *what*, young man?"

"It's something she should know right away, ma'am. I'm sure you would understand if you knew the whole story."

"Very well," Mrs Grant said in a mollified tone. "Who shall I say is calling?"

"Mr Vin-Maconochie. Just say it's Paul calling, please."

"Paul?"

"Yes please, ma'am."

Paul noticed that the clicking of typewriters in the background had stopped. He heard Mrs Grant calling out Anne's name. He could imagine the other girls staring at each other at this unprecedented breach of the pool's regulations. Then he heard Anne, breathless and nervous.

"Paul, you clown, I told you not. . . ."

"Quiet, wench. We have matters of great pith and moment to discuss. First let me say that I love you. . . ."

"*Paul*," Anne whispered desperately, "they're all looking at me."

"Let 'em look. Honey, my appointment has come. It's to *Carousel*. She's in the Far East."

"The Far East!"

"Don't shout. They're all listening to you too, I don't doubt. Meet me tonight and I'll tell you all about it. By the statue of Richard the Lionheart."

"Paul, where on earth's that?"

"Six o'clock. Don't be late. Cedric's giving a party tonight and he's invited us. No more now, Mrs Grant will be pawing at the deck and champing. I love you very much. Good-bye."

"But Paul. . . ."

"Remember Mrs Grant!"

Paul hung up with a sense of a mission well accomplished.

He had broken the Grant Barrier, compared with which the sound barrier was a mere hurdle, he had told Anne he loved her and he had arranged to meet her that evening. Romeo himself could have done no more.

Anne finished work at half-past five. She repaired her make-up, washed her hands, telephoned her mother to say she would be late, bought a new lipstick and asked a policeman the way to the statue of Richard the Lionheart and arrived at ten minutes past six. She was annoyed when she discovered that the statue was near her office on Millbank and she must have passed Paul at least once but she did not allow him to notice it.

"Come on," said Paul, brusquely. "We're picking Michael and Mary up on the way and they're always early."

"I'm sorry I'm late, Paul."

"That's all right. Most girls would have still been looking. Who is this person Mrs Grant? Anyone would think I was trying to ring up the Kremlin!"

"Oh, she was sweet when you rang off. She wanted to know if I was in any trouble and could she help. I hadn't the heart to deceive her so I told her about you. She wishes you luck."

"That's big of her."

"She said she guessed what was going on but she liked your voice, although she didn't believe a word you said."

Paul breathed over his knuckles and brushed them on his lapel. He was flattered to be told that he could charm women over the telephone.

"Bully for Mrs Grant," he said. "I told Michael that we'd meet them outside St Martin-in-the-Fields. I insisted on meeting you here and he insisted on meeting Mary where he always meets her so we split the difference. He's a most unoriginal chap. He always meets his woman in the same old place. He must know the pavement outside Swan and Edgars like the back of his hand."

Anne felt a momentary twinge of envy. She would have loved to have been a woman who always met Paul in the same old place.

Michael and Mary were waiting on the steps of St Martin's amongst the home-rushing crowds, the pigeons overhead, and the newspaper sellers shouting their curious international language.

"Right," said Paul. "Let's get a bus *du côté de chez Cedric.*"

Cedric lived in Stanhope Gate with his butler Thomas and his collections. Cedric was a kleptomaniac, though in perfect taste, and his collections were famous. His collection of glassware and drinking cups rested in Hepplewhite cabinets and enjoyed an international reputation. Cedric had champagne glasses of venetian glass, waxed leather blackjacks with silver rims, enamelled humpers, Georgian pewter tankards, and a scintillating array of punchbowls, chalices, tumblers and sets of glasses of soda metal and glass of lead with their stems fluted, chased, knobbed, serpentine, quatre-foiled and engraved. Cedric's collection was a museum dedicated to the art of drinking; his friends from the London clubs made pious pilgrimages to see it. *Country Life* published an article on it and thereafter Cedric received letters from elderly ladies in Perth, Western Australia, enquiring whether his collection included the Holy Grail and postcards from schoolgirls in Weston-super-Mare asking if he possessed the human skull from which Darius, the Great King of Persia, was wont to drink the blood of his slaughtered enemies.

Cedric had other collections, of snuff boxes, dragon china, walking-sticks, bullfight posters, Japanese armour, spinning-wheels and clockwork toys. He also had a large collection of friends whom he was pleased to invite to his house and to whom he explained his collections with their histories. Cedric was erudite without being pedantic and an arbiter of good manners who still preferred champagne from a tankard because it brought out the flavour. "Like Dr Johnson," Paul said, "only not so fat and argumentative."

Cedric himself met them at the door. He looked sternly at Michael.

"Never get into a habit with one woman, my boy," he said. "Before you know where you are you'll wake up and find yourself married to them and there's no greater habit than that. You may laugh. I've seen it happen too often."

Thomas, Cedric's butler, who looked and spoke like an

ex-flyweight champion of Donegal, poured sherry and madeira from cut-glass decanters which were part of the collection and Mrs Vincent, wearing a flame-coloured dress with a high collar, took Michael under her wing.

"Paul, darling you know lots of people, but you don't, Michael, so let me introduce you. Let's see. There's that round man from the B.B.C. whose name I can never remember. He won't do. The Admiralty have just banned his book about the Wrens. Then there's that big stuffed dummy who advertises that nauseating whisky . . . I know."

Mrs Vincent led Michael and Mary towards a tall man who was standing next to one of the most beautiful women Michael had ever seen but who was looking quizzically at his glass as though he were wondering how soon he could get it refilled. The man looked up as Michael approached. The face was unmistakable. It was Lieutenant Commander Robert Bollinger Badger, Royal Navy, otherwise known as The Bodger.

"Good God," The Bodger said. "It's Hobbes."

"Of course," said Mrs Vincent. "I'd forgotten you knew each other."

"*Know* him," said The Bodger, "I brought him up! How are you, Hobbes? How are you, Mary? I remember you from some time ago. Julia, you haven't met these two young people. This is Mary and this is Lieutenant Michael Hobbes. My wife, Julia."

"How do you do, Michael," Julia said. "You must be one of the cadets who gave Robert his grey hairs!"

"I hope not, ma'am."

Michael may have been rather naïve for his age, he may still have been shy and awkward when meeting a woman for the first time, but he had the true naval officer's instinct for a beautiful woman. He recognized a superb specimen when he saw one and Julia, The Bodger's wife, was the kind of woman at whom Michael would have unabashedly goggled in the street. She was almost as tall as her husband with jet black hair swept up to a coronet of curls. Her figure inside her black dress, her white shoulders, full red lips and black eyes with long lashes made Michael feel vaguely yearning. She looked perfectly composed; Michael could not imagine her ever being put out by anything. She would entertain midshipmen and admirals; cope with the water supply and the servants in a Maltese flat; and be hostess to the Royal Family without raising her voice.

The Bodger noticed Michael's face and the circle of men who were beginning to converge upon his wife, and grinned widely.

"You look surprised to see me, Hobbes," he said.

Michael recollected himself. "I am a little, sir. I thought you were in the South Pacific."

"The *what*?"

Michael blushed. "I must have made a mistake, sir. I thought you were R.N.O. in Nassau."

The Bodger let out a roar of Rabelaisian laughter which reminded Michael vividly of many occasions at Dartmouth and in *Barsetshire*.

"Did you really think I was off to be a beachcomber, Hobbes? Actually, you're partly right, I *did* get a draft chit to the South Seas and it gave me furiously to think for a while. However, there was one very simple way out of that. Julia and I went into this question of the South Seas in a big way. We drew up piles of graphs about copra and pearls and black men generally. We had statistics about the rainfall in Fiji and the number of red-headed men in Tonga and so on. It took the little Wren in my office some time to type it all. Then I sat down and wrote an official letter to the Admiralty recommending that an N.O. be appointed to look after this hive of industry. I damn soon got an answer saying that Their Lordships did not see any operational requirement for an N.O. in Nassau. After that, I went to see Jerry Leanover, an old chum of mine at the Admiralty, and that was that. It's just another case of what I was always telling you blokes about. There's always a way of making the other chap do what you want him to do without realizing it, if you'll only take the trouble to sit down and think about it!"

"Where are you going now, then, sir?"

"*Carousel*, as First Lieutenant and Defence Officer."

"Good heavens, Vincent and I are going to *Carousel* as well, sir."

"I've no doubt we shall meet a lot of friends there," the Bodger said. "I know the Commander, Jimmy Forster-Jones, very well indeed, and there's Ginger Piggant, as Senior Engineer and of course, Dickie Gilpin as Captain. The chap I'm supposed to be relieving was carted away in a strait-jacket a fortnight ago I hear. He had a nervous breakdown trying to sort out the messdecks. There's been so much special gear fitted in that ship, all of it in messdeck space, and none of it ever taken out. One of these days, probably in about two hundred years time, the boffins will get around to designing a special type of human being to live in warships. They'll all be about two feet high with arms six feet long. They'll never need anything to eat or drink. They won't even need air to breathe. They won't have families to give trouble, nor will they need mail, nor *leave*. They'll have about one hour's sleep a night when they'll put out a long prehensile tail and hook up on rails where they'll hang like bats until it's time for them to go to work again. They won't want women or alcohol or tobacco. They'll be a mixture of bat, Mormon, Puritan, and duck-billed platypussesses. . . ."

Julia turned to Mary. "I'm afraid Robert is well and truly on one of his hobby-horses now," she said. "We might as well stay here quietly until they remember that we're here. I like your brooch."

It was a silver pin carrying a naval crown in silver and small diamonds.

"Michael gave it to me last Christmas. He says it's my uniform. All naval wives and girl friends have one."

"It's certainly your uniform. Robert gave me one before we were married. He said he won it in a poker game! When are you going to get married?"

"I don't know. You weren't supposed to know about it."

"I guessed. And Cedric told us."

"*He* did?"

"He came to dinner with us last summer. I can hear him now. 'Julia, my girl,' he said, 'I'm very much afraid there's another good man gone there. If I know anything about such things, I fear those two are going to get married'!"

"Oh, he would!"

"I should get Michael to marry you as soon as possible. Robert and I were married when he was a junior sub-lieutenant. We hadn't any money so his father lent us a lodge in Scotland for our honeymoon. We only had four days and it rained the whole time. Robert always tells everyone that it was a splendid place for a honeymoon because we used to look out of the window, see that it was still raining, and go straight back to bed again!"

The Bodger looked over his shoulder. "Name of a name," he said, "they're giggling again!"

Cedric joined them. "Jolly hockey-sticks, Julia," he said.

"Hello, Cedric. We were just talking about you."

Cedric rolled his eyes and sighed. "That's just it. We've always got to remember that we're encompassed about by a great *cloud* of witnesses. D'you know, last week I went into Spry's to buy myself a buttonhole and within half an hour people were ringing me up asking me who I was engaged to! Oh dear, that poor B.B.C. man. Bodger's giving him the treatment. Shall we go and help him? I think not."

The Bodger had the round man from the B.B.C. hemmed in between the wall and a cabinet containing a huge samovar. The B.B.C. man's eyes were glassy; he stared, hypnotized, at The Bodger like a bird before a snake.

"The trouble with you people," The Bodger was saying, "is that you will *exaggerate* everything. You're not quite as bad as some of the newspapers but *all* of you listen to some matelot dripping about the Navy in some low pub or other and quote it next day as 'An Admiralty spokesman stated that. . . .' I'm just waiting for the day when *I'm* an Admiralty spokesman. . . ."

The Bodger drained his glass and beetled his eyebrows at the cringing B.B.C. man.

"Mind you," he went on, "we've got to be fair. The average N.O. meets a press representative in the wardroom and says to himself, 'Christ, who's this funny-looking cove with the scruffy shirt?' and gives him a splendid line of hot cock about the Navy. And yet he's the first to blow his top when he sees more or less what he told the wretched bloke printed in the paper next morning."

"Wherever two or three naval officers are gathered together," said Cedric, "they will talk shop."

"This is not quite the same as a wardroom, Cedric," Michael said. "There, you never get a reasoned argument. You get flat statements, followed by flat contradictions, followed by personal abuse."

Cedric's party began to settle down into its component parts. Julia was surrounded by a group of men including an elderly author who wrote novels about the upper classes for money in advance, a very drunk Lloyds underwriter, a man who shot rare jungle animals for Universal Aunts, and two acrobats who were third on the bill at the Palladium. Mrs Vincent was resuscitating with pleasant conversation the palsied limbs of the B.B.C. man. The Bodger had found a small unobtrusive man who had spent the Great War selling guns to the Serbo-Croats, who now ran a casino in Smyrna and held the monopoly for ouzo everywhere from Trieste to Damascus. The Bodger was charmed with him. Michael and Paul had joined each other again.

"I don't like the sound of Dickie Gilpin being in the chair when we get there," Paul said.

"Oh, he'll never remember us out of all those faces in *Barsetshire*."

"Don't you believe it. That man's got a memory like an elephant. You mark my words, he'll remember all about us when we get there. By the way, it's getting a bit late. I don't want to break up the happy party but I think we ought to be going. My mother is going to dinner with Cedric, The Bodger and Julia."

"Its extraordinary to hear The Bodger referred to as Robert, isn't it? Where shall we go?"

"I thought of trying a place George Dewberry recommended. . . ."

"God."

"No, it's quite legitimate. He gave me his membership card before he went to the Far East."

"Who is George Dewberry?" Anne asked.

"He's a mad pusser who was in our term at Dartmouth whose two interests in life were liquor and classical music. . . ."

"He was the boy who brought a bongo drum to one of Sonia's parties," Mary said.

"The man himself. He used to come back late at night tight as an owl and wake me up and ask me when did I think Sibelius was going to publish his eighth symphony. He became what's called a cool cat before he left. He asked me to get them to play 'Potato-head Blues' just for him. Imagine it!"

George Dewberry's club was in a street behind Maple's furniture store. A flight of grimy steps covered with scraps of newspaper and dirty milk bottles led down to the entrance. A young man sat at a window just inside. He did not bother to look at Paul's extended card but mouthed through the cigarette in his lips.

"Half a dollar. And another half a dollar for the cool quails."

Paul paid and they passed on to the door of the club itself.

"Remember," Paul said to Anne, "you're a cool quail. I've just paid for you."

"Man, that's real crazy," Anne said. Paul stared at her.

When they opened the door of the club a noise like the combination of tyres screaming at the limits of adhesion, mad dogs baying, and helpless human beings shrieking under some nameless torture, howled at their astounded eardrums.

"Siddown!" a voice yelled in Michael's ear.

They felt their way over to a table and sat down. Their eyes became accustomed to the atmosphere.

The room was crowded and filled with tobacco smoke. It was impossible to see the colour of the walls but pictures could just be distinguished through the haze. They were all photographs of negroes blowing, holding or sitting at musical instruments. Those negroes not actually blowing through an instrument bared their teeth in smiles of ferocious satisfaction. The band were sitting on a platform in one corner of the room; they were the photographs in the flesh. The dance floor was small and filled with gyrating couples who twisted and thrust each other and swung and dipped without disturbing the calm, almost monolithic, blankness of their faces.

"Paul!" Michael shouted above the music. "Did you say George Dewberry *recommended* this place?"

The band stopped suddenly while Michael was shouting and his last words rang round the room.

"Oh crikey," Michael said.

Two of the dancers came back to their table. The young man was wearing a blue and white sweater and black gaberdine slacks. His hair was crewcut except for a quiff in front. The girl wore her hair in a long pony tail, a pink sweater and electric blue trousers stretched tightly over her buttocks.

"Man, man, that was endsville," the young man moaned in an American accent.

"That was very nice," the girl said dreamily.

"Excuse me," Paul put in.

They turned and focused their eyes unwillingly on him, as though he had dragged them back from the delights of Arcadia.

"Yeah?"

"This is our first time here. I wonder if you could tell me the name of the tune they've just been playing, please?"

The young man looked at the girl.

"That was 'When I'm walking My Baby along South Basin Street Blues'."

"Oh. Thank you very much."

"The Armstrong version."

"I see."

"The number before that was 'Baby, Doncha Hear me Talkin' To Ya Blues'."

"Oh, thank you very much."

"And can you tell us the name of the band?" Michael asked. "Who's playing?"

The young man grimaced expressively at the girl, who grimaced back.

"Where ya bin all your life?"

"We're new here," Michael said, defensively.

"Ya want me to give ya the line-up?"

"Yes, please, if you would."

"Man, that's King Dirndl sitting in on trumpet and the guy in the sax chair he's Duke De Moinas an' that's Earl Easton with the liquorice stick, you wanta dig *him* when he breathes on that reed and Lord Lugrimace sitting by the keyboard. They're a bunch of cools."

"And the chap with the xylophone?"

"The *vibes*. That's Baron Bolo. The coolest."

"The chap on the drums. He seems pretty cool too."

"That's the Cardinal. Ya he's a cool heeler."

A negro waiter, in full evening dress with a white tie and tails, appeared beside the table.

"Two cokes, Pope," the young man said.

"Coke or coffee?" the Pope asked Paul.

"Is the coke cool? I mean, is the coke cold?"

"Nope."

"We'll have four cups of coffee then, please."

An upheaval was taking place on the stand. The band whose names read like an ecclesiastical and secular New Orleans Debrett were being replaced by four young men whom they all instantly recognized as friends of Sonia's. The four young men prepared to play the guitar, washboard, bass and piano. Two of them had been to Eton, one to Harrow, and the fourth to Winchester.

The first chords awoke a faint response in Michael's memory. He had surely heard that song before; when the chorus came he was certain. It was the song Lieutenant Chipperd had sung on the Beattys' last night at Dartmouth.

"And the pig got up and slowly walked away," sang the Old Harrovian, strumming the guitar.

"Walked *away*?" enquired the Old Wykehamist, from the piano.

"Walked away," answered the Old Etonians, on bass and washboard.

"And the pig got up and slowly walked away," sang all four.

"What's the name of this band?" Michael asked the young man.

"It ain't a band," the young man said scornfully. "It's a skiffle group. Piffle group, more like," he added, his American accent temporarily breaking down.

34

The Skiffle Group played and sang three more songs and the Debrett Band came back, this time accompanying a small boy of about twelve years of age whose singing excited the young man and the girl like a powerful drug, transporting them into a glassy-eyed state of trance. Meanwhile, the tobacco smoke drifted thicker, the Pope sidled between the tables, the band gave out short staccato yelps between chords, and the empty coke bottles stood like forests on the tables.

At half-past one in the morning, Paul rubbed his eyes with his hand and led the way outside.

"Let's get a taxi for goodness sake," said Michael. "This wind is cutting me in half."

Michael and Mary lay back in the taxi and watched the remote impersonal lights of London pass by. They saw a man's head and shoulders, the roof of a car, the top half of shop windows and the steady progression of buildings swinging past overhead. The buildings stopped and there were trees and then again more buildings. The taxi suddenly stopped.

"We're there," Michael whispered.

"Um?"

"We're there."

"Oh? Oh yes. Are you going to come in?"

"Yes, please."

Mary's flat was cold and quiet. Mary switched on lights, took off her coat and started to make coffee.

"Never mind about the coffee," Michael said.

Mary stopped, surprised at the authority in his voice.

"What do you mean? We've got to have *something*. You must be starving."

Michael went round the room and switched off the lights. He came close to Mary where she stood in the centre of the room, pale in the light from the window.

"No. Let's sit down. I want to talk to you."

They sat on the edge of the bed. Mary sat stiffly upright. She had never known Michael so peremptory. She was aware of his presence, of his sex, more strongly than ever before.

3

ALTHOUGH very few of the thousand servicemen lining the boatdeck rails of H.M.T. *Astrakhan* had ever left England by trooper before, they all knew that this was how it should be done.

Below them they could see a satisfactory crowd of wives, sweethearts and mothers weeping, waving handkerchiefs and holding up babies. Behind, some Military Policemen were keeping a look-out for any passengers who may have had second thoughts about travelling. At the jetty's edge, six men in brown overalls and bowler hats stood ready to let go the ship's lines. A brass band was playing "Good-bye Dolly, I must leave you," surrounded by a light fringe of newspaper sellers, telegram boys, florist's assistants, private detectives and a huddle of cynical cats.

When the ship's siren unexpectedly gave a long blast, the crowd on the jetty somehow recognized it for what it was, no idle testing, but the authentic leave-taking of a departing ship. The women waved ever more wildly. The Military Police closed the gangways as though to prevent even a rat leaving the ship. One of the men in bowler hats blew a whistle and the others spat on their hands and began to take turns of wire off the bollards. The last gangway was lifted and the last umbilical wire dropped clear. The siren exploded again and the ship slowly moved away in the wash of water swirled back by the screws.

All together, the women, the Military Police, the men in bowler hats and the messengers joined in a ringing cheer which was echoed and thrown back by the troops at the rails and swallowed up in the noise of the siren and the hooting of the tugs.

In a short time the ship was gone. A quarter of an hour after she had left it was as though she had never been. Nothing of the parting scene was left. H.M.T. *Astrakhan* with her two thousand passengers and crew was already another world and had gone where other worlds exist, out of this one.

Michael stood at the rail, looking back, until the dock-yard buildings were only distant smudges and the cranes had been lost in the background. Paul pulled his arm.

"Out finger, Mike," Paul said callously. "You'll see her again in eighteen months' time. Let's go and see what sort of cabin they've given us."

They were very lucky. The Purser's son had just entered Dartmouth as a cadet and the Purser gave all naval officers travelling in his ship, whatever their rank or seniority, the best cabins on A deck. The Army came next, officers of the Brigade of Guards and the Household Cavalry being given cabins on B deck, and the remainder, the hussars, dragoons and lancers, and the regiments of foot and line on C and D decks. (The R.A.F. fitted in as best they could on G and H decks; the Purser's home was on an airfield boundary and the Purser had long given up all attempts to replaster his drawing-room ceiling. As far as the Purser was concerned, the R.A.F. could just as well doss down in the hold.)

Michael's cabin had a bunk, a chest of drawers, a wardrobe, and a wash-basin. It was small but there was plenty of headroom. There was a large scuttle looking out on the boat deck and above all, it was a single cabin. Michael rapped on the bulkhead. It seemed solid. The Bodger had once warned of the dangers of thin trooper cabin bulkheads. Michael went next door.

"Not bad, are they?"

"Bloody good," said Paul. "After my last one, it's palatial."

The hollow sound of a gong floated along the passageway.

"Dinner. We don't have to dress or anything the first night."

The dining-room was a long compartment panelled in walnut. A row of chandeliers hung from a gilded and ornamental ceiling. The mahogany tables and chairs were bolted to the deck. The room had a faint atmosphere associated with white duck suits and pink gins, as though it were still populated by the ghosts of the civil servants, tea planters and bank managers who had sat and dined there on their way to and from leave in England.

The seating plan was made out by the Chief Steward who cared for nobody except the six parrots in his cabin and who abided strictly by protocol. At the Captain's table sat the Lieutenant Colonel, O.C. Troops, the C.O. Naval

37

Drafts, in the person of The Bodger, the Wing Commander in charge of R.A.F. personnel and the Senior Nursing Sisters. Outwards and downwards from the Captain's table the other officers sat in rigid seniority, wives taking the same precedence as their husbands, present or not.

The naval party were the first into the dining-room and found their various tables. The rest, not possessing that inbuilt lodestone which guides a naval officer to the food and drink in a strange ship, followed. Michael and Paul were joined by Tommy Mitchell, a lieutenant a year junior to them.

"How far are you going?" Michael asked him.

"Honkers. To relieve a character called Freddy Spink."

"Freddy Spink? He's in our term. What's he doing now?"

"Rumour's going round the bazaars that he's keeping a Chinese mistress."

"Freddy *Spink*?" said Paul, in amazement.

"Oh yes. He's engaged already, you know."

"I think I heard about it."

"Got engaged to a Wren while he was at Lee-on-Solent. Most unoriginal of him, we all thought. Her old man's a retired Captain and he didn't go much on it when he heard his prospective son-in-law was shacking up with a heathen Chinee."

"I can imagine."

The dining-room was filling up. The next arrivals were a plump couple, a Captain and Mrs Featherday of the Pioneer Corps, accompanied by their daughter Phyllis, an anaemic-looking girl of slightly mongoloid features. Then came a swarthy lieutenant of the Black Watch. The last member of the table gave the rest a foretaste of things to come.

He was a bald-headed captain of yeomanry who was jocularly addressed by officers on adjoining tables as Goldilocks. Goldilocks sat down and tucked his napkin into his collar.

"Well, well, well, well," he said, rubbing his hands. "What have we here? Let's 'ave a look at the menu. Must 'ave a butchers at the scoffcard," he added, aside, to Michael.

Goldilocks surveyed the menu.

"Could be worse. But we must have a little something to

wash it away with. Let's 'ave a butchers at the blood-sheet."

He took up the wine list.

"D'you fancy a little rat's blood to wash down your bangers, ma?" he asked Mrs Featherday.

"Well, what are we going to have Pibroch, me old jock and sporran?" he asked the taciturn Black Watch subaltern.

"If you leave your mouth open like that my girl," he told Phyllis Featherday, "the wind'll change and you'll stay like that for ever and then you'll never get a man!"

Conversation during the meal was a monologue by Goldilocks. He told jokes in Cockney, Welsh, Scots and Liverpudlian accents, explaining the point of each joke. He addressed the Black Watch subaltern as Pibroch so often that Pibroch he became for the rest of the voyage. Captain Featherday's face was beetroot red as Goldilocks pretended to be ignorant of the Pioneer Corps' existence. Mrs Featherday crumbled her bread nervously while Phyllis, in spite of her warning, remained open-mouthed.

After dinner, Paul said: "You meet them now and again."

"But all the way to *Hong Kong*!"

"Never mind," Michael said soothingly, "we'll have to think up some way of nobbling him."

"Let's have a drink. I need it."

In the bar they found the other naval officers travelling in *Astrakhan*. The Bodger was presiding and beside him were Mr Crayshaw, a Commissioned Master at Arms on his way to the barracks at Hong Kong, Mr Pebblethwaite, a Commissioned Writer Officer and Lieutenant (E) Bongo Lewis, a South African, both for *Carousel*.

"Let me get these," said The Bodger hospitably.

"How many sailors have we got on board, sir?" Michael asked.

"About thirty, most of them for Hong Kong and a few for *Carousel*. We've got a Chief G.I. so he'll give a hand with the rum and do all the regulating. We'll have a duty roster amongst us and the duty boy will muster the hands in the morning and do rounds of the troop deck at night. When we get organized a bit we'll have a few training classes. That's about all."

When the ship cleared Ushant and began her run south she ran into a full Atlantic gale. With her high top weight and small metacentric height *Astrakhan* had a slow, leisurely pendulum-like period of roll, remaining for some moments suspended at the extent of her swing before rolling back. Stewardesses hurried between cabins with basins. The Chief Steward's seating plan was ignored because there were only enough stewards who had escaped sea-sickness to serve those passengers who were also immune.

Astrakhan wallowed in the storm for three days until she rounded Trafalgar and passed through the Straits of Gibraltar into the Mediterranean when she steamed miraculously into calm weather, blue skies and warm sunshine. The passengers emerged on deck as joyfully as Noah after the forty days of rain.

It was not long before the passengers with shorter memories were sighing for the storm's return. The gale had been a continuing nightmare, aggravating every sense, but at least it had kept Goldilocks in check.

Within twenty-four hours Goldilocks had organized a deck-tennis league, a deck-quoits championship, a concert party, roulette twice a week, and bingo on alternate nights. His table talk was confined to new ventures for the passengers' entertainment. He trotted round the ship untiringly, cajoling or browbeating unwilling passengers to hazard their money, lend their dinner jackets, and sing their songs. His voice became the harbinger of inconvenience; where it was raised somebody found himself committed to something which he had not intended to do, did not like the thought of doing and which, when he came to reconsider the matter, he would be damned if he was going to do. But Goldilocks had an answer for every excuse. Nobody could plead another engagement. There were no other engagements except those arranged by Goldilocks. Nobody could plead illness. Goldilocks visited the sick bay daily and made a note of the attendance. Nobody could lie in his bunk. Goldilocks reproached all who did so with lack of communal spirit. The English, the most reserved of all races, responded all the more vigorously to the charge of being anti-social; young and old fell into Goldilocks's traps again and again.

Across the Mediterranean and down the Suez Canal, while the sun grew hotter, the passengers dealt each other cards and sang each other's choruses. Some of the more elderly passengers had not indulged in such an orgy of late nights for forty years but, spurred by the fear of being thought unsociable, they played whist, chased quoits and spun the roulette wheel until they dropped exhausted in their cabins at night.

Goldilocks's only failure was The Bodger. When invited to take part in the deck-tennis league, The Bodger's answer was quite definite.

"Deck *tennis*? In *this* climate? My dear old Goldilocks you want your head examined. I leave all that sort of thing to the pongos. Keeps 'em out of mischief. I intend to spend my afternoons in the best traditions of the service, inspecting the rivets in the deckhead of my cabin."

The Bodger retired to the bar with a strange gleam in his eye and the regulars there became aware that The Bodger had something on his mind.

The Bodger's moment came when the ship headed down the Red Sea. A following wind carried the ship's fumes through her and the cabins were like tiny dark ovens. The passengers' tempers grew thin. The lounge was like a forest dried in the summer and, ironically, it was Goldilocks himself who struck the spark. The fatal idea came to him while reading the scoffcard.

"Soup. Poached Cod. Bangers, spuds, mercy me. Chaps! I've got an idea!"

Captain and Mrs Featherday assumed a hunted look. The rest of the table ignored Goldilocks, except Phyllis Featherday, who gazed open-mouthed.

"We'll have an Inter-Service Pentathlon!"

"What do you mean?" Pibroch asked suspiciously. He fingered the black eye which he had got at the children's sports.

"Five sports. Teams from the Army, Navy and the Raff. Let me see. How about bridge, tug-of-war, deck-tennis, quoits. . . . We need another sport. . . ."

41

"How about Liar-dice?" Michael said innocently.

"*Liar*-dice! Exactly! Everyone can have two days to practise."

Goldilocks organized it. He persuaded the First Officer and the Purser to be judges and arbitrators of the *Astrakhan* Olympic Games. The Purser, who had been combating the idiosyncrasies of passengers for over thirty years without meeting anyone like Goldilocks, agreed to lend his presence and, if necessary, equipment.

The Army in general welcomed the idea of a Pentathlon. The R.A.F. were sceptical but consented to take part. To the Navy, however, the Pentathlon came as the last straw.

A meeting was held in the bar at midnight and a Hate-Goldilocks League was formed, with The Bodger as its President. The meeting was also attended by the Purser who had somehow come to hear of it.

The main resolution of the meeting was proposed by The Bodger and unanimously carried. Something horrible must now happen to Goldilocks, and quickly. The Purser offered the League certain articles he had picked up in Shanghai, Yokohama and Mobile, Alabama. His offer was gratefully accepted and the League left The Bodger to work out the details, whereupon a demoniacal smile spread over The Bodger's face.

The Games were officially opened by the O.C. Troops. An embarrassed Royal Norfolk Regiment subaltern in shorts and singlet ran twice round the boat deck with the Chief Engineer's torch. The O.C. Troops made a short speech and announced the first event, the Deck Tennis.

The Army's representatives had spent many hours under a broiling sun perfecting their game but the R.A.F. produced two unknown quantities, two Pilot Officers who had played lawn tennis together at Wimbledon. One of them won the singles and together they won the doubles.

The Bodger, who had watched Paul and Michael play deck tennis for the Navy from his deck chair, roused himself for the next contest, the Contract Bridge.

"What about prepared hands and tournament points and all that?" he asked Goldilocks.

"Oh, that's too complicated. We'll treat it as a whist drive, only we'll be playing bridge."

The Bodger sat down to shuffle the first hand, grinning like a tiger.

The spectators were chiefly interested in the table where The Bodger and Sam Crayshaw opposed Goldilocks and an Army Padre. The Bodger and Goldilocks were competent players who could normally win from their fellow officers, but Sam Crayshaw was a novice. A bid of two spades was to him the same as a bid of two pounds and he conducted his play on the famous first principle of Hoyle—"When in doubt, win the trick."

The Army Padre, on the other hand, was a player of a very different calibre, indeed he was thought indecently skilful at cards for a man of his cloth. His bidding was bold and cool. His card-playing was economical and well-judged. He noted the fall of every card, remembered the play of every trick and was renowned for the occasional psychic bid in which, it was rumoured by the malicious, he received more than earthly assistance. He was a formidable opponent.

"Forcing Two and Blackwoods, partner?" The Bodger asked pleasantly, as the first hand was dealt.

"Eh?"

"Or would you rather play the Vienna Convention?"

The Bodger glared at Sam Crayshaw who looked concerned until he remembered the coaching The Bodger had given him.

"That's O.K. by me, sir," he said stoutly. "But I'm partial to fourteen points for an opening, if you don't mind, sir."

The Padre picked up his cards and glanced at Goldilocks.

"Same as usual, partner?"

"Of course, Padre."

The spectators nodded significantly at each other; all agreed that the Padre and Goldilocks had won the first trick of all.

The cards fell evenly and small scores were made above and below the line by both sides. The Bodger played methodically. Sam Crayshaw went one down, doubled by the Padre. Goldilocks interspersed play with remarks such as "Never send baby to fetch home the beer" when Sam

Crayshaw trumped too low and "There are more men walking the Embankment because of that" when Sam Crayshaw failed to draw the last trump. The Padre, gauging the mettle of his opponents, brought off a couple of neat finesses and made game.

On a hand dealt by himself, Goldilocks's opening bid showed strength. The Padre had support. They bid swiftly to game and finally to a small slam which the Padre made. With one rubber and a small slam behind them, the Padre and Goldilocks were well ahead.

The Bodger ruefully gathered the cards for the next shuffle while players and spectators relaxed in the bitter-sweet chatter after a bridge hand. Suddenly, The Bodger's voice cut across the hum of voices.

"I say," he said, in a puzzled voice, holding up an ace and examining it, "I'm sure these cards are marked!"

Grimly, the Purser made his way across the hushed room. He took a card to the daylight and looked along its edge. He went back to the table, picked up another card and ran a finger over the surface.

"Yes," he said reluctantly, as though acknowledging a tragic fact, "they're marked all right. All the picture cards are nicked. What was the score on this hand?"

"Small slam," said Sam Crayshaw.

"Who dealt it?"

"I did," said Goldilocks.

The Bodger quietly put his cards back on the table. He looked Goldilocks full in the eye and, white-lipped, walked away. The rest of the Navy team, as though taking a cue, followed him. The Wing Commander leading the R.A.F. team went red in the face and then nodded to his team.

The Padre's cloth prevented actual physical violence but there was no question of abandoning the Pentathlon. Each service was determined to continue, under martial law.

The news of the marked cards travelled and a huge crowd watched the teams prepare for the Tug-of-War. (The ship's officers were also there; they had not had such amusement from the passengers since the Balinese rugby football team attempted to seduce the ship's nurses, all together and to the beat of gongs and drums.)

The crowd had come to see fair play and the spectre of the lynching post hung over the Army team as the Purser inspected their rope for anchors and their boots for spikes. When the Purser was satisfied, the Army beat the Navy and the R.A.F. comfortably in straight pulls.

Another large crowd assembled for the fourth contest, the Liar Dice, because The Bodger was the acknowledged maestro and there were few who could resist seeing a master in play. The Bodger and Goldilocks were again opposing each other and the crowd stood three deep behind them.

The first four rounds of the dice established that The Bodger was sadly out of form. His subterfuges were easily penetrated and he seemed unable to throw higher than nine or ten. After six rounds The Bodger had been penalized twice and the crowd thickened behind him, anticipating the fall of a giant.

After his second penalty, The Bodger threw for the next round, covering the dice with the leather cup. He threw two aces and passed them as a pair to the Squadron Leader on his right who threw a third ace. The three aces were passed and accepted as three tens. Sandy, the Royal Norfolk subaltern who had borne the torch, saw a chance of eliminating The Bodger and forced the bidding, calling a full house, aces on jacks. Paul took two dice and threw a fourth ace. A Flying Officer threw a queen.

Goldilocks was faced with a call of four aces and a queen. Two aces and the queen lay in view on the table but Goldilocks had not seen the dice under the cup. He hesitated before accepting the call, but reflecting that the Flying Officer had never lied yet, he took the cup and saw that there were indeed four aces and a queen. Goldilocks was now squeezed. The Bodger, sitting on his right, had originally thrown and must know what lay under the cup. Goldilocks's only course was to throw the queen and pass it as a king or as five of a kind, whatever the actual value.

The Bodger courteously picked up the queen and handed it to Goldilocks. The spectators, knowing The Bodger's predicament, appreciated the gesture.

Goldilocks threw, covered the dice, and called five aces.

"Cut-throat stuff this," said The Bodger. "I'll lift that on principle."

The Bodger lifted the cup. Five aces lay on the table. A murmur of awe ran round the spectators. They had just witnessed The Bodger eliminated from a liar dice game in seven rounds. Goldilocks could not stop himself smirking.

Instead of getting up from the table, The Bodger bent down and took off a shoe. Sharply, he cracked the heel down on the fifth ace.

The impact split the dice in half and a bead of mercury glittered across the table and fell on the deck where it splashed into several shining globules.

The Bodger stared at the shattered dice. Then, white-lipped, he rose from his seat and walked away. He was followed in order by the rest of the Navy and the R.A.F. teams.

Michael had a letter from Mary at Aden and he took it up to his favourite spot on the boat deck to read. When he had nearly finished it he was joined by Paul.

"Lonely heart's corner," said Paul.

". . . Then Anne came for tea on Sunday afternoon and we sat and talked. It was one of those times when you said you'd like to be a fly on the wall. . . ."

"Cedric's been invited to do a radio programme on his collections," Paul said.

"Oh, do shut up, Paul."

". . . I think of you every day at the funniest times, with all my love, from Mary."

Michael looked up and saw Paul regarding him intently.

"Does she still love you?"

"Yes."

"I gather Anne feels the same way about me. She sends you her love."

"Good."

Paul tucked away his letters and lay back in his deck chair.

"How peaceful it all is," he said, "now we've curbed the frumious Goldilocks."

"Did the Purser get his cards back?"

"The Bodger collected them afterwards. It was a pity

46

about the dice. The Bodger said it nearly broke his heart to smash such a perfect specimen."

"It was in a good cause."

"Goldilocks had a terrific blast from O.C. Troops. Old Bushy went on about the honour of the regiment and being blackballed from any decent club and so on. Pibroch told me about it. Goldilocks kept on saying, 'But *Sir* . . .' but Bushy wouldn't let him finish and drowned him out with 'making an apology to the Senior Service' and 'what would Kitchener have said.' He droned on for about half an hour."

"That'll teach him to ask The Bodger to play deck tennis on hot afternoons."

Goldilocks's eclipse left a gap in the ship's life, like the lancing of a boil. The passengers walked the decks without fear, confident at last that the next corner would not reveal Goldilocks with a new scheme. Goldilocks himself led a sheltered, almost monastic, existence. He read a library book a day and was exceptionally polite to the Feather-days. Best of all, he stopped calling the menu a scoffcard.

"Just as well," said Tommy Mitchell. "A few more days of it and I would have upped with my soup plate and fitted it over his ears."

Goldilocks's fall had another side effect. It left the younger male passengers more time to enjoy a traditional trooper entertainment which needed no organizing. Boat-deck romances were born, flourished and faded in a single night; the lifeboats were the scene of innumerable rendezvous, estrangements and reconciliations.

Tommy Mitchell was the foremost of the lifeboat cavaliers and his especial partner was a young blonde named Dolly who was on her way to Singapore to join her husband. Although Tommy Mitchell was never given any more information but that he was big and had a red face, the question of Dolly's husband fascinated him; he returned to it like a moth to a candle.

"But what does your husband *do*?" he asked one night.

"Oh, never mind about him, Tommy. Put your arms round me."

"All right. But why did you get married?"

47

"I got fed up with being at home and he asked me so I said yes."

"Gosh." Tommy Mitchell had thought that a proposal of marriage was a special, almost a holy, moment; this casual attitude awed him.

"He was always about the place on his last leave. I really had to marry him or Daddy would have gone quite mad. It made a change."

"Is he in the Army?"

"Tommy, don't *worry* about that. Kiss me."

"All right. But how long had you known him before you married him?"

"Oh, about six weeks."

"Gosh." Again, Tommy Mitchell rapidly readjusted his conceptions of a proposal; he had always thought one had to wait a decent interval. Tommy Mitchell thought vaguely about banns and things.

"What's he doing in Singapore?"

"Oh, let's not think about that. Undo me here."

"All right. But he will be meeting you when you get off the ship?"

"I expect so. If he's not there I'll hang around until he comes. *Now* kiss me."

"Gosh." Another of Tommy Mitchell's favourite mental pictures, that of a sweet young wife hanging on the rail for the first glimpse of her husband, vanished with the rest.

"Oh, you're so clumsy."

"But doesn't he write to you and all that?"

"Every day. They're terribly boring. *Now* kiss me properly."

"Gosh," said Tommy Mitchell, "all right."

The Bodger had overheard the entire conversation through his cabin scuttle. "For God's sake, Mitchell," he muttered irritably, "get in there and put the poor girl out of her misery."

Three nights out of Aden The Bodger and Sam Crayshaw were walking the boat deck when they heard a slap and a wail. A slap was hardly worth comment but a wail made them prick up their ears. A woman's voice came out of the night.

48

"No you *can't* be a Jack the Ripper. You're going to be a Pierrot and like it, so stop your snivelling."

"What's that?" The Bodger asked.

"The Children's Fancy Dress Party, sir," said Sam Crayshaw.

The words struck like a knell. Of all the social functions enjoyed by the passengers between Southampton and Hong Kong, the Children's Fancy Dress Party was the most dreaded. The Party made itself felt long before the event. The ship's shop sold out of papier mâché, string, thread, tape and pins. Curtains disappeared from the lounge and cloths from the dining tables. The cotton wool in the sick bay was guarded day and night by a staff who had endured fancy dress parties before.

The children were divided into categories according to age and prizes were awarded for the best dresses. Entries of twins, triplets or any higher multiples were permitted as single entries but in such cases the winners received a prize each. (None of the ship's officers would soon forget the scene on the previous voyage when the twin sons of a R.E.M.E. sergeant received a prize of one rubber ball.) Judging was done by the Captain himself and there had been occasions, according to the Purser, when even the Captain had barely made his escape from the lounge in time.

The question of what Phyllis Featherday should wear for the party provided a fresh and welcome subject of conversation at the table. Paul proposed Mata Hari. Captain Featherday was charmed with the idea but himself preferred Alice in Wonderland. Michael said that he had heard that the last prize for Phyllis's age group had been won by a Florence Nightingale. Pibroch did not agree with fancy dress on principle. Goldilocks, with a touch of his old self, suggested Lady Godiva or Salome. This for some reason annoyed Mrs Featherday who said that it was supposed to be a secret and Phyllis would go as Joan of Arc. Phyllis herself said that she did not want to wear anything; it was a prophetic remark.

The Bodger was persuaded by an evening's free whisky on the O.C. Troops to be in general charge of the party and he ordered the other naval officers to help him. The

49

task of controlling the entrants and presenting them in the correct order was given to Sam Crayshaw, the Commissioned Master at Arms.

"Just corral them outside, Sam," said The Bodger. "Unleash them one by one as I read out their names. You'll have some mothers to help you with the young ones and I've detailed Vincent and Hobbes as a fisting party to help you with the older ones. And for heaven's *sake* don't make them cry or anything. This is a lynching crowd we've got aboard this vessel."

"Aye, aye, sir," said Sam Crayshaw.

"If you need help, shout. The fisting party will be just inside the door."

"Aye, aye, sir."

On the afternoon of the Party, the first-class lounge was crowded with parents. Michael and Paul stood on either side of the door like night-club bouncers. The Bodger took up his position in the middle of the floor.

"Ladies and gentlemen! Your attention please! The first class is for boys and girls under five. The first entry is . . .", The Bodger glanced down at his list ". . . David and Kirstie MacGregor, The Bisto Kids!"

A large hand forcibly propelled two bashful but quite recognizable facsimiles of the Bisto Kids through the door. There was some applause, determinedly led by Sergeant Major and Mrs MacGregor, Welsh Guards.

"Christine Summerfield! Little Bo-Peep!"

There was more clapping and a cheer from the back where Fusilier and Mrs Summerfield, Royal Northumberland Fusiliers, were sitting.

"Beryl Frogat. . . ."

Beryl was wearing a small seaman's jersey and trousers made specially to her size with the words "Enos" chalked across the front of her jersey.

". . . An Old Salt!"

Beryl skipped across to join her mother Mrs Frogat, wife of Commander Frogat, R.N., in a general shout of laughter.

The next entries were a small boy and his sister. The small boy wore a pair of his father's grey flannel trousers rolled up and one of his father's sports jackets which came down below his knees. His face was covered in boot blacking and shaving cream and he carried a pipe in one hand. His sister wore one of her mother's dresses with a brassière outside it. Her face was smeared with lipstick and face cream.

"John and Deirdre Hampton. Left Alone for Five Minutes!"

Friends leaned forward to clap the backs of Squadron Leader and Mrs Hampton in the front row.

The Fancy Dress Party followed its ancient and traditional pattern. There was a Little Miss Muffet, a Dick Whittington, two Aladdins, several Little Jack Horners and some Sinbads, Robin Hoods and Cinderellas. There were also Pierrots, Gypsies, the inevitable Cowboys and Indians, and one Spaceman. Historical characters were represented by Nell Gwynn, Gandhi and Nelson. On the side of Natural History, there were several Brer Rabbits, a White Rabbit, and one Space-Animal. The Stage was upheld by Punch and Judy and by Charlie Chaplin. There was also a small bespectacled Matador.

The last class was for boys and girls between eleven and sixteen. The Bodger's voice had long grown hoarse. The Captain showed signs of strain. The bachelor passengers and ship's officers ranged round the walls began to despair of any excitement.

"Ladies and gentlemen," croaked The Bodger. "The last class is for boys and girls over eleven. Phyllis Featherday. . . ."

There was a scuffle by the door and Michael heard Sam Crayshaw's despairing voice.

"*Please*, Mr Hobbes, sir, give me a hand with this one!"

Michael and Paul swung round to see Sam Crayshaw and Phyllis Featherday in an apparently intimate embrace.

". . . Joan of Arc!"

"No, I'm not!" Phyllis cried. "I'm Salome!"

Wrestling herself from Sam Crayshaw's grasp, Phyllis Featherday sprang past Michael and Paul. She had a nightdress clasped about her and, throwing it away, she began to dance, shaking her hips and wriggling in a manner which The Bodger afterwards admitted was a first-class rendering,

51

considering the girl's age and experience, of an Algerian *danse du ventre*.

While the lounge remained thunderstruck, Phyllis cavorted across the floor, flexed her body in front of the Captain's astonished nose and disappeared back the way she had come.

At once, Mrs Featherday rose up and struck the amazed Goldilocks with her handbag.

"You *satyr*!" she hissed.

Recovered from their first stupefaction, the bachelors round the walls found their voices.

"*Encore!*"

The Bodger struggled to make himself heard above the uproar.

"Ladies and gentlemen! The next entry. . . ."

"We want Salome!"

"The next entry!" shouted The Bodger.

"To hell with the next entry!" roared back the bachelors round the walls. "We want Salome!"

The tumult died a little as the Captain was seen to bend and whisper to the O.C. Troops.

"That girl's got a future, Bushy."

"I should say so, sir. Shall we go on with the show?"

"No. Anything else would be an anticlimax, don't you think?"

The Purser, who had watched the show from a strategic position near the door, went away to the Chief Steward's cabin and drank whisky with him. Their shouts of "We want Salome!" and the drunken squawkings and flutterings of the six parrots kept officers in the neighbouring cabins awake until early the next morning.

Phyllis Featherday's *danse du ventre* was the sensation of the voyage. (It was judged by the ship's officers the best entertainment put on by the passengers since the night before Southampton when the wife of an R.A.M.C. captain did a strip-tease in the lounge and inadvertently sneezed off her brassière.) Mrs Featherday was mortified and obscurely blamed Goldilocks. Phyllis herself became a ship's celebrity and was surrounded by interested young men whenever she appeared. Tommy Mitchell was interested enough to suggest that Phyllis give a repeat performance of her *danse du ventre* in the privacy of his cabin. Goldilocks had another lecture from O.C. Troops.

With Goldilocks as impotent as Napoleon in exile and the Fancy Dress Party over, there were no more social events until the ship reached Singapore.

No leave was allowed until the families had cleared the jetty and the young bloods who were going on to Hong Kong watched the disembarkation with cynical eyes.

"Makes you think what a two-timing lot of twisters they all are," said Sandy, the Olympic torch bearer, bitterly. "Get Delilah there. Dig that shark skin outfit. It's about twenty times as much as I saw her wearing the night before last."

"Don't get all bitter and twisted," Paul said. "Put yourself in her husband's place. He wants to see his wife come down the gangway calm, chaste and exquisite. Not dashing down in her dressing-gown as though the lecherous lascars were still after her. Besides, he's got plenty of time to put two and two together and find out just what did go on in the good ship *Astrakhan*."

A huge Major appeared on the gangway and embraced Dolly. Tommy Mitchell blenched.

"Santa Maria! Is *that* her husband? Thank God I didn't shout good-bye!"

Dolly disengaged herself neatly and tripped away on her husband's arm without a backward glance at *Astrakhan*, for which Tommy Mitchell was grateful.

The Bodger came up on the boat deck.

"All right, men," he said. "Put your eyeballs back in their sockets. You can get ashore now. The ship leaves at eight o'clock tomorrow morning."

From the sea Singapore had looked a modern city but behind the tall buildings there were warrens of narrow streets with deep gutters and washing hung in lines from the rib-tiled roofs. There were sky-scrapers and sampans, barefoot beggars and American convertibles, Sikh taxi-drivers, Malayan girls with paper sunshades and traffic policemen with white boards like wings on their backs.

53

It was a city where so many different races lived that they could, and did, form a football league.

The party from *Astrakhan* started at the Raffles Hotel, the most luxurious hotel the city offered and the hub of fashionable Singapore, the kind of place, Paul thought, from which George Dewberry would have been thrown out.

They ended in a dirty bar separated from the street by a chain curtain in a quarter of the city which they suspected was out of bounds, the kind of place, Paul thought, where George Dewberry would have felt at home.

It was not a successful run ashore.

"They're all the same all over the world," said Paul. "You go ashore looking for a few drinks and some excitement. You don't know the place so you have to play it off the cuff. You get the drinks but you'd get more excitement in a morgue."

"We could try a bit further on," said Sandy in a tone of voice which made everyone say, "Let's go back to the ship."

A last bingo night and dance was held on the night before the ship reached Hong Kong. Bingo nights were afterwards one of Michael's chief memories of *Astrakhan*. Sam Crayshaw's voice calling out the numbers in an expert monotone voice:

"Eyes down for the next house. Sixty-six clickety click fifty-nine five and nine the Brighton line twenty-six two and six bed and breakfast shake'em up one and six sweet sixteen never been kissed seventy-six seven and six was she worth it oh dear me it's number three *legs* eleven line! Lady there says she's got a line check the numbers Bob."

In the party afterwards The Bodger recited "Eskimo Nell," a Q.A.R.A.N.C. girl lost part of her skirt, a Wing Commander received a black eye. Goldilocks was summoned before the O.C. Troops in the morning.

* 4 *

H.M.S. *Carousel* was a ship with a name and a history. She was the tenth ship of her name and her battle honours

54

included both Sluys and Guadalcanal. In the period from 1939 to 1945 her bows were blown off by a bomb in Malta, her back broken by a mine at Tobruk, and her stern cut in half by a suicide bomber in the Java Sea. Her other war damage was, for her, comparatively local; her foremast and gun direction position were shot away by a German armed merchant cruiser in the Indian Ocean, her wardroom was wrecked by a shell from a shore battery on the Normandy coast, and her forward seamen's messdeck was burned out when the projector burst into flames during a showing of "In Which We Serve."

The ship had been rebuilt and redesigned so often that there had grown up a popular notion in the Fleet that young constructors joining the Royal Corps were given *Carousel* to practise on, like a teething ring. Her armament changed from her original force of nine 6-inch guns, in triple turrets, to multiple batteries of anti-aircraft guns, by way of quick-firing radar-controlled 4-inch guns in double turrets. Her radar was modified at annual intervals. A helicopter landing platform was built on the quarterdeck and removed before it had ever known the beat of wings. Mine-laying rails were laid out along the main deck but laying ports were never cut in the ship's side. There were sudden changes, steps, drops, and inclines on every deck. Many pipes disappeared into bulkheads, never to reappear. Compartments existed all over the ship whose original purpose had long been forgotten and every passageway contained anonymous fuse boxes, plugs and brackets which baffled the ship's company. The ship's external appearance had changed so often that at last even "Jane's Fighting Ships" admitted defeat. *Carousel* was struck from the list of the other 8,000-ton cruisers of her class and given a special half-page of her own, her photograph being headed by the curt and aggrieved notice—"The silhouette of this ship is liable to radical change without warning."

Such a ship could be expected to be temperamental and *Carousel* was as unpredictable as a prima donna. Her steering gear was liable to inexplicable failures. She had a tendency to sheer to port when going astern and was skittish and playful coming to a buoy in a tideway. But

Carousel was too old and wise a ship ever to allow herself to get into serious difficulties. She handled like a fast motor boat, accelerated like a hurdler, and turned as quickly as a barmaid. She had never been known to run aground or collide with another ship and she had never damaged a jetty. She knew her way into Devonport better than her officers and went up the Hamoaze as confidently as an old mare approaching her stable.

The ship's temperament was reflected in her officers and ship's company. She was reputed to have the same effect upon her officers as old Istanbul had upon the suleimans; according to superstition, sooner or later all *Carousel's* officers became slightly, pleasantly, harmlessly, but definitely, insane.

"You'll like it here, Bodger," said Jimmy Forster-Jones, the Commander.

"I hope so, Jimmy."

"Everyone here is slightly round the bend. The chap you were supposed to be relieving thought he was a poached egg. We made him a huge piece of toast and he sat on it all day quite happily."

The Bodger, once more back in a seagoing wardroom with a glass in his hand, was completely at home.

"You haven't changed a bit, Jimmy," he said. "It's really good to see you again."

"And it's good to see you, Bodger. Seriously, we need you badly, to get some sanity back into those damn messdecks. We've only just commissioned and the troops are getting restless already. Don't blame 'em. About fifty of them have to live in spaces which the R.S.P.C.A. would be on your backs for keeping a dog in."

"The whole trouble," The Bodger said, confidently, "is that constructors don't have to go to sea in the ships they design. If they *did*, then we'd see a difference. Tell me, with all due respect and all that, Jimmy, I thought you were passed over?"

"I was, but almost immediately my Navigating Officer lost some C.B.s. It was partly my fault, because I didn't keep a close enough eye on him. I lost six months, got back into the zone, and was promoted next shot. It's a strange life. Now I must push off and introduce the rest of the trogs to the Captain."

"He was very civil to me just now."

"Oh, Richard's calmed down a lot. He's got a phobia against Chinamen. He hasn't been ashore anywhere yet except for official calls. Just the man to send to command a ship in the Far East, don't you think?"

Captain Richard St Clair Gilpin had not changed, except for the fourth stripe on his sleeve. He looked down his nose at Paul, who was being introduced by Commander (E), just as he had looked at him in *Barsetshire* years before.

"We've met before, haven't we, Vincent?"

"Yes, sir."

"Is that your best uniform?"

"I'm afraid not, sir."

"Great heavens, boy, when a young Lieutenant meets his Captain for the first time he tries for once in his life to look smart and not like a walking scranbag!"

"I don't think Vincent has had time to unpack yet, sir," Commander (E) put in soothingly.

"Maybe. Maybe. What job are you giving him, Chief?"

"Outside machinery, sir. Taking over from Cardew, sir."

"Ah. Well, Vincent, I don't need to tell you that your part of the ship is vital, Steering gear, refrigerators and all that sort of thing can have a big effect on the morale of the ship's company."

"I realize that, sir," said Paul, astonished that the Captain knew what machinery was in the Outside Department.

"We've had trouble from them in the past but now that you're in the chair I expect everything to work properly."

"Yes, sir."

"And never let yourself get the feeling that your efforts are going unnoticed."

"No, sir."

"Good. That's all."

Michael was waiting outside, with the Commander.

"Lieutenant Hobbes, sir."

"We've met before, haven't we, Hobbes?"

"Yes, sir."

"Is that your best uniform?"

"Yes, sir."

"You need a new one."

"Aye aye, sir."

"What job is Hobbes getting, Commander?"

"Boats and laundry, sir. For the first few months."

"Well, Hobbes, I don't need to tell you how important those two particular departments are to the morale of the ship's company."

"No, sir."

"A ship is judged by her boats and by the appearance of her libertymen, Hobbes. If the boats are dirty and late, and the libertymen are scruffy, the ship gets a bad name. We have a lot to do in this commission to give the ship a good name. I give you that thought to take away with you."

"Yes, sir."

"Good. That's all, Hobbes."

"Thank you, sir."

On his way along the passageway from the cuddy, Michael suddenly stopped. He had seen what he thought was a ghost. A midshipman was walking towards him.

"Hoy!" Michael shouted. "Your face is bloody familiar?"

The midshipman grinned. "You probably knew my eldest brother, sir."

"Tom Bowles?"

"That's right, sir."

"And you're his youngest brother?"

"Yes, sir."

"What's your name?"

"Andrew Bowles, sir. My other brother's name is Simon, sir. He's a sub-lieutenant."

Michael walked on, with a sense of shock. Tom Bowles's youngest brother in a midshipman's uniform somehow made Michael feel about ninety years old. He went up to the quarter-deck and into the wardroom feeling as though he ought to be on crutches.

Carousel's wardroom was a long room just off the quarter-deck, panelled in wood upon which hung photographs of the Royal Family and the inevitable wardroom Van Gogh prints. Michael caught sight of Tubby Rowlands, whom he was relieving, by the bar.

"I'm jolly glad you've come," said Tubby.

"How long have you been here, then?" Michael asked.

"Too bloody long. I was here all through last commission. I've been here two years and eight months."

"That *is* a long time."

"You can say that again, boy."

"Do you know what your next job is?"

"Haven't the remotest idea. Looney bin, I expect. That's where most people go after this outfit. I can't think why you didn't relieve me while we were still in the Med. I've just got out here and now I've got to go all the way back. Not that I mind, though."

"The ship's only just got out here?"

"Christ, yes. We've only just got worked *up*. We're only just out of the *egg*."

"What was the work up like?"

"It was hell, boy, hell. We came scooting out of the dock-yard with dockyard maties leaping ashore like rats leaving a sinking ship. I expect you'll find a few still on board if you like to look around a bit. Then we went to sea for a shakedown cruise and boy, was that a shakedown! It shook us all right! We had all our trials, noise ranging, degaussing, measured mile, turning and manœuvring, full power trial, radar calibration, the lot. . . ."

"But what kind of refit *was* this? It couldn't have been a full-scale one."

"God no, they just put that Thing on B gun-deck. Nobody's seen it yet. It's been covered with a tarpaulin ever since it's been on board. The boffins insisted that the ship go through all her party tricks. Of course we had *them* on board as well, crawling all over the place, most of them looking for the heads. I've never known anyone like boffins for looking for the heads, they must all have bladders like paper bags."

"You must have had quite a time. . . ."

"But wait. Behold, the half has not been told you. We repelled aircraft attacks, surface attacks, frogmen attacks and submarine attacks. We replenished a destroyer and a tanker replenished us. We've taken in oil fuel, fresh water, ammunition, potatoes. . . ."

"Potatoes. . . ."

"Vital, boy, vital. Must have potatoes. As I was saying, we took in stuff and gave out stuff at every point of the compass. We defended ourselves from attacks from above, below, right, left, north, south and up the chuff. We had ourselves a *whale* of a time."

"Sounds like it," said Michael admiringly. He knew that Tubby Rowlands was being anything but enthusiastic but, in spite of that, Michael found himself looking forward to *Carousel*. She sounded the sort of ship where at least something was happening all the time.

Michael looked around him. It was past twelve o'clock and the wardroom was filling up. It occurred to Michael that, though the actors were different, this same scene was being enacted at that time of day in every ship throughout the Navy. Just beside Michael a stout Gunner was reaching for his first gin of the day as eagerly as Tantalus grasping for the wine. Beyond him, two doctors were throwing dice for the first round and in the corner three lieutenant-commanders, one fat, one thin, and one with red hair, were staring bitterly into their glasses; occasionally one would direct on the others a stare of extreme loathing. Commander (S) was writing painfully in the mess suggestion book, sucking a stub of pencil and gaping at the deckhead for inspiration. The stewards were servings drinks as hostilely as though they hoped that they were arsenic. The Chief Steward was watching the chit book as closely as though it were drawn from his own bank account. A burst of laughter rose from a group which included The Bodger. The general level of talk began to rise.

"We've got a good crowd here on the whole," Tubby Rowlands said. "The Commander's quite a bright spark. The two and a halfs are a bit promotion-conscious but they're not a bad shower really. The new Jimmy's got quite a reputation as a player. . . ."

"The Bodger, you mean?"

"Yes. This is the first time I've met him. I left Dartmouth before he arrived. I think he's an old chum of the Commander's."

"He's certainly a player," Michael said.

"We can't have too many of them. Well, let's go and eat and then I'll show you the whole works. The laundry shouldn't worry you too much. All you've go to do is humour Number One Boy. He does all the work. Just see that the bloody Chinese don't start knocking each other off one dark night."

On the way out Michael saw Paul talking to a bunch of officers whom he guessed were engineers.

"I hope you've got all the usual vices, Vincent?" Ginger Piggant, the Senior Engineer, was saying.

"I think so, sir."

"Good. I must go and talk to The Bodger."

"What's he like as Senior?" Paul asked.

"Bloody good," said Cardew. "Doesn't mess you about. He has a hard time of it sometimes, explaining things to Commander (E) in words of one syllable. Chief's not a bad old stick but they didn't have most of the stuff we've got in this vessel in the *Victory* or the *Ark*, or wherever he got his ticket. Chief's one of the people commonly referred to as 'the old school'. I sometimes think he lost faith in the service when they dropped coal. He and Pilgrim get on like twin souls. . . ."

"Mr Pilgrim? Is he here?"

"Oh, yes. He and Commander (E) were boy artificers together. On guest nights they get drunk and tell each other what Jackie Fisher said to Nelson the day they introduced steam into the Navy. Let's go and see what enormity the Messman has perpetrated on us today and then I'll show you around. Everything's going like a box of birds at the moment so you shouldn't have too much trouble."

"I'm afraid you'll have to give me a pretty good run through," Paul said. "I'm not exactly an expert on steering gear and things like that."

"Oh, you'll learn, boy, you'll learn."

5

Top Flat (Back),
1003A Gloucester Road,
Hong Kong.

Dear Commander Royal Navy,

There is much happy joy with me in writing to you. Myself and fourteen nieces have many happy customers (navy officers special) in years gone by. Always I have tried to make satisfaction for my customers. For the rubbish of your ship myself and fourteen nieces clean your bottom. This is very special offer for navy ships for in normal times we take money for rubbish as well as bottom.

We make bottoms specially clean than all other for Royal Navy ship.

Myself and fourteen nieces,
Joan
(Mrs J. Ah Loo Tuck).

The Commander put down the letter and went next door to Commander (S)'s cabin.

"Cyril," he said, "how many nieces did Joan have when you were last out here?"

Commander (S) thought back to the high and palmy days when he had been a young lieutenant on the China Station. Life had been more leisurely, the girls had been prettier, and money had gone farther.

"I couldn't say off-hand," he said. "But I rather think it was about a dozen. Perhaps a few more. Why, how many has she got now?"

"Fourteen."

"These Chinese live a long time you know, Jimmy."

"Obviously. Joan's nieces last as long as Number One Boy's nephews."

The Commander went back to his cabin and found The Bodger waiting.

"What can I do for you, Bodger?"

"I had a compassionate requestman this morning. I wondered if you had any back history."

The Commander took out a massive file from a drawer

and laid it on his desk. "Let's have a look at my Domesday Book," he said.

"God, that's some tome you've got there, Jimmy!"

"It's got everyone in the ship's company in it."

"What are the numbers for, by some of the names?"

"Aha, that's their code rating in the Forster-Jones Scale for compassionate leave. It works like the Beaufort Scale. It's a quick way of letting the Old Man and me know what we're in for. Care to have a copy?"

"Surely." The Bodger picked up the sheet and studied it. It was headed "The Forster-Jones Scale for the Assessment of Nervousness in Wives. Why be in doubt, when you can know the worst?" The sheet was ruled off in columns, with a number and a corresponding explanation.

1. Married for years. No illusions left; likes the money but no use for hubby who can go abroad for as long as he likes, as often as he likes, and the best of British luck to him, provided he keeps up his allotment.

2. Happy on her own; can manage house and children herself. All relatives healthy and self-supporting. Realizes her husband is in the Navy and does not object to him doing his share of foreign service.

"To give 'em credit," said the Commander, "most of them are like that."

3. Can't manage the children but otherwise O.K. Needs husband to bash the brats periodically.

4. All right by day, but definitely misses something at night. Wants husband kept in easy bus distance with no night duty. Will suffer from the vapours unless this is done.

5. Lonely, hysterical and maladjusted; pregnant for Nth time (where N tends to infinity). Friendless in heart of overcrowded industrial town. Cancellation of foreign draft and immediate posting home recommended by a Dr Yehudi.

"Now you're getting warmer," said the Commander.

6. Going to end it all. Hears burglars in the house every night. No neighbours closer than next door. Requires husband (a key rating) flown home at once.

7. Knows what she married for and it was not for her husband to go gallivanting about with unmentionable Chinese girls. Wants him back the day before yesterday. (Doctor certifies return will be "most advisable and beneficial.") Will write to MP if not accommodated.

"Wait for it," said the Commander.

8. Has been going round with a Pole. Husband has anonymous letter. Horrible language, hard lying, divorce. Husband to be kept at home for court case.

9. Very naughty girl but has turned over new leaf. Husband has promised to accept and grow to love little blessing now on way. However, must be flown home now and stopped draft for five years to "cement" relationship.

"Then," said the Commander sadly, "will I strip my sleeve and show my scars and say, 'These wounds had I from compassionate cases'."

10. Psycho-neurotic, suicidal, nymphomaniac. Husband required day and night. No time for naval duties but must have pay. Constituent of Labour M.P.

"Jimmy, this is a masterpiece!" cried The Bodger. "Every divisional officer should have one. You should put it up for the old Herbert Lott Fund. You might get an award. Can I keep this?"

"By all means. Who is this bloke you're enquiring about?"

"Ordinary Seaman Gawn. He's in young Hobbes's division."

The Commander consulted his file.

"It's all right. He's number three. Ask Hobbes to come and see me."

Michael, however, was not thinking of compassionate cases. He was taking a shore telephone call on the ship's exchange. After the normal exhortations and reassurances from the ship's exchange operator, Michael heard a thin far-away voice, like a voice from the past.

"Hello. Hellohello. Is that Michael Hobbes? Operator, I thought you said I was through now? Hello?"

"Lieutenant Hobbes speaking," Michael said.

64

"That you, Mike? Spink here."

"*Who?*"

"Freddie! *Freddie Spink!*"

"Freddie!"

"The same. Tommy Mitchell told me you were out here now. It's about the only sensible thing he's said since he got here. Keeps burbling about women. What?"

"I thought he was supposed to relieve you days ago?"

"I know, old boy, that was the official plan but things are a bit complicated with the Barracks at the moment. They keep agitating about a wine audit we should have done. It's a long story and I won't bore you with it. What I really wanted to ask you was whether you can come ashore tonight? Have you seen anything of Honkers yet?"

"We had a few drinks last night. . . ."

"You come ashore with me and I'll show you around."

"I'd be delighted, Freddie."

"I'll see you in the Gloucester Lounge at half after seven, then."

"Can't you come on board here first and get up some flying speed?"

"I won't if you don't mind, old boy. I'm a bit fed up with the Grey Funnel Line at the moment and your vessel is a hot-bed of it. Is Paul there?"

"He's around."

"Ask him if he can come too."

"That'll be splendid, Freddie!"

"See you."

Carousel had a long naval tradition behind her in Hong Kong. Joan and her nieces had cleaned the boot-topping of every warship on the station within living memory and the Chinese tradesmen who came on board and set up stalls of lacquer work, brocades, silks and ivory in the Canteen Flat had orders from naval officers and ratings in their books dating back for more than thirty years. The tradesmen who came on board were merely the advance guard of a mighty battalion of shopkeepers who waited in the narrow teeming streets off the Gloucester Road for the Navy to come ashore. Hong Kong was the gateway to Communist China, a bright oasis on the extreme edge of a dark forbidden continent. It was the only port open to the Navy between Singapore to the south-west, and Japan to the north-east.

Neither Michael nor Paul had seen Frederick Augustus Spink for over three years. When they did see him, they hardly recognized him. He was wearing a pale beige Irish linen suit, a silk tie, light green nylon socks and white leather open sandals. As he sat in the Gloucester Lounge negligently sipping a German lager and smoking an American cigarette he seemed to Michael and Paul, in their heavy English clothes, the picture of the leisured oriental lounge lizard who may be observed in his natural surroundings in any first-class hotel lounge from Colombo to Honolulu. He had lost the greater part of his hair and the dome of his head was bronzed by the sun of Repulse Bay. He rose when he saw them.

"Michael! Paul! How nice to see you again!"

A Chinese waiter hurried to their table with two more lagers; Paul guessed that Freddie Spink was an old and valued customer.

"I can recommend this stuff," said Freddie.

"God, Freddie," said Paul, "what's happened to your hair?"

"Gone with the wind, dear boy. Penalty of the Orient. Now, how are you both? Well, I hope? Apart from being in love, of course. How's Mary? Does she still love you?"

"Yes," said Michael. "I hope so."

"And how about your light o'love, Paul? I've forgotten her name for the minute. I only got it through the grapevine the other day. *Anne?*"

"Bouncing," said Paul. He was intrigued by the new Freddie Spink. This was not the shy nervous boy who had been so frightened by everything that happened to him in *Barsetshire* and about whom The Bodger had had so many misgivings. He was now a mature man, so mature that Paul thought that perhaps he had gone to seed; there was a lassitude about Freddie Spink which suggested that he had already tried everything and found none of it worth finishing. He was blasé. Paul found himself more surprised and interested by the present Freddie Spink than he had

66

ever been by the old; Paul could say with truth that he had never really noticed Freddie Spink as a cadet.

"Anybody I know in your mighty ark?" Freddie asked.

"You might remember The Bodger," Michael said, casually.

"Is he really here? I heard he was. What a pity I'm just leaving. We need someone like him to brighten the place up."

"What about you, Freddie," said Paul. "What's this we hear about you marrying a Chinese girl?"

Freddie paused with his glass to his lips.

"*Eh?* What's all this?"

"Tommy Mitchell told us he was relieving you to save you from a fate worse than death with a Chinese tottie."

"So *that's* why he arrived so bloody early! I thought Their Lordships had got wise to one or two of my little activities. I can see how it all arose now. My uncle runs one of the better night-clubs on the Kowloon side, in fact the best night-club here. Whenever you see a first-class night-club you can bet it's run by a Spink. Fords make motor cars, Rothschilds manipulate money and we run night-clubs. My uncle is half Chinese and he introduced me to a Chinese family here and the daughter is an absolute honey. She went to Oxford and all that and she's one of the most charming girls you could meet anywhere. I used to take her about a bit, to the C.-in-C.'s ball and things like that. But I never intended to *marry* the girl."

"No, I don't suppose you would," said Paul.

"Oh, it's not on my side I can assure you," said Freddie. "It's *her* family who would never have allowed it."

"Why ever not?"

"What, let their daughter marry a naval officer, even though he does come from the best white-slaving circles? They aim a bit higher than that, I can tell you."

"How very disappointing," said Michael.

"Mind you," said Freddie, "I shan't be sorry to go. The social set, so-called, of this place, was beginning to get me down a bit. D'you know, when *Calypso* arrived on the station a couple of years ago she gave a cocktail party. Their Captain's Sec told me that it was like a party where the guests knew each other much better than the hosts. Which was quite true of course. The Locals gathered in groups and talked for two solid hours about people and events which the poor blokes in *Calypso* knew nothing about. And then a day or two later their Sec was at another party ashore and he met a girl who had been to their party on board. She didn't recognize him or ask him what he did for a living and she said 'My *dear!*' or words to that effect, 'we went to the most killingly boring party on Tuesday on that *boat* that's just come in. There were so many people there I knew that *really* I might just as well have gone to the Tennis Club. They had some terrible old red cocktails and the same old flags and things you see in all those boats.' Poor old Sec. I felt for him."

"Why for him particularly?"

"He was *Calypso's* Mess Sec. at the time."

"Cor blimey," said Paul, "you don't paint a very encouraging picture of Hong Kong."

"Ha, that's only one side, and the least important side. I'll show you how the other half lives now. Drink up men, and I'll take you on Spink's conducted tour of Hong Kong, licensed by Cooks and countenanced by the Board of Trade. I will be your Virgil through the dark underworld of this jewel of the orient."

"How many beers did you say you'd had?"

"A modicum, my dear Paul, a modicum. We step outside and regardez! Hong Kong by night!"

Hong Kong was blazing with lights. A stranger to the city stood amazed before them, like Sinbad at noon in the Valley of Diamonds. Lights poured and tumbled from the Peak in glittering waterfalls, archipelagos of lights, brilliant necklaces and pendants thrown on a velvet cloth. Headlights on the twisting Peak road shone out, were eclipsed and shone out again. The neon-lit Chinese characters were like signs traced in the sky by the glowing end of a magician's wand.

"Look at that sign," said Paul. "It probably means 'Soap' but in Chinese it looks like a magic formula."

"Actually, it means 'Girls'," said Freddie. "Let's go to Uncle's."

68

Uncle's was at the top of a flight of stairs which mounted between two buildings. It was a large room, lit by oil lamps which stood on small lacquered tables. The lamps were shaded by paper screens which were decorated with paintings of flowers, birds and fruit. The floor was covered with a carpet on which a huge dragon writhed and gaped its mouth at the door. The walls were curtained by folds of brocade cloth decorated in the same patterns as the lamp screens. The place smelled of spices and, Paul decided, money.

Freddie Spink crossed to one of the tables and before he reached it a Chinese had come from behind a curtain and placed a chair for him. Two more Chinese brought chairs for Michael and Paul.

"There don't seem to be any women about," said Paul.

"Patience, dear boy, patience. It's early yet. They won't turn up till later. Besides, we're on a drinking run tonight. You can't afford this place, anyway."

"Can't I?"

"No. Nor could I if it weren't Uncle's."

They ate clear soup, sour pork and dishes of savouries. Then they had chow ming and lychees and cups of China tea. Michael felt bloated. Freddie Spink talked about Hong Kong.

"Trade's good at the moment. This whole place is booming, you know. A lot of Chinese business men came here when the Communists took over China. They either had the choice of staying in China where they were likely to get their heads cut off any minute or go to Formosa where there's little scope. Or here. Most of them chose to come here. That's why there's so much building going on."

It was clear that Freddie Spink was completely at home in Hong Kong. He took them to quiet bars where Chinese in business suits were drinking tea; taxi dance halls where the girls could be purchased by ticket; dark caverns where Coca Cola, the only drink served, cost as much as whisky but included the services of a Chinese girl; and to garish places full of American airline pilots and thin girls in slit-skirt dresses. Freddie Spink was known wherever he went. Bartenders hurried to serve him when they saw him standing at the bar. Taxi-dance girls clustered round his table and rickshaw boys understood his directions.

"You seem to know where the heads are in every bar in this place," Paul said.

"I ought to," answered Freddie. "You know, I get the feeling there's a pretty powerful team ashore tonight. Are any of your wardroom ashore tonight?"

"Not that I know of," said Michael. "Nothing special, anyway."

Freddie Spink was not convinced. He was sure that somebody had been stirring up his favourite haunts.

"Everyone seems very excited tonight."

Freddie Spink was as sensitive as a great fish feeling the presence of an alien current in his own pool. He arranged his tour so that they arrived back at the dockyard at one o'clock.

"Well," he said. "That's that. I must go and say my tender good-byes now. I'm off to Australia the day after tomorrow."

"Whatever for?"

"I've got quite a bit of leave due to me and I thought I might go and see some relations. A friend of mine has offered me a lift in a plane so I might as well go home that way as any. It's almost as quick from here."

"Who have you got to say your fond farewells to, if you don't mind my asking?" asked Paul.

Freddie grinned. "I *have* got a little Chinese popsy here actually. I didn't know anyone knew about it. It shook me quite a lot when you mentioned it. Just shows, you can't fool the grapevine. Good night, fellows."

As Michael and Paul turned in at the dockyard gates, they saw that there had indeed been a powerful team ashore that night. Their attention was attracted by an uproar coming from the direction of the ferry. While they watched, a large crowd came running round the corner, headed by two rickshaws. In the leading rickshaw sat The Bodger, ringing a handbell and shouting "More revs! More revs!" Second by half a length and on the outside of the bend was the Commander who was waving a vast ivory fan and bellowing "Mush! Mush!" at the top of his voice. The rest of the crowd was made up of several yelling small boys, three or four sailors who had lost their caps, an empty rickshaw, a yellow mongrel, and, in the rear, two breathless members of the Hong Kong Constabulary.

★ 6 ★

"THIS new Jimmy," said Leading Seaman Jones, known to the messdeck as Hooky, "bit of a fire-eating *bas*tard."

"He's a —— menace," said a swarthy Able Seaman called Golightly sitting opposite. "Trooped me yesterday for a —— haircut."

"How's that, Golly?" enquired the rest of the messdeck.

Golightly glanced round to make sure of his audience. "I was standing outside the —— Regulating Office when along comes the Jimmy. Get your hair cut Golightly, he says. I've just *had* it cut, I says. Well, get it cut again, he says and stand a bit closer to the razor this time. I thought——"

Able Seaman Golightly relished the laughter of the messdeck.

"And then he says, what you doing standing outside the Regulating Office anyway, he says. Why ain't you working in your part of ship?"

"So what did you —— say to him, Golly?"

"I said, this *is* my part of ship, outside the Regulating Office."

The Bodger's personality had swept through the messdecks and life of *Carousel* like a breath of cold fresh air. The organization of a ship and the care of sailors was The Bodger's profession and he had had nearly fifteen years experience in it. The tools of his trade were a knowledge of the Navy's resources and an ability to study men; The Bodger read the sailors' faces as accurately as his predecessors of two hundred years had read the clouds to predict the wind. The Bodger understood the sailors' chief needs and he knew how far the Navy's official organization could satisfy them. The Bodger knew better than anyone on board the structure of authority and comfort which it was the First Lieutenant's duty to build and he set about building it as confidently as a skilled carpenter making a cabinet. His first concern was the state of the messdecks. He discussed the habitability of the ship with the Commander who agreed that while nothing could be done about the numbers of men on board, the surroundings could be made more pleasant.

"We can't make them any bigger," The Bodger said, "but at least we can make them a damn sight cleaner."

"Well that's a start anyway. I can't give you any more hands I'm afraid, but. . . ."

"That's all right, Jimmy. I don't need 'em. I'm going to bear down on the ones I've got."

The Bodger began a series of lightning rushes along the messdecks. His visits, like those of a meteor, were unpredictable and shattering. Just as the messdeck sweepers were settling down to their second afternoon cup of tea, The Bodger would appear with Chief Petty Officer Marks, the Messdecks Chief. The messdeck sweepers, who regarded their job as a quiet number awarded for long service and good conduct, staggered under the impact. However, they had all met keen First Lieutenants before and they resolved to weather the storm, humouring the new Jimmy, until The Bodger's first enthusiasm had evaporated. But The Bodger kept up his first pace and the messdeck sweepers realized, first with surprise and then with horror, that they had misjudged their man; this First Lieutenant's first enthusiasm was not going to evaporate. The Bodger was at last gratified to hear the sounds of scrubbing whenever he passed a messdeck or a bathroom.

One morning The Bodger heard not only scrubbing, but Beethoven. The Bodger paused in his stride and looked inside the messdeck. Behind a row of lockers a tall young sailor was whistling while he scrubbed the bulkhead. He stopped and stood upright when he saw The Bodger.

"This place is coming on quite a bit," said The Bodger encouragingly.

"Thank you, sir. But all I'm doing is picking up the odd pebble or two while the great ocean of dirt lies all untouched before me, sir."

"Eh?"

"This place must have been designed to be uncomfortable and dirty, sir."

The Bodger sensed in this young stripling a spirit akin to his own.

"The trouble is, sir, naval constructors don't go to *sea* in the ships they design."

Now that The Bodger had found a kindred spirit his first impulse, paradoxically, was to crush it. The Bodger beetled his eyebrows.

"You leave the design of the ship to those whose business it is," he said crushingly, "and get on with the cleaning of it."

"Aye aye, sir."

"I haven't seen you before. What's your name?"

"Darnay, sir. Ordinary Seaman Darnay, sir. I'm normally a quartermaster, sir, but the proper messdeck dodger has gone sick. He says he's overworked, sir."

The Bodger snorted. "A likely tale. Are you a National Serviceman?"

"Yes, sir."

"Well let me give you a bit of advice before you go finding out how the other half lives. Don't go bothering the other chap about his job in the Navy. Nine out of ten times it's all he can do to find out about it himself without having to worry about you. Understand?"

"Yes, sir."

"And incidentally, I may be wrong but I'm sure the second movement of the 'Emperor' is in *G* major."

The Bodger strode loftily away. That's fixed him, he thought.

"You 'eard," said Chief Petty Officer Marks to Ordinary Seaman Darnay. "Pick up yore little pebble and get started on that ocean."

The bathroom next door belonged to the stokers and from it music was also coming, not a concerto but a simple country air, and its composer less likely to be Beethoven than Rabelais.

"Oh Mrs Porter what shall I do?" sang a voice in a shrill, uncertain falsetto, "Can I spend my next weekend with you? Can I bring my three-badge oppo too?"

73

The bathroom door was obscured by a large ventilation trunking and the headroom was insufficient for anyone but a dwarf to stand upright. When The Bodger climbed in and crouched inside, the singer, a tubby stoker with "N.O.R.W.I.C.H." on the pocket of his shirt, who had been polishing the washbasins, politely put away his cloth and waited for The Bodger to comment on his bathroom.

"What's your name?"

"Crab, sir."

"Why've you got Norwich written on your shirt?"

"It's me home town, sir. And it's what I always write on the back of me letters to me wife, sir."

"Norwich?" The Bodger was baffled. He had heard of S.W.A.L.K.—"Signed with A Loving Kiss" and I.T.A.L.Y.—"I Trust and Love You" and even of B.U.R.M.A.—"Be Undressed Ready My Angel"—But N.O.R.W.I.C.H. defeated him.

"All right, I'll buy it. What's it mean?"

"Nickers Off Ready When I Come Home, sir."

"Ah. Stupid of me. Bit stuffy in here, isn't it? Is the ventilation working?"

"Partly, sir. We put in a defect but the electricians is too busy at the moment, sir."

"I see." The Bodger observed the discoloured paint on the bulkheads, the cracked mirrors, and the rust which lay on the deck under the basins.

"Lot of rust about," he said.

The Bodger looked at a small screen bulkhead near the showers. The white paint was streaked with long red trails of rust. Stoker Crab followed The Bodger's eye.

"Now take that bulkhead, sir. A month ago I scraped that bulkhead, sir. I scraped it to the bare metal. Then I wirescrubs it, gives it two coats of detel red and one of yellow chromate. Then I finished with two coats of white paint. It looked beautiful, sir. And now look at it. Makes you want to cry. It's like painting the Forth Bridge, this bathroom, sir, honestly. When I first see it, I tell you struth it made me 'ackles rise. Sometimes when I looks round me at the end of a hard day's work, sir, I feel I want to sit on the deck and sob like a little child, sir!"

"How many good conduct badges have you got, Crab?"

"Three, sir."

"I'll see what I can do about the ventilation."

"Thank you sir, and if you could slip a word to the painter, sir, we could get a bit extra paint and make a job of this place."

"I'll see, but first you want to get all that rust off."

"Aye aye, sir."

"Well, what you waiting for?" said Chief Petty Officer Marks to Stoker Crab. "Hadn't you better get on with yore Forth Bridge before it breaks yore heart?"

The Bodger went to visit the Deputy Electrical Officer. The D.L.O. lived in a brightly lit and well ventilated office on the main deck. There were four electrician's mates and a petty officer sitting at the desks. The Bodger remarked how all electrician's mates were either lanky with long hair and glasses, or with cropped hair and pimples.

"Eric . . ." The Bodger began.

"I *know* what you're going to say. Ventilation. Bodger, you see that large green tome at the end of the shelf there? That's the only book on that shelf *not* full of ventilation defects. Seriously, Bodger, I'm at my wit's end to find blokes to keep abreast of current defects without bothering about back numbers."

"But unless we have ventilation in these bathrooms we might as well wrap up painting them," said The Bodger. "The condensation is so bad in some places they're absolutely weeping. They're not only scruffy, they're unhygienic."

"I know. And since it's you Bodger, I'll make a special drive. I've been meaning to have a blitz on ventilation. I'll do my best."

"Thanks, Eric."

The Bodger also visited the Senior Engineer. He entered the Engineers' Office gingerly. As an executive officer in the very heart of the engineers' capital, it behoved The Bodger to walk warily. The Bodger knew of some executive officers, the Gunnery Officer in particular, who never entered the Engineers' Office at all but did all their business by proxy, through emissaries. The office was full of drawings, gloves, torches, messengers, overalls, ringing telephones and the largest tea-urn The Bodger had ever seen. The Bodger had not believed such tea-urns existed outside the Victoria and Albert Museum. Above Ginger's desk was a large notice, hand-painted on wood:

"Their Lordships feel it their bounden duty upon national and professional grounds to discourage to the utmost of their ability the employment of steam vessels as they consider the introduction of steam is calculated to strike a fatal blow at the Naval supremacy of the Empire."

Lord Melville, 1st Lord of the Admiralty, 1828

Ginger seemed pleased to see The Bodger.

"Wotcher, Bodger. What can I do for you? If it's more hands for store ship, you can't 'ave 'em."

"No, it's not that, Ginger. It's bathrooms. I wondered if something can be done about all the valves and things in them. They're as rusty as hell. I know we're not supposed to paint the working parts but could they be greased or something? I don't know what any of them are for, but I bet over half of them are seized up right now."

"Bodger, I'd love to have every valve in the ship shining. But I can't. No hands."

"No hands? But the engine-room department is. . . ."

" . . . One of the biggest in the ship. I know, but just let me demonstrate something." Ginger pulled out a sheet of paper. "Now, just watch this. There are three hundred and sixty-five days in the year. Right? Now, everyone sleeps for eight hours out of twenty-four which comes to roughly a hundred and twenty-two days a year. Don't interrupt. That leaves two hundred and forty-three. They get thirty-two days leave each year. Two hundred and eleven. They don't work on Sundays, fifty-two, nor Saturday afternoons and make and mends, another fifty-two. Which brings us down to a hundred and seven. One moment. I've calculated that the length of time they all spend up at requestmen and defaulters comes to twenty-three days a year. Eighty-four left. Then there's going to the sick bay, nineteen days, payment and mismusters for payment, seventeen, and divisions, nine. That leaves thirty-nine. Then there's holi-

76

days. They get Christmas Day, Boxing Day, Good Friday, Easter Monday, Whitmonday, August Bank Holiday and Nelson's Birthday off. Seven. Making thirty-two working days in the year. But wait, what's this? All the rest, the rum issues, hearing warrants, slops issues, sports parties, extra make and mends, clear lower deck for entering and leaving harbour, going to naval stores, Captain's rounds, kit musters, collecting laundry, patrols drawing and returning webbing equipment, all *that* comes to thirty-*three* days a year. So out of a whole year I get minus one day's work. I've got well over a hundred ratings in this department and I get *minus* one day's work from each one of them. Except in a Leap Year, of course, when I proff and get no work at all. . . ."

"All right, Ginger, I take your point. . . ."

"*However*, since it's you asking, Bodger, I'll bear down on this very thing. We'll have a big blitz on it. It's been in the back of my mind for some time."

"Thanks very much, Ginger."

"Stay and have a cup of tea, Bodger."

"Well, that's a very civil thought, Ginger."

"All done by steam, you know."

The Bodger made himself felt in the ship in other ways. It was he who persuaded Joan to muster her nieces in two ranks at Sunday divisions and have them inspected by the Captain. It was also The Bodger who put the American destroyer *Hiram J. Salt* in her place during *Carousel's* exercise with the American Fleet.

On their last run ashore in Hong Kong, the Commander and The Bodger had shared a bar, for a short time, with some Americans. The Americans were drinking Scotch whisky alternately from the bar and from thermos flasks which they had brought with them. They wore T shirts, Bermuda shorts and dark glasses. The leader of the party was addressed by all present as Wilbur and The Bodger understood from his conversation that Wilbur was the Commanding Officer of the destroyer U.S.S. *Hiram J. Salt* and that he had a poor opinion of the Royal Navy's ability to maintain a fleet train at sea and in particular to transfer such elementary fluids as oil fuel from ship to ship. Jimmy

Forster-Jones had barely succeeded in removing The Bodger in time.

"He must have seen something nasty in Piccadilly Circus when he was two," The Bodger said loudly.

When The Bodger read the signal detaching *Carousel* from the main exercise to refuel *Hiram J. Salt* he howled gleefully.

"Yonder's Wilbur!"

The Bodger went away to consult with the D.L.O. and the radio artificer in charge of the ship's broadcast.

As First Lieutenant, The Bodger was in charge of refuelling at sea and he prepared very carefully for the event. He had long conversations with the Bos'un; the rest of the wardroom could hear snatches, the Bos'un saying "Two trough method" and "jackstay method" and The Bodger saying, "Of course, *if* we had self-rendering winches. . . ."

The day could not have been better chosen for The Bodger. The exercise had started in rough weather and a heavy sea was still running on the third day when *Hiram J. Salt* began her approach from *Carousel's* port quarter.

The Bodger had his team ready on the boat deck: the Bos'un with a whistle and an anxious expression, the Chief G.I. holding the line-throwing gun and wearing a red luminous waistcoat like a medieval knight's breastplate, the Chief Bos'un's Mate with lungs ready inflated to bellow orders, the crane-driver hoping someone would remember to tell him what was happening and not leave him (as last time) to guess for himself, a party of sailors ready with the lines, a telephone rating, flags and boards. Mr Pilgrim stood near by with his Chief Stoker and a huddle of depressed-looking stokers. Mr Pilgrim was looking wistfully at the crane-head as though he were longing for the old days at Scapa when they coaled *Irresistible* in six hours, ten minutes.

The Bodger glanced for the last time over his arrangements, at the hose slung in its two cradles, the men on the topping lifts, and the lines rove through blocks on the boatdeck. The Bodger ran over the sequence in his mind: gun-line, messenger, distance line with coloured markers and the telephone cable, hose line, and then the hose itself.

All was ready and dependent upon *Hiram J. Salt* and upon Wilbur.

Hiram J. Salt approached confidently, perhaps, in the opinion of *Carousel's* ship's company who crowded the upper deck to watch, too confidently. On the bridge, the Captain muttered anxiously.

"He's one of these Grand Prix drivers obviously. Midshipman, ring up the engine-room and tell them I want absolutely steady revs from now on."

"Aye aye, sir," said Andrew Bowles, who was midshipman of the watch.

The Commander stood on the bofors gun deck below the bridge and looked down on the boat deck.

"This," he told himself, "should be a guinea a minute from now on."

Hiram J. Salt's bow bit deeply into the sea and threw a solid curtain of spray over her superstructure. She was near enough for the watchers in *Carousel* to distinguish the figures on her bridge and the cluster of men at the fuelling point amidships. A negro cook was sitting on a stool by the after screen wearing that expression of supercilious disdain which small ship sailors reserve for coming alongside larger ships. The negro cook exasperated The Bodger.

"A murrain on his black hide," The Bodger said.

When *Hiram J. Salt* was level with *Carousel's* quarter-deck her bows unexpectedly swung towards *Carousel*. The destroyer wavered uncertainly and at last turned away and began to open out from *Carousel*.

"*Now* what's he up to?" said the Captain irritably.

"He's turning away, sir. Going to go round again," said the Navigating Officer.

"I can see *that*. But why?"

A telephone rang at the back of the bridge. Andrew Bowles answered it.

"From the First Lieutenant, sir, suggest we make a signal to *Hiram J. Salt,* Matthew, eleven, three, sir."

"What's that? I don't know the reference."

Andrew Bowles consulted the telephone.

"The First Lieutenant says it's 'And said unto him, Art thou he that should come, or do we look for another?' sir."

79

The whole bridge exploded into laughter, as though The Bodger's suggestion had put *Hiram J. Salt's* antics back into perspective again.

"Right," said the Captain, "make that to our friend right away."

"Aye aye, sir."

The Navigating Officer put up his glasses. "*Hiram's* signalling, sir. Can you read that, Signalman?"

"Just getting it, sir. Message is . . . Sorry . . . Quartermaster . . . has toothache . . . here . . . I . . . come . . . again. Sorry, quartermaster has toothache here I come again, sir."

"Very good."

Hiram J. Salt approached for the second time at almost half the speed, so slowly that the Captain grew impatient.

"Come on, man, we can't stop here all day."

As *Hiram J. Salt* crept up to *Carousel's* side, The Bodger held up his thumb. A hand behind a scuttle in the bridge superstructure acknowledged the gesture. *Hiram J. Salt* plunged and swooped at her slower speed and was at the extent of a roll when *Carousel's* upperdeck loudspeakers burst into raucous music.

"One for the money!"

Wilbur lifted his head from the voice-pipe.

"Two for the show!"

Wilbur cocked his head enquiringly at his First Lieutenant.

"Three to be ready and *go cat go!*"

Hiram J. Salt swung nearer *Carousel* and her bow rose and fell sharply.

"Rock! *Rock!* ROCK EVERYBODY!" roared *Carousel's* loudspeakers. "Roll! *Roll!* ROLL EVERYBODY!"

Wilbur handed his cap to his First Lieutenant and did an impromptu dance on the wing of his bridge. The music faded as the two ships came level.

The crack of the line-throwing rifle was like a race starting-gun. The spidery white line soared out over the water. The distance line was hauled in and passed forward to the destroyer's fo'c'sle. The telephone was connected and Ordinary Seaman Darnay, the telephone rating, began to test communications. Meanwhile *Hiram J. Salt's* sailors, led by the negro cook, hauled in the hoseline, *Carousel's* sailors eddied to and fro, the Chief Bos'n's Mate barked sharply, the crane-driver swore monotonously, and The Bodger grew purple in the face.

Hiram J. Salt were having trouble. Twice they attempted to haul away the hoseline at the run and twice they were brought up short. Wilbur leaned over the bridge rail and shouted at the negro cook through a megaphone.

"Satchmo, is you is or is you ain't a *cook*?"

"Will you say again all after 'Goddam limeys,' please," said Ordinary Seaman Darnay.

"Roll on my —— twelve," said the crane-driver fervently.

"Just as I thought," said the Commander. "A guinea a minute."

Apart from his duties as First Lieutenant The Bodger was also Defence Officer and responsible for the ship's damage control. He had organized a few minor exercises but he had discovered that the only ratings taking part were one watch of stokers and E.R.A.s, and the shipwrights; the rest of the ship's company were unaffected and uninterested. The Bodger resolved to remedy that and, with the Captain's permission, organized a full-scale exercise while the ship was at sea.

Michael's action station was on the Gun Direction Position, but when the Captain saw him there with the rest of the G.D.P. crew he objected to the crowd.

"Too many bloody people up here," the Captain said. "Hobbes, go down to one of the section bases and see what's going on. It won't do you any harm to see how the other half lives."

Michael made his way down the ladders to the Canteen Flat where Bongo Lewis was in charge of Number One Damage Control Section.

A motley rabble of stokers, electrician's mates, shipwrights, E.R.A.s, stewards and sick berth attendants choked the flat outside the Base. A Chief Stoker was standing on a hatch cover calling out names and ticking them off on a board. Michael could see no order or rote in the roll-call but one by one men crept furtively away to unknown destinations and for unnamed reasons.

Inside the Base itself were Bongo Lewis, a stoker on the switchboard, an E.R.A. wearing a pair of headphones, and a miscellaneous rating, who might have been a cook or a steward, crouched in a corner smoking a cigarette.

Bongo was speaking on the telephone and grimacing at the bulkhead.

"I don't think that's possible, sir. . . . If you remember, we tried it last time, sir. . . . No, we couldn't get it out for days. . . . But *sir*. . . . Aye aye, sir."

Bongo replaced the telephone and looked despondently at Michael.

"Christ Almighty," he said. "Commander (E) wants to exercise taking a pump down the Naval Store and pumping it out. Last time we did it, it broke somebody's foot and got jammed down there. We had to burn away a stanchion to get it out."

The loudspeaker on the bulkhead hummed, and spoke.

"All sections, this is H.Q. One, report when your sections are closed up and in Damage Control State One."

The stoker on the switchboard, who had the name "Yorky" in white paint across his shirt pocket, came to life. He picked up a telephone and made two switches.

"This is D.C. Base One section closed up and in Damage Control State One," he said, without consulting Bongo Lewis or even asking any other person for information.

"All sections, this is H.Q. One, test communications."

Yorky began to test communications. He settled down to the job in comfort, as though he understood it perfectly and knew that it would take him at least an hour.

" 'C' Fire and Repair Party," he said, "this is D.C. Base One, testing communications, how do you hear me?" He paused and looked up at the deckhead. " 'C' Fire and Repair Party this is D.C. Base One, how do you hear me?" He paused again. " *'C' Fire and Repair Party, this is D.C. Base One, how do you hear. . . .* Hello, that you Jumper? Yorky here. How's yourself? Loud and clear? Loud and clear also. Cheers, oppo." Yorky reset the switches and made two more. " 'A' Magazine Flood, this is D.C. Base One. . . ."

"It's pointless testing communications really," Bongo said to Michael. "There's never anything wrong with the telephones. The trouble is getting somebody to speak on them the other end. This section is so big once people get away from the base you can never find them again. They just disappear like water in the sands of the Nile. It's all right for people like Paul. His base is next door to his cabin and he's got everything all round him. I have to keep half a dozen hands outside the door here so I've always got someone I can send right away. Who are you?"

The crouching figure in the corner stood up.

"I'm a . . ."

"Take that cigarette out of your mouth!"

"I'm a steward, sir."

"Yes, but *what* are you?"

"I'm the runner, sir," the steward said shamefacedly, as though he were confessing to some loathsome disability.

"The runner! Didn't know we had one. Well, run round to the Chief Stoker in the Capstan Flat and tell him to start getting his pump down into the Naval Store. We'll be needing it."

Bongo sat down and put his feet up on the table.

"It always takes them a quarter of an hour to get themselves sorted out in H.Q. One," he explained to Michael.

Michael looked outside. He was repelled by the hostile stares of six stokers who were squatting on the deck. They all wore blue overalls with their names painted across the pocket. Michael noticed that the names fell into clearly defined groups. There were names of purely geographical significance, such as Scouse, Geordie and Jan; alliterative or traditional names, such as Bomber and Dusty; and names referring to their owner's physical properties, such as Lofty. Michael was intimidated by the stares and withdrew his head. But he had been noticed.

"Who's that ——, Scouse?"

"Some —— from the upper deck."

"What's he —— doing here?"

"—— goofing."

83

"Cor ——."

"The ship will shortly be listed to an angle of ten degrees. This is being done to give damage control parties experience in working under action conditions," snarled the broadcast. The stokers outside sucked their teeth.

"First they list the ship so we can all learn to walk —— sideways," said Scouse, "then I suppose they'll go astern so we can all walk —— backwards."

Michael watched the heel indicator. It was already beginning to swing. Yorky was still testing communications.

"Paint Store this is D.C. Base One. Testing communications, how do you hear me? *Paint* Store how do you hear me? Eh? Can you hear me that's all I want to know. Well, pull your finger out lad, I haven't got all day. Loud and clear, Roger."

"The ship has just received a torpedo hit starboard side forrard. All sections report damage."

Without a break in his voice, Yorky put himself through to H.Q. One.

". . . This is D.C. Base One. Torpedo hit starboard side forrard. Free flooding between eighteen and sixty-eight frames, up to five deck, starboard side. Flooding boundary being established from seventy-two frame forrard. Free surface in Communications Branch messdeck, cofferdams now being rigged. Complete electrical failure forrard of ninety-seven bulkhead. Two small fires in the Acetylene and Dope Store and one in the Forward Cold Room now under control. Firemain break both sides at eighty-four bulkhead being isolated at a hundred and three bulkhead. Casualties unknown. More assistance required with medical aid, pumps and fire-fighting equipment. Got that? Well, why the bloody hell don't you listen? What's the use of me spieling away here? I say again. Torpedo hit starboard side. . . .'

"He's done these exercises before," Bongo said to Michael apologetically.

"Yes, I can see that," Michael said admiringly. He looked at Yorky with newly-awakened eyes; he realized, for the first time, that he was in the presence of greatness.

The E.R.A. wearing the headphones was covering a large

board with hieroglyphics in coloured pencil. He seemed absorbed in his task, dwelling on each symbol with loving significance. Bongo poked him.

"What are you doing, Bodily?"

Bodily removed his headphones.

"Incident Board, sir," he said.

"I *know* that. What's that thing there?"

"Electrical fire in the Forward Compressor Room, sir."

"Did you report an electrical fire in the compressor room, Higgins?"

"No, sir," said Yorky.

"Scrub that out. You must keep the Incident Board *accurate,* Bodily."

"Yes, sir."

"For exercise, for exercise, fire in the Forward Compressor Room."

E.R.A. Bodily looked reproachfully at Bongo Lewis.

"I should have known better," Bongo said to Michael. "Bodily's done these exercises before, too."

D.C. Base One, this is H.Q. One, rig portable pump in G Naval Store.

Yorky twirled a handle.

"Rig portable pump in the Naval Store."

"What's that?" shouted the voice at the other end of the line. Michael could hear the tinny sound from where he stood.

"Rig portable pump. . . ."

"Who's a chump?"

"Now don't be funny, Wings, rig portable pump. . . ."

"What pump?"

"The message is 'Rig portable pump. . . .' "

"I know, I *know!*" yelled the voice excitedly. "I know what the bloody message is and my message to you is 'Get knotted!' "

Yorky held the dead telephone for a moment. Then he looked round and Michael was surprised to see him blushing.

"I'm sorry, sir. I got the Chapel by mistake."

"Never mind, they're doing it anyway."

"D.C. Base One, this is H.Q. One, for exercise, for exercise, flood 'A' Magazine."

"Now get this one right, Higgins," said Bongo. "We don't want any more trouble with Mr Broad."

Yorky repeated the message.

"You may think this all a bit of chaos, Mike. . . ."

"Oh, not at all."

"But it's surprising, if you have enough of them the troops do get the idea eventually. But you've got to keep on at it, just like everything else. It's no good having an exercise once in a blue moon, everyone's forgotten where everything is. You've got to have lots of exercises. Trouble is that it's usually the engine-room department who get clobbered for them. They close up while every other bastard in the ship goes to standeasy. . . ."

A flying figure scattered the stokers by the door. It was Slim Broad, the Commissioned Gunner. Bongo's welcoming smile faded when he saw Slim Broad's face.

"That's the second time I've caught that moron on the flooding cabinet swinging off on the valves," Slim Broad said grimly. "You might get the buzz to your blokes that this is an *exercise*."

"Message from 'C' Pump and Flood, sir! Will you send an S.B.A. down to the Naval Store quickly, sir, the Chief Stoker's hurt himself with that pump."

The ship will shortly be closed down to Action! State One to exercise attack by atomic warfare."

"They're always trying to make you do without —— food," Scouse said bitterly. "Now they're trying to make you do without —— *air* as well."

★ 7 ★

MICHAEL, Paul and Tim Castlewood, the Sports Officer, were walking the quarter-deck. The quarter-deck, after dinner, was the recognized time and place for officers to promenade and take the air.

"I wonder how they're getting on down in the laundry?" said Tim Castlewood casually.

"What do you mean?" Michael demanded. As Laundry Officer, he was sensitive to the subject.

"I must pay a visit there some day. I want to see the machine that crushes the buttons on my shirts."

Paul saw his cue joyfully. "And the machine what drills holes in my pants. . . ."

"*And* the gadget that puts brown stains on my collars. . . ."

"Now *look*. . . ."

"It's all right, Mike. I'm only getting at you. Laundry officers are *always* got at."

"I'm getting fed up with it."

"It has been a little erratic in the past, Mike, you must admit."

"Only once. That was that bloody feud."

Michael had known nothing of laundries when he joined *Carousel*. His first visit had been a terrifying experience. He was met by the Laundry Manager, a Chinese known as Number One Boy, who led Michael through a succession of dark, steamy caverns containing small, weird machines which were like nothing Michael had ever seen before. Tiny pistons worked to and fro, spouting steam. A press like a giant hand descended with a vicious sizzling. Chinese faces, inscrutable, indistinct, peered at Michael through the gloom. After that first visit Michael left the running of the laundry to Number One Boy and confined himself to standing rounds once a week, and sending in his own laundry every day.

Michael heard of the laundry feud from The Bodger.

"Hobbes! One of your bloody Chinamen has disappeared! Get down there and find out what Number One Boy's been up to!"

Number One Boy had been up to nothing. It was two of his nephews (all the laundry boys were Number One Boy's nephews) who had been causing trouble, Number One Boy explained.

The Chinese on the collar-shaping machine had a long feud with the Chinese who worked the shirt-presser. Michael could not uncover the original cause of the dispute but

Collar-Shaper Boy had confided to Spin-Dryer Boy, his particular friend, that it was his intention to murder Shirt-Presser Boy. The news travelled down the subterranean corridors of the laundry to Shirt-Presser Boy and made him wary. The rest of the laundry boys observed the feud dispassionately; sooner or later the laundry would need either a new Collar-Shaper Boy or a new Shirt-Presser Boy. Nor was Number One Boy himself concerned. He had a nephew in Hong Kong who could work either machine. (He would, however, have preferred the feud to smoulder until the ship reached Hong Kong so that the new nephew could take over with the minimum of delay.)

As the weeks of the feud passed, Collar-Shaper Boy gained a moral ascendancy; he seemed to exert a subtle, enervating influence upon Shirt-Presser Boy. Day by day, the laundry's collars were more superbly turned out, the shirts more poorly finished. Shirt-Presser Boy was moody, listless and lackadaisical. The grin on Collar-Shaper Boy's face grew broader and he flexed his fingers eagerly. Number One Boy wrote to his nephew in Hong Kong.

But one morning, a wonder came to light in the Laundry. Shirt-Presser Boy appeared for work. Collar-Shaper Boy did not. Michael could not penetrate further than the fact that one evening a Collar-Shaper Boy had been at work and the following morning none had appeared. Number One Boy pointed to the idle collar-shaper as proof.

"No piecee collar," he said. "Boy gone no work."

Down the gangway, Michael could see a Chinese loading towels into the spin-dryer and keeping his face turned towards the shirt-presser. The message had been passed that Shirt-Presser Boy intended to exact revenge on Spin-Dryer Boy for the part he had played in the feud with Collar-Shaper Boy. Number One Boy was not concerned; he had a nephew in Hong Kong who could work the spin-dryer.

"I must go down there one day," Paul said. "I want to see the thing that shrinks my overalls."

"Oh, drop it," said Michael. "I don't suppose your department is all that hot either."

"By no means."

Paul, too, had his problems. Outside Machinery embraced

88

all the machinery in the ship which was not covered by definition in other departments. Its scope ranged from the capstan forward to the steering gear aft, and from the fresh-water tank on the main mast to the fresh-water pumps below the stokers' messdeck. "All the odds and sods," as Ginger explained it to Paul. Paul's chief assistant was an aged mechanician named Fogarty, a Yorkshireman and a philosopher. It was Fogarty who taught Paul an ancient engineering truth.

"All machines like to be visited, sir," said Fogarty. "Even if you don't *do* nothing, they likes you to stand and look at 'em."

Paul discovered that there was much in Fogarty's theory. Paul found that it paid him to make a daily round of his department and he performed it religiously, as though making a daily obeisance at each individual shrine.

Fogarty had no truck with modern methods of maintenance. To each emergency call he took a hammer and a handful of cotton waste.

"There's only two reasons why it don't work," he explained to Paul. "The seamen have bunged it up wi' paint or it's stuck."

Fogarty had yet another remedy.

"If it still don't work, Ah fetches a bigger hammer."

Paul had one responsibility about which neither he nor Fogarty could do anything. Paul visited it every morning but was not permitted to do more. It had been fitted by the dockyard before the ship left England and it stood on the fo'c'sle, motionless, tarpaulined and sinister. The ship's company nicknamed it The Thing and forgot it until The Bodger, reading signals in the wardroom log, indirectly drew attention to it.

"Goddamn a thousand damnations! Talk about security! No wonder the Americans get cheesed off with us."

The Communications Officer, who sensed an attack on his department, assumed mental guard.

"What's the matter, Bodger?"

The Bodger ignored him. "Just put me in a sealed room ashore somewhere and give me nothing to read except the *un*classified *un*restricted signals published every day and

I'll bet within a week I could tell you the name of every ship in the harbour, its training programme, and its state of readiness for war. Give me a *fortnight* and I could tell you the name of the Chief Cook and the crew of the Captain's gig!"

"Oh come, Bodger. . . ."

"Goddamn it man, you can get a list of ships from the *football* fixtures! Here's somebody wants some more duffle coats. They're hardly likely to be going to the Equator, are they? And here's *Tadpole*, being visited by the C.-in-C. with his flag flying and getting fuel from a lighter and giving an R.P.C. all on the same day. It doesn't take an Einstein to work out what they're doing, does it? Quite correct, they're leaving the station. All you've got to do is lie off the Limoun Pass in a submarine and monitor a couple of wavebands and after three weeks you could go home with a better idea of the working of the station than the C.-in-C. himself!"

"What's the excitement, Bodger?" asked the rest of the wardroom.

"For months," said The Bodger, "we've had that Thing on the cable deck. It's so damn secret we're not even allowed to touch it, let alone know what it is. And now this signal, in plain language, says 'Mr Merrydown, of Admiralty, trials party of three, and one press representative will be joining *Carousel* a.m. Tuesday for duration of trials. Request usual facilities.' I *ask* you!"

"It does seem to be a slip-up in the drill," the Communications Officer admitted. But the rest of the wardroom were intrigued by the chance of actually seeing The Thing.

"You don't mean they're actually going to let us have a look at it?" said the Gunnery Officer. "I thought it was all 'for Kremlin eyes only, burn before reading' stuff."

"I wonder if there's anything at all under there?"

"That reminds me Bodger," said the Commander. "Will you look after the boffins when they arrive? Give them cabins and see they don't fall through any holes in the deck. One of them is supposed to be a very important chappie. He's the only man in the U.K. who knows how it works."

The Bodger allocated cabins, arranged a boat and forgot

about the whole matter until a very stout man in a green sports coat and grey corduroy trousers stopped him in the passageway after breakfast one morning.

"I say," said the man in the sports coat coyly, "could you tell me where to go to spend a penny please?"

The Bodger's jaw dropped open.

"A what a what?"

"Spend a penny, please?"

The Bodger tossed the penny to and fro until it dropped.

"You must be the trials party?"

"Right. My name is Merrydown. We've just come on board. . . ."

"But where are the rest?"

"On the quarter-deck."

The other members of the party were standing on the quarter-deck by a pyramid of suitcases, tape recorders, tripods and strangely-shaped leather cases. Mr Merrydown introduced them.

"Masterson. Known to everybody in A.R.L.E.F. as Bat. This is his show really. He designed it."

Bat Masterson was a tiny man with white hair which shot straight up from his head.

"Beetle, D.E.E.M.E.D.'s representative and Cowplain, from Barwick and Todhunter's, the makers."

Beetle had horn-rimmed spectacles and khaki shorts. Cowplain was bald-headed and had a figure which reminded The Bodger of a Conference Pear. The Bodger shook hands.

"Stephen Ropehead, naval correspondent of the *Daily Disaster*."

Stephen was wearing a chrysanthemum-dotted purple shirt and a green Tyrolian hat. The Bodger shook hands with a wince.

"Don't I know your face?" he asked sternly.

"I covered the fire in *Voluminous* and the mutiny in *Wave Osteopath*. You may have seen me then."

"No, it wasn't then. I'll remember later."

"Or perhaps it was the wreck of the *Snarkfish*? Or you weren't a witness in that incest case were you?"

"No. No. No. Proper Jonas, aren't you?" The Bodger said. "Gentlemen, the midshipman of the watch will show

91

you your cabins and I'll have a steward to collect your gear."

"Is this a happy ship?" The Bodger heard Stephen ask the quartermaster as he went down the hatch.

The news of Mr Merrydown and his party flashed round the ship and a large crowd gathered round The Thing on the first morning at sea when Bat Masterson was seen approaching.

Bat Masterson had longed for an appreciative audience all his life. Conscious of the intent eyes upon him, he very deliberately loosened the guy-ropes and carefully took off and coiled down the lashings. He twitched the edge of the tarpaulin and then, with a quick tug, uncovered The Thing.

Cynical as they were and scornful of anything designed by the Admiralty, the sailors (and their officers gathered discreetly in the rear) could not restrain a gasp of awe and admiration. If Bat Masterson had designed The Thing, then the man was an artist. It resembled a harpoon gun but was bigger and more robust, as though its harpoons were armed with atomic warheads. It looked as light and fragile as a spider's web but as strong as steel scaffolding. Its long barrel leaped from a pedestal as graceful as a woman's throat and tapered to a sharp antenna-like point. The butt was a solid block studded with gauges and coloured levers. In spite of their long sojourn under a tarpaulin the paintwork and the glass were still bright and shining. It was a beautiful Thing.

There were two bucket seats upholstered in red leather by the breech. The Conference Pear climbed into the lower and Bat Masterson into the upper. They pulled several of the levers and studied the gauges. The Thing began to hum and slowly revolved through an arc of a circle. The barrel depressed and elevated again. By means of a small joy-stick Bat Masterson controlled The Thing as effortlessly as a conductor waving a baton.

"O.K. Bat?" Mr Merrydown called up from the base of The Thing.

Bat Masterson, assured of his audience and determined not to waste a minute of the limelight, gestured impatiently.

He began to demonstrate The Thing, playing upon it like a sensitive instrument. The Thing was incredibly quick, one moment inching round, snake-like and menacing, and the next lashing suddenly in a half-circle, making the sailors watching drop back a pace.

"Are you all right, Bat?"

Bat Masterson bared his teeth in a grimace of exasperation. The barrel quartered the sky, waving gently like an insect's feeler, then locked rigidly as though it had scented a target, and tracked steadily across the horizon. The Thing accelerated until it was spinning rapidly on its axis and Bat Masterson was indistinguishable except for his flying white hair.

"Are you all right, Bat?"

The spinning slowly stopped. Bat Masterson reset the levers. The hum died away. Bat Masterson and the Conference Pear climbed down.

"—— lovely," said the sailors. "But what's it —— for?"

The Bodger had the same sentiments. Cautiously, he sounded Mr Merrydown.

"Quite an impressive thing, isn't it?" he said, cunningly. "What *is* it exactly?"

But Mr Merrydown was not to be drawn. "Can't tell you that, I'm afraid," he said. "This is just a prototype. If it works we'll build a bigger job ashore and if that's a success we'll make another shipborne one. Then we'll go back on shore again and finally we hope to have something for service in the Fleet."

"But how long will that take?"

"Years, old boy, years. Rome wasn't built in a day, you know."

Mr Merrydown walked away, chuckling.

"Today's beautiful thought," said The Bodger.

The ship settled quickly on her passage to the trials area. Conditions on the messdecks and wardroom of *Carousel*, a ship isolated in a tropical climate for most of the year, were ideal for the growth and flowering of individual idiosyncrasies; any man who had a mole or wart in his nature found a fertile atmosphere in which to develop it.

Every messdeck had its mouth-organists, rug-makers, marquetry-workers and ship-modellers. Everyone had some means of leisure employment; those who did not knit, or embroider, or write pornographic poems, sat in corners and grew beards or contemplated suicide. In the wardroom, the P.M.O. opened a file on any officers whose behaviour he considered was trespassing nearer than the norm to insanity. The file swiftly included most of the wardroom. The P.M.O. wrote brilliantly reasoned letters to *The Lancet* upon environmental insanity.

A large canvas swimming pool was erected on the fo'c'sle, fed by water from the firemain. In the dog watches, there was deck hockey and clay pigeon shooting on the quarter-deck, boxing on the upper deck, judo and weight-lifting on the boat deck and all over the ship naked sun-worshippers stretched themselves out, burning themselves a darker mahogany brown. Spin-Dryer Boy disappeared one night.

Bat Masterson's skill with The Thing had made him one of the most popular men on board and such was his personal standing that his invention was nicknamed Miranda. Every morning a large crowd watched Bat Masterson put Miranda through her paces. The sailors came to know all her tricks and recognized all her characteristic sounds. Above all, the sailors enjoyed Bat Masterson's *pièce de résistance*, when he spun Miranda like a top until he himself became invisible but for his flying hair. The performance was always rewarded by a round of clapping, shouts of "Encore" and, from the Instructor Officer (who was a balletomane) "Bis!" Bat Masterson flourished under the applause; he would bow to each side and descend, flushed and smiling, each silver hair on his head standing rigid with gratification.

At dawn after a week at sea the Navigating Officer informed the Captain that the ship was in position for the trials, midway between Wake Island and the Marianas and more than two hundred miles from the nearest land.

The Captain, who was looking through binoculars at a small brown cloud on the horizon, grunted disbelievingly.

"I'm not so sure about that, Pilot," he said. "What do you make of that cloud over there?"

"I would say it was a cloud, sir."

"Would you! I would say it was land."

The Navigating Officer made a pretence of looking again. It was an important part of his job to humour the Captain in the very early morning.

"It can't be land, sir. I'm sure it's a cloud."

"Trouble is that it's almost in the sun and I can't make it out clearly. But I bet it's land."

"There isn't any land there, sir," said the Navigating Officer aggrievedly. The Captain was blaspheming against everything the Navigating Officer held sacred.

"I *know* it's land."

The Navigating Officer heard, in his inmost soul, the sound of the veil of the temple at H.M.S. *Dryad* being rent from top to bottom.

"We'll go and have a look anyway." The Captain took a bearing. "Come round to zero four five. I've got a feeling in my water there's something funny going on over there."

As they came nearer it was obvious that it was no ordinary cloud. It was isolated on the horizon, a single stain on the hard blue sky. It changed shape very slowly, elongating and gaining height. It appeared to be hanging over the surface of the sea. At about ten miles distance the Captain could see that the cloud was in fact mushroom-shaped, consisting of a broad hazy head supported on a thick black column.

The starboard look-out stiffened and shouted.

"Green four five sir, large eddy on the sea, sir!"

"*Look* at that!"

Broad on the starboard bow, a gigantic eddy swirled and subsided again, as though a huge mouth had opened in the sea.

The Captain ran his finger along the bridge rail.

"Volcanic dust, or something like it."

From two miles, the cloud's components could be seen clearly. The mushroom head was a dense dust haze and the stalk was a rain of boulders and lava. Beneath the falling, erupting boulders, not more than fifty feet high, but plainly visible, was an island.

"What did I tell you, Pilot!" cried the Captain jubilantly. "It's land after all! The damn thing must have been forced up from the sea bed. If we came back here tomorrow there probably wouldn't be a sign of it. Pass the word to that press representative. This is right up his street."

The ship began to swing wildly off course.

"Thirty of port wheel on, sir!" shouted the helmsman. "Can't hold course, sir!"

"*Hard* a port!"

"Hard a port, sir. . . . Wheel's hard a port, sir! Ship's not answering, sir!"

"Very good. Midships."

"*Midships*. . . . Wheel's amidships, sir."

Carousel spun like a toy boat in a bath. On either side swelling eddies surged up and shoals of fish swirled to the surface and were dragged down again. Solitary waves, lead-coloured and as much as twenty feet high, reared and fell onto the upper deck. *Carousel* had been caught in an oceanic convulsion like the birth pang of the planet itself.

Fine dust drifted and settled on the upper decks and superstructure and the Captain found time to think of the Commander's face when the watches fell in to scrub decks.

"Senior Engineer on the telephone, sir. He'll have to shut down the main engines soon, sir, the sea temperature's over a hundred, sir. . . ."

"Main switchboard report two turbo-generators off the board, sir. . . ."

Stephen Ropehead appeared on the bridge and the Navigation Officer rolled a frenzied eye at him.

"Here you are! Put this in your damned scandal sheet!"

Stephen looked at the thundering column of boulders, the huge livid waves leaping and plunging at random in every direction, and the yellow banks of dust. He shrugged his shoulders.

"No human interest," he said.

The ship swung her stern to the island and the Captain seized his chance.

"Hard a starboard!"

"Sea temperature's still rising, sir. . . ."

"*Full* ahead together! *Bugger* the sea temperature!"

Black smoke poured from the funnels as the chief stokers in the boiler rooms ordered more sprayers. Shuddering along every girder and plate as she strained round in her turn, the ship fought clear and, still accelerating, glided into cool blue water.

"Half ahead together."

The bow wave dropped. The boiling wake subsided. The Commander appeared on deck and glared in disbelief at the dust on the quarter-deck.

"Let that be a lesson to us, Pilot," said the Captain. "Mind your own bloody business until after breakfast!"

The ship returned to normality so quickly that it was difficult for the Captain to believe that the volcanic island had not been a phantom; only the cloud, now far astern, remained as proof that he had not dreamed the whole incident. The dust, however, was not a trick of imagination. It lay thickly all over the ship and the seamen had to use hoses to wash it off.

Mr Merrydown appeared on the bridge.

"Pity we couldn't have avoided the dust, Captain," he said severely. "It's very bad for the works."

The Captain remembered. "The trial! I'd forgotten about it. What are we to do now, Pilot? We obviously can't have it here."

"We can go north about fifty miles from here, sir, and still be in the area. It brings us a bit nearer the shipping routes but it should be pretty clear. It's been published in the Notices to Mariners."

The Captain snorted derisively. "Fat lot of good that will be. If you want to keep anything a secret, publish it in Notices to Mariners. We'd better close up radar. We'll start the trial at nine-thirty. What do you want us to do, Merrydown?"

"We'd like to fire the first one with the ship stopped, Captain. Then at low speeds, working up to as fast as you can go, steaming on a north-south line. Then we'll do the same thing on an east-west line. Finally we'll fire with the ship circling. After that, Bat and I will correlate the data and decide whether we require another set of readings."

At nine-thirty, Bat Masterson stepped proudly up to Miranda, like a conductor mounting his rostrum. All the other mornings had been rehearsals; this was the performance. Bat Masterson and the Conference Pear climbed into their seats, made switches, set levers, and waited for Miranda's tuning noise, warming the intricate circuits and relays in her interior. But Miranda remained passive and silent. Patiently, like a rider whose horse is being fractious, Bat Masterson went through Miranda's starting routine again. But still Miranda refused to start. The sailors watched with bated breaths; their hearts were with Bat Masterson.

"What's the matter, Bat?" Mr Merrydown shouted from the screen.

Bat Masterson ignored him and set himself to start Miranda. No theatre organist practising for an audition, no lathe operator turning out jobs against the clock, could have rivalled Bat Masterson's performance in the following minutes. He pounced from knob to lever and from lever to switch. He set gauges to zero and levers to maximum. He reset gauges to full deflection and levers to neutral. He tried every permutation and combination of the controls. But Miranda remained unresponsive.

At last, red-faced and unable to meet the eyes of the sailors, Bat Masterson climbed down and opened a small tool box set in Miranda's base. He took out a crank and inserted it in a hole in the side of the pedestal.

"Well, goddamn my old sombrero," said The Bodger. "It's a starting-handle!"

But the starting-handle was of no more use than anything else. Bat Masterson and the Conference Pear both tried. But Miranda refused to start.

Paul and Mechanician Fogarty—with bundle of cotton waste and a hammer—waited at the base of the pedestal. Although neither of them knew anything about Miranda, they had both felt that they ought to be there.

"What's the matter, Bat?"

Bat Masterson turned and gestured hopelessly. He was almost in tears.

"I don't know. She's never done this to me before."

Mechanician Fogarty tired of the inaction. He strode forward firmly and struck Miranda a resounding blow on the barrel with his hammer. Immediately Miranda hummed into vibrant, chuckling life. Bat Masterson and the Conference Pear leaped into their seats and tried out the controls. Miranda functioned perfectly, performing all her set pieces, even to spinning like a top; she had recognized the hammer blow of a master.

"Thank God for that," said the Captain. "Can we start now, Merrydown?"

"As soon as you're ready, Captain."

"Anything on radar?"

"Scan clear of all contacts in long range, sir."

"Very good. All right, Merrydown, it's all yours. The ship's stopped and we're heading north."

"Right. We'll fire the first one on a bearing of red three zero."

Bat Masterson brought Miranda to a bearing of red three zero. As soon as he had set the bearing and bent himself to the firing circuit, Miranda trained herself to a bearing of green three zero. Again Bat Masterson brought her to point on the port bow and again, slowly but inexorably, Miranda swung round to starboard.

"What the hell's wrong now," the Captain muttered.

"What's the matter, Bat?"

"She's preset to green three zero. It must be the computer."

"Does it *matter* whether it fires to port or starboard?" the Captain asked.

"Not at all, Captain. All right, Bat, we'll fire the first one on *green* three zero."

Bat Masterson made one more attempt to point Miranda on red three zero but Miranda was adamant.

"Check radar," said the Captain.

"Scan clear of all contacts in long range, sir."

"Very good. Go ahead, Merrydown."

Bat Masterson held up his thumb. The Conference Pear, in the lower seat, held up his thumb. Beetle and Mr Merrydown held up their thumbs and all the sailors standing in rows in the background held up their thumbs. Mr Merrydown completed the count-down.

Whatever her other shortcomings, Miranda fulfilled all expectations in her moment of truth. The cable deck, A gun deck and Miranda herself disappeared in a pall of black smoke. The thunder of Miranda's mighty voice rolled away into the sky and the violence of her recoil shook *Carousel* from end to end. When the smoke cleared Miranda and Bat Masterson and the Conference Pear could be seen spinning like a top.

"God*damn* my old sombrero!"

"Are you all right, Bat?"

"Scan clear of all contacts in long range, sir."

"Red rocket fire on the starboard bow, sir."

"What's that?"

"There's another one, sir."

"Does this thing fire a red rocket when it lands, Merry-down?"

"No. The nose cap stains the water yellow."

"My Good God," whispered the Navigating Officer, piously, "we've hit some poor bastard. Right in the middle of the Pacific! With the press on board too!"

Through his binoculars the Captain could see the thin tracing of a rocket on the horizon. As he watched, it was followed by another and by a puff of black smoke.

"Scan clear of all contacts in long range. . . ."

The Captain's face distorted in a hideous grimace of rage.

"*Somebody* tell that man to stop making *bloody* stupid reports before I go in there myself and . . ."

The Navigating Officer sprang into the Radar office. He found Able Seaman Golightly, the R.P. rating on watch, conscious that there was some upset on the compass platform, studying his plot and anxiously turning the tuning dials.

"I think the set's off tune, sir."

The Navigating Officer controlled himself. "*Now* you tell us," he said coldly.

"Contact zero-two-nine," reported Able Seaman Golightly suddenly, "forty-five thousand yards, moving slowly left, range closing, sir."

"That must be the nose-cap," said Mr Merrydown.

"Nose-cap be damned!" the Captain retorted. "That's a ship and there'll be hell to pay if your damned machine's hit it! Well, we'll go and see. Come round to zero-two-nine," he said to Michael, who was Officer of the Watch.

Michael took a professional pride in bringing the ship to her new course with the minimum of helm orders. Besides, he was conscious that Stephen was watching him.

". . . Midships, steady."

"Midships, steady, sir. Zero-two-six, sir."

"Steer zero-two-nine."

Michael lifted his head from the compass.

"Hobbes," said the Captain, "never give a helmsman the order 'Steady' unless you're within two degrees of your course."

"Aye aye, sir," said Michael, his cheeks burning. He could see Stephen grinning. The Captain, too, had noticed Stephen; he had a momentary vision of the headlines—"Navy's secret weapon strikes innocent ship"—"Another Lucky Dragon?" For a moment the Captain sighed for an old-time sea captain's power of permanent arrest.

Miranda had been cleverer than any of them. There was indeed a ship over the horizon, on Miranda's exact firing bearing. She was a small coaster, heading east but apparently stopped and rolling in the long Pacific swell. She had black sides and a red funnel with a black band. Her two masts were covered with flags and lines of washing hung on her quarter-deck. With her high bow and tapered stern, her flying flags and her perky funnel, her whole appearance suggested ruffled dignity, like a hen who has been suddenly sprayed with water. The sea around her was stained yellow.

The Chief Yeoman of Signals put his telescope to his eye.

"She's wearing the Liberian flag, sir," he said.

"What signal is she flying?"

"Can't read it, sir. Most probably Liberian swear-words," the Chief Yeoman added, under his breath.

"We'll send away a boat to pick up the nose-cap and give them a couple of bottles of whisky. That should make our peace with them. Pass the word to the First Lieutenant to lower the seaboat."

Carousel stopped three cables from the coaster and lowered the whaler. As the boat crept over the intervening water, *Carousel's* ship's company studied the coaster.

A crowd had gathered on the coaster's upper deck to

stare at the cruiser. One figure stood out amongst them.

"What an Amazon!" said the Navigating Officer.

She stood well over six feet in her leather sea-boots. Her flaxen hair hung down to her waist in two plaits like hawsers. She wore a vast pair of blue overalls gathered by a length of rope. The whaler's crew had noticed her too.

"Talk about the Widow Twanky," said Stephen, who had slipped past The Bodger and into the boat at the last moment. His eyes were gleaming at the prospect of a world scoop.

The Widow Twanky put her hands to her lips. Even at that distance they could hear her voice as plainly as though she were in the whaler.

"What language is that, I wonder?" said Stephen.

"Swedish," said Bat Masterson, unexpectedly.

The Widow Twanky spoke for some time.

"What's she saying?" asked Andrew Bowles, who was the midshipman of the boat.

"She says go away."

"I'll hold up the whisky bottles," said Stephen. "That should soften her."

The Widow Twanky spoke again.

"What's she saying now?"

"She's telling you what to do with the whisky bottles."

"Ask her if she's seen the nose-cap."

Bat Masterson shouted the question over the water. The Widow Twanky gave a short answer.

"What does she say?"

"She's telling you what to do with the nose-cap."

The whisky bottles, however, had attracted the attention and approval of at least one other member of the coaster's ship's company. A tiny man in a moustache and an apron was hovering about behind the Widow Twanky. He was gesturing towards the whaler.

"He wants us to go round the other side."

"Let's do that then," said Stephen. "I want to go on board."

Bat Masterson eyed the Widow Twanky. "Do you think that's wise?" he said.

"Of course. I'll show them my press-card."

There was a jumping ladder hanging down the coaster's side and Stephen began to climb up it. When he reached the top there was an outraged bellow and a scuffle. Stephen described a parabola. They heard him yell as he hit the water.

"He *would* go, you see," said Bat Masterson.

The Bodger was watching through a telescope. "I've just remembered who that bloke is," he said. "He was an ordinary seaman doing his National Service when I was Jimmy of *Voluminous. There* he goes. How *splendid!*"

Meanwhile, the Widow Twanky was glaring down at the whaler's crew from the top of the ladder. Close to, she looked even bigger; they could see that she had a faint blonde moustache and forearms the size and colour of cured hams.

"What's she saying now?"

"She says that one was lucky. The next one won't be."

A small scuttle opened below the jumping ladder. A bucket appeared on the end of a rope. They could see the tiny man's face, his moustaches working in extremity. Andrew Bowles put the whisky bottles in the bucket and the whaler pulled away. The Widow Twanky kept up a flow of conversation as they pulled back to the ship.

"What was all the shouting about?" the Captain asked.

"She didn't mind being fired at," said Bat Masterson, "but she did object to the nose-cap carrying away most of her washing."

"—— good old Miranda," said the sailors, when they heard about it.

★ 8 ★

ONE of the finest natural harbours in Japan is the little fishing haven of Suki Yaki which, until the arrival of the United States Navy, was known only for the beauty and generosity of its women and for its local stew, cooked on a shovel.

Suki Yaki's boarded sidewalks, numerous bars and rows

of single storey buildings had a nostalgic Yukon flavour which appealed to the American sailors who quickly transformed Suki Yaki from a poverty-stricken town struggling to recover after Japan's defeat into a town enjoying a gold rush. The gold was indeed there, in the pockets of passing Americans, and the Japanese, male and female, exerted themselves to dig for it. The citizens of Suki Yaki abandoned fishing with alacrity and instead sold liquor, cameras, souvenirs, and each other's bodies.

The décor of the bars, which were open twenty-four hours a day, depended upon the whims of their owners. They had exotic names, the more exotic the name, the more squalid the bar. They advertised by neon signs and posters (in which they were given the lead by the U.S.N. Fleet Club which carried above its door the legend: "Through These Portals Pass The Finest Goddamn Fighting Troops In The World").

Carousel was welcomed to her berth by an all-Negro military band, a flower-decked float carrying the current Miss Suki Yaki, and most of the population of Suki Yaki. Once ashore, *Carousel's* officers and ship's company became tourists. They bought armfuls of silks and brocades. They went on excursions to porcelain factories, damascene showrooms and the Japanese opera. Commander (L), who was something of a collector, filled his cabin with wood-cuts. Ginger Piggant, Mr Pilgrim, and the D.B. Chief Stoker had a steam bath and were scrubbed and pounded by giggling, nude Japanese girls. The Captain and his Heads of Departments attended a Suki Yaki party, with geishas, given by the Mayor and Corporation.

Paul and Michael visited a cultured pearl farm a few miles outside Suki Yaki. Their guide was a gold-toothed Japanese in a dirty white jacket, black cotton trousers and sandals. He showed them the process of grafting a piece of mussel shell, round which the pearl would form, into an oyster. They saw the wicker cages in which the treated oysters were lowered into the water. The guide discussed the art of grading and sorting pearls.

"Pearl can be *any* colour," he said. "Golden, cream, white, grey, blue-black. One among many thousands is found the beautiful dark pink with perfect shape, then it is valued exceeding high."

"What about the black pearl?" Paul asked.

"Black pearl is freak of nature, sir. Black sheep of pearl family. It is mishap occur when spawn or other thing interfere between core bead and pearl covering. Best way to enjoy pearl is to wear. Human skin gives oil to pearl and more brilliant beauty. To tell *real* pearl from false, *watch!*"

The guide picked up a pearl and placed it between his teeth. He bit and the pearl shot across the table.

"Glass," said the guide. "Glass smooth, pearl rough."

He picked up another pearl and bit it. This time the pearl stayed between his teeth.

"Pearl."

The guide displayed strings of pearls, graded for size and colour. The pearls rippled through his hands like a shimmering rope of many beautiful colours. Michael and Paul, dazed by the lights of so many pearls, bought two necklaces. They had them wrapped in tissue paper and braced themselves for the taxi ride back to Suki Yaki.

The road was pot-holed and curved and at some of the worst bends the U.S. Navy had posted signs: "Horn Curve." On one of these bends their driver neglected to sound his horn. A stout young man in a straw hat flung himself off the road as they bore down on him. Although he looked nothing like an officer of the Royal Navy, Paul recognized him.

"George! Tell him to stop, Mike. It's George Dewberry!"

The fat young man picked himself up and made for the car.

"Just what did you. . . . *Hello* Paul! And Michael! How are you, men?"

They shook hands. "You fellows in *Carousel*?" George Dewberry asked.

"How did you guess?" Paul said.

"Where've you been hiding yourself, George?" Michael asked. "We've been here nearly a week and we haven't seen anything of you."

"Oh, I've been around," George Dewberry said, distantly. He seemed embarrassed by the others' curious glances.

It was the first anybody had seen of George Dewberry. Michael had made enquiries about him but he heard only rumours of "That mad pusser. Gone native. Shacking up with a Japanese tottie somewhere." Michael had scarcely believed it. The George Dewberry whom he had known as a cadet and later as a sub-lieutenant would have been as likely to have had a mistress as Little Lord Fauntleroy. Now, George Dewberry had a Pickwickian paunch, rimless spectacles, tobacco-stained fingers and, it seemed, a Japanese mistress.

"I heard you'd gone native, George," Michael said.

"Not quite, but bloody nearly. Where are you all going now?"

"Back to town. We're going on a run. Do you want to come? You ought to be an expert on this place."

"I am," said George Dewberry simply. "If you'll give me a lift in your vehicle. I think I'm safer inside it. Come and have dinner up at our grot and then I'll show you something of Suki Yaki."

"We're in your hands, George."

The taxi turned off before reaching Suki Yaki and began to climb into the hills. Paul observed how the land was cultivated to the last inch. The fields of maize grew not merely to the road but to the very walls of the houses. Not even the steepest hillsides were wasted; the crop grew in terraces which followed the contours of the hills and every hill was crowned by a clump of green. The taxi stopped outside a low Japanese house.

"Golly," said Paul. "This is beautiful."

The house stood in a garden made in the classic Japanese manner. To the untrained Western eye the garden seemed carelessly laid out, even disorderly, but its skill lay in its disorder. Maples and pines stood in groups which soothed the eye and led it from one pattern to another. Gravel paths and banks of moss drew the garden together into a whole. A small stream flowed under stone bridges into a wide shallow pool where large goldfish moved in the shadows. Between two trees the sharp silhouette of a mountain jutted into the sunset. The garden was hushed and quiet except for the sound of the running water.

"Let's go and see what atrocity Jasonsan has got for us," said George Dewberry.

It was a strange meal. When Paul thought over it afterwards he was reminded of the Mad Hatter's Tea Party. The meal was served by Jasonsan, an old Japanese in a white coat. The table was bamboo and was covered by a bright green cotton cloth. Down the centre was spread the largest collection of sauces, spices, chillies, pickles and mustards Paul had ever seen. The centre-piece of the collection, a jeroboam of tomato ketchup, a gigantic bottle, was decorated with three gold lace stripes, wound round its gargantuan belly.

"Harry, the Base Officer here, was passed over last June," George Dewberry explained. "We had a Feast of the Passover. Everybody was flat drunk for two days, even Jasonsan. Harry said that even if *he* couldn't have three stripes his bloody sauce bottle could. Incidentally, if you feel like tomato sauce, fellows, don't use that bottle." George Dewberry caught Michael's look. "You'll meet him."

George Dewberry squinted at the menu. "What are we on tonight? Eggs to order." He clapped his hands and Jasonsan came in with a full bottle of whisky and three glasses. "Two boiled eggs, Jasonsan, and fill up the glasses."

"Two boiled egg, sir."

"Can I have mine poached?" Michael asked.

"Egg boiled, sir," Jasonsan.

"But can't I have mine poached?" As a guest, Michael was anxious not to be difficult, but the menu *did* say "to order."

"Egg boiled, sir," said Jasonsan firmly.

"Oh, all right, two boiled eggs."

"The same for me," said Paul quickly, having learned from Michael's example. "And can you make them four-minute ones, please?"

"One egg four minute. Two egg eight minute, sir."

"I see. You do them in series, not parallel."

"Two egg pallallel, sir."

George Dewberry leaned forward. "Look old boy," he said anxiously, "don't make any jokes about the food while you're here. They're just not appreciated."

The door through which Jasonsan had retired was thrown violently open again.

"Hah! I see strangers! Good morrow, George!"

"Good evening, sir. Would you excuse mine and my guests' rig please, sir?"

"*But* yes!"

A tall Lieutenant Commander in mess dress stood in the doorway. Paul noted the broad red beard, the vast paunch, the bloodshot blue eyes, the hand resting on one hip, and tried to remember where he had seen that figure before.

Henry VIII was followed by another, much smaller, Lieutenant Commander who could only be a Welshman. His jowl was blue-back as though coal dust had been in-grained in it at birth and his face was twisted in a scowl, as though from many hours of dodging punches in the arc lights and tobacco smoke of a big fight. George Dewberry introduced him, inevitably, as Dai.

Henry VIII and Dai sat at the top of the table and Jasonsan served them with boiled eggs. As Jasonsan withdrew, Dai pursued him and caught him up at the door.

"Silence man!" said Dai. "Will you not whistle at meat!"

Dai returned to his seat and battered in the top of his first egg.

"Fishy it is," he said, after the first mouthful.

Meanwhile, Henry VIII decapitated his egg with one stroke of a knife and consumed it in three mighty spoonfuls.

"A friend of mine," he said to Dai, "used to go about the place looking for a piece of paper."

"Indeed," said Dai.

"After he read a piece he used to say 'This isn't it' and throw it away."

"In*deed*."

"He was quite difficult to live with. You couldn't put a piece of paper down without him snatching it up, reading it and saying 'This isn't it'."

Jasonsan removed the debris of the eggs and brought pork chops, brown peas and, astonishingly, rhubarb. Henry VIII covered his plate with tomato ketchup while Dai looked disgusted.

"One of these fine days," he said, "we will be having honest God's meat."

"Toffee papers, lavatory paper, it was all the same to him. He read them all and said 'This isn't it'."

George Dewberry, Michael and Paul ate in silence. Jasonsan brought welsh rarebit and clear tea.

"Fishy it is, man," said Dai.

". . . He took a party of sailors to the *Daily Disaster* offices and made an exhibition of himself. Had indigestion for weeks. Then they took him away to Netley and certified him. . . ."

Paul and Michael drank their tea as quickly as possible. George Dewberry led the way outside.

". . . At last they gave him his discharge from the Navy. When he saw it, he read it and said '*This* is it!'"

"Indeed."

"You may think they're all a bit cuckoo," George Dewberry said.

"Oh, not at all," said Paul.

"You should have seen them when I first got here. We used to have a guest night once a week, not that we ever had any guests, and Harry always thought it was time the goldfish were given a work out. He used to leap in and chase them while Dai stood on the bridge singing 'Men of Harlech' in Welsh."

Their taxi-driver, who seemed to know George Dewberry, was still waiting for them and drove them into Suki Yaki.

George Dewberry led the way from bar to bar without hesitating and without appearing to pause for thought. There were no aimless wanderings, no pavement conferences; George Dewberry proceeded as though on hidden tramlines.

They drank beer and the floor-shows were always strip-tease. Every bar had a matchbox with its name printed on it and a map of the town.

"They're very useful if you can't remember where you've been the night before," George Dewberry said.

After the sixteenth bar, glass of Japanese beer and exhibition of Japanese womanhood, Michael began to falter.

"I'm sorry George, but I don't seem to have the stamina for this. You've worn me out."

"Never mind. Perhaps I'll see you again sometime. How about you, Paul?"

Paul hesitated. Michael had spoken for him as well but he refused to admit that he had been drunk to a standstill and walked off his feet by George Dewberry.

"I'm game," he said. "The night's just starting. It's only just after ten."

"I know," said Michael, "but we started at half-past six."

"Well what about it? Are you two coming?"

Something in George Dewberry's cool manner maddened Paul.

"*Come* on, Mike."

"Oh God, all right."

George Dewberry walked rapidly down a side street to a dark doorway over which shone a neon sign: "The Hot Squat."

"The Hot Squat" was a long room with a stone floor and walls decorated with pictures of fauns, satyrs and centaurs painted on the bare brick in shades of dirty pink and puce. The bar and the room were both empty. Had Paul and Michael looked in by themselves they would have certainly gone somewhere else, but George Dewberry seemed pleased.

"Good, we've got it to ourselves. There's an American top-sergeant who comes in here sometimes. Let's wake 'em up. Hoy! Mamasan! Where are you, you mother of all whores! Girslan!"

George Dewberry's voice had the same magic action as the Pied Piper's. There was a rustling and a bustling and the room filled with girls, tripping, dancing, flinging their arms round George Dewberry.

Michael felt himself lifted off his feet and carried to a chair. His shoes were removed, his collar loosened and a hot towel pressed on his forehead. He saw Paul nearly submerged in girls, also having his forehead bathed. A special chair was brought for George Dewberry and he sat in it surrounded by girls, like Bacchus with attendants. Although, as a customer of long and respected standing,

George Dewberry had the majority of the girls' attention, he still seemed unsatisfied.

"Where's Mimi! Mimi!"

A tall Japanese girl came out from behind some curtains at the back of the bar and sat down by George Dewberry. She was wearing a European evening dress but she had the golden skin and almond-shaped eyes remembered in a thousand legends of old Japan. Her eyelashes were long and swept upwards and her lips were pouted and red as cherries. She seemed aware of her beauty and displayed it as though she were conscious that she was destined to give pleasure.

"Zut *alors!*" said Paul. "Where did you find her, George?"

"In here."

"I'll be damned."

"Oh, you make me sick. There's such a lot of rubbish talked about Japanese women. Just say the word 'Japan' to most people and they immediately think '*Geishas*'. They come ashore expecting tinkling samisens, fluttering fans and Madame Butterflys up every side street. And when they find it's not quite like that they take one look at the old woman who comes to do the laundry, say 'Aroint thee witch' and take to the bottle instead. Mimi's not a geisha. She's a whore. Aren't you, Mimi?"

Mimi nodded and smiled.

"Well, I won't argue with you, George," Paul said. "You're obviously an expert."

"I know a fair amount about it. I was thinking of going R.A. at one time. Lot to be said for a Japanese wife. They understand men."

"I can imagine," said Michael.

"Mimi, meet my friends. She's got the best-looking bottom in all Suki Yaki. Haven't you, Mimi? She doesn't speak English very well but she's got the message."

George Dewberry pinched affectionately. Mimi wriggled and dimpled with pleasure. Michael felt outraged, as though he had just seen someone tweak the Mona Lisa's nose.

"Now. What are we going to have? Don't take any notice of all those bottles. You can have beer or saké. Or you can have Mamasan's own speciality, 'Kiss of Fire'."

"God, what's that?"

"Equal parts of whisky and vermouth with chrysanthemum seeds sprinkled on top."

"Blimey, is it an aphrodisiac or an abrasive?"

"Couldn't say, never tried it. Personally I've had enough beer for one night. I'm going to have saké. Mamasan brews quite a good drop up in the bathtub. Real Prohibition hooch. I can recommend it."

"I'll have saké," Michael said. "What are you going to have?" he asked the girl nearest him.

"Whisky, Mac," said the girl.

"Saké for me too," said Paul. "How about you?" he asked the girl next to him.

"Whisky, Mac."

"You can see the American influence, can't you? Suki Yaki is the Forty-Ninth State."

Mamasan, the large jovial Japanese woman who ran the bar, brought the drinks. The whisky was in small pony glasses and the saké in a china teapot surrounded by thimble-sized cups.

"Aragato, Mamasan," said George Dewberry. "Shall I be mother?"

He poured the saké into the cups. It was steaming hot and tasted of earth, rice and caraway seeds. The girls drank their whisky straight and replaced their glasses on the tables expectantly. Michael was suspicious.

"I wonder if that's really whisky?"

"Oh, it's whisky all right," said George Dewberry. "They don't go in for the layer trick or cold tea here, although quite a lot of them do. Taste it yourself and see."

Michael tasted it. It was certainly whisky.

"Tastes a bit peculiar though."

"That's Genuine Old Highland King Victoria VIII Scotch. Made in Tokyo. Not a drop sold until it's two days old."

George Dewberry sipped his saké with the air of a connoisseur.

"Did you see anything of old Freddy Spink while you were in Hong Kong? The last time I heard of him he was running a highly successful taxi-dance and call-girl racket."

"He showed us over his empire."

"I rather liked old Fred. He and I saw eye to eye on a lot of things. I met one of his uncles the other day, the chap who runs that big night-club on the hill. I didn't take you there tonight because I got the buzz that the Yank M.P.s are getting interested in it. It's due for a temporary shut-down. All the best people get drunk there."

Mamasan brought more saké and small pieces of salted fish, scented cheeses and olives cut and filled with mint. Michael thought the saké a pleasant and sociable drink; one drank it like tea and it had the mellowing effect of alcohol.

"Let's have some music," said George Dewberry. "Mimi, let's have a song! I've rather been neglecting Mimi with you fellows around."

Mimi and the other girls stood in a circle and sang a plaintive Japanese song, clapping their hands and swaying their bodies.

"What's it called, George?"

"I've no idea. They always sing it when I'm here. They know it's my favourite."

Paul stretched his legs. "What a life of bliss you lead, George. Here were we thinking poor old George an exile in foreign parts, and all the time you've been having these orgies."

"I think if it wasn't for Mimi and the other girls I'd go round the bend. The chap I relieved had to be put away. He thought everything he ate tasted of castor oil."

"Haven't you got out of Suki Yaki all the time you've been in Japan?"

"I've had an occasional trip up to Kure but that's only once every three months or so. And I did manage a week in Kyoto. That was well worth while."

"Where's that?"

"On the way to Tokyo from here on the main island. All the American tourists go there. It's the sort of Japanese Oxford, Stratford-on-Avon and Edinburgh all rolled into one. It was the only major city that wasn't bombed by the Americans during the war, because of it's historical value or something. It convinced me that no European ever will know the first thing about how a Japanese mind works."

113

"Oh come, if you lived here long enough you'd be bound to get to know them."

"So you say. But the last time I was in Kure I met an old boy who's worked out here for Dunlops for thirty years and he said he still hasn't started to understand the Japanese. They can make gardens like people in England would never dream of. I saw the Emperor's gardens in Kyoto and parts of them came straight out of the Wizard of Oz. But a good many of these people think the bigger a hypodermic needle is the better the injection will be."

George Dewberry was unaware of the interest he was arousing in Michael and Paul; they were both trying to reconcile the man they saw now with the boy they had known. At Dartmouth George Dewberry had been one of the dullest young men in the term, who got drunk at every opportunity and wrote regularly to his family, receiving in reply detailed lists of the numbers of British fauna slain in his absence. Paul wondered what George Dewberry's family would say if they could see him in "The Hot Squat".

"They take such incredible pains over things, too. The chaps who make that damascene stuff sit cross-legged all day long hammering tiny cuts into pieces of metal, about five hundred cuts to the inch."

The girls began to play games with match-sticks. They solved their own puzzles with lightning speed, leaving Paul and Michael baffled. George Dewberry, however, solved the tricks almost as quickly as the girls themselves.

"You've obviously got this business all buttoned up, George."

"I know. Perhaps I should have been a Japanese procurer instead of a naval officer. I sometimes wonder why I joined the Navy. When I first joined I was still getting the weight. It was a novelty and I suppose I enjoyed it. Now I've got the weight and I'm beginning to wonder where the hell I'm carrying it. Do you remember that first night I got drunk at Dartmouth?"

"Perfectly."

"Vividly."

George Dewberry grinned. "Do you know *why* I got drunk? It was the big day of the Royal Visit. When I saw those divisions and the brass and all the shouting and tumult I thought this is too much for me. So I went out and got myself thoroughly honked."

"George, you're getting quite maudlin!"

"I know. I shall be in tears soon. The big thing I've got to decide now is whether to go into that little back room with Mimi. If I don't I shall have to stop coming here or Mimi will lose face. Or she'll go off with that American top-sergeant. Let's have some more saké."

"Not for me," Michael said decisively. "I've had enough."

George Dewberry finished his saké and stood up.

"Well," he said, "there are one or two things I must do. See you again sometime. Best of British luck in your mighty vessel."

Taking Mimi by the hand, George Dewberry went through a door at the back of the bar. He seemed to take the party spirit with him. One by one the girls got up and sat at the other end of the room. They were no longer interested. Michael and Paul were merely customers who looked as though they were going soon; George Dewberry had been somebody of special importance.

Michael and Paul went outside. The night life of Suki Yaki was in full swing. They met parties of sailors walking arm in arm, singing and supporting each other, negro patrolmen swinging their truncheons, and crowds of Japanese staring into the lighted shop windows. A neon sign flashed "Silver Dollar! Clean Girl!" and another "Savoy Suki Yaki! Stateside Drinks! You Try!" Loud music blared across the street.

The Navigating Officer was the only officer in the wardroom.

"Hello you two!" he said. "You're back very early?"

"We've had enough beer for one night, sir," Paul said. "We met a chap in our term who showed us Suki Yaki in a big way and told us what peculiar people the Japanese are."

"They're certainly that. They're the most peculiar people I know. I was a prisoner-of-war out here for two and a half years."

"That must have been pretty tough, sir."

"You never knew which way they were going to jump next. I was down in Macassar for most of the time. There were thousands of us and only a few soldiers and one officer guarding us. I'll never forget the day that bloke was relieved. We were all lined up and told we had to cheer him out of camp. Those with caps would wave them in a circular motion, all same Cheer Ship. Those without caps would go through the motions. Any man who made a sound would be shot. That foxed us a bit but we weren't in any position to argue the toss so we lined up and cheered the bastard off. Without making a sound. It was only after the war that I found out that the chap had got the idea from a film of King Edward VII's coronation. He wanted to be cheered in the same way. The reason we weren't allowed to make a sound was because the film was a silent one!"

The Navigating Officer finished his whisky. "I must away and arrange some bail for the Commander and The Bodger and the rest of the boys."

"Why, what have they been doing, sir?"

"Half the wardroom were in some sleazy night club that was raided tonight. Good night."

The next morning, there was a commotion in the streets of Suki Yaki. Every American walked plainly with a chip on his shoulder. There were several bar-room fights with Commonwealth troops before lunch. Americans in passing boats shouted at *Carousel's* gangway staff.

"What's gotten into our American allies?" The Bodger wondered.

George Dewberry had struck back at his rival, the American top-sergeant. On the large placard outside the U.S. Fleet Club which stated "Through These Portals Pass The Finest Goddamn Fighting Troops In The World" there was an amendment to the word "Pass". A bold stroke of Mimi's lipstick had cancelled the letter "A" and substituted the letter "I".

116

"NAVAL Officer Rapes Typist," The Bodger read, aloud.

The rest of the wardroom, reading the other Sunday newspapers, pricked up their ears.

"He Was Like An Animal Says Girl In Citizens Advice Bureau."

"After you with that, Bodger."

"Anybody we know, Bodger?"

"No. Some pilot or other. Listen to this. 'The Judge said that the evidence to follow was likely to prove unpleasant and anyone who wished to leave the court could do so now. No one left.' In evidence the girl, a nineteen-year-old typist from Stockton-on-Tees, said: 'He took me for a ride in his sports car and *possessed* me on the Guildford by-pass'."

"Crikey, I didn't think that was possible!"

"Love will find a way, Padre."

"I screamed and shouted for help but the engine was still running."

"After you with that, Bodger."

"You can have it now. I've got to go and look at the midshipmen's bloody journals."

The other lieutenant commanders in *Carousel* had been delighted to hear of The Bodger's past experience at Dartmouth and in the Cadet Training Cruiser. They had unanimously voted him the man most likely to succeed as officer in charge of midshipmen's training, better known as Snotties' Nurse. The Bodger was not reluctant to take the job, indeed he enjoyed it, but it sometimes tried his patience to have to correct the midshipmen's journals on a hot afternoon, after a curry lunch.

The midshipmen's journals were intended to be a record of their service in diary form, with appropriate sketches, charts and diagrams. They were presented to The Bodger for inspection once a week and to the Captain once a month. Some of the journals were well done, but others made The Bodger wonder whether his successors at Dartmouth were achieving anything at all. The Senior Midshipman, Jeremy James Waffard, nicknamed Soapy by the Gunroom, was something of an artist and his journal (although The Bodger disliked the boy personally) gave The Bodger many moments of private amusement. Andrew Bowles's journal, on the other hand, was barely readable. There were grammatical errors and spelling mistakes in almost every line and the sketches were only just adequate. But The Bodger was tolerant with the boy because he recognized that Andrew Bowles was labouring under a tragic and unavoidable disadvantage; shy and rather slow himself, Andrew Bowles was following in the footsteps of two brilliant elder brothers. The Bodger took the trouble to give Andrew Bowles a special talk about journals.

"You've got to get the right idea about this journal business, Bowles," he said. "It's not just another thing thought up by Their Lordships to make your life more of a misery. There's a definite purpose behind it. Sooner or later every officer, if he wants to get on in the service, has got to learn how to *notice* things, with an enquiring mind. He's also got to learn how to express himself clearly and distinctly on paper. It grieves me to say it, but in peacetime one of the few ways an officer can make his name is in the quality and quantity of his paperwork. You've only got to look at some of the dreadful *jargon* you read in a lot of the 'Orders' and official letters which are being pushed around the place now to see the results of muddled and stereotyped thinking and hence muddled and stereotyped writing. Quite apart from all that, if you write up your journal properly it'll give you an enormous amount of amusement in years to come. I often look through mine and howl with laughter at myself. The Commander was telling me only the other night that he's still got his journal because it's got two things in it which he's always finding useful, the complete words of 'The Ball of Kerriemuir' and a recipe for paint to put on ships' boats that's better than anything else he's seen. See what I mean?"

"Yes, sir."

"Now let's have a look at yours. See, this is what I mean. Thursday, 19th. 0900, anchored. Where? You know, and I know, that it was off New Guinea but put it in all the same. Here again, 'sent away seaboat'. It doesn't say what for. For all your journal tells us we stopped one day, lowered a seaboat just for laughs and steamed on our way rejoicing. There's a lot of things which have happened this commission which you don't even mention at all. You might have described the way we rigged the motor-cutter for diving when the Commander went down to find Lady C.-in-C.'s engagement ring. And what courses we steered to keep clear of that typhoon. The Captain didn't just pick a course with a pin, you know. There's a quadrant in every typhoon configuration which you steer for to keep out of trouble. There's lots of things. I could go on and on. The concert party. The banyans. The dinner party we gave for the chief who offered to shrink the Chief Steward's head free of charge. You've hardly mentioned Miranda and that island that appeared. There's plenty of learned gentlemen in the Royal Society who would have given their right arms for your grandstand view of that. Got the idea?"

"Yes, I think so, sir."

"Good. Now sketches. This one of the weather forecast areas of the British Isles is all *right* but we're not *in* the British Isles, we're in the Far East. And this one of pipe markings is O.K. but it's not very original, is it? I can get a dozen much better ones from the Senior Engineer any day of the week. You must try and cultivate a newspaper-man's outlook about this. Try and make your sketches relevant, up to date, interesting and informative. Even a map of Hong Kong showing the bars and their prices would fill all four functions, although I don't suppose the Captain would go much on it. See what you can do any-way, Bowles."

"I'll try, sir."

With Soapy Waffard, The Bodger had a different approach. The Bodger thought Master Waffard too clever by half.

"Hm. What's this?"

"It's a map of Hong Kong, sir. It's got the name at the bottom, sir."

"Yes."

It was a very good map, The Bodger was forced to

concede. It was complete with contours, streets, even soundings in the harbour; every street was named and every
mooring buoy marked. It was indeed a superlative map
but The Bodger was careful not to show approval; a little
praise went a long way with Master Waffard.

"Looks like an elephant's turd. What's this next one that
looks like a dissected sheep's heart?"

"It's an isometric drawing of a boiler feed regulator, sir.
You remember we did our engineering time last month, sir."

"Of course I remember."

Actually, the fact had escaped The Bodger's mind
completely. The Bodger wished he could remember what
"isometric" meant. He studied the drawing. Again, it was
well done; The Bodger had no doubt that Ginger would
say that it was as good as any of the ship's drawings. The
Bodger turned to the text.

"Writing could be improved a bit." Waffard's writing,
The Bodger reflected, was probably the most legible in the
ship; it was almost mechanically legible.

"Too many adjectives."

"Aye aye, sir."

"It's not too bad, though. Still a long way to go before
it's any good. Try and remember you're writing a journal,
not an Admiralty Fleet Order."

"Yes, sir. Sir?"

"Yes?"

"Could you tell me anything about Dhon Phon Huang,
where we're going next week, sir? I can't find anything
about it anywhere, sir."

"Ask the Navigating Officer. That's his part of ship."

"Aye aye, sir."

After Soapy Waffard had gone (probably, The Bodger
suspected, to read up his Seamanship Manual), it occurred
to The Bodger that he himself knew nothing of Dhon
Phon Huang either. The Bodger brushed the dust off the
wardroom encyclopedias and in the volume entitled
"Deodorant—Frier," between *Dholgore* and *Dhwalagiri*, he
found *Dhon Phon Huang*.

"Dhon Phon Huang," The Bodger read, "a native princi-
pality on the lower southern edge of the Indochinese

Peninsula. Pop: 250,367 (1826). Exports: opium, hashish, slaves. A backward and barbaric port on the delta of the Houdun River believed to have been first founded by stragglers from the armies of Genghis Khan. Governed since the earliest times by a hereditary chieftain known as The Huang, who is hostile to foreigners. Huang the Terrible (1818-1895), who begat 453 bastards, one for each day of the Dhonese Year, was responsible for the massacre of forty missionaries in 1863. The missionaries were cooked and eaten in the palace amidst scenes of extravagant excitement."

"Name of a name," said The Bodger admiringly. "This Huang must be quite a player!" He went to ask the Navigating Officer for more information.

The Navigating Officer was in the chart-house, poring over a chart and looking disgruntled.

"Bodger, you're about the fourteenth person who's asked me about that *damned* place this morning. I tell you I don't *know* yet. I've got to read it up. All the Far East Pilot says is 'Not recommended for ships above 5,000 tons. The Dhonese are expert smugglers and armed guards should be posted day and night'. I've only just got the chart of the place from Droggy."

"Let's see. Is this what Captain Cook saw from the horizon in 17-something or other?"

"Oh no, it's the latest. Not that it's much help. The place hasn't been surveyed."

The Bodger was impressed. "That's pretty efficient of Droggy," he said. (The Bodger had often noticed that, when a ship was isolated at the end of the earth and all normal mail had come to a stop, bills still arrived from Gieves Ltd and charts from the Hydrographer of the Navy.)

"What exactly *is* this shindig we're going to?"

"It's the Dhonese New Year. It's like our New Year's Eve, the Fourth of July and Mardi Gras all rolled into one. It lasts a week. Apparently the Communists have got their eye on Huang and his merry men and someone in Honkers thought it would be a good idea for the R.N. to be represented there. Nobody's ever been there before. Just look at this passage up to the city. There's a bloody great kink half-way up, like Bechers Brook. . . ."

"The Canal Turn, you mean."

"The Canal Turn then. There doesn't seem to be a leading mark or a buoy the whole way and the greatest depth of water, *marked* that is, is six fathoms. It may be much shallower for all we know. I only hope to Christ there's a pilot."

There was certainly a Pilot. He was rowed from shore by forty oarsmen in a ceremonial silver barge. The barge was sixty feet in length and was a magnificent craft. The rubbing strakes were of burnished silver and jewels shone in the canopy over the Pilot's head. The oarsmen dipped their oars to the time of a silver horn, blown by a man standing in the sternsheets. Above all flew the Pilot's flag of rich red cloth and silver thread.

"Here's your pilot," the Captain said to the Navigating Officer. "Looks like something out of 'Anna and the King of Siam'."

The Dhonese Pilot was the most bizarre figure ever seen on *Carousel's* bridge. His face was the shade of sun-soaked teak and was carved in planes of strength. He stood only about five foot in height but he had tremendous thighs and shoulders. His cap was flat and red, like a cardinal's, with silver designs worked on it. He wore a short red sarong and a red cape which hung open to reveal his mighty brown chest. His feet were bare but his mouth was determined and his eye commanding. The Captain recognized an equal.

The Pilot was accompanied by three other men, one very short and the other two very tall, with shaved heads and long polished swords.

The Pilot bowed. The Captain and the Navigating Officer bowed. The very short man bowed and, pointing to himself, said: "Interpreter".

The Captain pointed at the two men with swords.

"Who are they?"

"Huang executioner." The Interpreter made an expressive downwards sweep of his arm. "Slow sailor—*zut!*"

The Captain thought about the swords. He was sure he had read something somewhere about the implications of naked weapons on the bridge of H.M. Ships and Vessels.

"Well, I suppose we'd better get on with it," he said. He nodded. The Dhonese Pilot mounted the bridge parapet and stood with his legs apart and his arms folded. The Navigating Officer took up his position by the voice pipe and the two executioners placed themselves behind him. The Captain grinned.

"Watch it, Pilot," he said. "Slow sailor—*zut!*"

The Navigating Officer allowed a thin smile to cross his face.

"Half ahead together, one hundred revolutions."

Carousel began to move ahead. Suddenly, the Dhonese Pilot shot out his right arm. The Navigating Officer hesitated. The executioners shifted their grips on their swords.

"Come to starboard, Pilot," the Captain said quietly.

"Starboard fifteen."

The ship's head swung. The Dhonese Pilot pointed ahead.

"Midships."

After several alterations, one of them through ninety degrees, the Navigating Officer realized that the Dhonese Pilot's hand signals were not directional but were intended as helm orders. The Navigating Officer was forced to admit to himself that this exotic-looking pilot had a very accurate grasp of a cruiser's handling qualities in confined waters. Again and again, the arm gestured at the exact moment when the Navigating Officer himself would have ordered a helm movement. Between them, the Navigating Officer and the Dhonese Pilot navigated very successfully. The executioners relaxed their grips.

At the mouth of the estuary the shoreline had been low-lying swamp and mudbanks but farther inland the ground began to rise and the banks closed in. A range of hills lay ahead and *Carousel* was steering directly towards them. The Dhonese Pilot shifted his stance. His hand signals were smaller and more frequent.

Presently *Carousel* passed into a narrow gorge cut into a hillside. The fairway was not more than a cable across and the bottom was shallow. The Navigating Officer wondered how so small an outlet could convey the water volume of a river, which by the size of its estuary, must be at least the size of the Thames; then he realized that they must have chosen only one of the many faults in the hill formation, almost certainly the most navigable. The Navigating Officer began to have more confidence in their outlandish Pilot.

The Navigating Officer looked up and saw that *Carousel* was apparently steering into a solid hillside of rock. It must be the Canal Turn.

"Very bad place," explained the Interpreter.

The Navigating Officer privately agreed. The hillside loomed closer so that the men on *Carousel's* bridge could see the individual boulders in its face and the bushes near its summit. The Dhonese Pilot seemed unconcerned, although *Carousel* with her complement of eight hundred souls was steaming at six knots towards sudden and final ruin. At the last moment, before *Carousel* must have dashed herself on the rocks, a clear channel appeared to port. Still the Dhonese Pilot made no movement. The Navigating Officer looked questioningly at the Captain but the Captain shook his head and nodded at the Dhonese Pilot. The Navigating Officer tightened his lips; this, he said to himself, will separate the men from the boys.

At last, the Dhonese Pilot extended his left hand and *Carousel* wheeled swiftly into the channel. The Dhonese Pilot took off port wheel before a layman would have expected him to and ordered starboard wheel. *Carousel* slid on a straight course with ten of starboard wheel on. A new respect came into the Navigating Officer's eyes.

"Clever chaps, these Chinese," he muttered. "This bastard's even heard of canal effect."

The Navigating Officer caught the Dhonese Pilot's eye and was astounded to see him grinning. The truth flashed on the Navigating Officer. In the Dhonese Pilot's eyes it was he, the *Navigating Officer,* who was the beginner, not to be trusted in pilotage waters! The Navigating Officer's temper rose. This man comes on board, looking like something escaped from the Chelsea Arts Ball, with his Chu Chin Chow henchmen, and then gives him, the Navigating Officer, a graduate of H.M.S. *Dryad,* and a professional seaman whom the Admiralty had passed as competent to handle their biggest ships, an object lesson in ship handling. The Navigating Officer now understood the meticulous hand signals and the exaggerated movements to indicate changes of speed. It occurred to the Navigating Officer that he might have been in real danger from the executioners.

Meanwhile, the Captain could not prevent himself feeling a strong rush of relief. He had summed up the Dhonese Pilot and, ignoring the ancient rule of "Pilot's advice but Captain's orders" he had decided that the Dhonese Pilot was the best man to guide the ship. But, when the Captain remembered that hairpin bend, he was heartily glad that fortune favoured the brave.

"Worse than Shimoneseki," he said to the Navigating Officer.

"Much worse, sir." The Navigating Officer could feel the sweat cooling on his brow.

The channel widened into a land-locked bay. The city of Dhon Phon Huang lay at the northern end. *Carousel* dropped her anchor and her ship's company looked out upon a sight which had not changed since the time of Marco Polo.

The Captain studied the shoreline with more than usual attention. There were few landfalls the Captain had not made, few coastlines he had not seen from seaward, and few seaports he had not visited. But Dhon Phon Huang was a new one. The Captain was probably the first man-of-war captain to have penetrated so far up the channel for several hundred years.

The city was uncompromisingly oriental. There were no signs of Western influence, no oil company and soft drink hoardings, no modern buildings, no cars. The city was untouched by hand, a vintage piece. Its skyline was of temples and trees and towers. The silver barges with high prows by the quay might have carried Sinbad himself to catch the magic fish which became beautiful maidens at the cast of his net. The golden temple dome behind the trees might have been the Roc's egg and those wharves might be the wharves of old Cathay where silk and sandal-wood were unloaded by merchants who travelled as far as Samarkand. The Captain thought that *Carousel's* sailors would cause a sensation ashore.

Before the Captain had made any official calls, before even the mail had come aboard, The Bodger received an invitation. Hand-written on excellent writing paper, it smelled faintly of lavender and made The Bodger beetle his eyebrows in disbelief.

Dear Robert,

You won't remember me so there is no need for you to rack your brains. But I know you because I was at your christening. I was bridesmaid at your grandmother's wedding and Julia's grandmother was my greatest friend when we were girls.

I shall expect you to take tea with me this afternoon at my house. My First Elephant will be waiting at Huang Steps at a quarter to four. Come in uniform. I cannot *abide* your dreadful naval dog-robbers.

Yours sincerely,
Emily Several-Strickland.

"Several-*Strickland*! First *Elephant*! *Dog*-robbers!"

The Bodger's first thought was of a hoax. He suspected the Commander. But when he read the note a second time he was convinced it was genuine; it was too fantastic not to be. Also, the name Several-Strickland had at last stirred a dim memory; The Bodger could remember as a school-boy going to tea with a mad red-haired family who lived in a huge house twenty miles away. The boys of the family had dared The Bodger to ride a pony bareback and the eldest girl had blacked The Bodger's eye.

There were no motor cars in Dhon Phon Huang. The townspeople walked, more important citizens had donkeys, and the most important had elephants which reflected their owners' taste and finances as accurately as motor cars. The British Consul's elephant, for example, was a splendid animal. It was silver grey in colour and from its silver-tipped tusks to its blue-tasselled tail it had Rolls-Royce written all over it. Emily Several-Strickland's First Elephant, too, was a majestic beast. It was kneeling on the jetty, its eyes fixed on The Bodger with a look of malevolent appraisal. The Bodger's transport caused some facetious and ribald comment from the other officers in the boat.

"Please pass, running in," said the Padre.

"Bet she won't do more than twenty in third," said Eric the D.L.O., who had once participated in the Monte Carlo Rally and still dined out on the story.

"Make sure you face the right way, Bodger," shouted Ginger. "This is one of the reversible ones with old-fashioned reciprocating legs."

As The Bodger approached, the mahout, who was dressed in clean white linen shirt and trousers, let down a small set of steps. The Bodger mounted into the howdah, which was also stamped with its owner's personality. The cushions were covered in embroidered silk and the windows were lace-curtained. Sachets of lavender hung in the corners and in a rack was a month-old copy of *The Tatler*. A metal horn, like a goad, lay in a rest and The Bodger picked it up curiously, so uncovering a notice which read: "Don't *fiddle*".

The Bodger enjoyed the ride. The elephant's back put him high above the hurly-burly of the streets. The Bodger looked down on a scene which might have come out of a travel film. There were old women holding chickens, stalls full of pink, fly-covered slices of meat, swarthy faces which burst into huge smiles at the sight of The Bodger, in uniform, swaying on top of the elephant. The Bodger looked across the roofs to the hills at the end of the city. The houses ended abruptly and the elephant rolled along a garden path. The garden had been laid out by an expert. Tropical flowers, flame red and brilliant yellow, grew in banks and slopes and clusters of colour. Here and there, The Bodger recognized familiar faces.

"Goddamn," he said, "hollyhocks!"

The First Elephant stopped, and knelt, in front of a low white house with a veranda. The Bodger had no time to examine it. An imperious voice called from inside.

"Come in, Robert. One more minute and the tea will be spoiled."

The Bodger hurriedly handed his cap to a butler who stood at the door and entered a long room which showed its owner's years of service as a missionary. The furniture was a hotchpotch of bamboo, mahogany and tubular steel. On one wall hung, in succession, a worked sampler commemorating Victoria's Diamond Jubilee, an aquatint of Salisbury Cathedral, an oil portrait of a Malayan pirate, and a rose crayon drawing of a sleeping mongoose. At the far end of the room, bolt upright in a hard straight-backed chair, sat Miss Emily Several-Strickland.

She was plainly one of those fabulous, and formidable, English females who did not allow the peculiar habits of foreigners to alter their own way of life in the least particle. They grew snapdragons in the jungle, took afternoon tea with scones and thin sandwiches in the middle of revolutions, and conducted Sunday school classes, with verve and enthusiasm, on mountain tops. They considered divorce worse than murder, read *The Times* faithfully and minutely, pampered their dogs and dispatched their menfolk dispassionately, almost implacably, to endure incredible privations in every remote corner of the globe. Emily Several-Strickland had her family's red hair. Her nose was angular and thin. Her skin was like powdered parchment and her eyes were searching, as though she was wondering whether The Bodger had washed his neck before coming to tea. Her greeting was typical.

"Come and sit down, Robert. Let me see your hands."

The Bodger bashfully held out his hands; he was glad that the Commander could not see him.

"A very fine pair of hands. You're obviously a very capable man. You're better-looking than your grandfather. He didn't drink. You obviously do. I like a man who drinks. If my father had not been a teetotaller he would have lived another forty years. Old Huang would never have *dreamed* of eating a fellow-alcoholic."

Miss Several-Strickland poured two cups of tea while The Bodger wrestled with his voice.

"Really, ma'am?"

"The present Huang's grandfather ate my father, you know."

The Bodger's cup rattled involuntarily in the saucer.

"Oh yes," said Miss Several-Strickland. "With mango sauce. My father was considered quite a delicacy. But I get on very well with young Huang. Probably because we have that bond in common. Huang gave me Manweb, my butler."

128

"That's a very odd name, ma'am," said The Bodger, desperately seizing on the one intelligible part of this lunatic conversation.

"I saw it on a van at home once and I couldn't *imagine* what it meant so I called my butler after it. Manweb is a judo expert. He could break your arm between his thumb and forefinger if he liked. I find him very useful to throw people out of my garden at this time of the year."

"Do you get much hooliganism during the festival?"

"Oh no. Just a little quite innocent fornication."

The Bodger's last mouthful of tea remained suspended in his throat; his face contorted in a painful rictus of incredulity and shock.

"It does spoil the flower-beds so. You'll like Huang. I've asked him to give your ship's company the more presentable virgins when you visit his palace on Saturday."

With difficulty, The Bodger disposed of the mouthful of tea which seemed to have lodged half-way down his throat for almost as long as The Bodger could remember.

"That's very kind of you, ma'am," he said breathlessly.

"I've always felt it quite wrong that English girls should be expected to be virgins when they marry. It puts them at a disadvantage from the very start. The girls here serve an apprenticeship in the temple first. For most of them it's their only way of saving up for their dowry. I'm sure Julia would agree with me."

The Bodger blushed a deep consuming red.

"Good heavens, I'm embarrassing you, boy."

"Oh, not at all, ma'am." The Bodger struggled to change the subject; there was no knowing what detail this woman would go into next. "The tea is rather hot. I suppose it's the local growth?"

"Nonsense, it's Joe Lyons' Don't let that old humbug of a Consul persuade you that the tea they grow here is better. I get it by the bushel from England and Manweb treads it out with his feet."

"We're giving a cocktail party on board tonight. I wonder if you would care to come as my guest, ma'am?"

"I should be delighted, Robert! What time?"

"Half-past six. There will be boats from Huang Steps."

"It's years since I went to a party on board a ship! Oh, *certainly* I shall come! How very kind of you to invite me." Miss Several-Strickland pursed her lips and closed her eyes reminiscently and The Bodger had the lunatic thought that perhaps the last wardroom cocktail party Miss Several-Strickland attended had been given by Captain Cook.

The old lady opened her eyes. "Do you still drink gin in the Navy?"

"The old brigade do. Most of the younger generation drink Horse's Necks."

"Horse's *Necks*!"

"It's brandy and ginger ale, ma'am."

"Strange service, the Navy. I'm told they pay you more now. That's a bad thing. Officers in the services should be able to support themselves. They should have a substantial stake in the country. The people of England haven't forgotten Cromwell's Model Army."

Miss Several-Strickland looked pointedly at a small ormolu clock by her chair. The Bodger rose to his feet. Miss Several-Strickland accompanied him back to the elephant.

"Be careful of the local liquor, Robert," she called, as The Bodger swayed down the path on the First Elephant's back. "Huang's got a head like rock, like his father, but he forgets that not everybody else has."

The Bodger began to warm towards Huang; he sounded like a first rate fellow.

When The Bodger returned to *Carousel* the first boat-load of libertymen were being laid out in rows along the upper-deck. The two junior doctors, Hamish Maclean and Alastair Campbell, with stethoscopes and stomach pump, were examining the corpse-like figures.

"Jings," Hamish said to The Bodger, "they've all been drinking Mickey Finns. There was only one could speak and he said he had one pint of the liquor ashore and remembered no more."

The Bodger looked along the line of unconscious faces. He noticed that the line included representatives from most of the messes in the ship. Royal Marines, stokers, electricians and cooks lay next to each other in happy alcoholic abandon.

"Here's the Chief Steward. He probably hasn't come off

shore drunk since he was a boy. Look at him. Like a baby. Mike Hobbes was the Officer of the Watch and he says he's never seen a quieter boatload in his life."

"Oh well," said The Bodger. "We'll get our own back tonight."

Carousel's cocktail party was attended by Huang himself and by the polite society of the city. It was the most oddly-assorted company ever to gather on *Carousel's* quarter-deck and the party was the biggest social occasion in Dhon Phon Huang since the consumption of the forty missionaries, nearly a hundred years before.

"They still talk about that," said Miss Several-Strickland, who was wearing a hat which made the gangway staff feel that their day had not passed unrewarded. " 'Missionary' means 'very tasty' here, although its been corrupted to 'Yummaree'. To a Dhonese, 'Yummaree' means anything splendid, or enjoyable, or worth waiting for. Let me point out some of the local celebrities for you, Robert. That woman in the dreadful hat and the bangles over her breasts is the mistress of the deportment school for the temple girls. And that funny little man with the sad face is Huang's Prime Minister. He wanted to be a farmer, poor man, but his family have always been Prime Minister so he had to be. There's Huang himself at the end. *Such* a handsome boy. . . ."

Huang was talking to the Captain and the British Consul through the Interpreter. His dark eyes looked out over the guests and to the shore as though he could see the endless plains over which his forbears had galloped with the sun on their backs and the cloak of Genghis Khan in front. He wore a long red silk robe and held a Horse's Neck in one hand. With the other he fondled the hair of a naked Dhonese girl. He said very little but concentrated upon the drinks. A steward stood with a tray which Huang steadily, as the party progressed, emptied. The Captain and the British Consul stopped their conversation to watch him, in awe. Huang finished the tray and his feet were still as firmly planted upon the quarter-deck and his eyes as levelly fixed on an empty horizon.

Meanwhile, Ginger Piggant entertained the mistress of

the temple deportment school and the Commander consoled the Prime Minister. Executioners with bared swords stood at intervals round the quarter-deck. "Slow drinker—*zut!*" said the Navigating Officer to the Dhonese Pilot.

★ 10 ★

NEW Year was the most important festival in the Dhonese calendar and the Dhonese set themselves to enjoy it with a single-mindedness which would have made a feasting Roman emperor pensive. The rules of Saturnalia held sway, no man could be punished and no woman was unapproachable. Maidens who had resisted all year gave way in a single night. The temple girls did a brisk trade. Fireworks seared the sky every night and the streets were bright with flaring torches. Processions of dragons, masked men and dancers threaded the narrow streets of the city, kites with long streaming tails flew above Huang's palace and young men and girls danced to the throbbing of gongs, drums and cymbals. *Carousel's* sailors watched the festivities with goggling eyes, finished their drinks and, led by Number One Boy's nephews, joined in.

A full programme had been arranged. *Carousel's* Royal Marine Band beat the retreat on Huang Steps in spite of an unseasonable cloudburst. The ceremony brought tears of nostalgia to Miss Several-Strickland's eyes, and was respectfully reviewed in the Dhonese press the next morning as a rain-making rite of supernatural efficiency. The ship's football team were soundly beaten by a team of Huang's executioners in a game which lasted nearly five hours, a banquet of fried chicken and rice wine being served at half-time in the Prime Minister's house which was over two miles from the ground. The boxing team, however, beat Huang's boxers by eight fights to nil, Huang's boxers being, in their opinion, unfairly handicapped by being forbidden to use their feet. The ship was open to visitors every afternoon. Everything movable was locked up or lashed down and the denuded decks were crowded with curious Dhonese fingering the sailors' uniforms and exclaiming at the guns.

On the third day the Commander organized a children's party in the traditional manner. It was the first children's party in Dhon Phon Huang's history, and it passed into the city's mythology. Hordes of screaming children swooped down the slides on to the quarter-deck, and rode on saddles fixed to the gun barrels. Small boys enthusiastically punched the midriff of an inflated diver's suit while the Chief G.I., hidden behind the bulkhead with a microphone, made groaning noises. The ship's company dressed up as pirates and presided over the sideshows, served tea, and separated knots of struggling small boys.

"Just look at 'em, sir," said the Master at Arms breathlessly to The Bodger from beneath his layer of grease paint and his eye patch. "Kids is just the same all over the world."

Miss Several-Strickland told The Bodger afterwards that *Carousel's* party for the poorer children of the city had more effect on Huang's foreign policy than the whole weight of an army division supported by the U.S. Seventh Fleet.

The climax of *Carousel's* visit was a banquet given by Huang himself. Huang's performance at *Carousel's* cocktail party and their own experiences ashore had made *Carousel's* ship's company cautious. The ship appreciated that this would be no banquet for weaklings. The Bodger gave the selection of the wardroom party his personal supervision.

"We've got Commander (E) and Commander (L)," he told the Commander. "Myself, Pilot, Guns, Slim, Broad, Scratch, Mr Pebblethwaite, the two Docs and Eric. And Ginger's selecting a team of plumbers."

"God," said the Commander, "that's certainly the first eleven. If Huang manages to knock out that lot, we'll give up and join the Toc H."

"Pity you can't come, Jimmy. I've a feeling this will be your sort of run ashore."

"No, I've got to stay on board if the Old Man's going ashore. I'm very surprised he's going, actually. You know what he's like about the Yellow Peril. He and Commander (L) have given Western civilization ten years at the outside."

"I didn't know El-san was a Yellow Peril fan."

"Rabid," said the Commander.

The ship's company were also taking Huang's banquet seriously. The Master at Arms drew up the list himself. The Chief Petty Officers and E.R.A.s messes were included almost to a man, the Royal Marine barracks provided a strong contingent and the Master at Arms hand-picked the remainder from the ship's defaulters' lists. The Captain himself led the party which, when mustered on the jetty, was the most formidable expedition the ship had ever put ashore on a single evening.

The banquet party were profoundly impressed by Huang's palace.

The palace gates were of bronze wrought into intricate designs of dragons, horses and elephants. The dragons' eyes were blood red rubies and the elephants' tusks were of inlaid ivory. The gates were flung open as *Carousel's* party advanced and the Prime Minister stood waiting to welcome his master's guests.

The Prime Minister led the way along a paved path between fountains and flowering magnolia trees. Lanterns hung in the branches and servants stood with torches to light the way.

"Good heavens," said Commander (L), "this man's quite civilized."

Huang's dining hall was under the great golden dome the Captain had seen from the ship. It was a vast apartment floored in marble with mosaics set in the walls. Latticed windows opened on to the garden and the music of plucked strings floated out from a small gallery in one wall. Cushions were placed for the guests and the walls were lined with serving girls.

Commander (L) was interested in the mosaics.

"I wonder what they're doing as far east as this?" he said to Commander (E). He examined the nearest mosaic appreciatively and the girl standing under it was flattered. She smiled and wriggled her hips. But Commander (L) was quite oblivious of her.

"Strange to see them here. They look almost Greek. Or Persian perhaps." The girl smiled delightedly. "I must have a closer look later on."

The ship's company were also intrigued by the mosaics.

"Cor," said Able Seaman Golightly hoarsely, "look at 'em! Better than —— Pompei!"

The Captain sat on Huang's right hand with the officers on either side of them. The Bodger sat next to the Prime Minister and the ship's company ranged themselves in a huge circle round the hall. The meal began.

Huang's banquets were on an Olympian scale. Each guest had a whole chicken and large bowl of rice wine to himself. The carcass of an animal the size of an ox was brought in steaming and reeking on a spit, and was placed in the middle of the floor. An executioner with bared sword stood ready to carve.

"Oh God, I bet I get the eye," The Bodger muttered.

The Prime Minister awoke from the trance of apparently fathomless gloom in which he had been sitting and called to the executioner. The executioner nodded and, with a lightning lunge and twist, carved out the nearest eye and brought it, still smoking, on the end of his sword and offered it to The Bodger.

The Bodger looked at the terrible eye glaring at him from the end of the sword and felt his stomach make a complete revolution. But smiling delightedly, The Bodger accepted the ghastly eye and carried it towards his mouth. As he did so, he squeezed the eye like an orange pip. The eye soared over The Bodger's shoulder and out of the nearest window, while The Bodger put his hand in his mouth and munched ostentatiously, nodding and smiling, as though his evening had just been made complete.

"Bravo Bodger," breathed the Captain, who had been watching surreptitiously, with his heart in his mouth.

The drinking bowls were filled and Huang caught the Captain's eye. The Captain at last recognized the vaguely familiar tune the band were playing. The company rose for the Loyal Toast. Huang, obviously feeling that the occasion called for some added comment, spoke to the Interpreter, sitting behind him.

"Lord Huang say 'Cheers'," said the Interpreter.

The Captain inclined his head in acknowledgement.

"Tell Lord Huang 'Cheers' to him too," he said gravely.

The message was translated for Huang who was delighted

and ordered the bowls to be refilled. Huang drained his own bowl and spoke again.

"Lord Huang say 'This wine made in his grandfather's time'."

"Tell Lord Huang it's very good."

"Lord Huang say 'Because of this wine his grandfather have four hundred children'."

"Tell Lord Huang congratulations."

Huang beamed and ordered the bowls to be refilled.

Mellowed by food and by quarts of rice wine served by shapely serving girls, *Carousel's* sailors began to warm up. The roar of conversation was interrupted by feminine squeals and shrieks. A girl broke away from clutching arms and ran giggling out of the hall. The Captain looked anxious but Huang was pleased and ordered that sailor's bowl to be refilled. The Captain thought it time to talk of diplomacy. He had been fully briefed by the Chief of Staff in Hong Kong.

"The usual sort of line, Dickie," said the Chief of Staff. "Give him a few words about Anglo-Dhonese solidarity, S.E.A.T.O., and a bit about the U.S. Seventh Fleet. *You* know the usual sort of guff as well as I do. You might talk about imperialism, balance of power, White Man's Grave and all that. Wogs love talking about White Man's Grave. It may not do any good but at least it won't do any harm. *You* know the sort of thing. Just give him the idea that we're all right with him, on his side, so that if he cares to put something up to the United Nations he might, in five years' time, get a printed circular about when the bar opens and all that. But for heaven's sake don't *sign* anything. We're still sorting out the mess left by one of your predecessors who went to a party in Macao and exchanged the whole Eighth Destroyer Flotilla for five per cent of the year's opium takings. The trouble is," the Chief of Staff had said mournfully, "that it would have been a bloody good bargain for Their Lordships."

The Captain took a long draught from his bowl and opened diplomatic relations; he was conscious that he was upholding a long tradition. The Royal Navy has influenced the foreign policy of the country for centuries.

"Tell Lord Huang the British are very happy to be here and to be welcomed to Dhon Phon Huang. We hope that this visit will be the first of many and that Dhon Phon Huang will not feel isolated in the middle of unfriendly countries."

In styling himself "Interpreter" the Dhonese who acted in that capacity for Huang had exaggerated his own talents. He was capable of translating an exchange of simple courtesies and greetings. A high-level diplomatic conference, however, was beyond him. But the Interpreter was frightened of losing face with his master, who was already waiting for enlightenment. The Interpreter did his best.

"Lord Huang is pleased you like Dhonese girls."

The Captain tried again.

"My government is anxious to reassure you that they have Dhon Phon Huang's position very close to their hearts. Can I inform them when I return that Lord Huang feels friendly towards the British Government?"

Huang was watching the Captain with curiosity; it seemed strange to him that this Englishman should trouble to raise a subject which Huang took for granted.

"Lord Huang say 'Not to worry. He himself will choose girl for you'."

"Perhaps you have had delegations from other countries? I have no power as far as politics go but anything I may say will have an influence on affairs in London."

Huang frowned while the Captain's words were translated. Then his brow cleared and he looked at the Captain with respect; his grandfather had once told him about the English qualities of Empire building and founding settlements.

"Lord Huang say he is very sorry not to know strength of British sea captain. He will choose *two* girls!"

The Captain gave it up. (Later, when the Chief of Staff asked how it went, the Captain thought over his conversation with Huang and said: "Oh, they're pro-British all right.")

Huang, too, had tired of diplomacy. He clapped his hands and a team of acrobats wearing baggy trousers, like Cossacks, tumbled out on to the floor.

Some of *Carousel's* sailors were themselves expert gymnasts. The long hours in the dog watches at sea had made some of them as good as many stage artists. But even they had to admit that Huang's acrobats were better than any they had seen. They jumped, pirouetted, locked arms and formed human structures containing as many as nine or ten men balancing upon each other's shoulders.

It was inevitable that at least one sailor would wish to take part.

"Oh, God Almighty, trust Jolly John," groaned The Bodger when Stoker Crab staggered from his cushion and began to lurch about on the fringe of the acrobats' activities. The acrobats took the sailor's interruption in good part. They clustered round him, seized him under the armpits and, swiftly mounting upon each other, hoisted him to the top of a pyramid of ten men. Crab babbled in horror. The pyramid swayed, shook, and dissolved. Crab fell like a plummet into the arms of two acrobats who caught him and swung him, unharmed, on to his feet. Crab tottered to a window and was sick in the garden.

Released from the tension, the sailors finished their bowls in one gulp and The Bodger, looking round the hall, began to realize that Huang's banquet was going to be a run ashore to tell his grandchildren about. He glanced at the Prime Minister and was astonished to see him weeping; the Prime Minister turned on The Bodger a look of such absolute despair, as though his heart were loaded with a thousand dolours, that it chilled The Bodger's blood.

"Cheer up, old sport," said The Bodger. "Have a drink." The Prime Minister shook his head wordlessly; his eyes were dark, brimming pools of agony.

"Oh well, I'll have one then," said The Bodger. This, said The Bodger to himself, is as bad as sitting at a mess dinner next to a teetotal Royal Marine with toothache.

Again, Huang clapped his hands. The acrobats skipped out and their place was taken by a wrinkled old man who wore a simple gown and appeared to be searching for something. He looked inside the folds of his robe, peered up the sleeves and turned up the hem. Then he shrugged his shoulders and threw out his arms. A pigeon appeared in each hand. The pigeons fluttered to the roof of the hall and flew out. While the old man looked at his hands in mild surprise, two more pigeons materialized. Still apparently dumbfounded at the incredible things which were happening to him, the old man produced pigeon after pigeon, as though they grew from his hands. At last the old man snapped his fingers and the supply of pigeons came to an end but when the old man examined his hands again he was horrified to find they now contained two ivory balls. In vain the conjurer worked his hands, snapping them and rubbing them together as though to be rid of the spirit which possessed them; with every movement a fresh ivory ball appeared until each hand held six. Aware that they were watching a conjurer of genius, the sailors roared approval every time a new ball appeared. The old man seemed encouraged and was not so infuriated when his hands began to produce balls of different colours which he rolled along the floor towards his audience. The Bodger stopped one and examined it. It was solid ivory. It seemed impossible that the old man could have concealed so many about his person, to say nothing of the pigeons. When The Bodger looked up again the old man was plainly calling for a volunteer. The Master at Arms himself, rather unlikely a member of the Magic Circle, stepped forward amongst catcalls from the sailors.

"Now make him disappear!" called an anonymous voice. "*Bluidy* Jaunty!"

The old man had a showman's instinct for his audience. He held his fingers to the Master at Arms' nose and clapped him on the back. A stream of copper coins fell from the Master at Arm's nose. The old man held his hand to his mouth in dismay and dodged behind the Master at Arms' back whereupon a second stream fell from the seat of the Master at Arms' trousers. The sailors rolled on their cushions, tears in their eyes.

Shamefacedly, the old man shook hands with the Master at Arms and as their hands disengaged a silk scarf appeared. The old man flapped the scarf, drew it through his fingers and wrapped it round one arm. Huang leaned forward attentively.

The old man waved the scarf from side to side. While the audience watched every movement the scarf slowly stiffened into a flat board which the old man stood on one end on the floor. Then the old man climbed up and sat on the scarf with his arms folded. He bowed, slid down, waved the scarf in sweeping arabesques to show that it was once more a scarf and disappeared, before the amazed audience could properly appreciate the trick their eyes had just seen.

"Well," said The Bodger, "that's the nearest to the Indian rope trick *I'm* ever likely to see."

When sailors have been drinking for some time and have been provided with entertainment their thoughts inevitably turn in one direction. Not long after the conjurer had finished *Carousel's* sailors began to shout the war-cry which The Bodger had been subconsciously expecting but which, now that it had actually been raised, made him wince.

"Bring on the dancing girls!"

The dancing girls, who had been watching the party's progress from behind the latticed windows, were only too willing. They had seen the reception given to the tumblers and to the conjurer and they realized that here was an audience which might have been sent in answer to prayer, from Buddha himself.

At a signal from Huang, the girls made their entrance.

The dancing girls were well up to the standard set by the conjurer. They wore short silk tunics unbuttoned at the front and, as the sailors took care to observe, nothing else. Their routine had the most hardened sailor gripping his cushion; here and there sailors were being held down by their friends.

"Lord Huang say this is dance done by maidens at New Year hoping for husband."

"Looks like plain strip-tease to me. Tell Lord Huang it's a very beautiful dance."

When the dance was at its height, the girl who had been standing under the mosaic which Commander (L) had admired bent forward to refill Commander (L)'s drinking bowl. It was her pleasure as well as her duty to serve him and, besides, had he not directed upon her a glance which, in Dhon Phon Huang at the New Year, could mean but one thing? She leaned close to him and looked languish-ingly into his eyes.

Commander (L), hazy and befuddled by bowl after bowl of rice wine and sharing with the Captain an ancient fear of a Chinese invasion of the West, looked up through a miasma of alcohol to see an oriental face glaring at him with an expression which he construed as malignant hostility. Alarm bells rang in Commander (L)'s mind. He gave a shriek of panic.

"It's come! They're here!"

Commander (L) leapt to his feet and set off on a long swerving run down the hall. Hitching her sarong and grit-ting her teeth, the serving girl gave chase. The Captain was too involved with Huang to notice; the conversation had taken an alarmingly mercenary turn.

"Lord Huang say he give one *thousand* virgins for your ship."

The Interpreter had a brilliant memory of business English.

"C.O.D." he added, triumphantly.

The Bodger watched Commander (L) jinking and side-stepping through the dancing girls and was sober enough to think it odd but too tired to enquire into reasons. His bowl was full, the dancing girls made pleasant erotic patterns in front of his eyes, and the sailors were obviously enjoying themselves. The Prime Minister was weeping on his shoulder and Commander (L) appeared from time to time, like a comet, trailing girls. The Bodger was content.

The Commander met the returning banquet party on the quarter-deck.

"How did it go?" he asked The Bodger.

"It was very . . . very. . . ." The Bodger put his hand to his eyes and searched for the word. "It was very . . . yummaree yummaree," he said at last.

AFTER two years in the Far East, *Carousel's* commission came to an end. The last days were crossed off the make-shift calendars which had been put up all over the ship and *Carousel* prepared to go home. The Bodger wrote to Julia, sealed the letter, and, after some thought, printed N.O.R.W.I.C.H. on the flap.

Michael was especially pleased with life. It was the last day in Hong Kong. Tomorrow the ship left for Singapore and home. The bar was open and the mail had just come on board. Michael had two letters from Mary and two bills. He had thrown the bills through the cabin scuttle and was settling to read Mary's letters when Paul poked his head round the cabin door.

"Hi Mike," he said. "Did I tell you Cedric is doing his own television programmes now? All about his collections. My mother says Cedric thinks it's the funniest thing that ever happened. He's been offered I don't know how many thousands to write his life story for the *Daily Disaster*. Cedric's got a good mind to do it. Says it'll serve them right. How's Mary?"

"Fine. Just fine."

"I can see you'll be next in line for the marriage stakes."

"Oh. I wouldn't go as far as that. How's Anne?"

"Dunno. Haven't heard from her for about a month. *When* she *condescends* to write to me, I'll let you know how she is. *Bloody* woman, here am I wearing my fingers to the bone writing to her and does she answer? Does she hell! There's only one thing for it! We must celebrate the Feast of the Passover at the mess dinner tonight!" The idea fired Paul's imagination. "I'll even make a speech. I'll vilify woman and all her works! The Scarlet Woman! Oh Babylon, Babylon, daughters of Babylon. . . ."

Paul went away, much cheered by the thought of his speech. Michael shook his head and returned to Mary's letter.

When Paul rose for his speech, it was amongst cheers from the bachelors and prolonged booing from the more senior members. The civilian guests who had been invited for the evening looked dismayed as the mess began what sounded like a tribal chant.

"Up! *Up!* UP! Up! *Up!* UP!"

Paul climbed on to his chair and crouched under the low deckhead.

"Mr President sir, honoured guests, gentlemen," he began solemnly. "I rise to speak to you tonight on a very grave issue, one which touches us all very closely and which has not yet been examined in sufficient detail in this mess. . . ."

"*Keep* it clean, Paul!"

"Such is my intention. Gentlemen, I propose to speak to you tonight on the subject of *women*. . . "

"Man, *man*, dat's fighting talk!"

". . . and their proper place in a civilized society. First of all, there are certainly *some* things for which women are indispensable. . . ."

"Now what could those be?" The Bodger pondered aloud.

". . . granting those, why should women be accepted as first-class citizens in a civilized society? They only have a limited sense of values. They are incapable of looking to the future. They can't look objectively at a certain course of action. They will vote for one man because he has a nice face or, worse still, because their husbands vote for him, and they won't vote for another because they've heard he makes his wife do all the washing-up. Women are not civilized because civilization depends to a large extent upon reason and women are unreasonable. If women were given complete control of government we should be back to barbarism in a decade. . . ."

"Ah, but it's a *lovely* way to die!"

"Women have no conversation, by which I mean reasoned comment. They can *gossip* and they have a certain amount of general knowledge but they have no conversation in the true sense. Anyone who's listened to a roomful of women will know what I mean. Like the crackling of thorns under a pot!"

As always, the mess were impressed by anything which smacked of the Bible; The Bodger often remarked upon

143

the power of the Old Testament in bolstering up a weak
wardroom argument.

"Every Saturday night at sea we drink to sweethearts
and wives. Why?"

"You want I should tell you?"

"I should say that being married in the Navy is nothing
to congratulate yourself about. Married men are the curse
of the Navy!"

"Hear hear!" shouted the bachelors fervently, in unison.

"They get married in a fine rolling frenzy, *knowing* the
penalties of being married in the Navy and then they spend
most of their married life belly-aching because they haven't
got enough money and they don't have enough time with
their wives."

Paul could sense his audience growing restless and began
to wind up his argument before they actually began to
throw things.

"Sweethearts, so called, are no better. They're merely
apprentice wives, learning the job and getting ready for
Der Tag. They expect as much as a wife and give even
less. There's only one thing for it! I wonder more people
don't do it. Keep a mistress. You know exactly where you
are then. You can choose her like a tailor and change her
like a library book. . . ."

Anything further Paul might have said was swallowed
up in the uproar and it was only after several moments'
violent work with his gavel that the Commander succeeded
in making his voice audible.

". . . I think Mr Vincent has his supporters on both sides.
Mr Vincent will therefore stand the President and Mr Vice
a round of port!"

After dinner, the Commander took off his mess jacket,
lined up three whiskies and sodas on the lid of the piano,
and sat down to play. A group collected round him. After
some preliminary strumming, for hymn tunes were not
his forte, the Commander began to play "Eternal Father
Strong to Save". The group recognized the tune.

"It nearly broke her father's heart . . ." sang the group
by the piano. "When *Lady* Jane became a tart. But blood
is *blood* . . and race is *race*, and *so* to save the family's

144

face. . . . Her *father* bought her a cosy retreat . . . on the shady side of *Jermyn* Street."

Michael took up a handy position near the bar with the hard core of drinkers who regarded songs and party games as mere fripperies. This was the part of a mess dinner that Michael enjoyed most. His stomach was satisfied, his glass was full, and there were interesting conversations going on all around him.

"Next August," Commander (L) was saying, "I shall have been in the Navy twenty years. And I'll have spent ten of them waiting for boats."

The Bodger raised his glass to the Padre. "For all the saints, Padre," he said. "Cheer up, young officers always like to sit next to the Padre at dinner. They want to show off their agnosticism."

"I don't know why you should act so disappointed, Paddy," Alastair was saying to the dental surgeon, Paddy McGeogh. "You ought to know that nymphos never have a proper orgasm."

"How should I know? Toothwrights only study as far as the waist."

"If you really want your leave messed about," Mr Pilgrim was saying to Commander (E), "join the engineering branch and have it done by experts. I've still got some leave due to me from when we paid off *Ramillies*."

"I hear your bofors magazine got flooded again the other day, Slim," said Tim Castlewood.

"Yes," said Slim Broad bitterly. "I said to him, some may flood that magazine *quicker*, and some may flood it *deeper*, but *no one*, I said, floods it so *regular*. . . ."

"That piano's a bit battered, isn't it?" Paul said to the Navigating Officer. "Can't we ditch it and get a new one?"

"We can't do that, boy! My God, that piano was presented to us by the *Carousel* Boy's Paper and if anything happened to it there'd be hell to pay! It gave us a nasty scare the Christmas just before we commissioned. We were giving a children's party sponsored by the *Carousel* Boy's Paper and about half an hour before they were all due to arrive we had everything ready and then someone remembered the piano. Nobody could think where it was.

Hadn't seen it for ages. I'd only just written to the Editor, too, wishing 'em all a happy Christmas and saying how much we enjoyed playing their piano. At last, just as we were getting desperate, the Bos'un pulled his finger out and remembered where he'd put it. It was down in the electrical spare gear store. The duty part of the watch only just got the thing out in time. Of course, the Commander was sweating the big drop. Any bad publicity for the Navy in a thing like the *Carousel* Boy's Paper would probably muck up recruiting for a whole generation."

"I can imagine that," said Paul. "Can anyone else play it?"

"The Commander's the only one who understands it. A lot of the notes are missing and you have to be a bit of a Rachmaninov to remember which they are. The Commander's not bad but he's not a patch on the last TAS Officer we had here. He was brilliant. A second Carroll Gibbons. Bloke called Morton. We used to call him Jellyroll in memory of the immortal."

The group by the piano were still singing. Paul could hear their refrain high over the thunder of the conversation.

". . . It's even rumoured, without malice. . . . She had a client at the Palace. . . ."

At the other end of the bar, Bongo Lewis and a party of engineer officers had set up in opposition.

"Oh Sir Jasper do not touch *me* . . ." they were singing. "When I'm lying in bed with nothing on at all. . . ."

Michael was on his third whisky. The future looked even brighter. The conversation still eddied around him.

"What's happened to the P.M.O.? I haven't seen him around the last couple of days."

"They've taken him away. He thought everybody was making notes about him. He had a complex about it. Guess he was just a poor crazy mixed-up P.M.O. That's the new P.M.O. over there, standing on his hands."

Several officers were balancing on their hands on chairs in the middle of the room. Others were placing armchairs in lines and preparing to dive head-first over them. The Editor of a Hong Kong evening daily was trying to turn a somersault on a chair without touching the ground.

"Oh Sir Jasper do not *touch*. . . ."

"That chap's going to break a leg, I can see that coming a mile off."

The group by the piano were singing another song, led by a prominent Hong Kong banker.

"The portions of a woman which excite a man's *depravity*," sang the prominent Hong Kong banker, "are fashioned with considerable care. For what may seem at first a simple little *cavity* . . . Is really an elaborate affair. . . ."

Just like a normal guest night, thought Michael. He noticed that many of the senior officers present were surrounded by junior officers of their own branch. The senior officers were listening and the juniors were talking. A mess dinner was the recognized service time for telling a senior officer what you thought of him, for what The Bodger called "Pounding the Boss's Ear". It was also the recognized time for stories, bibulous, fabulous, and libellous.

"Old Jellyroll was quite a character," said the Navigating Officer. "He was one of the few naval officers who're members of the Athenæum and one morning when he was feeling a bit hangoverish he happened to be sitting next to the Archbishop of Canterbury at breakfast. Hangovers used to make Jellyroll ravenous and when he started digging into his breakfast the Archbishop looked over his newspaper and said: 'Young man, you must be hungry'. Old Jellyroll couldn't see very well at that time of the morning, he hadn't even figured out which day of the week it was and he had no idea who this old codger was so he said: 'Sir, if you'd had nothing between your teeth for twenty-four hours except a tart's tongue and a toothbrush *you'd* be hungry too!'"

"Golly," said Paul. "When was he retired?"

"Beginning of this year. He got a job in Hollywood at first, playing the background Rachmaninov while the heroine threw herself off the cliff and that sort of thing but he chucked that and came back to London. Playing the piano in a night-club now. Says he's never enjoyed himself so much in all his life and wishes he'd started years ago."

The Commander had left the piano to replenish his glasses.

"The white feather is not dead by any means," he said to Andrew Bowles who, with the rest of the gunroom, had been invited up for the evening. "I'll never forget once during the war when I was on leave in the country staying with a friend of my father's. A chum of mine and I went out for a day's shooting and we were standing about in some pub or other, in plain clothes, when in comes the most belligerent-looking woman you ever saw. She looked the sort that opens bazaars and generally hunts the local foxes and her husband into their graves. She was wearing a W.V.S. badge and must have scaled at least sixteen stone. This dame gave us the once-over, snorted, and went out. We thought no more about it. But she came back in about half an hour and gave us each a matchbox. We opened them and there was a white feather! When our host saw them I thought he was going to drop dead with sheer rage. He rushed after her and told her things about herself which I'm sure she never suspected. I gathered she was one of the old boy's neighbours and he'd been waiting for years to tell her what he thought of her. She just crept away without another word and I bet the foxes and her husband had a hell of a time for the rest of the war."

"What were you actually doing at that time, sir?" asked Andrew Bowles, who was well aware that the story was by no means complete.

"I was doing a spot of clearance diving. My chum had just got the D.S.C. a week before. He's a stockbroker now, of all things. I don't know what he's like broking stocks but he was a bloody fine diver."

". . . They shouldn't have magazine floods and sprays anyway. They should just have zip-fasteners in the bulkheads."

". . . I believe that chap *has* broken his leg."

"Oh Sir Jasper do *not*. . . ."

The Captain, who was also a guest of the mess, was talking to the Sub of the Gunroom.

"There are times," said the Captain, "when honesty is certainly not the best policy. When I was a midshipman I once went in a party to look over a coal mine. On the way back I met the Sub of my Gunroom who had been playing golf. The Sub told me to take his clubs back to the ship. When I came across the gangway carrying the golf-clubs, the Commander said to me: 'Been playing golf, young Gilpin?' and I, like a fool, said: 'Oh *no* sir, I've been down a coal mine'. I got a month's stoppage of leave."

The Sub of the Gunroom, who had heard the story twice before, laughed until it seemed that he must do himself an internal injury; he had already taken the story's moral to heart.

"Oh Sir Jasper *do.* . . ."

A mountain of officers in the middle of the wardroom collapsed in a pile of waving arms and legs, taking with it two tables and some chairs. The pile dissolved, leaving one prone, motionless figure, the Editor of a Hong Kong newspaper.

"*That's* a broken leg all right."

"Oh Sir *Jasper.* . . ."

The stewards watched dispassionately from behind the bar.

"Never mind, Jacko," said one. "We've done the first six years. It's all downhill now."

In a corner of the room a solitary figure was trying to stand on his hands. Periodically he fell and, giggling, tried again. The Captain's Secretary was pouring Kummel on to his forehead in the hope that it would trickle into his mouth. A large stain was spreading over his shirt front. The Bodger, hair on end, and a trouser leg and half his boiled shirt ripped away, eyes gleaming with the light of battle, pounded the bar and demanded a double Harpic and soda.

"Oh *Sir.* . . ."

Breakfast was served in funereal silence. The stewards walked like Agag with black coffee and iced tomato juice. At eight o'clock the prominent Hong Kong banker walked into the wardroom. The Chief Steward eyed him coldly. When he saw officers eating, the prominent Hong Kong banker stopped.

"What time is it?"

"Eight o'clock, sir," said the Chief Steward icily.

"Yes, I know, but what time? Day or night?"

"We are serving *breakfast*, sir," said the Chief Steward.

The prominent Hong Kong banker clapped a hand to his forehead and disappeared.

"Obviously a lost weekend," remarked Paul. "Lost night, anyway."

"Beats me how he could sleep," said Mr Pebblethwaite. "I was kept awake all night by the sparrows walking about on the upper deck."

"They didn't worry me," said Slim Broad. "It was the cockroaches marching about on the bulkheads. When I did get used to it, they'd all break step and I'd be wide awake again."

"There's one with a wooden leg in my cabin."

"This is getting too bloody humorous for this time of the morning," said Michael. He picked up his coffee and his newspaper and went into the ante-room. He settled in an armchair and a deep weariness overtook him. Paul joined him a minute later.

"I feel a bit of an idiot this morning, Mike."

"Not unusual, surely?"

"Don't be that way. I found all Anne's letters in my cabin when I got back last night. Some idiot put them in my cabin during the evening and didn't tell me about it. So everything's O.K. now."

"Splendid."

"Do you know what I did after I'd read them?"

"How the hell *should* I know?" said Michael wearily.

"I sat down and wrote to Anne proposing to her!"

"Ye *Gods*! After that speech! Did you post it?"

"Yes."

"Oh well, we'll just have to hope for the best. With **any** luck she won't be able to read your writing."

PAUL'S wedding took place in London and was voted a huge success by everyone (even by the three hundred people who waited in the Brompton Road for an hour in pouring rain to see Cedric, the national television personality, who was an usher). Anne was given away by her father and had six bridesmaids. Michael was best man.

Michael bought books in the Charing Cross Road which explained a best man's duties. They varied in detail (some suggested the ring should be kept in the left-hand side pocket, others in the right) but upon one point they were all agreed: the Best Man always made a speech. The thought weighed upon Michael and a stranger looking at them both as the day of the wedding came nearer would have taken Michael for the groom and Paul for the best man.

Michael met the Maconochies at the wedding rehearsal. Anne plainly took after her father's side of the family. Mr Maconochie, soon to become Lord Brothferry, was short and dark, with bushy black eyebrows from under which he peered shyly at strangers, like a bushman staring wonderingly from a thicket at the foreign white men. He dressed in sober grey suits and permitted himself the vanity of wearing shoes with built-in heels which added to his height; he found them a great help in dealing with young employees recently down from Oxford and Cambridge. Wolverhampton and Sunderland were the only towns of substance in the British Isles in which he did not own a hotel. He seemed to be mortally afraid of Mrs Vincent.

Mrs Maconochie was a stocky woman with fair hair which stood out in bunches on either side of her head. Her legs were like pillars upon which she planted herself sturdily and uncompromisingly. She had blue eyes, set wide apart, and a wide mouth tucked in at the corners, giving her an expression, Paul thought, like a calculating cow. It was Mrs Maconochie who conducted the tribal negotiations over the marriage settlement.

Mrs Maconochie was the matriarch of a large dynasty of Maconochies who had been brought up to regard invitations

to family occasions as Royal Commands; they would no
more have ignored one than they would have ignored a
police summons. The Maconochie believed in strength in
depth and Mrs Maconochie was supported by a battalion
of greater and lesser Maconochies who travelled to London
by rail, road and air from hotels all over England.

Paul's family were more simply represented. There was,
first of all, his mother, then a peripatetic uncle who had
made the journey from Monte Carlo against his doctor's
advice, and finally a cousin named Nigel who designed
fireplaces and looked like an older and more dissipated
version of Paul himself. But what Paul's side of the church
lacked from his family was more than made up by the
uniforms, gilt buttons and medals of *Carousel's* wardroom
and ship's company, the tweed suits of the officers' ladies,
the Paris models of the ship's company's wives, and Number
One Boy's red and white striped Hawaiian shirt.

The Navy singing surprised the vicar and made the five
guineas which Mr Maconochie had paid for the services
of the choir seem an unnecessary expense.

The wedding went without a hitch. Anne looked lovely
on her father's arm. The bridesmaids appeared demure.
Michael, contrary to expectations, had the ring ready.
Mrs Maconochie wept and was supported by the female
Maconochies. Paul spoke up, as Cedric said afterwards,
as though the padre was conducting the service from the
mast-head. Anne came down the aisle on Paul's arm. Both
sides of the church collected their hats and handbags while
the happy couple were photographed with the guard of
honour. Then all drove away to drink Maconochie champagne.

The first person Michael met at the reception was Commander J. P. Leanover, R.N.

"Don't I know your name?"

"*Hobbes*, sir."

"Of course. You were the young man who was so keen
on going to *Carousel*."

"Well, actually sir. . . ."

"Must confess I thought it very funny of you to want
that particular ship so much. She hadn't a very good

reputation at the time, you know. Everyone there seemed to be going round the bend."

"I *was* aware sir. . . ."

"Still, that's all changed now. You and your compatriots seem to have made a new ship out of her."

"I'm glad that we. . . ."

"My dear boy, it's the success story of the year! That visit to Dhon Phon, or wherever it was, changed the face of the Far East! Half of our department have been promoted on the strength of it! Must say I didn't know Dickie Gilpin had a talent for diplomacy. The First Lord looks a new man. The civil servants have even got a new office block approved. Well, next time you want a job, you know where to come. Any time, as long as it's not during Goodwood."

"Thank you very much, sir."

"Don't thank me. We always try to give people what they want."

Commander Leanover drifted away to have his glass refilled. Michael looked round the room and caught sight of a face he had not seen since his sub-lieutenant's courses. It was Colin Stacforth, who was talking to a plump, cheerful-looking girl with a large mouth. Michael was willing to bet that she was either a nurse or a Wren.

"Michael!" said Colin Stacforth. "After all this time! You haven't met my wife. Jenny this is Michael Hobbes, an old friend of mine from Dartmouth and the Training Cruiser days. He's just been serving with Paul in *Carousel*."

"Oh yes," said Jenny, "you're in Tom Bowles' term, aren't you? The Bodger was your training officer."

A Wren, Michael told himself; not a bad guess.

"I'm afraid I didn't even know you were married."

"Oh, it's all quite legal," Jenny said. "I've got lines to prove it!"

"I've got a little out of touch in the last year or so. When were you married?"

"How long is it, darling?"

"One month and four days," said Colin Stacforth promptly.

"Did you do the whole commission in *Carousel*?" asked Jenny.

"Almost all of it."

"When Daddy was promoted he thought he might go to *Carousel* to relieve Richard Gilpin but he was too junior. You normally have to wait quite a long time for a command as a Captain nowadays," said Jenny. "Who is your Commander?"

"Jimmy Forster-Jones."

"Oh yes, I've met him. He was quite senior for the job. I expect he'll be promoted after what he's done for the ship. He's being relieved by someone very junior, who used to be Daddy's First Lieutenant in *Voluminous*. And then he was Flags to C.-in-C. Antarctic. You might know him. Christopher Smythe? He was Communications Officer when you were in the Cadet Training Cruiser."

"Jenny knows the Navy List backwards," Colin Stacforth said proudly.

"Yes, I can see that," Michael said.

"Are there many of the term here today?"

"There's quite a good turn out. Of course it's quite an occasion when a bachelor as hardened as old Paul gets married. Everyone comes to see what the girl's like who's pulled it off. I don't see Raymond Ball anywhere. I know he had an invitation."

"I don't expect he feels much like celebrating," said Jenny. "Haven't you heard?"

"Haven't I heard what?"

"He had a row with the C.O. of his submarine and got thrown out of submarines."

"His C.O. had a reputation for being difficult to live with. He'd been a submarine C.O. for ten years. Had about nine years in as a lieutenant-commander. Passed over a year ago in December. Colin, darling, there's Richard Gilpin. We must go and say hullo. He was on the Staff Course with Daddy," Jenny added to Michael.

Michael watched them go. There, he thought, goes a typical naval officer and his *typical* wife. He noted Jenny's complete change of manner as she talked to the Captain. There seemed to be an appropriate Jenny for every occasion, a "young wife, eager, naïve but backing her husband to the hilt, Jenny" for Colin's superiors and a "nice girl, what's your poison, say when, have you heard, Jenny" for Colin's contemporaries. Most probably there was a third "seniors into the boat last and out first, Jenny" for Colin's juniors. Michael imagined them both in twenty years' time, when Colin would be a Captain and Jenny would be ruling the wives' roost with a rod of iron and four gold stripes on her handbag. The picture depressed Michael.

Michael saw Tom Bowles standing on the edge of the crowd. Although Michael had not seen Tom Bowles for some years he had heard all about him. The Golden Boy of the Training Cruiser had developed into the bright star of the present generation. Tom Bowles passed out top of his pilot's training course, distinguished himself in two squadrons, and had been chosen to fly at the Farnborough Air Show. Leader of the Fleet Air Arm aerobatics team, graduate of the Empire Test Pilot school, favourite of the press, he was quickly becoming one of the best-known officers in the Navy. He had grown a blond beard since Michael had last seen him and, as he stood head and shoulders above the crowd, he reminded Michael of a young Viking.

"*Hello*, Mike," Tom said. "It's nice to see you again."

"Hello Tom, how are you getting on these days?"

Tom Bowles grinned. "Well, I'm not very popular with Their Lordships at the moment. I crashed the prototype of that new night-fighter last week. So now I've got a draft chit to Dartmouth. As a divisional officer. Imagine me as a '*sir*', teaching all the trogs!"

"So help me God!" said Mrs Vincent who had appeared at Michael's elbow. "Its the first time I've seen Paul in his uniform at home and it will probably be the last. Who are all these dreadful people? I'm sure I don't know them and I can't imagine the other team knowing them. They must be some of Cedric's friends gate-crashing. I met an incredible little man masquerading in your uniform just now who said he was a *Double Bottoms* Officer! That's vintage Cedric Friend! Michael, I came to tell you, Paul thinks it's time we started to make speeches and read telegrams and things."

The Maconochie telegrams were traditional. "Best Wishes For Your Future Happiness, Auntie Florence and Uncle

Samuel"; "May Good Luck Follow You Through Your Life Together, Cousin Edie and Boxer"; "May All Your Days Be Happy Ones, Auntie Ruth." *Carousel's* telegrams were also traditional, in their way. "May All Your Troubles Be Little Ones, P.M.O."; "Best of Luck Dynasty-wise, Cedric"; "Every Conceivable Happiness, Pilot"; "Fight The Good Fight, The Bodger"; "Best Of Luck In Your New Commission, The Wardroom Officers"; and from Commander (E), the Senior Engineer, and the Engineer's Office, "Your Attention is Drawn to B.R. Sixteen brackets Fifty close Brackets Engineering Manual Precautions Before Opening Unventilated Compartments."

Michael's speech followed. Michael had prepared a careful speech with several witty jokes and comments. Lying in bed the night before the wedding Michael had run over his speech in his mind and had thought it uncommonly funny. But when he came to speak, Michael could not remember a word of it.

"I'm not really sure what the best man ought to say," he said. "It's no good giving the bridegroom any advice. It's too late. He's already made the fatal mistake! All I can really do is direct his attention to the B.R. mentioned in the telegram, particularly where it says that all officers and ratings and other persons concerned are to make themselves familiar with the precautions, and advancement of engine-room personnel will be made conditional on their possessing a good working knowledge. . . ."

Michael went on to congratulate the bridesmaids on their turn-out and to propose a toast to them. Michael's speech went surprisingly well although, as he reflected, a best man had the most tolerant and well-disposed audience of anyone in the world except a bridegroom.

Paul was almost completely tongue-tied. He restricted himself to thanking his mother for bringing him up, his fellow officers for keeping sober, at least until the wedding was over, and his bride for consenting and turning up to marry him. Then Paul stopped and blushed. For the first time Michael understood that the old Paul with whom he had joined the Navy and with whom he had enjoyed so many happy times had now gone for ever. The thought crossed Michael's mind that he might try it himself; he looked round for Mary.

"Here I am. Cheer up, Michael," said Mary. "Anyone would think *you* were getting married, you look so doleful. I thought you were going to ignore me."

"I'm terribly sorry, honestly. I've been quite busy."

"I thought your speech was jolly good."

"Did you really?"

"Yes, did you have it all rehearsed?"

"Oh yes, I knew exactly what I was going to say."

"You liar, Michael." Mary grinned. "I bet when you got up you hadn't the vaguest idea what you were going to say."

"Of course I *did*! Not perhaps in so many *words*, but. . . ."

Mary laughed. "Never mind, it was a jolly good speech."

"When would you like me to pick you up tonight?"

"Michael, you haven't changed a bit!"

"What do you mean?"

"You change the subject so quickly. I always used to find it difficult to keep up with you. One moment you'd be saying something wonderful to me and the next you'd be talking about the car. And the other way round."

"Well, we mustn't get in a groove."

"No, but you were so sudden."

"Right. We'll see Paul and Anne off and I'll go and change and pick you up at six o'clock. How's that?"

"That would be lovely, Michael."

Before he went, Michael said good-bye to The Bodger.

"Well, young Hobbes," said The Bodger breezily (he had met a good many old friends at the wedding). "Got your next appointment?"

"No, sir. I thought of going to see Commander Leanover next week."

"Good God, don't do that! He'll write things down on bits of paper and get 'em all mixed up and you'll find yourself in the one job you didn't want. Go and see Gwladys, his secretary. She runs the department. It's Gwladys who does all the officers' appointments in the Navy. Go and see her."

"Do you know where you're going, sir?"

"I'm not going anywhere. I'm retiring. Don't look so

157

surprised. I've been thinking of it for some time. I've been thinking of retiring from the Navy ever since I joined but of course I never meant it. But I do now."

"What are you going to do outside, sir?"

"No idea. Something will turn up, I've no doubt. What I would really *like* to do would be a gamekeeper or a factor for somebody."

Michael tried to imagine The Bodger in leggings, carrying a gun under his arm and chasing after poachers, but he found it impossible. His imagination could not encompass it.

"I'm very sorry you're leaving the Navy, sir," he said.

"Oh, I've had a good run. I would do it again if I had the chance. But the Navy's changed radically since I joined. There's probably a future in it for the people joining it *now*, but for those of us who knew it years ago it's changed out of all recognition. We haven't got enough *fanatics* in the Navy now. People who don't give a damn about brass hats or pensions or *married quarters* or anything else, who just do it for the sheer love of it. Most of the people who joined with me would still have done it for half the money. Of course, most of them could afford to. Nowadays we're getting people who've chosen the Navy when they might have chosen banking or stock-broking or *local government*, whatever that may be. That's not the right way to approach it. There are very few of my term left now. Those who weren't killed in the war are, ironically enough, banking or stock-broking. Still, enough of all that. I'll just go and seize Jerry Leanover before he climbs down the front of my wife's dress and we'll shout Hallelujah at young Vincent from the top of the stairs."

It was a perfect time to be back in London. The whole city breathed of spring. The parks were pale green, the plane trees in bud, dogs gambolled, there was tennis in the evenings, and damp tables outside the small restaurants in Chelsea and Notting Hill Gate.

Michael drew in a deep breath. He was experiencing one of life's supreme pleasures, that of walking, bathed, shaved and wearing a black tie, along a quiet street on a cool spring evening with a girl in an evening dress on his arm.

"Oh boy, oh boy!" Michael jogged up and down. He leaped into the air, executed a makeshift *entrechat* before he landed. He was still wearing the glow of Maconochie champagne. "I feel good. Where shall we go tonight?"

"How about Toni's?"

Michael whistled. "O.K. Let's go all nostalgic. We'll have minestrone, spaghetti, Chianti and pretend we're just married. . . . I mean, just starting out on our affair."

Toni's was still the same. Toni himself pretended to recognize them and gave Mary a rose, as he had done on their first visit. He gave all the other couples roses too, as he had been doing for more than twenty years. The couples sat gazing at each other, all wearing the unmistakable aura of awakening, wondering, first love. Michael thought them a touching sight; he observed them sardonically, as an experienced performer looks upon the first efforts of beginners.

Michael finished the first bottle and ordered another (to Toni's surprise; most of his customers were as new to wine as they were to love and treated them both gingerly, as though they were explosive). It was one of Michael's rare evenings, when his head grew clearer as he drank, when thoughts of great philosophical significance filled his mind, and when nothing in the world seemed impossible.

"You *have* changed, Michael," Mary said.

"In what way?"

"I think the Navy's done something for you."

"Done something *to* me, you mean."

"You've got more poise now. Is that the right word? Do boys have poise?"

"I've got more *money* now, if that's what you mean."

"Michael, do be serious. I mean you're more confident. Much more. I thought your speech today was jolly good. I couldn't imagine you doing that before you went away. You were a bit dull. But now. . . ."

"Now what? Do go on. If there's one subject I can go on discussing for hours it's me."

"That's what I mean. Before you went away you wouldn't

159

have said that. You seem to have expanded and got tougher."

"I had to, my dear. *Carousel* was only two steps removed from the *jungle*. You know, when I look back on myself a few years ago I think, cor blimey, what a bloody idiot you were then. And then I think, never mind, you're not such a bloody idiot now. And yet I wouldn't be surprised if in a few years I look back on myself now and see that I'm *still* a bloody idiot. What was that place you were talking about? I suppose I ought to feel guilty at not taking the bridesmaids out but I don't. Come on, let's hit the trail."

Mary laughed as she bent down to pick up her handbag. "What's up now?"

"You remember what I said about changing the subject."

"Oh, very well."

"Haven't I been here before?"

"Yes. It was the place you said George Dewberry recommended. It's under new management now and terribly fashionable. Debs get their names in the papers here. My dear, everybody goes here."

"Does it matter that I'm not a member?"

"No. We've got to pay ten bob each to get in anyway."

"*Have* we?"

"Oh dear, is that too much, Michael?"

"Too much! *You're* speaking to someone who's loaded for bear. I'm a mean hound dog and tonight's my night to howl."

Michael put his finger to his mouth and whooped.

"Michael, please, just say you're in the Navy. The manager's got quite a soft spot for naval officers."

"Golly, that's unusual! Normally you say you're in the Navy and they start calling up the bouncers right away. The mere mention of the initials 'R.N.' puts ten per cent on everything, drinks, car insurance, magistrates' fines, the lot."

The club had been redecorated and renamed "The Capricorn Light". The photographs on the walls had been replaced by heavy curtains. The floor was now carpeted and the room was lit by small shaded sconces. A bright bar occupied one corner. The dance floor was its original size but the band platform was empty except for a tubby little man absent-mindedly rippling his fingers over the piano keyboard. The whole room had the subtle but perceptible atmosphere of sophisticated patronage. This was plainly where the very best people got drunk.

The clientele showed more clearly than anything else the change in the club's fortunes. Pony tails and jeans had given way to evening dress, though it was still early and most of the tables were unoccupied.

"Nobody's here yet," Mary said.

Michael looked round. All the men he could see were obviously naval officers.

"Nothing but riff-raff," he agreed. "You pop off now and ditch your coat and do your face and I'll get a table."

The Manager himself came forward. Michael recognized him immediately. It was someone he had not seen since he was a cadet. It was Mr Sammidge, the Commissioned Catering Officer in *Barsetshire.*

"Good heavens, it's Mr Sammidge!"

Mr Sammidge looked furtively over his shoulder. "If you please, sir, my name is Rinaldo, now."

"Dear me, I'm so sorry."

"That's all right, sir. It's Mr Hobbes, isn't it?"

"Good heavens, you must have an astonishing memory!"

Mr Sammidge shrugged modestly.

"It pays, sir, it pays."

"You own this place, Mr . . . Rinaldo?"

"I collected a few friends together when I left the service and started here. That's the Captain's steward, Knowles, behind the bar and Lieutenant-Commander Morton, at the piano. Everyone calls him Jellyroll now."

"I hear you're doing well here."

"Can't complain, sir. Let me find you a table. I'll put you near the floor."

"I didn't know you knew Rinaldo?" Mary said, as she sat down.

"Chap I used to know. It's astonishing how you meet people."

Towards midnight the club filled up for the floorshow. The band arrived and several couples danced. Rinaldo had a reputation for engaging the best artists available and he had at that time engaged a dancer of international fame. In the space of one year "La Pompadour" had risen to the top of her profession. Her name was known as far afield as the Far East.

Michael considered himself an expert on strip-tease. He had watched discarded feathers, beads, veils, and even snakes, all over the world. He had tucked notes beneath navels in Istanbul, trafficked for strange webs and pinched naked bottoms in Tangier, and had admired the universal shape of woman from Piccadilly to Suki Yaki by way of Dhon Phon Huang. Michael had seen many dances but after a few moments of "La Pompadour" he acknowledged that he was witnessing one of the finest.

La Pompadour's face was veiled and her body clothed in layers of gauze which she shed without breaking the rhythm of her dance. The dance was enticing, perfectly timed. Michael thought it quite beautiful.

As the dance progressed and more of "La Pompadour" became visible, Michael felt a faint twitching of memory. The twitching grew to a turmoil. Michael racked his brains. When at last the ultimate veil was dropped and "La Pompadour" stood revealed, Michael remembered.

"La Pompadour" was Phyllis Featherday.

At the same time, Michael had another thought, blinding in its certainty and in its irrelevance.

"Mary," he said, "will you marry me?"

In the morning, Michael woke to the sound of tyres swishing through water. He got up and went to the window. The weather had broken. It was hard to imagine the street outside as the one down which he had skipped the previous evening.

Michael rubbed his chin. He tried to remember something The Bodger had said, years ago. "If you want to make up your mind about a woman, sleep with her. There's nothing like it for separating the sheep from the goats." Once again, The Bodger had been absolutely right. Michael made up his mind to marry Mary the minute it could be arranged. He dressed and went out to look for a shave.

Michael walked thoughtfully, thinking of the term who had joined the Navy with him. They were now separated all over the world. Some of them were even dead. Some he had met, others he had merely heard of; most of them could hear but not see each other, like troops thrashing through thick jungle.

When Michael became conscious of his surroudings again, he found blue sky, and Euston Station. He had walked the rain away.

The station was in a state of excitement. Flags hung over the roadway, officials were bustling about, and a large crowd lined the station approach.

Michael did not enquire the reason for the crowd. He joined it and was content to wait until something happened.

A black car flying the Royal Standard swept through the crowd and drew up at the station entrance. The crowd cheered and several small children waved flags.

Once the reason for their assembly had passed, the crowd dispersed. A woman with a shopping bag who had been standing next to Michael jogged his arm.

"That was nice, wasn't it?" she said. "I always stop to see Them go by. Sets me up for the day. I shall have to tell Irene—that's me daughter—I seen 'em when I git home. Fair crazy on Them she is." The woman turned and looked squarely at Michael. "*He* used to be in your mob, didn't he?"

"Yes," Michael said. "Yes, he was."

"Well, cheer up then. He might make you an admiral some day."

"He might," Michael admitted.

Michael walked on. After a few yards he stopped, so suddenly that a man cannoned into him from behind.

"Watch where you're going, chum."

Michael paid no attention. He was examining himself in a shop window. He was still wearing evening dress, with a grey top coat and no hat. He was unshaven and his eyes were bloodshot.

Michael addressed himself to the shop window. "How the *hell* did she know?"

DOWN THE HATCH

Salvador Dali tells a fable of a sardine
on the seabed who, seeing a submarine
pass overhead, says to his children:
"There goes our revenge: a great tin
made of sheet-iron in which men, covered
in oil, are held inside, pressed against
one another."

THE pictures on the walls of the Admiral's private office were all mementoes of a long career in submarines. By the door there was a group photograph of his submarine training class: three rows of grinning sub-lieutenants and a bearded training officer. Next to it was the Admiral's first command coming to a buoy in Portsmouth Harbour; her elementary wireless aerials and angular conning tower had not been seen at sea for many years. More submarines followed, a string of them, growing longer and sleeker through the years. The last picture of the sequence was the barrel-sided submarine depot-ship which had been the Admiral's last sea-going command. The other pictures were a mixed collection: a periscope photograph of a broken-backed Italian cruiser sinking against a pale Mediterranean sunset; a fox-terrier wearing a sailor's cap; and a startling picture of a submarine returning from her last patrol, flying the Jolly Roger, with her ballast tanks ripped in great gashes where a Japanese destroyer's screws had raked her.

The Admiral was not a sentimental man but he had held on to his pictures. They had travelled the world with him, survived all his removals and, he hoped, would go with him into retirement.

The Admiral himself was something of a celebrity in the Submarine Service. He had married very young and to the envy of his contemporaries, capturing by far the best-looking of the Admiral's daughters to come out between the wars. He had had a stormy career, so stormy that many of his friends regarded it as a miracle that he had ever achieved the rank of Rear-Admiral; his enemies attributed it to a triumph of matter over mind. He had trampled roughshod over his opponents. He had never toned down his scorn for superiors he thought incompetent. Tact and finesse were unknown to him; he had achieved everything by brute driving force. His tactlessness had led him to one court martial, two D.S.O.s, and three lung-splitting cheers from every ship's company he had ever commanded. He was of the school who learned about men rather than machines and who put charity before technique. But now the old fires were damped. The Admiral was left with a row of medal ribbons and his pictures. He often thought of retiring from the Navy and sitting for an agricultural constituency in the West of England.

The Admiral's favourite view was from his office window (he had coveted the view since he was a sub-lieutenant). From where he was standing he looked out over the submarines where they lay at their trots. The nearest submarine was charging her batteries; a plume of spray and steam rose from her after-casing and the Admiral could hear the thumping of her main engines against his window. Ahead of her another submarine was loading torpedoes. The Admiral could see the dull blue shape of a torpedo being lowered into her hull.

The furthest submarine was the longest and largest of all. She overlapped her neighbours at both ends. Her tall fin soared above the stubby towers of the rest. She was painted dead black except for the white identification numbers on her fin and she was plainly brand new. The Admiral looked at her like a father recognizing his favourite daughter.

The Admiral allowed himself to gloat over her for a minute and then, as though struck by a painful memory, scowled and turned away from the window. The Captain who was standing on the other side of the desk braced himself apprehensively.

Captain S/M was the Admiral's opposite in temperament. He was what was known in the service as "a charmer". He was in command of the submarine squadron which operated from the base and he was well used to the Admiral's moods. He had often been the sounding board for the Admiral's hobby-horses. But it was not often that he was so peremptorily summoned into the presence. Captain S/M guessed that the Admiral must have something pretty serious on his mind.

"Sometimes," the Admiral began, sadly, "I really wonder

166

why we bother. We've all fought for years to get the Navy a new submarine instead of a new block of offices. We've fought, and beaten, every government department. We've fought every branch of the Navy. We've fought everybody from the Ministry of Pensions to the Y.M.C.A. to get this damned submarine. At last we got her approved. We got her designed, we got her started and now, by God, we've even got her finished. In spite of sympathy strikes, wildcat strikes, token strikes and every other bloody kind of strike. At last we got H.M.S. *Seahorse*, God bless her and all who sail in her. Admittedly she's obsolete. She was obsolete before she was even designed. That's not the point. The point is that we've survived the worst the trade unions can do, we've survived two changes of government, three changes of First Lord and four financial crises to get her. And now that she's finished her work-up and is ready to join the fleet, what happens? We find we can't choose a captain for her. The whole thing is taken out of our hands. We get some passed-over bumpkin nobody's ever heard of. . . ."

"Oh, not exactly, sir," Captain S/M put in tactfully. "He was my Torpedo Officer in my first command."

"Has he ever commanded a submarine himself?"

"He had an old V-boat just after the war, sir."

"Exactly! An old *V-boat*! *Seahorse* is not an old V-boat! She's the best submarine we've got now and the best we're likely to have for a damn long time! What's this man been doing all these years?"

"I gather he was training cadets for a while, sir. Then he had a job in the Admiralty and one in Bath. And he was Jimmy of a cruiser in the Far East for a commission, sir."

"Why did he leave submarines?"

Captain S/M blushed. "I understand it was because he wrote 'Quoth the Raven' in the visitors' book after dining with the Admiral, sir."

The Admiral's manner softened. It was a coup worthy of himself when young.

"Who was the Admiral then?"

"Admiral Creepwood, sir."

"Ah yes, I know him well. And Flora too, come to that.

Her curried shrimps once gave me the worst attack of Malta Dog I've ever had. But that's beside the point. This man may be an excellent trainer and a first-class pen-pusher. He may be an excellent First Lieutenant in a cruiser. He might even be something of a gastronome but why, *why* send him here to command *Seahorse*? I've got a list of submarine captains as long as my arm, any one of whom could take her."

"Sir, can't you. . . .?"

"I've tried, I've tried. But Their Lordships are adamant. But why, that's what I cannot understand?"

"It may have been, sir. . . ." Captain S/M hesitated.

"May have been what?"

"It may have been your remarks to the First Lord about new blood in submarines, sir."

"But I meant the *submarines*, not the officers! Oh my God," said the Admiral plaintively, *"when* will I learn not to talk to politicians like that? Their minds just don't work like other people's."

"I think this man will be all right, sir, when he gets back into practice."

"He'd better," said the Admiral.

The new Commanding Officer of H.M.S. *Seahorse* was at that moment walking along the jetty towards his submarine. He was a stout, red-faced man with a shock of black hair which was just beginning to go grey. He walked with an unconcerned but hopeful air, as though he expected at any minute to be offered a drink. His name was Lieutenant-Commander Robert Bollinger Badger, D.S.C., R.N., but he was known throughout the Navy as The Artful Bodger.

Nobody looking at The Bodger's jaunty step and nonchalantly-pursed lips could have guessed that inwardly The Bodger was as nervous as a frightened kitten. As Captain S/M had told the Admiral, it was several years since The Bodger had commanded a submarine and now, by some ironical twist of circumstance (The Bodger had long ago stopped trying to unravel the mystical processes which decided officers' appointments in the Navy) he had once more been given command of a submarine. Furthermore, his new command was not just any submarine, but the latest, the fastest and the most expensive the Navy possessed.

Looking at *Seahorse*, The Bodger could see that he had been entrusted with a thoroughbred. Her lines rose smoothly from her low tapered stern to her high flared bows. Her sides had none of the gratings and awkward projections of older submarines. Her fin seemed to grow from her body in a clean proportioned sweep. Even The Bodger's predecessor, a venerable submarine captain who had been appointed to stand by *Seahorse* while she was building because he had an unsurpassed way with dock-yard officials, had been moved to remark that she seemed a reasonable design.

The Bodger was pleased to notice that the trot sentry was ready to salute him and was wearing a clean pair of gaiters. As he mounted the narrow gangway, The Bodger felt that, after an unconscionable length of time in the wilderness, he was coming home at last.

The rest of *Seahorse's* officers were waiting in the ward-room. They had all met the new Captain and they were agreed that he seemed a reasonable fellow but they knew that first appearances in submarines often turned out to be wrong. They realized, equally, that their social and professional lives during the coming commission depended to a very large extent upon the Captain's personality. The history of the Submarine Service abounded in stories of the brilliant and kindly men who had commanded sub-marines. But there were also darker tales of evil-tempered or eccentric men who had driven their officers, and par-ticularly their First Lieutenants, over the edge of break-down. The wardroom were well aware that, for them, the new Captain was more powerful than Caesar and more terrible than Jehovah.

The Bodger dexterously flicked his cap so that it slid along the chart-table and wedged itself behind the echo-sounder. Then he parted the wardroom curtains and, while the rest stood up, sat down in "Father's Chair", at the end of the table.

Seahorse's wardroom was typical of many in the Submarine Service. A central table was flanked by seats, upholstered in blue plastic material, which could be converted into bunks. The bulkheads were panelled in light polished wood which was broken up in several places to allow passage for pipes and valve handwheels. The spaces between the bunks were fitted with cupboards and drawers and, along the top of one bulkhead, a bookcase. A barometer and a clock were set into the woodwork above Father's Chair and a deep depth-gauge faced them on the opposite bulkhead. The whole space was slightly smaller than the driver's cab of a long-distance locomotive and, at sea, provided the living, eating and sleeping space for six men.

"About time the bar was opened," The Bodger said.

The wine cupboard was quickly opened and glasses and bottles set out on the table. The wardroom noted the remark; the Captain's policy about the bar was vital.

The Bodger raised his bubbling glass.

"Here's to us. Whores like us."

"Cheers, sir," said the rest of the wardroom, cautiously.

"Well now," said The Bodger. "I've managed to thrash out most of our programme for this term with the Staff Office. It's not very exciting but it could be much worse. Tomorrow, we're going to sea for exercises by ourselves. This is for my benefit, to give me a chance to get a grip on things again. But if anyone has any ideas about any particular evolution, now's your chance. How about you, Number One? Have you got anything you feel strongly about?"

"Not really, sir, though we might have another go at things like putting out a fire in the battery, sir. We weren't too good at that during the inspection."

"Good, we'll certainly do that."

Frederick Wilfred Garnet de Zouche Burnham, the First Lieutenant, once delighted his kindergarten teacher by confiding that he wanted to be an angel when he grew up. The kindergarten teacher, a kindly soul, had thought it a heavenly idea. The family, however, had thought differently. By tradition only the second son joined the Church. Young Wilfred, the third son, was therefore delivered, scarcely protesting, up to Dartmouth at the age of thirteen. He was a shy, fragile child with long fair hair, a thin nose and green eyes. He had quickly acquired the nickname of Vera, a name which still returned to haunt him whenever members of his term were gathered together. But the boy with the ethereal looks and the frail physique had won a reputation for survival; he had served with three of the toughest and most unpleasant captains in the Navy List and he had never been logged nor goaded into losing his temper. The First Lieutenant of Wilfred's first submarine had been driven into the arms of the psychiatrists by a captain who asked him, every morning at breakfast throughout a two-year commission, whether he felt well. Wilfred had watched and noted and said nothing. The Bodger suspected that his new First Lieutenant had qualities of withdrawal which made him immune to the boorish habits of people whom he considered his inferiors.

"How about you, Chief? All parts taking an even strain in your part of ship?"

"Yes, sir."

Derek Masonwyck, the Engineer Officer, was the wardroom's senior lieutenant and oldest inhabitant. He had joined *Seahorse* before she was launched, before she had even been a ship and was still several hoops of steel on a wet, windy slipway. He had stood by her while she grew from a shell into a submarine. He had watched and advised while she was transformed from an imaginary conception, represented by lines on thousands of drawings, into a solid entity with life and dimensions. He was a small man, with hunched shoulders as though from much crouching in the basements of submarines. He alone of the wardroom had known The Bodger when he had last been in submarines and while he remembered The Bodger as an excellent fellow, he had yet to be convinced of his qualities as a submarine captain. The Bodger recognized that Derek would probably be the hardest member of the wardroom to win over.

"Well, if nobody has any ideas about tomorrow, we'll leave that and see how we get on on the day. The day after tomorrow we set off for Oozemouth to show the flag. The idea is to show the great British public that we actually have got a submarine that Nelson didn't fly his flag in. . . ."

"Oozemouth?" said Dagwood Jones, the Electrical Officer. "I had a great-aunt who lived there once."

Dagwood Jones had a sharp, ferret-like face and black hair brushed straight back on his head. A degree at Cambridge, at the Navy's expense, had left him unusually erudite for a naval officer and he still wore a faintly donnish air, as though he were merely present in *Seahorse's* wardroom to lend a little tone to what would otherwise have been classified as a thieves' kitchen. He had a waspish sense of humour and a disrespectful choice of words which had often run him foul of senior officers.

"She used to breed miniature pekingeses and was a wizard at the horses," said Dagwood. "She made a lot of money in half-crown bets. My mother told me the biggest wreath at the funeral was from the local bookie!"

"Have we got charts of Oozemouth and all that, Pilot?"

"Oh yes, sir. Everything's under control in that line."

Lieutenant Gavin Doyle, R.N., was the ship's Navigating Officer and lady-killer. He had thick curly black hair, blue eyes, full lips and a reputation of which Don Juan himself might have been envious. Gavin's taste for fast sports cars and svelte girl-friends provided gossip for most of the Wrenneries in the Service.

The last member of the wardroom, who had not spoken and who in fact very rarely spoke, was Rusty Morgan, the Torpedo Officer and the ship's sports officer. He was a large, placid officer with red hair and a pleasantly freckled face. He was a particular friend of Dagwood's, being as good-humoured as Dagwood was prickly. He had played rugby football for Dartmouth and for every ship and shore establishment he had served in since and was now on the verge of a Navy trial. The Submarine Service thought of him as a resoundingly good chap and the finest open-side wing forward to join submarines since the war.

"We'll stay six days in Oozemouth," The Bodger went on, "and sail immediately for Exercise 'Lucky Alphonse'. That lasts three weeks. After that we get a fortnight's main-tenance here and then go off to the Equator somewhere to do something for the boffins, but that hasn't been settled yet. And that's as far as the Staff Office crystal ball goes.

By the way, Number One, I almost forgot to tell you, we've got a Midshipman R.N.V.R. joining us for training. He's a National Serviceman and I understand he's pretty green. I don't know exactly when he's joining. . . ."

There was a knock outside and the curtain was flung aside. The Bodger's jaw dropped open.

Framed in the doorway was a very parfait young naval officer. His doe-skin uniform still had its virginal sheen, his patches were dazzlingly white, his buttons blindingly bright, his cap stiffly grommeted, and his face was composed in a grimace of concentration. Just visible behind him was the dazed countenance of the trot sentry.

The apparition gave The Bodger an elbow-cracking salute.

"Midshipman Edward Smythe, R.N.V.R., come aboard to join, sir!"

The Bodger recovered himself.

"Ah. Ah, yes. Do come in."

"Aye aye, sir!"

The Midshipman seated himself in the one vacant chair and fixed The Bodger with a stare of furious zeal. The Bodger was disconcerted.

"Do take off your cap and hang it somewhere, old chap," said Wilfred.

"Aye aye, sir!"

The Midshipman whipped off his cap and held it, peak forwards, on his lap. The Bodger winced.

"Slow down a bit, Mid. Relax. What are you going to have?"

"What am I going to have, sir?"

"Yes, what would you like to drink?"

"Oh. Can I have a glass of beer please, sir?"

"Beer?"

"Beer?" The wardroom looked at each other as though the Midshipman had asked for a draught of hemlock.

"We don't keep beer," Derek said mournfully. "We haven't got room for it."

"Can I have a glass of sherry, please, then?"

"Sherry?"

Dagwood began to search in the wine cupboard.

173

"Sherry, sherry, sherry. We've got a bottle somewhere. Derek won one in a raffle."

"Have a horse's neck, Mid," said The Bodger kindly. "It's brandy and ginger ale."

"I'm afraid I've never tried brandy, sir."

"How old are you, boy?"

"Twenty, sir. Nearly twenty-one."

"Nearly twenty-one and you've never tried brandy," said Dagwood.

The wardroom gazed at the Midshipman as though he were an aborigine newly emerged from the remotest depths of the Matto Grosso.

"Anyway, you've come just at the right time, Mid," said The Bodger. "Always join a new submarine when the bar's open. Softens the blow a bit. On both sides."

"I'm sorry I didn't come earlier, sir. I only heard about it as I was going into lunch. I didn't get an appointment or anything. Someone just stopped me and told me."

Wilfred snorted. "Good heavens, you never get *appointed* to any submarine. You just think to yourself, I think I'll relieve old Charlie in the good ship *Venus*. So you stand up at the bar inboard and when anyone asks you what your next job is you just say, *I'm* going to relieve old Charlie in the good ship *Venus*. You keep saying that and after a month or two a little man calls you into his office and tells you, in the strictest confidence, that your next job is to relieve old Charlie in the good ship *Venus*!"

"Don't you believe it, Mid," said Dagwood. "If you do that you'll find yourself in a boat day-running from the Outer Hebrides with a Quaker wardroom and a Captain S/M whose wife you insulted at the last Summer Ball! No, the answer is to get a monk's habit and walk around the depot-ship, genuflecting every fifteen paces and chanting from S.G.M.s. . . ."

"I'm afraid I don't know what S.G.M.s are, sir."

"S.G.M.s stands for Submarine General Memoranda. Equal to but under the *Koran*. Every night at sunset the duty submarine staff officer climbs up to the roof of the Admiral's office and rings a bell whereupon all submariners all over the world turn and face Gosport while the chapter

174

for the day is read out. My God, you'd better bone up on S.G.M.s, Mid. When a submariner is buried he's laid out like a Crusader with his sword in one hand and his copy of S.G.M.s in the other!"

The Bodger saw the beginnings of panic in the Midshipman's face.

"Now that we're all together for the first time," he said firmly, "I want to make a few points about the way I intend to run things in this boat. I don't intend to do this again. I hope this will be the last time I'm going to talk in this rather pompous manner. As you all know, I've just come back to this after rather a long absence. I'm out of practice and I look to you for your full support while I get my eye in again. My way will probably be quite different to the way you did it in your last boats. But different boats, different cap tallies and I expect you to back me up in whatever I'm doing. I shan't hesitate to replace any officer who doesn't. In return, you can be sure that I will back you up all the way. I think that's enough for general matters. Now for particular things. Drinking. Your wine-bills are no concern of mine unless you choose to make them so. All of you, except the Midshipman, are sufficiently experienced to know when enough is enough. When I first joined submarines we weren't allowed to drink down in the boat while we were alongside the depot-ship. We had to do all our drinking up in the depot-ship where Commander S/M could keep an eye on us. I'm not suggesting any such arrangement nor do I intend to set an arbitrary limit on how much or what you drink but you can be sure that I'll come down like a ton of bricks on any officer I find drunk on duty. Now, smoking while dived. Various captains have various ideas on this. I'm going to try a new way and abolish the old 'One All Round' idea altogether. I'm going to allow smoking anywhere in the submarine while dived except in the control room, where there will be no smoking at all unless the submarine is on the surface. I don't know how it will work but we'll see as we go along. In the meantime, as I said earlier, I've got a bit of leeway to make up and I shall need all your support. We shall have the eyes of the whole Submarine branch on us the whole time, but

175

I think with a bit of luck we should have a very good commission."

The wardroom picked up their glasses again. Fair enough, they said to themselves.

★ 2 ★

WILFRED leaned over the after end of *Seahorse's* bridge, drew in a deep breath, and cupped his hands.

"*Midshipman!* What's happening down there? What's the delay?"

The Midshipman, very self-conscious in his brand-new yellow lifejacket, was still too new to have developed the submarine casing officer's superb disregard for the oaths and exhortations hurled at him from the bridge. He looked up nervously.

"Just coming in now, sir," he said.

"Well chop chop! We were supposed to be singled up five minutes ago."

"Aye aye, sir." The Midshipman turned to the leading seaman in charge of the party on the after casing, a squat, swarthy man named Gorbles who wore a prophet's beard and had been handling berthing wires on the casings of submarines for years.

"Can we hurry it up please, Gorbles?"

Leading Seaman Gorbles spat leisurely into the creek. "All ready now, sir."

The Midshipman relayed the news to the bridge and was rewarded by a furious scowl from Wilfred.

"Don't you worry about them up there, sir," Leading Seaman Gorbles said, confidentially. "They got nothing better to do. You be like the Torpedo Awficer, sir. When they shouts at you, tell 'em to go and take a running poke at a rolling doughnut."

Seahorse was ready for sea. Everyone was now waiting for The Bodger who, true to the tradition of submarine captains, was standing on the jetty, brief-case in hand, delaying going aboard his ship until the last moment.

An impressive committee had come to see The Bodger off, consisting of Captain S/M, Commander S/M, the duty staff officer, several heads of departments in the submarine depot, a few captains of other submarines, and a quartermaster with a bosun's call waiting to pipe The Bodger over the side. "Sir Bedivere and friends," said Dagwood, watching from the bridge.

The Bodger knew exactly why he had such a large and high-powered audience, gathered like vultures, to see him off. They were all curious to see how the new boy would shape. The Bodger suspected that they had all come half-hoping to witness a startling display of ship-handling. The Bodger could even see the figure of the Admiral, watching from his office window.

Commander S/M glanced at his watch. The other submarine captains assumed an expectant look. Captain S/M shook hands with The Bodger.

"Good luck, Bodger. It'll all come back to you."

"Thank you, sir."

The Bodger sensed the same expectancy when he reached *Seahorse's* bridge, where Wilfred, Gavin, Derek and Dagwood were waiting to report their departments ready for sea. The Bodger knew by their faces that they too were curious to see their new captain perform. Even the sailors busy taking in the gangplank, although they moved unconcernedly, were plainly conscious of a change of management. Down below, the control room watch devoutedly hoped that the new boss would not hit anything.

"Right, Number One," said The Bodger. "Let's go."

Wilfred waved a nonchalant hand forward, and again aft. The breast ropes dropped. The Union Jack at the bows was struck. The Bodger seized his microphone.

"Slow astern port. Slow ahead starboard."

The water whipped and frothed round the stern.

"Port screw going astern starboard screw going ahead sir," intoned the Signalman. When the ship was manœuvring alongside, it was the Signalman's duty to stand at the back of the bridge and report to the Captain the actual— as opposed to the ordered—movement of the screws. It was not a part of his profession that the Signalman took seriously; he had long been convinced that nobody listened to a word he said. "One of these days," he frequently promised himself, "I'll say, Both screws dropped off, sir, and I bet no *bastard* takes any —— notice."

Seahorse's stern swung away from the jetty. The Bodger caught the swing and the submarine backed slowly out into the main harbour, the Signalman keeping up a steady monotone commentary. The committee on the jetty watched her go and then broke up, feeling vaguely cheated.

The Bodger could not have picked a more testing occasion for his first day. It was a fine sunny spring morning and everyone who had any business on the river was afloat. A dockyard tug shot across *Seahorse's* stern as The Bodger completed his turn. A ferry passed close down the starboard side as The Bodger was lining up his ship for the harbour entrance where, just outside on the western sand-bank, a dredger was lying half-way across the channel. A motor boat crammed with sightseers darted in front of *Seahorse's* bows as she picked up speed. The Bodger could hear the guide's voice over his loudspeaker.

". . . Here we have a bit of luck, ladies. Here we have H.M.S. *Seahorse*, the Navy's latest submarine. You can see the ship's company all wearing life jackets in case the submarine sinks. . . ."

Outside in the main channel, The Bodger twice had to slow down as sailing boats tacked across his bows.

"All right for some," said the Signalman bitterly, as he watched a yacht glide by. "Not like Jolly John, in Daddy's yacht here."

By the time *Seahorse* cleared the outer buoy, The Bodger could feel sweat on his back, his legs were aching, and he realized with some surprise that his whole body had been fiercely tensed, with every muscle knotted, since *Seahorse* left her berth. When he came down from the bridge, leaving Gavin on watch, The Bodger felt as though he had run a Marathon.

"Coffee, sir?" said the Steward, as The Bodger sat down.

"That's the most civilized suggestion I've heard today."

"Just coming up, sir."

The Steward was the ship's company's equivalent of

Gavin Doyle. He was a dramatically good-looking young man with curly blond hair and a dimple on his chain. His face had a quality of innocence which, framed in a sailor's uniform, made nine out of ten girls feel, as they expressed it in their letters, funny all over. The Steward's private mail was the largest of any on board and was almost entirely composed of letters written on green, pink, or pale blue paper, perfumed, and with crinkled edges. They earned for the Steward the nickname of Mr Wonderful and gave the ship's company, to whom Mr Wonderful passed most of his mail, some of their most enjoyable reading.

"What's the matter with that signalman?" The Bodger asked, as he stirred his coffee. "He keeps muttering and grumbling in the background like a sort of Greek chorus."

"He's in love with a policewoman, sir," said Dagwood. "He's taken her out every leave for two years and last leave he tried to kiss her. Apparently she immediately seized him in a sort of judo grip and nearly broke his back!"

The Chief Stoker appeared at the wardroom door. The Chief Stoker was a giant Irishman with a broad beaming red face. He weighed nearly eighteen stone and had a belly laugh which could tremble a glass of beer at ten paces.

"Trim's on, sir," he said to Wilfred.

"Thank you, Chief Stoker."

"That reminds me," said The Bodger. "In future, I want the trim put on before we leave harbour. And go to diving stations and open up for diving as soon as we get outside. Mid, you'd better go with the First Lieutenant and see how to open up for diving."

Most of the machinery outside the engine room of the submarine was maintained by a tiny bald-headed man with huge projecting ears who was known by the traditional submarine title of the Outside Wrecker. The Outside Wrecker was a Lancastrian and leg-spinner for the ship's cricket team. He had a poor idea of any officer's knowledge, particularly non-technical officers, and when he walked through the submarine with Wilfred he leaped forward to check every valve and system himself, as though the First Lieutenant's touch would infect the metal.

"When yer openin' oop fer divin'," he told the Midshipman, "yer gettin' the boat ready to dive. There're certain things which moost be open and others which moost be shut. If yer miss one out, she won't go down and if she does happen to go down, she won't coom oop!"

"I see," said the Midshipman.

". . . And if yer in any bloody doubt whether to open or shut it, fer Chris-sakes leave it shut."

"I see."

There was still one thing puzzling the Midshipman. He ventured to ask the Outside Wrecker.

"What's the trim, please?"

"It's what the Jimmy makes a balls oop of," said the Outside Wrecker cryptically and sidled off towards the artificers' mess.

The Midshipman decided to put the same question to the oracle himself.

"Every time we go to sea," said Wilfred, "I work out a little sum about how heavy the boat is and how much water to have in the tanks. I give the figures to the Chief Stoker and he makes sure the right amounts of water are in the right tanks. That's what he means by 'The trim's on'."

When they got back to the wardroom, The Bodger said: "Mid, go up and relieve the Navigating Officer and dive the submarine when I tell you."

"Aye aye, sir." One of the cardinal rules drummed into the Midshipman as an ordinary seaman had been: "Obey the order first, ask questions afterwards."

Gavin was surprised to see him.

"Hello, old boy. Come up for a bit of freshers?"

"No, actually I've come up to relieve you."

"Oh." Gavin thought for a moment. "Oh, splendid. Well, let me see now. We're a mile inside the diving area, steering one-nine-four, both telegraphs half head, four hundred revolutions. Patrol routine, 'Q' flooded, radar in the warmed-up state. Only one ship in sight, that's that one, and she's going away. O.K.?"

The Midshipman, to whom the traditional catechism of the officer of the watch's turnover was so much gibberish, swallowed and said: "Yes, but I've got to dive the submarine!"

"Bully for you, boy. Don't pull the plug until I get down there, will you?"

"No, I won't, I promise."

Gavin softened. "D'you know how to do it?"

"I-I haven't the faintest idea."

"It's not all that difficult. When the Boss tells you to dive the boat, all you've got to do is tell the look-out to clear the bridge, shut the voice-pipe cock, take a quick look round to see if you haven't missed anything and then climb into the hatch yourself. Just on your right you'll find a little tit. That's the diving klaxon. Press the tit twice. You must do it twice. If you only do it once nothing'll happen. Then all you've got to do is shut the hatch before the cruel sea comes in. Got that?"

"Yes, I suppose so."

"Right. It's all yours. *Don't* look so worried, boy. You've got lots of time. This boat takes so long to dive you've got time to walk round the bridge and have a quick drag after the main vents open. Don't forget, *two* presses on the tit."

"No. I mean . . . yes."

Gavin disappeared and the Midshipman was left in command. He looked about him as though he expected the gigantic bows of a liner to crash into the submarine at any minute. But, as Gavin had indicated, the horizon was almost empty. The Isle of Wight lay far astern. A fresh wind was blowing from the south-west. There was no swell, only short waves with plenty of white horses to hide the feather of a periscope. It was, though the Midshipman could not appreciate it, perfect submariner's weather.

"Nice day, sir, isn't it?" the look-out remarked conversationally.

The Midshipman noticed the look-out for the first time. He was a young sailor in a duffle coat and a woollen ski-cap on which "Ripper" was embroidered. He had a perky, Cockney face which suggested costermongers' barrows, programme sellers at Lords and jellied eels.

"Yes it is," said the Midshipman.

"This your first submarine, sir?"

"Yes."

181

"It's a *hell-ship*, sir," said Ripper earnestly.

"*Is* it?"

"I should say so. It's. . . ."

"*Midshipman,*" The Bodger's voice crackled over the broadcast. "*Dive off the klaxon!*"

While the Midshipman remained paralysed, Ripper leaped round the bridge, shut the voice-pipe cock, collected the binoculars and vanished inside the tower. All at once the Midshipman found himself alone, the last man on the bridge of a submarine about to dive. It was the loneliest moment of the Midshipman's life.

The klaxon button was where Gavin had described it. The Midshipman pressed it twice and far below, as though on a different planet, he heard its sound in the control room. At once, there was a roar of escaping air from outside the submarine, the engines stopped, and there was silence, in which the Midshipman could hear his breath rasping through his throat as he struggled with the top hatch.

The hatch would not budge. In a frenzy the Midshipman seized the handle and pulled with all his strength. The hatch swung shut with a violence which knocked the Midshipman off balance. One of the clips removed his hat and dealt him a stunning blow on the head. He had not been prepared for the complete blackness when the daylight was shut out and he hung on the ladder, unable to see, dazed by the blow on the head, incapable of finding the clips and appalled by the thought of the sea by now rising steadily up the outside of the tower.

"Here, sir."

The Midshipman felt Ripper's hands guide him to the clips. He tightened them and slipped in the securing pins.

The Bodger was already at the periscope when the Midshipman reached the bottom of the ladder.

"Well done, Mid," the Bodger said, without looking up. "Bloody good for the first time."

Standing at the bottom of the ladder, rubbing the bump on his head, the Midshipman experienced a soaring exaltation of his spirit; he felt, for the first time, a proper member of the ship's company. The Midshipman in that moment, was unwittingly bitten by the submariner's disease. It was an affliction which would remain with him all his life and would make him run to the rail whenever he saw a submarine pass by and stand a-tiptoe when they were named.

The day's dive was The Bodger's first opportunity to put his new ship's company through their paces and it took the ship's company only a short time to realize that they had taken on board a Caesar. Standing in the control room while his ship's company raced round him, The Bodger took his ship and made it jump through hoops. They practised putting out a fire in the main battery and restoring electric power by emergency circuits. They exercised the hydroplanes and the steering gear in emergency control. The Chef was required to put out a fire in his galley. The engine room staff rigged emergency methods of pumping and flooding. The Steward steered the ship, while the Coxswain operated the switches in the motor room. The Chief Stoker and his store-keeper, a lanky, saturnine stoker called Ferguson, laboured to bring up fantastically-shaped pieces of spare gear which had not seen the light since the day they were installed. After two hours of it, the ship's company felt as though they had been put through a wringer.

"If this submarine was an animal," said Leading Seaman Gorbles, "we'd have the R.S.P.C.A. after us."

"Keep silence," said the Coxswain.

"Aye aye, Swain," said Leading Seaman Gorbles.

Leading Seaman Gorbles disliked the Coxswain. Most of the ship's company disliked the Coxswain but not because he was the ship's master-at-arms and responsible for disciplinary matters, nor because he was also the ship's catering officer and responsible, under the First Lieutenant, for the amount and variety of the sailors' food. Other submarine coxswains suffered under these disadvantages and still remained popular and respected men. It was not in his professional but in his private life that the Coxswain offended. The Coxswain had, in the distant past before he became a Coxswain, got religion. The normal submarine sailor regarded religion as something to be used when strictly necessary, at its proper time and in its proper place, classifying it in the scale of usefulness after Eno's Salts but before an appendectomy. They mistrusted anyone except a padre who looked upon it in any other light. It was perhaps this mistrust which led to a poem being pinned on the control room notice board on the day *Seahorse* commissioned which defined the ship's company's attitude to their Coxswain.

> "This is the good ship *Seahorse,*
> The home of the bean and the cod:
> Where nobody talks to the Coxswain,
> Cos the Coxswain talks only to God."

When *Seahorse* surfaced after her day's exercise, The Bodger felt as invigorated as though he had just had a cold bath and a massage. He knew now that he had the structure and potential of a very good ship. All that was needed was to breathe it into life. He was also selfishly pleased with his own performance. He had gained in confidence with each minute. The old commands, the familiar submarine street-cries, had all come back to him, as Captain S/M had predicted they would. Having laid his first foundation, he could safely pass on to the next item.

"Now," he said, rubbing his hands. "Let me see some of the correspondence."

Rusty, who was the ship's correspondence officer, guiltily brought out a file marked "Captain to See". The worst moment of any submarine correspondence officer's day was the moment when the Captain called for the correspondence pack. It nearly always meant trouble for someone.

"Yes," said The Bodger doubtfully. "The one I'd like to see is the 'Captain *Not* To See' pack. I always had one when I was Black Sebastian's correspondence officer. Who on earth are the EetEezi Catering Company?"

"They supplied the food during our contractor's sea trials, sir," said Rusty.

"Why have we got a letter from them still in here? Ditch it. What's this *gauge* all this stuff is about?"

"It's a gadget for the distiller, sir," said Derek.

"Have you all seen it?"

"I think so, sir."

"Well, take all this rubbish away and put it in your own pack. I don't see anything about this place we're supposed to be going to tomorrow?"

"I've made a special pack for that, sir."

Rusty handed The Bodger a bulky pack marked "Ooze-mouth—For Sunny Holidays."

The Bodger rubbed his chin. "I see we're open to the public every day from two to six. Is that O.K. with you, Chief?"

"It should be, sir," said Derek. "We haven't got anything big on, unless something expensive happens on the way there."

"Good. I don't see any visits from schools or sea cadets here?"

"We haven't fixed that yet, sir."

"That *must* be done, right way. We'd better have a Schools Liaison Officer. Dagwood. . . ."

"Sir?" said Dagwood, apprehensively.

". . . You've been selected from a host of applicants. As soon as we get there, I want you to go ashore and ring up every school in the place and ask them if they'd like to send a team down. Ask them all—sea cadets, girl guides, Band of Hope—everybody. Give the local crêche a ring, too. They may have some embryo submariners for all we know. This is supposed to be a flag-showing visit and we're going to show the flag if it kills us. I don't give a damn about the general public. They've all seen too many gloomy films about submarines and they're only coming to satisfy their morbid curiosity. But the schools are a different thing. Unbelievable though it may be, that's the Navy of the future you're looking at, under that disgusting school cap and behind those indescribable pimples. You give a boy a good time when he comes to visit your boat and he'll remember it all his life. So schools and sea cadets are the number one priority, no matter when they want to come and no matter how many they want to bring. They won't want very much, no detailed descriptions or anything like that. Just being in a submarine will be enough. And if they don't give the ship a cheer when they leave you can take it that the visit's been a failure. So don't forget. It's Billy Bunter, Just William and the Fifth Form at St. Dominic's we're after. Mum, Dad and Uncle Henry can look after themselves. It'll need a bit of organizing, Dagwood. We don't want them all at once and yet we don't want the boat looking like a Giles cartoon twenty-four hours a day for six days. Think you can do it?"

"Oh yes, sir."

"I'm told we'll have some boffins, too, from some Admiralty Research Establishment or other. You'd better deal with them, Chief. They're the worst of the lot, of course, but go easy with them. They've been sitting on chairs so long the iron has entered their souls."

Dagwood relished the last remark on the boffins. He had been a little overpowered by The Bodger's speech on Billy Bunter *et al.* but now he was relieved, and delighted, to see in The Bodger the gleam of a dry sardonic sense of humour.

"Have we got a press hand-out?"

"Yes, sir. S/M had a couple of thousand run off before we left."

"Has it got a photograph?"

"Yes, sir."

"Splendid." The Bodger began to turn over the papers in the "Oozemouth" pack. "Football against the police. Cricket against the fire brigade. Badminton against King William IV Grammar School. Visit to a brewery. Visit to a chemical works. Visit to an oil refinery. Reception in the Mayor's parlour. Free tickets to *We Couldn't Wear Less* at the Intimate Theatre. Darts against the 'Drunken Duck'. We're going to have our work cut out, men."

As The Bodger sifted through the invitations, he began to understand that the City of Oozemouth had exerted itself to be hospitable. There were honorary memberships of yacht clubs, tennis clubs and golf clubs; free tickets for plays, concerts and dances; and a card for every member of the ship's company entitling him to travel free in municipal transport when in uniform.

"What's this, supper and classical records with the Misses English-Spence, for two sailors? Have we got any classical music fiends, Dagwood?"

"I think the Radio Electrician and the Chef know a bit about it, sir."

"The Chef! Good God! Well, there we are. Obviously we're going to have to wave the old flag until we drop. What time do we get there, Pilot?"

"Nine o'clock tomorrow morning, sir," said Gavin.

At nine o'clock, in a light drizzle of rain, *Seahorse* reached the fairway buoy and passed up the channel to the City of Oozemouth. In spite of the rain, they were cheered all the way up. The main road which ran close to the water's edge for part of the way was packed with drenched holiday-makers. People perched on the roofs of cars and leaned from windows to wave. The inner harbour was swarming with sailing boats and pinnaces. *Seahorse's* black hull moved among them like a shark's fin in a shoal of minnows. A sodden sea cadet band was playing on the jetty as *Seahorse* secured.

"Zero hour," said The Bodger. "Synchronize your watches, men."

★ 3 ★

"But don't you get terrible claustrophobia?"

"No ma'am, only thirsty."

"But I thought you got rum?"

"Yes ma'am, but not enough."

H.M.S. *Seahorse* was open to the public for the first day and the citizens of Oozemouth were determined to make the most of the first submarine to visit their city since the day the war ended, when a German U-boat stupefied the local coastguards by surfacing next to the fairway buoy and hoisting a white flag. A squad of policemen with linked hands held back a surging, thrusting mass of holiday-makers, sea-cadets, tradesmen and seamen from neighbouring merchantships. Behind the public, mustered in ominous phalanxes, were the First Seven Schools.

Dagwood had spent a lurid two hours on the port harbour-master's telephone immediately *Seahorse* had secured. He had discovered that there were forty-two educational establishments in Oozemouth and district, ranging in size and denomination from Oozemouth Secondary Modern School, with over a thousand pupils, to Miss Elizabeth Warbeck's Academy for Daughters of Gentlewomen in Reduced Circumstances, with ten girls. Bearing in mind The Bodger's strictures on the subject of Billy Bunter, etc., Dagwood had telephoned them all and every school had said it would like to bring all its pupils. Dagwood had made a swift calculation. Forty-two schools, in six days, made seven schools a day.

The First Seven Schools had arrived and were being held back by the brute force of the police, assisted by depressed-looking men in faded sports-coats and ginger moustaches and large women in tweed suits and pork-pie hats, who were circulating amongst the tide of coloured school caps, squashed velour hats, satchels, hockey-sticks, and straw boaters like cow-hands at a round-up. A gigantic nun, wearing a headdress reminiscent of the Medici, was laying about her with an implement which seemed to The Bodger, watching in horrified fascination from *Seahorse's* bridge, to be a crozier. Hats, caps and satchels were falling into the harbour in a steady rain and were being retrieved by an old man in a blue sweater and three days' growth of white stubble. The old man had not had such a day in his small boat since the time the brewer's lighter came apart at the seams and four dozen barrels of assorted beers went floating out on the ebb tide.

When, suddenly, the Seven Schools broke through the police cordon and swept towards the gangway, the Bodger hurriedly left the bridge and went down to the wardroom where he poured himself a stiff whisky and followed it with another. The only other person in the wardroom was Gavin, who was pretending to study a chart.

"What are you doing, Pilot?" The Bodger asked him.

"Sailing plan for Exercise Lucky Alphonse, sir."

"Never mind about that just now. Get up top and start showing people round."

"Yes, sir."

Shortly there were shrill screams from forward, where Gavin had run into a party of girls from the Secondary Modern School.

Left alone, The Bodger was settling down to enjoy his whisky when he became aware of a rich north country voice resounding from the control room outside.

"Bah goom," said the voice, "Ah wish Ah had a quid for every time Ah've whanked one of these."

Cautiously, The Bodger peered round the corner of the wardroom door.

The speaker was a tubby cheerful-looking little man in a brand-new checked sports coat and a blue shirt open at the neck. With him was a lady who was plainly his wife and there were four children, two girls who looked like their father and two boys who resembled their mother, standing in a row which reminded The Bodger of a cocoa advertisement. It was clear that the tubby little man needed nobody to show him around. He was fingering the shining handles lovingly and passing his hands knowingly over the air valves. He sniffed, and a delighted smile of nostalgia spread over his face.

"Eeh, it hasn't changed a bit! Diesel an' cabbage an' sweat!"

"*Bert*," said the wife.

"Maria, Ah was in these things for four years before Ah married you an' they were the best years of mah life. Ah was Outside Wrecker and Ah remember one day off Sicily we 'ad something loose in the casing an' the Captain asks for volunteers to go and fix it. So the Engineer and me goes up and fixes it. When we got down again the Captain said to me, Biggs, he said, thart a brave man, Biggs. If an aircraft'd come while ther were up there Ah'd have to have dived without you. And Ah said, No tha wouldn't, Ah shut off t'panel afore Ah went, tha *couldn't've* dived. He just looks at me and when we got back he recommends me for warrant officer!"

The Bodger enjoyed the story. It had timing, punch, and a moral. Just as The Bodger was returning to his whisky he heard a small girl who was being held up to the after periscope by her mother squeal: "Look mum, it's in technicolor!"

A black scowl wiped away The Bodger's indulgent smile.

Up on the casing, in steady rain, Petty Officer Humbold, the Second Coxswain, was showing a party of the general public round the upper deck. The painting and care of the outside of the submarine were the Second Coxswain's own particular responsibility. He was the Torpedo Officer's right-hand man when the submarine was entering or leaving harbour. He was a broad-shouldered, bullet-headed man with a torpedo beard and a pugnacious manner, as though he might at any moment punch his audience on their respective noses.

"Up there," said the Second Coxswain, pointing at the gangling figure of Ferguson, the Chief Stoker's storekeeper, who was standing in oil-skins, boots and gaiters by the forward gangway, "we have a sailor who's known as the Trot Sentry."

The small band of the general public gazed at Ferguson, who was alternately blowing on his hands and making marks in a saturated note-book to note the number of visitors boarding the ship.

"He ain't good-looking, but like me and unlike you he's only here because he's gotta be."

"Why haven't you got a gun?" asked a tall pale man in a cloth cap and a plastic raincoat.

"Can't afford one," said the Second Coxswain shortly. "Forrard, we have the anchor and cable. We've got one capstan, that's that little drum. . . ."

"What's your job in this submarine, mister?" asked a youth in a black leather jacket and a crash-helmet.

"When the submarine dives, I run forrard as fast as I can and hold its nose. Back here, we've got the tower, where the awficer of the watch keeps 'is lonely vigil. . . ."

"Don't you get claustrophobia in a submarine?"

"Only when I laugh," said the Second Coxswain grimly.

In the engine room, Derek was entertaining the party of boffins. The Admiralty Research Establishment had provided an assorted collection of representatives, who were led by a senior scientist. There were four physicists, two marine biologists, three metallurgists, a specialist in wave formations, and a visiting professor from Harvard.

Derek led the way on to the engine room platform. In front of them were two panels of gauges, one for each engine, and all about them were the valves and systems for starting, controlling and stopping the engines. The party looked around in silence for a few moments.

"Holy Cow," said the visiting professor from Harvard, at last. "Rock-crushers!"

Derek bristled. He had cherished these engines from their earliest days. He had watched them grow from bare skeleton frames, lying on a shop floor, to thundering monsters capable of driving the submarine across the world.

"They're a little more than that," he said coldly.

"Tell me," said the Senior Scientist, "do you go everywhere dived?"

"No. When we're on passage we go on the surface. In peacetime anyway."

"Do the engines give you much trouble?" asked one of the metallurgists.

"Only when the Chief E.R.A. has a wash."

"I beg your pardon?"

"It seems to be traditional that the Chief E.R.A. of a submarine never washes at sea. If he does, something goes wrong with the engines to get him dirty again."

The Wavemaker looked at the tangle of pipes around him.

"How do you figure out all these pipe systems? They don't seem to lead anywhere."

"Actually, these systems are better than most," Derek said. "They've been planned on a mock-up first, before they were ever put into a submarine. Most submarine systems look as though they were designed by Salvador Dali. Of course, they were put in under the old Olympic System."

"The *Olympic* System?" The Senior Scientist shook his head.

"The fastest dockyard matie won, sir. Every morning while the submarine was building the men from the various dockyard departments lined up on the dockside holding their bits of pipe. Then when the whistle blew they all doubled on board and the man who got there first had a straight run. The others had to bend their pipes round his. The beauty of the system was that it didn't matter what size the pipes were. If the electrician was particularly agile he could put his bit of quarter-inch electric cable in first and watch the boiler-maker bend his length of eight-inch diameter special steel piping round it."

"*Really?*" said the Senior Scientist.

"Yes," said Derek, looking the Wavemaker, who appeared to be sceptical, defiantly in the eye. "Now, gentlemen, was there anything in particular you wished to see?"

One of the physicists had a special request.

"May we see the distiller, please? I've been designing a special gauge for them and I would love to see where it's actually got to go."

Derek showed them the distiller. The Physicist was thrilled.

"I'm *so* glad we saw that," he said. "Do you know, I've been designing them, and writing letters about them, and giving advice about them for a long time and this is the first time I've actually seen one!"

Good God, Derek said to himself.

"How stable are these boats in rough weather?" the Wavemaker asked.

"Pretty good. The fin keeps them more or less dry, not like the older boats with low towers. The stability has to be pretty carefully worked out, of course. We do a trim dive in the dockyard basin after every refit. Occasionally they make a mistake. One boat I went to sea in very nearly capsized. We heeled over to about fifty degrees and stayed there. I thought we'd all had it."

"Of course," said the Wavemaker, "in a case like that we've got to differentiate between actual *danger*, and mere *discomfort*."

Derek ground his teeth and repressed an almost overwhelming urge to howl out loud.

"Now, is there anything else, gentlemen?"

The Senior Scientist looked sheepish.

"I wonder. . . ."

"Yes, sir?"

"I wonder. . . . It seems silly but . . . I wonder if you could

192

explain something I've always been puzzled about. . . ."

"Yes, sir?"

"How exactly does a submarine dive?"

"Well sir, all along the outside of the boat we've got a row of very large tanks, called main ballast tanks. They're open to the sea at the bottom and closed at the top by very large valves, called main vents. When we open the main vents, the sea rushes in at the bottom and the air rushes out at the top, the submarine in effect shrinks in volume, displaces less water and therefore becomes heavier and therefore sinks. When we want to come up again we shut the main vents and blow the water out with compressed air. That makes the boat sort of swell again, displaces more water, become in effect lighter, and up she comes again. All done by Archimedes' principle, sir."

"Archimedes?"

"You remember the chap, sir," said the Wavemaker. "He lived in a barrel."

"Ah yes," said the Senior Scientist.

In the control room, the Schools Liaison Officer was explaining technical matters to a crowd of schoolboys. Keep it simple, The Bodger had said. Dagwood began his address on first principles.

"These levers raise and lower the periscopes, and these open and shut the main vents. The main vents are. . . ."

"Solenoid-operated, I suppose?" said a treble voice, casually.

"Huh?" Dagwood was thrown out of his stride. "As a mater of fact, they are. This is the starter for the L.P. Blower. . . ."

"It puts the final bit of air into the ballast tanks after surfacing," said another treble voice confidently. "Naturally you wouldn't use air from the bottles for all of it. You would use only enough to get you to the surface. H.P. Air is too precious in a submarine."

Dagwood felt the hair on the back of his neck prickle with the first cold feeling of foreboding.

"Quite right," he said. "Now this. . . ."

"The Germans used to use the exhaust gases from the engine starting instead."

"*Did* they?" said Dagwood.

"Yes."

A very small boy whose face was almost entirely extinguished by hair and by an enormous blue school cap said: "What would you do if the submarine began to drop towards the bottom, sir?"

Dagwood thought rapidly.

"I would go hard a port, or hard a starboard, and full astern. That would tend to bring the bows up."

"And if that didn't work, sir?"

"Blow the forrard main ballast tank."

"And if that didn't work?"

"Blow *all* main ballast tanks."

"And if that didn't work?"

Dagwood had by now the attention of everyone in the control room; there was a hush as they waited for his answer.

"That would work all right," he said finally. But he did not feel that he had convinced anybody.

Far aft in the after torpedo space, Leading Seaman Miles, the torpedo rating in charge of the compartment, was being asked the same question by another schoolboy.

"What would you do," the questioner's voice was charged with drama, "*if the submarine began to hurtle towards the bottom of the sea completely out of control?*"

"Face aft and salute, lad," said Leading Seaman Miles easily.

Just aft of the control room, Leading Seaman Gorbles was explaining a delicate point to two schoolmasters.

"These are heads. What you call lavatories. There's one for the officers, one for the petty officers and one for the sailors. That's democracy."

One of the schoolmasters had a dim memory connected with submarine toilets.

"Are they easy to work?"

"Dead easy. You just flush 'em. In the old days it was a bit tricky, you had to blow 'em over the side. You had to ring up the control room and ask the awficer of the watch before you did it. We used to get fed up with that rigmarole after a bit so we used to ring up and say: 'Shit?' and they said: 'Shoot!'"

194

In the fore ends, the Midshipman was explaining the escape system to Miss Elizabeth Warbeck, her niece Miss Sarah Warbeck, and the ten daughters of gentlewomen in reduced circumstances. Miss Elizabeth Warbeck was a tiny but staunch lady, with the perky air of a gamecock. Her eyes were sharp and interested in all she saw, her cheeks were rosy and her silver hair was drawn into a bun. The ten daughters of gentlewomen in reduced circumstances were uniformly dressed in grey tunics and berets.

But the Midshipman was chiefly interested in Miss Sarah Warbeck. He had first seen her, or rather a part of her, when she came down the fore hatch. The Midshipman had then discovered one of the least-publicised advantages of a submariner's life. No matter how tight her skirt nor how circumspectly she lowered herself, a girl descending through the fore hatch of a submarine was forced to display her legs.

The Midshipman had tactfully averted his eyes but could not prevent himself seeing enough of Miss Warbeck to whet his interest.

"This is an escape hatch," he said. "This is where you see John Mills and Co looking terribly brave on the movies. You let this trunking down and flood up the compartment until the pressure inside is equal to the sea pressure outside. Then you can open the hatch and duck under the trunking and go on up to the surface."

The Midshipman paused and glanced quickly at his audience to see how they were taking it. He was gratified by Miss Sarah Warbeck's solemn expression.

"Of course in wartime," he went on, "all this would be removed to save weight and the hatches would be secured from the outside with clips."

"But that's not fair!" said Sarah Warbeck indignantly.

The Midshipman gave a sad shrug, as though to say, That's the way the ball bounces.

"They have to be secured otherwise depth charges might blow them open. And anyway there wouldn't be anyone there to pick you up even if you did escape."

"I think that's a swindle!" said Sarah Warbeck hotly.

The Midshipman gave another shrug, as though to say, Ah well, that's the way the cookie crumbles.

"Shall we look at the rest of the submarine?"

On their way they passed Gavin and a party of prefects from a girls' grammar school. The prefects were fully-developed wenches, under their school tunics. Gavin was having difficulty in keeping them to the point.

"This is the Petty Officers' Mess," he announced.

"Is this where you live?"

"No, I live in the wardroom. The Coxswain lives here, and the Chief Stoker and. . . ."

"Ooooh, do look at the beds, darling. . . ."

"*Bunks*, Maureen darling. . . ."

"Not very big, are they?"

"Not big enough for two, *darling*. . . ."

". . . And the Stoker Petty Officer and the Second Coxswain. . . ."

"It's a good job you're all *men*!"

"Do you ever get kleptomania?"

"*Claustrophobia*, darling."

"Barbara, you coarse thing!"

". . . And the Electrical Artificer and the Radio Electrician and the Torpedo Instructor. . . ."

"Who was that *gorgeous* man in white tabs. . . ."

The gorgeous man in white tabs was enjoying the effect his remarks were having on Miss Elizabeth Warbeck and her niece. Their minds were now filled with pictures of black swirling water, explosions, feeble lights, and men struggling for breath. Miss Elizabeth Warbeck looked with compassion upon the Midshipman; he seemed so young to die.

They visited the galley next. The Chef was there in person, splendidly dressed for the occasion in a white apron and a tall white hat. The Midshipman was thankful that the Chef was not wearing his usual working rig of football shorts and bare chest, because the Chef was luridly and comprehensively tattooed. His tattoos included the words "Mild" and "Bitter", one over each nipple, and a dotted line round his throat, inscribed "Cut here". He also had an assortment of sailing ships, dragons, butterflies, crossed swords, naked women, and "Mother" in a halo of laurel leaves, on his arms.

"Where did you get all those tattoos?" asked Miss Elizabeth Warbeck.

"Hong Kong, ma'am, Singapore, Yokohama, all over the place, ma'am."

"I think they're terrific," said Miss Elizabeth Warbeck warmly. The Chef was charmed. He showed them over his tiny galley.

"How many chefs do you have on board?"

"Only me, ma'am."

"Only one Chef? For how many men?"

"Nearly seventy, ma'am."

"Good gracious!"

All day long the noise of battle rolled in *Seahorse's* passageways and living spaces. The general public tramped determinedly through, fingering, pointing, gazing through the periscopes, and exclaiming to each other at the marvels they saw. On the jetty, a queue a quarter of a mile long awaited their turn. Derek, who was duty officer, sat in the wardroom feeling like a goldfish in a bowl and trying to ignore the whispers and the shuffling feet behind him. At last he was driven to his bunk and he lay there with his curtain drawn. But the more curious members of the public ventured into the wardroom, pulled the curtain aside, and peered at him. Derek ignored them and concentrated on his book. It was a submarine story, just published, by a popular writer of novels.

"A submarine in harbour," Derek read, "is a lifeless, dead thing. It lies quiet, waiting, but with the hidden menace of a sheathed sword. . . ."

* 4 *

THE first comedian was a bulky man in a pale blue suit which hung baggily from his shoulders.

"A funny thing happened to me on the way to the theatre tonight!"

The second comedian was a thin man in a pale green suit gathered very tightly at the waist.

"A funny thing happened to you on the way to the theatre tonight?"

"Yes. I met a man who had fourteen children!"

"You met a man who had fourteen *children*?"

"He said his wife was deaf!"

"He said his wife was *deaf*?"

"Yes. Every night he said to her, Shall we go to sleep, dear, or what?"

"Ha! Every night he said to her, Shall we go to sleep, dear, or *what*? Go on, Jimmy."

"I'm goin' on. And every night she said, What?"

"Ha ha! Every night she said, What? Ha! Smashin' audiences you get here in Oozemouth, eh Jimmy? Smashin' audi. . . ."

"I fell out of my bloody cradle laughing at that one!" shouted a voice from the dress circle which Gavin, sitting in the front row of the stalls, recognized as that of Leading Stoker Drew, of H.M.S. *Seahorse*.

"Turn it up, mate," said Jimmy. "I wouldn't knock the broom out of your hands if you were working. Did I ever tell you the one about the old lady who saw an elephant eating cabbages in her front garden, 'Arry?"

"No, Jimmy, you never told me the one about the old lady who saw a *hephalump* eating cabbages in her front garden. . . ."

The Intimate Theatre was an Edwardian relic. The gas-light had been superseded by electricity but the chandelier in the foyer, the red plush seats, the gilded scroll work along the rim of the dress circle and the engraved glass on the box office window still remained. The theatre was a period piece. As the "Empire Palace", it had billed Marie Lloyd and had staged the provincial runs of *Floradora* and *The Belle of New York* to packed houses. But the visitor in search of nostalgia would have been disappointed. The glory had long since departed. The stage of the Intimate Theatre was now inhabited by bored girls who exhibited their bodies on revolving pedestals for twelve pounds a week and by comedians who ground out jokes about sexual perversion. The theatre was due to become a supermarket at the end of the year.

Jimmy and Harry finished their patter. The orchestra struck up. Jimmy and Harry shuffled to the centre of the stage, sang two choruses of "Underneath The Arches", waited for applause and, disappointed, shuffled off. The orchestra struck up again. A line of chorus girls galloped on and began to swing their legs mechanically at the audience. Leading Stoker Drew gave an appreciative howl and was helped from the theatre by two large men in shirt-sleeves.

"What do you think, Rusty?" said Gavin.

"Pretty starved-looking lot. You can count the ribs on that end one."

"I like the second one from the end, though. The small dark one."

"What do you say then, shall we try back-stage?"

"We'll see. Getting back-stage in one of these places is like trying to break into the Kremlin. We'll have to play it off the cuff."

Three hundred yards away from the Intimate Theatre, in the same street, The Bodger, Wilfred and Dagwood had disposed of the Mayor's clear soup and grilled sole and were preparing to attack the Mayor's roast duck.

The dinner for the Captain of H.M.S. *Seahorse* was a civic occasion. The City of Oozemouth had laid out its best dinner service, polished its best silver, chilled its best hock, warmed its best claret, and decanted its best port. The Mayor and Mayoress were there in person, supported by a goodly muster of aldermen and their ladies. The Bodger, for his part, had changed into mess dress with miniature medals and a clean white stiff shirt. He had also brought Wilfred and Dagwood as moral support.

"I've been to these things before," he said to them, as they sat in the Mayoral limousine which was bearing them towards the Mayor's parlour. "You'll get a first-class dinner and vino, but the conversation will drive you up the wall if you don't watch it. Do either of you know anything about boiling soap or smelting copper?"

"No, sir."

"You will, by the end of this evening. That's the sort of

199

thing these characters are pretty hot on. By the way, I've been boning up on a little local colour. Oozemouth United got to the semi-final of the F.A. Cup last year. The Oozemouth Festival Orchestra is second only to the Liverpool Philharmonic amongst provincial orchestras, though you'd better say for the sake of argument tonight that it's the best. Oozemouth makes the best electric light bulbs in the world and remained loyal to the Crown during the Civil War. That's about all I've managed to pick up."

"Thank you very much, sir," said Wilfred and Dagwood gratefully.

After the initial commonplaces about the weather, the traffic, and the criminal financial policy of the government had been exchanged, it suddenly became clear that The Bodger had seriously misjudged the conversational range of his hosts. While The Bodger was shyly admiring the delicate colouring of the Goldbeerenauslese in his glass, the conversation took an unexpected and vaguely hostile turn.

"Commander," said the Mayor. "Tell me something I've always wanted to know about submarines."

The Bodger composed himself to answer the usual chestnuts on claustrophobia and escape from sunken submarines.

"Why do men, like yourself for instance, go into submarines? What sort of man would do a thing like that?"

The cue was taken up at once by an alderman sitting further down the table whom The Bodger later discovered was the city's most prosperous undertaker.

"It is condemned in Holy Writ," said the Undertaker stridently. "Thou didst blow with Thy wind, the sea covered them: they sank as lead in the mighty waters. Exodus, fifteen, ten. And again," the Undertaker's voice rose thrillingly, "And their persecutors Thou threwest into the deeps, as a stone into the mighty waters. Nehemiah, nine, eleven."

A ripple of agreement ran down the table.

". . . Hear hear, Jeb. . . ."

". . . Took the words out of my mouth. . . ."

". . . Pure weapons of destruction, that's what they are. . . ."

". . . Should be banned. . . ."

"Nasty underhand things," said the Undertaker's wife.

Wilfred, sitting next to her, thought it time to change the subject.

"That was a jolly good show in the F.A. Cup last year," he said, brightly, "I mean, getting as far as the semi-finals. . . ."

Wilfred's voice trailed away into silence when the Undertaker's wife looked at him.

The Bodger had been taken off guard by the unexpected and spiritually well-documented attack. He felt his way cautiously towards an answer.

"I don't know that it's up to me to say whether we should have submarines or not," he said. "The fact is, we've got them, everybody else who can afford them has got them, and lots of people who can't afford them would very much like to have them. As to why people go into submarines, that's very hard to answer. You might just as well ask why do people become missionaries or shoplifters. I suppose the extra money has something to do with it but I'm sure that basically it all comes down to the question of which would you rather do, run your own firm, however small, or help to run someone else's, however big. Would you rather be a small cog in a big machine or a big cog in a small machine. Most of our ship's company are big cogs in a small machine. They're nearly all specialists. They have clearly defined jobs and in most cases they're the only man for that job, although all of them can do the basic things in a submarine which everybody should be able to do. Take the chef as an example. His actual rate is Leading Cook. In a cruiser or an aircraft carrier he would probably be in charge of a watch of cooks, one cook in over a dozen. But in *Seahorse* he's not just *any* chef, he's *the* chef. He's one of the ship's personalities by reason of his job, if nothing else. Everyone in a submarine has a much greater *identity*, if you see what I mean, than his counterpart in general service. Everybody in a submarine has a much better idea of what's happening. In an aircraft carrier I don't suppose more than ten per cent of the men on board know what's going on at any given time. But in a submarine news goes round in a matter of minutes. The chart is on the chart-table in the control room most of the time. Anyone passing by can see where we are and where we're going."

"Yes," said the Mayor. "Yes, I see what you mean, Commander. But I'm still of the opinion that it's a pity we have to make use of such things. I've never trusted all these new-fangled inventions. . . ."

"Oh, but the *idea* of a submarine is not new at all, Your Worship," said Dagwood, manfully stepping into the breach (while The Bodger thankfully resumed his meal; he had noticed that everyone else had already finished). "It's true that the first really practicable submarine in the modern sense, the Holland boat, only went to sea at the beginning of this century. But Robert Fulton built a perfectly workable one during the Napoleonic Wars. And even earlier than that, at the beginning of the seventeenth century, a Dutchman called Cornelius van Drebbel made one which was propelled by oars. He even took King James the First down for a dive in it!" Dagwood warmed to his subject; he had done a deal of research into the history of submarines. "Leonardo da Vinci had a design for a submarine. . . ."

"Ah!" cried the Undertaker triumphantly. "But he kept it a secret, didn't he? He was afraid of the use evil men would put it to!"

"Yes, that's true," Dagwood admitted, wishing he had never mentioned Leonardo da Vinci.

"And they besought him that he would not command them to go out into the deep. Luke, eight, thirty-one."

"When are the Oozemouth Festival playing again?" Wilfred enquired of the alderman sitting opposite him.

"Which league do they play in, lad?"

While his seniors wrangled, the most junior member of *Seahorse's* wardroom was being very well entertained. Having dined very successfully *en famille* with Miss Elizabeth Warbeck and Sarah, the Midshipman had ventured to ask Sarah back to the submarine for a drink. To the surprise of them both, Miss Elizabeth Warbeck agreed.

Derek was very glad to see them. The public had gone, except for some odd pockets of sea cadets who were being mopped up by the duty watch. He was bored with his book (the hero's submarine was plunging, out of control, towards the bottom of the Timor Sea, the hero being baffled) and he was bored with being by himself while the rest were ashore.

Recognizing the situation at a glance (Derek had been entertaining ladies in submarines while the Midshipman was still at his preparatory school), Derek knew exactly what was required of him. He opened a panel in the wood-work by his bunk and made a cunning two-way switch, installed by the builders at his personal request, which simultaneously extinguished the white lighting and replaced it with two dim red lights in opposite corners of the ward-room. He switched on Dagwood's tape recorder which began to play soft dreamy music of the kind defined by Dagwood himself as "Eine Kleine Smooch Musik". Lastly, he opened the wine cupboard, took out some bottles and clinked them invitingly.

"Chez *Seahorse*, we never closed," he said to Sarah. He was vastly taken with her. He admired the Midshipman's taste.

"What'll you have?"

The Midshipman and Sarah were both a little taken aback by the speed and facility with which Derek had converted the wardroom into a very fair facsimile of a sordid night-club.

"Well, I don't know what to have," Sarah said. "What have you got?"

"Anything you like."

"Except beer," said the Midshipman.

"How about some Contreau, Sarah?"

"Yes, that would be nice. But only a small one."

"We don't have small ones here."

Conversation came reluctantly at first, so reluctantly that Derek had to work hard to keep it going; he began to wonder indignantly why the Midshipman had bothered to invite Sarah down to the boat at all. But after a time the conversation started to flow freely, so freely that Derek began to feel superfluous. When the Midshipman took Sarah's hand and the conversation lapsed altogether Derek wished that he could tactfully retire to bed. But there was nowhere for him to go. Sarah was sitting on his bunk.

Derek's dilemma was solved by the arrival of Gavin and Rusty. They had succeeded in penetrating back-stage at the Intimate Theatre and had carried off two members of the cast, Gavin a brunette called Rita and Rusty a large blonde called Moira.

Rita was one of the occupants of the revolving pedestals. She was twenty-eight and had been occupying pedestals, wings and window ledges in the nude since she came to London from her native Birmingham at the age of twenty. She had never been very intelligent academically but she had already sized up Gavin. His technique, which had laid waste so many hearts, rebounded from her as though from bloom steel. She had already made the decision not to make any decision about the evening's outcome but to wait and see.

Moira was a female xylophonist and a minor celebrity in the show, her name actually appearing on the bill, in the bottom right-hand corner. She might have been beautiful but for her size. She was like a good-looking girl seen through a magnifying glass. She was wearing a black satin skirt, a white nylon blouse through which a pink brassière was just visible, gipsy-dangle ear-rings, a jewelled Juliet cap and chunky wedge-soled sandals. She carried a red plastic handbag and exuded a musky scent which reminded Derek of magnolias and a heavy head-cold. She made herself at home at once.

"Oooh, this *is* nice! This *is* cosy. *Womb*-like, ain't it, Rita?"

"Yes," said Rita shortly.

"Are you the captain?"

"No," said Derek. "I'm the engineer officer."

"Oooh, I bet you're a clever chap. I'll have a drop of the Pope's telephone number, if you don't mind. With splash."

"I'm sorry?"

"Vat 69, *dear*. You mustn't mind me, it's listening to Jimmy and Harry every night, you start to talk like them. Two shows a night, six nights a week, it's enough to send you screaming up the wall. It took my old man like that. He's in a home now, you know. What's the captain like?"

"He's a very nice fellow," said Derek.

"Where's he now?"

"Having dinner with the Mayor."

"Ooooh, *posh*."

Derek and Moira were left to carry on the conversation by themselves. The Midshipman and Sarah gazed at each other. Rusty said nothing. Gavin kept Rita under a steady predatory stare. Rita ignored everybody.

"I don't know how you find your way about one of these things, really I don't."

"It's all quite logical when you know what to look for."

"You clever thing!" Moira gave Derek a playful tap on the wrist which left him numb to the elbow.

"What do you do in the show, Rita?" said Sarah, suddenly.

"I pose in the nude," said Rita, coldy.

"Oh."

"Don't you mind her, dear." Moira bent to whisper confidentially to Sarah. "It's the *draughts*!"

When the taxi stopped outside her lodgings, Rita jumped out quickly.

"Thank you very much, Gavin," she said. "I've had a lovely time."

"Will I see you again?"

Rita shrugged. "Possibly," she said distantly. "Good night."

Gavin watched her run up the steps, open the front door, and disappear.

"What happened, sir?" said the taxi-driver. "Somebody bite her?"

When Moira's taxi stopped outside her door, she leaned over and kissed Rusty on the cheek.

"You're sweet. Are you married?"

"No."

"Come up and have a cup of coffee."

"Oh well, I don't. . . ."

"Come *on*, I'm not going to bite you!"

Moira's room was at the top of the house. As they crept up the stairs, Moira said: "Shush, don't wake my landlady. I call her Exide. She keeps on after all the rest have stopped. Oh dear, there I go again."

There was only one chair in the room and it was covered with clothes.

"You sit on the bed and I'll go down and get some coffee."

Rusty sat down on the bed. After a few minutes' thought, he lay back and closed his eyes. It had been a long day. Rusty drew the counterpane up to his chin and fell asleep. When Moira came back, only the top of Rusty's head was visible above the counterpane.

"Cor Blimey O'Reilly, wakey wakey!"

Rusty stirred.

"Come on, just because you're a submariner you needn't stay submerged all the time!"

The night before *Seahorse* sailed from Oozemouth the wardroom gave a cocktail party to return hospitality. The Steward marshalled rows of bottles and glasses on the chart-table and donned a white coat himself. The Chef resumed his tall hat and fried six pounds of chipolatas. The Petty Officer Electrician and his party rigged coloured lights along the casing. Miss Elizabeth Warbeck came during the afternoon and decorated the wardroom and the control room with flowers. The Mayor and Corporation attended with their wives and were followed after the last performance by the cast from the Intimate Theatre. The Midshipman and Sarah sat quietly in a corner of the wardroom. Jimmy and Harry pinned the Undertaker in a corner of the control room and told him jokes. Moira played "When the Saints Come Marching In" on a line of glasses. The Mayor was heard to remark that submarines were a fine invention.

"In fact I'll go further, Commander," he told The Bodger. "We'll be damned sorry to see you go tomorrow."

But when the morning came, it did not appear that *Seahorse* would go after all. A dense mist covered the harbour. Visibility was not more than a hundred yards. The mournful lowing of ships' sirens sounded through the fog. The Bodger would not normally have considered going to sea but there was another consideration.

"When have we got to be in position for 'Lucky Alphonse', Pilot?"

"We're supposed to be dived in our area by noon tomorrow, sir."

"How far have we got to go?"

"Almost four hundred miles, sir."

"Well, we'll wait a little longer. When the sun gets up properly it may melt this lot away. I'll have another look at nine o'clock."

At nine o'clock it seemed that the mist was thinning. The sun could be seen as a bright spot in the grey fog. The Bodger could see almost as far as the other side of the river. He decided to go to sea.

With radar operating, siren blasting and extra look-outs posted, *Seahorse* crept down harbour. Opposite the main road, where the channel narrowed, the fog clamped down more thickly than ever. The Bodger was forced to stop. He could not see *Seahorse's* casing from the bridge.

"What's the sounding now?"

"Four fathoms, sir. . . . Three and a half fathoms. . . ."

"We must be getting damned close to that main road."

"I think I can hear a car now, sir," said Wilfred.

The Bodger listened intently. He was sure he could hear a car, too. His doubts were resolved a few moments later by the squealing of brakes, a tearing crash of metal and a loud splash.

The mist momentarily thinned and the men on *Seahorse's* bridge looked down upon a small green van which was submerged in water up to the windscreen. The driver was climbing out when he noticed *Seahorse* materializing out of the fog. He shook his fist and bellowed at The Bodger.

"My dear chap," said The Bodger mildly. "Hadn't you better start sounding your horn?"

5

EXERCISE "Lucky Alphonse" was the biggest and most
important fleet exercise of the year, being planned to last
three weeks during which time one hundred and eighty
ships of fourteen nations would steam over an area stretch-
ing from the Denmark Straits to the Canary Islands and
four hundred and fifty aircraft would take off from airfields
scattered between Dakar and Reykjavik. The villains, or
attacking side, were Pink. The heroes, or defending side,
were Blue.

"Just as I thought," said The Bodger when he saw the
Exercise Orders. "Nuclear Cowboys and Indians."

The Exercise Orders, when first issued, were thought to
be a little too bulky, particularly for ships which had small
operations rooms, but by brilliant cutting and inspired
paraphrasing (at the risk of losing some of the nuances of
the language) the Combined Staffs had succeeded in reducing
the final edition to one more manageable volume equivalent in size, without Amendments, to the first two volumes
of the London Telephone Directory. Amendments followed
the Orders themselves at weekly intervals although many
ships received the Amendments some weeks before the
Orders. One destroyer from Rosyth received neither Orders
nor Amendments but still acquitted herself with distinction
in the Exercise; her Captain, a firm churchman, taking his
part from the Second Book of Kings and Hymns Ancient
& Modern.

When The Bodger received his copy he read the first page,
where he noted the date the Exercise started, the last page,
where he noted the date the Exercise finished, thumbed
hopefully through the rest (once, as a young midshipman,
The Bodger had come across a brand new ten shilling note
in a copy of *Orders for Disabling Fleeing Luggers, Smacks
& Jolly-Boats* published before the war), wrote "Action—
Navigating Officer" on the cover and then pitched the
Orders on Gavin's bunk and forgot about them.

The ship's company, and the officers, had all done fleet
exercises before. They knew the form: days of waiting, a
few brief hours of excitement, and more days of waiting

for the exercise to end, which it normally did twenty-four hours early because the planning staff had run out of incidents and wanted to catch the midnight train to London. But "Lucky Alphonse", under The Bodger, was not just another exercise. The Bodger's drive began before *Seahorse* left harbour. The polished fittings on the bridge and the casing were painted black and the wires, guard-rails and ladders were landed. A full outfit of torpedoes was loaded and a false deck of stores laid out along the passageways. The periscopes were realigned, the torpedo tube firing mechanisms overhauled, and the radar sets re-calibrated. When she finally left, *Seahorse* was stored for war.

When the ship was on patrol, The Bodger left nothing to chance. The submarine surfaced for nothing. The batteries were recharged by snorkelling and the rubbish which accumulated inside the submarine was fired into the sea through the gash ejector. The Bodger watched the smallest details, to the extent of personally supervising the weighting of the rubbish bags before they were ejected. "I once followed a Yank submarine three hundred miles across the Arctic, just by the ice cream cartons," he said.

The Midshipman was given a special job of his own.

"I want you to make out a Recognition crib, Mid," The Bodger said. "Get out *Janes Fighting Ships* and write down the tonnage, water-line length, funnel height and mast-head heights of every Blue ship in the exercise. When you've done that, write down by each ship any special features she may have. Almost every ship has something. The arrangement of the gun turrets, prominent radar aerials, lattice masts, cutaway quarterdecks, side lifts on the flight deck—anything I'll be able to recognize quickly through the periscope. Got it?"

"Yes, sir."

The Midshipman sat down with *Janes Fighting Ships* and began work. It was only after The Bodger had left the wardroom that he ventured his question.

"Why am I doing this?"

"Recognition mostly," said Gavin. "And ranging. The Boss ranges on the heights of things. That's why he wants the height of funnels and radar aerials. He may be able to range on them when he can't see the actual mast itself."

"Oh."

The Midshipman returned to *Janes* with a renewed feeling that he was indeed a tenderfoot on a strange range. Hard though he tried to gain experience he was again and again reminded that he was now in a private world, incomprehensible to outsiders, demanding techniques and knowledge of its own. When the Midshipman tried to trim the submarine, for instance, his first attempts were disastrous.

"Have a go at the trim, Mid," The Bodger said with a cheerful smile one morning when *Seahorse* had been on patrol for two days.

"Aye aye, sir."

The Bodger remained in the wardroom, mentally crouched in the slips, his eyes fixed on the depth gauge and his finger-nails drumming on the wardroom table.

"There's only one way for the chap to learn and that's by doing it by himself," said The Bodger to the rest of the wardroom, his face drawn in agony and his eyes straying again to the depth gauge. Almost at once he hit the control room deck at the double as the submarine, hitherto in perfect trim, responded to the Midshipman's tentative experiments by heading purposefully towards the bottom, a thousand fathoms below.

The rest of the wardroom were unnerved by the spectacle of their captain torturing himself in the sacred name of training. Wilfred, who was Trimming Officer and the most experienced trimmer in the ship, took it upon himself to give the Midshipman a special lecture on trimming.

"First of all," he said, "you've got certain things to help you trim. There's the depth gauge. That tells you how deep you are. There's the bubble on the inclinometer. That tells you whether you're level or not. And then there's the bathythermograph which tells you about the sea outside, but let's not worry about that for the time being. You've got two planesmen, to keep the boat at the right depth, and level. The ballast pump, to shift water into and out of the boat, and the trim pump which shifts water round and about the boat. You use all these things when you're trimming. There are people who can trim by the seat of their pants. They've been doing it so long they can tell what's wrong just by looking. But there's one sure-fire way anyone can use."

"What's that?" the Midshipman asked, soberly conscious that he was being initiated into one of the world's obscurest sciences, a mystery understood only by a tiny number of people.

"Go to a hundred feet if you can, where it's relatively calm and peaceful. Slow down. Put the wheel amidships. Put the planes amidships. Then watch the depth gauge. If you're light, the boat will rise. If you're heavy, the boat will sink. So you pump or flood, using the ballast pump. Always get the bodily weight right first. Then watch the bubble on the inclinometer. If it runs forward you know you're light forrard and heavy aft. If it runs aft, you know you're heavy forrard and light aft. So you pump water whichever way you need with the trim pump. It's useful to remember, always pump towards the bubble. Eventually you should get to the state where the boat stays at the right depth and the bubble stays amidships, without using the planes. You see, you may have been keeping depth before but the planesmen may have been sweating blood to keep you there. What you're trying to do is to achieve a state of neutral buoyancy so that the boat has no tendency to go up or down."

"Where does 'Q' tank come in then?"

" 'Q' has got nothing to do with the trim. It's either empty or full. It's an emergency tank which you flood when you want to go down in a hurry. Then you blow it out when you reach depth. The things that have an effect on the trim are the weight of fuel, water and stores, the number of people on board, the density of the sea water, and whether the boat is speeding up or turning under wheel or firing torpedoes. Even the weather up top has an effect down to a certain depth. Mind you, once you've got a good trim that doesn't mean it'll last for ever. You might run into a patch of denser sea water, people move about, the weather might get a bit rougher. You've got to keep at it the whole time."

"As well as looking through the periscope," said The

Bodger, who had been listening unobtrusively from the passageway. "I'd rather you had a bloody awful trim and kept a good look-out." The Bodger had been struck by a curious common factor in the reports of dived submarines which had collided with surface ships. In many cases the First Lieutenant, the Trimming Officer, had been on watch at the time of the collision and had been obsessed with the trim, taking a couple of gallons from one tank and putting a couple of gallons into another, while all the time the *Queen Mary* and the entire Home Fleet bore down on him at thirty knots.

The Midshipman took The Bodger's remarks to heart. He was indeed a little too zealous. The following afternoon the Midshipman was at the periscope by himself. It was the dead time of the afternoon. The planesmen yawned in their seats. Everyone except the watch was asleep. The Bodger himself was in his cabin, lightly dreaming of fat aircraft carriers steaming towards him on steady courses, when he was awakened by the sound of water flushing into "Q" tank. The deck was tilting and the depth gauge already showed seventy feet.

"Six helicopters, sir!" cried the Midshipman.

The Bodger's eyebrows rose.

"Six choppers!"

Seahorse was three hundred miles from land and had met nothing but merchant shipping for three days.

"Have you blown 'Q' yet?"

"Oh, no sir, I'm afraid."

The depth gauge was showing a hundred and twenty feet and the needle was still swinging rapidly. The Outside Wrecker, on the blowing panel, had the look of a man about to explode into a thousand pieces.

"Blow 'Q'. Sixty feet."

At periscope depth again, The Bodger searched sea and sky meticulously.

"Damned if I can see any bloody choppers," he growled.

The Bodger shook his head.

"Either you've got stereoscopic eyes or I'm going blind in my old age, Mid."

"I'm very sorry, sir."

"That's all right. You did the right thing. Always go deep for six choppers. Especially in the middle of the bloody Atlantic," The Bodger added, to himself.

The Bodger left the periscope, climbed back into his bunk and composed himself for sleep. Just as he felt the warm comfortable recession of his senses, the deck tilted once more.

"They're back, sir."

The Bodger gave the shame-faced Midshipman a curious look. Again he searched the sky. Again, he could see nothing but a wheeling seagull and the eternal grey waves rolling towards him at eye level.

"You feeling O.K., Mid?"

"Yes, sir. They're there, sir."

"Oh, I'm sure they are." The Bodger looked again. "Ah. . . . Wait, I see them. Is that them?" The Midshipman looked through the periscope and nodded. Flying steadily eastwards, looking neither to right nor left, were six large geese in line ahead.

The Bodger conceded that they did resemble helicopters to an untrained eye but the control room watch had not heard a better joke since the Coxswain got food poisoning. The helmsman tittered. The Outside Wrecker smirked. Ripper, on the foreplanes, grinned at his depth gauge. Even the Radio Electrician, a naturally sombre individual, sitting at the after planes, permitted himself a faint enigmatic smile.

"Never mind, Mid," The Bodger said. "Always go deep first and ask questions afterwards."

Nevertheless, The Bodger could not avoid a feeling of disquiet. The affair of the Six Geese smacked suspiciously of bird-watching and bird-watching through the periscope was the submariners' traditional symptom of impending insanity. In The Bodger's experience, the feathered friends were normally followed closely by the men in white coats. The Bodger had once served with a captain who was actually murmuring: "Strange to see black-backed gulls so far south" while a Japanese destroyer threshed past two hundred yards away. The Bodger resolved to keep a sharp eye on the Midshipman.

But when he had thought more deeply about the matter, The Bodger was not very surprised that the Midshipman should make mistakes on the periscope. The periscope was much more than a complicated optical instrument and to use it successfully required much more than mere good eyesight. A periscope demanded the ability to deduce facts from limited data, the ability to see a whole room through the keyhole, in short it demanded "the periscope eye". The task was hard enough in daylight. At night it was trebly difficult. Here again, the Midshipman provided the control room watch with some much appreciated entertainment.

The night following the affair of the Six Geese the Midshipman came on watch with Wilfred while the submarine was snorkelling to recharge the batteries. The Midshipman had no sooner taken over the periscope for the first time when he rang the "Stop Snorting" Alarm and ordered "Q" flooded. Once again, The Bodger tumbled out of his bunk.

"What's up, Mid? Luminous shite-hawks?"

"Aircraft dead ahead sir, coming straight towards!"

"Golly." The Bodger scratched his head. "Funny we didn't get any indication of it before. Was it lighted?"

"Very bright red light like a port wing light, sir."

"Did you see anything, Number One?"

"No, sir." Wilfred, too, was perplexed. It was a clear night with a sharply defined horizon and excellent periscope visibility. Surely he could not have missed a brightly-lighted aircraft?

"Well, we'll stay down for half an hour or so and see what happens."

After half an hour The Bodger brought *Seahorse* back to periscope depth. As the periscope broke surface The Bodger swivelled round in a quick sweep.

"There's your aircraft, Mid," he said, at once. "It's Mars."

The Midshipman blushed; what with flying geese and hostile planets, The Bodger must be beginning to think him a little touched in the head. But The Bodger seemed quite unconcerned about it.

"It's quite understandable," he said. "It's by far the

brightest star in the sky and it could well be an aircraft light. Don't worry Mid, there's many a good submariner stopped snorting and gone deep for Mars or Venus, let me tell you. As I said before, I'd much rather you went deep unnecessarily a thousand times than stayed up once too often and got us clobbered by an aircraft. Go deep first, ask questions afterwards."

The ship's company were grateful to the Midshipman. He provided them with almost their only source of innocent amusement as the days of the patrol crept by. They had already settled to the strange twilight existence of a sub-marine on patrol. They slept through the day and came awake at nightfall for the one hot meal of the day which was normally cooked and eaten while the main engines were running to charge the batteries. Twice a day they went to maximum depth to take bathythermograph readings of the sea layers. The rest of the time was spent patrolling at periscope depth.

The passage of time was marked by the changing of the watches. Beards grew longer and more unkempt until the control room took on the appearance of a depression bread-line. The bread itself was harder and the slices grew smaller—as the crusts went mouldy and were cut off. The submarine ticked over in a somnolent state similar to a mass hibernation.

Seahorse's patrol position lay across a main shipping route and The Bodger stood at the periscope and watched the big tankers come up over the horizon, their huge slab sides and superstructures as big as blocks of flats gleaming white in the sunlight. The Bodger practised attacks on them. They made perfect targets, steaming on steady unalarmed courses, the massive hydrophone effect of their propellers pounding over *Seahorse's* sonar. They seemed quite un-aware of a submarine's presence. If any of them ever noticed a suspicious flash from the sea as the sun caught the revolving glass of the periscope they showed no sign of it. Some of them passed less than a quarter of a mile from *Seahorse* and The Bodger was often unable to see anyone on watch on the bridge at all.

On the fifth day, The Bodger became concerned about

the lack of contacts and moved to the extreme westward of *Seahorse's* area. The Bodger reasoned that the expected Task Force would assemble far out in the Atlantic to the westward and move eastward towards Ushant. A signal at midnight from ComSubPink confirmed The Bodger's theory. By dawn on the sixth day The Bodger was waiting on the westward edge of his area. It was, appropriately, the Midshipman who made the first sighting.

The Midshipman looked very closely before he mentioned it to Wilfred. He could not afford another mistake. If this turned out to be a fishing vessel or a floating spar of wood, he would never live it down.

"Number One, would you come and have a look, please? I think I can see the mast of a destroyer!"

Wilfred was at the periscope in one bound.

"O.K. I've got it. Call the Captain!"

The Bodger was delighted.

"That's well done, Mid. That's a good sighting. It's a destroyer all right, large as life. I can just see the tip of his funnel as well. We're fine on his port bow. No, he's just altered towards. But he's still a long way away. Number One, pipe 'Attack team will be required in ten minutes' time'."

Leading Seaman Gorbles, the sonar watchkeeper, had been giving negative reports in a regular monotone voice. Suddenly, his voice went up a semitone.

"Possible H.E., bearing two-seven-zero. Faint transmissions on the bearing."

The Bodger was jubilant. "That's us! Blood for supper! Let's have a butchers."

The Bodger took the second pair of earphones and listened as Leading Seaman Gorbles quartered the sea with sweeps of his set. The Bodger could hear the unmistakable throbbing of the destroyer's hydrophone effect, known in sonar parlance as "H.E.", and the eerie pinging transmissions of its asdic set. Leading Seaman Gorbles had already begun his long recital of new hydrophone effects and bearing changes, couched in the esoteric dialect of the sonar world, which would continue until all the sounds had faded and the sea was empty once more.

". . . H.E. louder, two-seven-two, moving right. Revolutions one-two-zero, classified turbine. Transmissions on the bearing, transmission interval varying. *Second* H.E., two-seven-nine, transmissions varying. . . ."

The destroyers were still searching without contact. While their transmissions remained random and disconnected, a submarine could assume that it had not yet been detected. The Bodger went back to the periscope.

"It's them all right. I can see them now. It's two destroyers and there's something else behind them. . . . Can't see what it is, but it's a lot of ship! And *more* of them. . . . My God a whole bloody forest of masts! It's the Task Force, not a doubt about it."

It was indeed the vanguard of the Task Force, spread out over a front of more than thirty miles. The Task Force had been assembling for the past two days, the earliest arrivals killing time in refuelling, carrying out asdic sweeps and narrowly avoiding collisions.

The main striking element of the Task Force was the two aircraft carriers H.M.S. *Great Christopher* and the U.S.S. *Little Richard*. *Little Richard* was almost three times as big as *Great Christopher* and was the largest warship the world had ever seen. Rumours of her fantastic size had even percolated as far as *Seahorse* and the messes were buzzing with sailors' yarns about her, that she was so big that the Captain went round Sunday divisions in a Grand Prix Ferrari, that her hangars were so large that she carried two squadrons of B.52s, that she was so long that there was a bus service from one end of her to the other, and that her flag deck was so high that her signalmen wore oxygen masks. By any standards she was a formidable ship. The Bodger was anxious to make her acquaintance.

Little Richard was only the hub of a vast armada made up of *Great Christopher* and four smaller carriers, five guided-missile cruisers, three orthodox cruisers, seven escort and radar picket groups, and a fleet train of four tankers and a supply ship.

Occupying last place in the Task Force was the motor yacht *Istagfurallah*, the property of an oil-bearing Sheikh. She was present quite by chance, her owner only hearing of "Lucky Alphonse" through his sailing master who was given complete details of the exercise in a Naples bar. The Sheikh had arrived at the assembly point first and had courteously greeted each fresh arrival by dipping his ensign, the house flag of San Remo casino, and by a display of fireworks. *Istagfurallah* had passed unchallenged because each new captain who saw her had decided that she must have been included in an Amendment he had not yet received. Her presence was in fact appreciated, if only for the firework display she provided every night. Her only other quirk was her habit of hoisting inexplicable signals according to the passing whim of the Sheikh. At the present moment she was flying "Am preparing to repel boarders" and a small white pennant inscribed in gold with a verse of the Koran.

By breakfast time, the major units had completed fuelling, the escort groups were in position, and the Task Force moved off on an easterly course. *Istagfurallah* flying the International signal "You are standing into danger".

Ten miles ahead, and directly in the path of the Task Force lay S.555, Exercise Callsign: Eskimo Napoleon, H.M.S. *Seahorse* (Lieutenant-Commander R. B. Badger, D.S.C., R.N.).

*   *   *

Watching the Task Force's advance, The Bodger felt like a bandit waiting to ambush a ponderous wagon train. ". . . Four, five, *six* escorts. And behind them two carriers. Name of a name. . . . That's the biggest carrier I've ever seen! It's. . . . It's indecent! They're not even zig-zagging. Nearest escort is . . . let's see . . . four miles away. God, talk about Johnny-Head-In-Air! You'd thing they were out for a Sunday afternoon jolly. It's always the same with these frigates. Give them a fine afternoon off Portland with the First Eleven up in the Asdic Office and they're good kids. But you wait until they've been at sea a few days and they've had a bit of rough weather and there's any old Joe Bloggs on the set and then you see a difference! They wouldn't know a submarine if it came up and asked them for a light. . . ."

"Periscope's been up fifteen seconds, sir," said Wilfred.

"Right. Let's have another listen." The Bodger donned the earphones.

By now the attack team had closed up and were waiting for the attack to begin. The control room was crowded with men standing by instruments, plots and counters to help The Bodger with his attack.

"That's a funny H.E." The Bodger said.

"I think he's got a chipped propeller, sir," said Leading Seaman Gorbles. "I can't get a rev. count on him. He's staggering his revs."

"Dead crafty," said The Bodger.

The Bodger took the periscope again.

"Now here's a character who looks as though he knows what he's doing. I do believe it's our friend with the chipped prop. Yes, it must be. Well, here goes. Bring all tubes to the action state. Stand by for the first range and bearing of the target. The target is *Little Richard*. There can't be anyone else that size. . . ."

With the first range and bearing of *Little Richard*, the stop watches were starting, the first situation put on the fire control plot and the first entry made in the attack narrative. The attack was under way. Meanwhile, The Bodger returned to the ship with the intriguing propellers.

"I don't like the look of this man. He's got the attack flag at the dip. He's got a sniff of us. Ah, he's turned away. His pennant number is F.787. Somebody get out the exercise bridge card and see who that is."

"It's H.M.S. *Windfall*, sir," said Wilfred. "Frigate converted from a destroyer, sir."

"Who's her captain?"

"Captain J. A. S. Persimmons, D.S.O. and Bar, D.S.C. and Bar, R.N., sir."

"Black Sebastian!"

The Bodger put up the periscope handles with a snap.

"I'd forgotten he was in this exercise!"

The Bodger caught Wilfred's eye.

"That," he said sombrely, "puts a different complexion on it *altogether*. With Black Sebastian in the hunt this is not going to be as easy as I thought.'

"Black Sebastian!"

The control room echoed the words. So might souls abandoned in hell have whispered the syllables of Prince Lucifer's name.

★ 6 ★

CAPTAIN Jasper Abercrombie Sebastian Persimmons, D.S.O*., D.S.C*., R.N., known in and out of the submarine service as Black Sebastian, was a living justification of the principle of setting a thief to catch a thief. An ex-submariner himself, he had become the finest anti-submarine captain afloat. His knowledge of submarines and their capabilities and his insight into the mind and thoughts of a submarine captain made him a deadly opponent.

There had often been speculation inside the submarine service on the cause of Black Sebastian's return to general service. The popular theory was that the number of submarine officers Black Sebastian returned to general service through nervous breakdowns became too great a drain on the submarine service's manpower.

Whatever the reason, Black Sebastian now hated submariners with the unreasoning, implacable hatred of a renegade for his former companions. His hatred had made his perceptions keener. Just as Captain Ahab, with almost supernatural accuracy, could foretell the presence of Moby Dick, so Black Sebastian, by nothing more than the pricking of his thumbs, could feel the presence of a submarine. "I can *see* a periscope at five miles," he once said, "and I can *smell* a snort at ten."

It was no idle boast. Black Sebastian had proved it again and again, flushing a submarine from cover where his rival escort captains had drawn blank. Now, as he swept across the van of the Task Force, Black Sebastian sensed the familiar tingling which told him he was close. Although his asdic operator had only caught a fleeting contact and had been unable to classify it, Black Sebastian knew in his bones that he was getting warm.

Sixty feet down and three miles to starboard, The Bodger was well aware of his danger.

"Sonar, give me constant reports on that H.E. Designate Black Sebastian."

"Designate Black Sebastian, sir, roger. Black Sebastian, three-five-five, moving rapidly right, transmissions varying."

The Bodger's attack was already nearing completion. The attack team had re-created from the stream of bearings and ranges The Bodger had given them a plan picture of what The Bodger could see through the periscope. They had also made predictions and deductions which The Bodger could not see and fed them into the calculation. Now, the final firing bearings were approaching solution.

"Black Sebastian fading, zero-zero-five."

"He'll be back," said The Bodger. "Bugger him. Up periscope."

An attack on a task force through a defending screen was the supreme test of a submarine captain's skill and judgment. It was also a severe strain on his temper. Captains had been known to trample members of their attack teams underfoot and physically to assault their trimming officers if the periscope dipped below the surface for an instant. With such captains, an attack was such excellent entertainment that the sailors who were not in the attack team drew lots for the privilege of standing in the passageway whence they could hear the sound-track. The Bodger was using the smallest periscope for periods of five seconds, just long enough to take one all-round look and a range and bearing of the target. While the periscope was down, The Bodger paced the control room, crossing from the periscope to the plot, from the plot to the sonar room, and from the sonar room back to the periscope, executing as he went a nervous, jerking hop and jump, like an abbreviated Hungarian mazurka. He wiped the palms of his hands on the seat of his trousers each time before seizing the periscope handles.

"Bodger Agonistes," murmured Dagwood.

The Bodger was in a perfect attacking position, if the Task Force maintained its present course. He had no need to manœuvre to close the track, nor was there any danger

of him being overrun. He was like a swordsman who
need do nothing except allow his opponent to run upon
his weapon.

"*Surely* they must zig soon. I'm bloody certain Black
Sebastian got a sniff of us."

"Black Sebastian faded. Last bearing zero-two-zero."

"I wonder what that crafty old bastard's up to now?"

Black Sebastian was huddled on the starboard wing of
his bridge, scowling at the sea. He was a very tall man
with a hooked nose and a broad black beard. His complexion was pale and his eyes shadowed in deep sockets
and he had the pointed ear-tips and arched eyebrows of a
Rubens satyr, but his face lacked the same jolly devilment.
His whole appearance suggested a powerful but hostile
personality. As he leaned over the rail and studied the
disposition of the Task Force, he looked like the re-
incarnation of a medieval torturer, or one of those terrible
figures of the Inquisition who would eat a good dinner
and go downstairs to watch their servants with fire and
rack extort a recantation.

"We've gone too far."

Black Sebastian's Navigating Officer was a very brave
man, the only man in *Windfall* who dared to question
the Captain.

"I think it more likely we'll find him ahead of the Task
Force, sir," he said. "After all, sir, we're only five miles
inside the first submarine area. . . ."

"*I tell you we've gone too far you incompetent nincom-
poop!* He's got past us. We'd better get back there before
he does any damage. Starboard thirty. . . ."

Windfall and her two wing escorts wheeled back towards
the Task Force.

"Five degrees to go, sir!"

The Bodger was nearing his moment of truth. *Little
Richard* now filled the whole of the periscope aperture.
The Bodger could see every detail of her mammoth sides
and superstructure, the aircraft ranged on the flight deck
and the men moving around them. The Bodger felt that

he only needed to get just a little closer to be able to read the names on the backs of their overalls. Swinging right, The Bodger could see *Windfall's* silhouette lengthening on the horizon as she turned. He's clicked, thought The Bodger, but he's just too damned late.

"On, sir!"

"Shoot!"

"Stand by One . . . Fire. Stand by Two . . . Fire." Wilfred steadily counted off the torpedoes. The submarine shuddered as they left the tubes. A new sound, an angry buzzing like the wine of a nest of infuriated hornets, invaded Leading Seaman Gorbles' ears.

Windfall's asdic operator also picked up the sound and timidly, like a man who knows his voice will release an avalanche, he reported it.

"Torpedo H.E., three-one-five, moving right, sir."

"*WHAT!*"

Black Sebastian's roar shook the bridge windows. He stood stock-still, his lips trembling, his fingers clenching and unclenching, and for one delirious moment *Windfall's* action bridge team thought their Captain was about to drop dead of a stroke. But they had underestimated their man. Black Sebastian may have been temporarily un-balanced by fury but in the few seconds which had elapsed since he heard the report of the torpedoes he had seen *Little Richard's* emergency turn to comb the torpedo tracks, he had estimated the torpedoes' probable course, and he had already calculated the possible position of the submarine.

"Steer two-six-zero."

"*Contact*, sir, probable submarine, two-six-five!"

Black Sebastian recovered himself in time to prevent an undignified yell of triumph.

"Now we've got him! Steer two-six-five." He glowered round his bridge action team. "If he gets away, I'll break the lot of you," he said sincerely.

Like many large ladies, U.S.S. *Little Richard* was quick on her feet. But she was not quick enough. *Seahorse's* six torpedoes, set to run deep, spread out and enveloped her

223

in a wide fan, passing ahead, underneath and close astern of her. The torpedoes were expendable and ran on until their fuel was exhausted and then sank. For exercise purposes, however, they had done their work. *Little Richard* had been sunk, or at best, badly damaged.

The Bodger could not resist remaining at the periscope to witness the results of his handiwork until Leading Seaman Gorbles' voice recalled him to more pressing matters.

"Black Sebastian regained, louder, moving left, zero-four-zero. Transmissions constant, transmission interval four thousand yards. *In contact, sir!*"

"Let's get the hell out of this," said The Bodger. "Flood 'Q'. I think we've overstayed our welcome as it is."

It would be foolish to stay gloating at the periscope and run into the arms of the escorts, like a man who carried out the perfect bank robbery and was still there admiring his own brilliance when the police arrived.

Just before the periscope dipped, The Bodger caught a glimpse of Black Sebastian and his two henchmen. They made a brave sight, approaching at full speed, their quarter-decks almost submerged in the soaring wakes, their bows flinging spray over the mastheads, and the attack flags whipping at the yard-arms.

"Cor crikey," said The Bodger admiringly. "They've got their tails up now and no mistake. . . ."

"Black Sebastian zero-three-five, bearing constant, transmissions constant, transmission interval two thousand five hundred yards, *attacking, sir!*"

"Blow 'Q' sir?" asked Derek, looking anxiously at his depth gauges, which were unreeling as though demented.

"Not yet. Where's the layer here?"

"Marked one at two hundred and fifty feet, sir," said Wilfred. "Slight one at five-fifty."

"Seven hundred feet," The Bodger ordered. "Planes hard a-dive. Lose the bubble Coxswain."

Seahorse dropped like a bird with folded wings. No asdic set was needed to hear Black Sebastian now. The ghostly bats' squeaks of his transmissions could be heard plainly against the hull. Black Sebastian was coming down upon them like Sennacherib himself. The Bodger had the eerie sensation that he could feel the man's personality reaching down to grapple him. The Bodger made up his mind.

"Blow 'Q'. Full ahead together. Hard a starboard!"

Seahorse slipped sideways and downwards in a tight circle which took her underneath the heart of the Task Force where The Bodger stopped the shafts. *Seahorse* glided on under her own momentum, leaving behind her a curling wake of turbulent water which made an excellent asdic target. Black Sebastian's henchmen pounced gleefully upon it and began to weave their complicated ritual patterns above it.

"Black Sebastian very faint, one-seven-eight, no transmissions. Lost contact, sir."

Now what the hell's he up to? The Bodger asked himself.

"They sought it with thimbles, they sought it with care," said Dagwood, aloud.

"They threatened its life with a railway share," continued The Bodger, grinning. "Fall out the attack team."

Black Sebastian admitted himself nonplussed. He lashed himself, and his asdic control crew, with his self-reproach. He had committed one of the basic errors of warfare. He had underestimated his opponent. The juicy target upon which he had urged his group had been whipped away and a dummy substituted. Black Sebastian did not believe for a moment that his group were investigating a real contact. He understood very well what the submarine captain had done. It was a manœuvre Black Sebastian had practised many times himself. Furthermore, the submarine captain, whoever he was, had jinked the right way, diving into the middle of the Task Force where Black Sebastian was baulked by the train of surface ships.

Remembering that lightning evasion, Black Sebastian began to wonder about the submarine captain. There were very few submarines in the exercise with such a turn of speed.

"Pilot, get me the bridge exercise card."

Black Sebastian ran his eye down the list of submarines. "H.M.S. *Terrapin*, H.M.S. *Angelfish*, *Farfarelli*, the Italian. *La Veuve*, the Frenchman. The Nuclear Job. *Seahorse . . . Seahorse*."

It was too late to chase through the middle of the Task Force now. Black Sebastian decided that it would be better to wait in the rear. Sooner or later, the submarine would come up and then, Black Sebastian thumped a fist into his palm, he would be waiting. Black Sebastian signalled that he had lost contact and withdrew to the rear of the Task Force. He could see an American escort group on the far side taking up the search where he had left off.

"And the best of All-American luck to you too," growled Black Sebastian.

Between Black Sebastian and the Americans, H.M.S. *Great Christopher* was preparing to launch aircraft.

"*Great Christopher* about to launch aircraft, sir," said the Navigating Officer.

"I can see that, blast you. If they'd flown off that search at *dawn*, when they bloody well should have done, they would have kept that submarine down until we got past. As it is, against the sort of submarine these vermin are building themselves these days, they're pissing against the wind, that's all they're doing."

Looking like an Inquisitor faced with a more than usually obstinate heretic, Black Sebastian hunched himself in his bridge chair and settled down to wait.

The Bodger raised his glass.

"Well, men. Here's to Black Sebastian, bless his cotton socks."

"Cheers, sir," said the rest of the wardroom. It was very rare for any of the wardroom to drink during an exercise but, as Wilfred said, it was not every day you crashed an escort screen at its strongest point, fired six fish into the largest warship afloat and got clear away again.

"We'll stay here for a couple of hours," The Bodger said. "See if the shouting and tumult dies down a bit. Then we'll hop up and make our damage report. I've just realized, we didn't even make an enemy sighting report."

"I think it's just as well, sir," said Wilfred. "That would have given us away before we'd even had a chance to get close."

"Probably. What course did we estimate the Task Force was steering, Pilot?"

"Due East, sir."

"Well, we'll steer that for a bit. With any luck we might get another shot!"

"That must have given Black Sebastian something to think about, sir," said Dagwood. "I'd love to have seen his face when he realized he'd lost contact."

The Bodger shook his head. "We haven't finished with him yet by a long chalk. Black Sebastian isn't the sort of man who gives up as easily as that. You've got to appreciate that he isn't really exercising with you at all. He positively hates you. He wants to see us and all submariners wiped out for good. He looks upon us as vermin, to be stamped out on sight. The most important thing to realize about this whole business is that the best anti-submarine weapon the Navy's ever had and is ever likely to have is the personality of the escort captain. It all comes down to human terms in the long run. I remember a fellow who commanded a frigate during the war telling me that he only actually *saw* a U-boat once, after they'd forced it to the surface in the Atlantic. He said that when he saw that *shape* lying there on the water, he quite literally saw red. His first impulse was to charge down on it and ram it and batter it to death, shoot all the survivors and hang any that he missed from the yard-arm at once. Now, when a man like that manages to control himself and harnesses the energy he generates to a frigate's ship's company, *that's* when people like us have got to look out! Black Sebastian is like that. He's the kind who never gives up. He'll chase up every disappearing radar contact and investigate every echo. He makes everyone's lives a misery to them but he gets results and when he *does* get a submarine . . . he'll stay with it until Doomsday."

Just before noon, The Bodger yielded to Gavin's suggestion that they go up for a sextant shot of the sun's meridian altitude. *Seahorse* came up to a hundred feet while Leading Seaman Gorbles listened carefully all round for any sign of hydrophone effect. Hearing nothing, *Seahorse* rose cautiously to periscope depth. The Bodger had no sooner taken his first look through the periscope when he flooded "Q" and ordered a depth of seven hundred feet again.

"Jesus!" he said. "It was some kind of bloody yacht, stopped about twenty yards away! It was so damned close that all I could see through the periscope at first was a row of bloody rivets!"

At noon, Black Sebastian got up from his chair and stretched. If he was a submarine captain, he would be coming up just about now.

"Old *Istagfurallah* is very excited about something, sir," said the Navigating Officer.

"What's that?"

"He seems to've got some bee in his burnous. . . ."

Black Sebastian snatched up his binoculars. *Istagfurallah* was steaming excitedly round in small circles, firing off salvoes of fireworks and sounding long blasts on her siren.

"I'll tell you what he's got, you cretin!" bellowed Black Sebastian. "He's got a submarine! While we sit here in several million quids' worth of frigate with our thumbs in our bums a flea-ridden Sheikh squatting on his prayer-mat does everything but gaff our target for us! Look at them!" Black Sebastian gestured at his wing escorts, nosing industriously about on each side. "Bloody square-eyed addicts with free-flood ears, goggling all day long into their infernal idiots' lanterns and flapping their ears at a lot of clicks and bangs! They should get out into the fresh air for once where they can see what's happening! My God, we're going to be too late *again*!"

The spectacle of Black Sebastian and his two henchmen closing him at maximum speed was too much for the Sheikh. It had been a disturbing morning all round. First, an infidel periscope had broken the sacred hour of noon and nothing discommoded a true believer more than being spied on by strangers at his devotions. Now he was menaced by three Touareg frigates, the Forgotten of God. It was too much. The Sheikh swung round and withdrew to the south. Flying a banner which read: "Go Home Lawrence" the Sheikh disappeared rapidly over the horizon and took no further part in the exercise.

"*Now* we'll get him!" cried Black Sebastian. The Sheikh had given them an excellent datum position.

But The Bodger was not to be caught a second time. He went deep, lay very low, and like Brer Rabbit, said nothing. Black Sebastian searched vainly for six hours and then withdrew under instructions from the flag-ship. When The Bodger returned to periscope depth in the late evening, he found a clear sea and sky.

There were also three signals. Two concerned a gauge for the distiller and The Bodger threw them away without letting the details register on his mind.

"Here am I," he said, "trying to put one over the best anti-submarine captain in the service and they send me signals about distillers."

The third signal, however, caused The Bodger's eyebrows to shoot up. The suddenness and brilliance of The Bodger's attack on *Little Richard* had thrown the planning staff ashore into some understandable confusion (mixed with resentment that The Bodger had presumed to create an incident while they were still setting up the counters on the plotting floor). The third signal was from Com-SubPink and read: "Proceed at best speed".

The Bodger thought for a moment, replied: "Where?" and set *Seahorse* snorting at maximum speed to the eastwards.

In two hours the answer returned from ComSubPink: "Exercise Area Banana."

The Bodger stroked his chin and came back with a shrewd thrust: "Am in Exercise Area Banana."

"I can almost hear the wheels turning," The Bodger said, as he turned into his bunk.

At midnight, the Petty Officer Telegraphist decoded the top secret priority signal: "Remain on patrol in Exercise Area Banana."

"Ah . . . *splendid* exercise," said The Bodger.

At one o'clock in the morning a Coastal Command aircraft returning off task over the Bay of Biscay picked up a small intermittent radar contact. The contact was at extreme range and the aircraft did not have sufficient fuel to make a proper investigation. It was hardly enough evidence on which to begin a submarine hunt. But it was more than enough for Black Sebastian.

★ 7 ★

AT half-past two Black Sebastian was shaken by the bridge messenger.

"From the Officer of the Watch, we're at the position now, sir."

"Very good."

Still fully dressed, Black Sebastian swung out of his bunk and went out on to the bridge.

"We're at the aircraft datum position, sir," said the Navigating Officer.

"I know," said Black Sebastian brusquely. He crossed to the wing of the bridge. It was a very dark close night. The stars were obscured by a low ceiling of cloud. Below him Black Sebastian could just make out great white lines of foam racing out to *Voluminous* who was keeping station three cables away on the starboard beam. All ships were darkened. Or supposed to be darkened.

"Make to *Voluminous*: You have a bright light showing from your sea cabin."

"Aye aye, sir."

Black Sebastian came back into the compass platform.

"He's not here," he said. "If I was him I would be going like a bat out of hell. We won't find him just yet. How many look-outs have you got, Officer of the Watch?"

"Two, sir."

"Double them. How long has the radar watchkeeper been on watch?"

"An hour and three-quarters, sir."

"Have him relieved. And relieve the sonar watchkeeper as well. I want everyone fresh. We can expect him any time from now on and I expect he's pretty tired by now."

Black Sebastian knew from his own experience the effect on a submarine ship's company of snorting at top speed for most of the night. If there was any time for catching a submarine napping, it was between two and three o'clock in the morning.

"I bet there's not a man on watch in that submarine who hasn't got his eye firmly fixed on the clock. Make to *Voluminous* and *Octopus*: Cease operating radar. Switch on navigation lights. Keep radio and sonar silence."

The three ships were already steaming too fast for their asdic sets to be of much use but Black Sebastian had a poor idea of the mental capabilities of his fellow captains.

"I wouldn't put it past them to go spoiling everything with their eager beaver transmissions. They've been reading too many text-books and listening to too many lectures. Come down to twelve knots. I want to have a listen."

The escort group had barely eased to twelve knots and the fresh asdic operator had hardly taken his seat when Black Sebastian's heart was made glad within him.

"Steady H.E., one-one-zero, sir."

Black Sebastian steadied his voice.

"Classify."

"Possible submarine diesel, sir. Too fast for a rev. count, sir."

"Let me hear."

Black Sebastian listened to the steady, unmistakable rumbling and let out a sigh.

"That's him. . . ."

"From *Voluminous* and *Octopus* sir, Have contact, classified snorting submarine."

"Acknowledge. Now we'll just follow." Black Sebastian rubbed his hands. "Until the water gets nice and shallow. . . ."

Black Sebastian had described the position in *Seahorse* exactly. Rusty and Dagwood were on watch and heartily tired of it. Rusty was on the periscope and Dagwood was marking the plot and both were longing for the next forty minutes to pass when they would be relieved by Wilfred and the Midshipman.

"Any sign of that light-house yet, Rusty?"

"Not a thing. Nothing but those three merchantmen. Wait a minute, that might have been the loom of a light just now. Trouble is that it's so bloody dark that half the time I don't know whether I'm looking at the horizon or not. I have to keep coming back to those merchantmen to fix myself. We'll have to tell the Boss about them soon, Dagwood. They're getting quite close. Yes. . . . There it is again!"

Rusty stared at the loom of the light. It was less of a loom than a slight lifting of the darkness on the horizon.

"Yes, that's it definitely. Half a minute while I try and get the time. Group flashing four every fifteen, or thereabouts. How about that?"

"Sounds like it. I'll tell the Boss."

The Bodger came awake as the first footstep touched the sill of his cabin door. The long days with little sleep had fined down his perceptions; he awoke now to the sound of an eyelash fluttering.

"What bearing is it?"

"Zero-seven-six, sir."

"Good. We must have made better time than I thought. The tide must be with us. Anything else in sight?"

"Only three merchantmen, sir."

"*What three merchantmen?*"

"About five miles astern, sir. . . ."

The Bodger sprang from his bunk as though galvanized by a sudden tremendous current. He thrust Rusty away from the periscope, looked in it for a moment, and then raced to the sonar room. The watchkeeper, a somnolent rating named Perkins, snapped rigid in his seat at the sight of the Captain and began to operate his set industriously. The Bodger seized a pair of earphones and listened intently.

"Stop snorting! Action stations! Attack team close up!" The Bodger turned on Rusty and Dagwood. "Do you know what you've done, you cloth-eared clowns? You've delivered us up into the hands of the Anti-Christ!"

"H.E. faded, sir."

Black Sebastian's face creased in an executioner's smile. "Hah, they've woken up at last. Action stations. We'll get him now, once and for all."

Rubbing the sleep from their eyes, *Seahorse's* ship's company dragged themselves to their action stations. The Bodger stood at the periscope scourging them into their places with his tongue. Leading Seaman Gorbles' voice took over on the sonar broadcast; there was no need to tell him where the greatest danger lay.

"Black Sebastian two-eight-three moving right transmissions . . . on the bearing. . . ."

Leading Seaman Gorbles' sleep-drugged brain translated the information passed to him by the sonar automatically. His training had been so drilled into him that he could have passed sonar bearing changes while in a hypnotic trance.

It was almost too late for The Bodger to evade Black Sebastian, but not quite.

"Black Sebastian moving right two-eight-seven. . . ."

The Bodger had one last manœuvre up his sleeve. "Port thirty. Steer two-nine-zero."

". . . . Transmissions constant, *attacking, sir.*"

"Full ahead together!"

". . . Two-eight-eight. . . ."

"What's *Windfall's* keel depth, somebody?"

"Seventeen feet, sir," said Wilfred.

The Bodger made a rapid addition of *Windfall's* keel depth and the height of his own fin.

"Keep eighty feet."

As *Windfall* closed on her final attacking course, *Seahorse* darted towards her at full speed, passed directly underneath her, swayed in her wake while the noise of her passage clamoured against the pressure hull, and slid astern of her.

". . . Black Sebastian all round H.E. *very loud.* . . ."

The Bodger guessed that Black Sebastian would probably turn to port and turned to port also. He could not go deep. They were now less than fifteen miles from land and the water was already beginning to shallow.

"Unless we're bloody careful," The Bodger announced to the control room at large, "Black Sebastian's going to land us high and dry. What's the tide doing, Pilot?"

"Setting round the point, sir," said Gavin. "Quite strongly too, sir."

"We'll stay doggo and let the tide carry us quietly away."

"But oh, beamish nephew, beware of the day," said Dagwood to himself, "if your Snark be a Boojum. For then you will softly . . . and silently . . . vanish away."

Dagwood sighed. It was not nearly so funny at three o'clock in the morning.

"Lost contact, sir."

"Yes, I thought you had," Black Sebastian said bitterly.

Once again, he pondered on the nature of his enemy. These bursts of speed could only be done by a handful of boats in the exercise. That narrowed the field. But the last burst, right under the attacking frigate, narrowed the field still more; it could only have been done by a certain type of captain. Black Sebastian had felt the submarine pass underneath him, through the very soles of his feet, and he had to admit himself taken aback. It had been such a flamboyant, theatrical gesture; one might have expected it from Metro-Goldwyn-Mayer, but not from a modern submarine captain. Black Sebastian studied the bridge card again. Once more, *Seahorse* caught his eye.

"Badger." Black Sebastian pursed his lips. "Badger. Never heard of him."

Black Sebastian's memory could not recall a young sub-lieutenant who had joined Black Sebastian's submarine straight from his training class and who had refused to be crushed by his captain's personality.

"What's the tide doing, Pilot?"

"Setting strongly to the north, sir."

"He's bound to be carried by the tide whether he likes it or not. So we'll drive him. Between the tide and the land and the three of us, we should get him eventually. Operate radar."

"We should be getting up to the twenty fathom line any time now, sir," Gavin said.

"That's all right," said The Bodger. "We're allowed to go over it in this exercise. We're supposed to act as in war. And with Black Sebastian breathing down your neck, it is. Keep sixty feet."

Seahorse planed upwards.

"What time does it get light?"

"Just before six o'clock, sir," said Wilfred.

"Another two and a half hours of darkness. I hope that will be enough. Up periscope. What's this? Looks like a fishing fleet. How's your French, Dagwood?"

"Not too bad, sir."

"We'll be needing it. Right, Number One, I want to do an old-fashioned gun action surface. I want to get up there, but quick. I want a single white light to go on top of the fin. And a whistle. Have you got a whistle?"

"I can get one, sir," said Wilfred.

"Get it. Rusty, you'll surface the boat. Have you ever done a gun action surface?"

"No, sir."

"All you've got to do is let go the upper lid when I blow the whistle. Now let's have a pressure in the boat. Open 'Q' inboard vent and blow 'Q'."

"Open 'Q' inboard vent and blow 'Q', sir," said the Outside Wrecker, who knew exactly what to do. This was quite like old times.

Air poured into "Q" tank and out through the open vent into the submarine until the barometers showed an excess pressure of more than two inches.

"That's enough. Let's have a sailor with the light following up the Torpedo Officer."

"Here's the whistle, sir. It belongs to the ship's football team."

"Splendid! Ready?"

"Yes, sir. Ready to surface."

"Stand by to surface, full ahead together, planes hard a dive! *Dive* man," said The Bodger to the Coxswain, who was looking round incredulously.

Seahorse began to sink.

"Blow all main ballast!"

Air pressing into the tanks slowly counteracted the effect of the hydroplanes. *Seahorse* stopped sinking and began to rise.

"Planes hard a rise! Switch on navigation lights."

Under the combined effect of hydroplanes and the main

ballast tanks, *Seahorse* rose like a cork. While the upper hatch was still under water, The Bodger blew the whistle. Rusty let go the hatch and rose up with the rush of escaping air. A spectator would have thought that *Seahorse* had surfaced with Rusty already on deck.

"Chop chop with that light!"

The single light was rigged and switched on. The bow lights were already burning. From a distance, *Seahorse* quickly became indistinguishable from the mass of fishing vessels pressing all around her.

"Still no contact, sir."

"I don't believe it! She *must* be there! There's nowhere else she could have gone!"

"She might be among all those fishing vessels, sir," ventured the Navigating Officer.

"When I want your advice I'll ask for it!" Black Sebastian crossed to the radar screen. "Radar, did you count the echoes of that fishing fleet?"

"No, sir?"

"Well, why the devil not?"

"But sir, there's *dozens* of them, sir! I'd be all *night* counting them, sir!"

The radar operator's voice faltered when he discovered the Captain was actually looking over his shoulder. The Captain's voice sent chilly shivers up and down the radar operator's backbone.

"Now look here. When I tell you to count radar echoes, you count radar echoes. I want to know if an extra one appears or one of them disappears."

"Ay-aye aye, sir."

"We seem to be attracting quite a bit of attention, sir," said Dagwood.

Voluble Gallic cries of alarm were coming out of the night.

"So we are" said The Bodger. "What're they saying?"

"They want to know who we are, sir."

"Quite right, too. Tell them we're the Mademoiselle de Paris, two days out of Montmartre."

Dagwood translated to the nearest fishing vessel. More vehement shouts sailed out of the dark.

"I don't think that was the right thing to say, sir."

"Why not?"

"They seem to think we're a Russian submarine, sir."

"Good God, that's the unkindest cut of all! You'd better tell them who we really are. And tell them those ships out there are really the Russians. Who's the Officer of the Watch now?"

"I am, sir," said Wilfred.

"I want to stay up here as long as it's dark. Keep in the middle of this fishing fleet but try not to hit any nets or anything. You'd better try and smell of garlic and fish, too. Have you got a beret?"

"I'm afraid not, sir."

"Pity. You'll just have to hum a few snatches of the 'Marseillaise' now and then. Let me know if Black Sebastian comes too close or if he looks as though he's got us. Dagwood, have you got your tape-recorder handy?"

"It's in the wardroom, sir."

"You'd better get it warmed up. I want to use it."

Seahorse remained inside the fishing fleet (contrary to Admiralty Instructions, but The Bodger was a desperate man) until dawn and then dived. Black Sebastian and his two henchmen probed cautiously along the fringes of the fishing fleet but their radar was defeated by the multitude of echoes and their sonar listening was confused by the water disturbances under the fishing fleet. The two henchmen moved out to seaward, pinging disconsolately as they went. Black Sebastian stayed with the fishing fleet, like a terrier refusing to leave a rat-hole. Just after dawn he was rewarded by a contact.

"Underwater telephone, sir."

Black Sebastian lifted a weary head. "Put it over the bridge broadcast."

There came a hollow roaring, as though Neptune himself were clearing his throat, and then unmistakably the throbbing of drums, the wailing of a clarinet and the cheeky metallic voice of a calypso steel band singer.

"*Where* did the naughty little flea go? Nobody know, nobody know!"

Black Sebastian glanced round his bridge team. They were all poised, ready to start the attack again.

"Where did the naughty little *flea* go? Nobody *know*, nobody know!"

The bridge action team tensed.

"Where did the *naughty* little flea go? *Nobody* know, nobody know!"

"Switch that thing off," said Black Sebastian. "Pilot, give me a course to rejoin the Task Force."

At breakfast time, The Bodger sat down to as fine a grilled sole as he had ever set eyes on. Two bottles of whisky had procured fish for breakfast, lobster for supper, and three bottles of a violent purple vin ordinaire.

"I'm very grateful to Black Sebastian," The Bodger said. "If it hadn't been for him we'd be sitting down to the same old bangers and train smash. It's almost worthwhile meeting him again."

But they did not meet Black Sebastian again. They did not in fact meet anyone again. One day they saw an aircraft pass low on the horizon and on another day they investigated a target which proved to be a whale factory ship, but the main battle had passed them by. From time to time they intercepted signals which plotted the path of the Task Force eastwards and northwards as the submarines, one by one, rose to attack it like dogs leaping at a bear. The rest of the time they spent waiting for the signal which would release them.

As soon as the magic signal was received, submarines popped to the surface all over the Western Approaches and set off determinedly towards hot baths, liquor and women. Most of them arrived together and the water around Spithead was soon churned into a foam by submarines of various nationalities queueing up to enter the channel, getting in each other's way and sending each other fatuous signals.

Seahorse joined the queue with her control room watch singing their home-coming song: "First the Nab and then the Warner, Outer Spit and Blockhouse Corner" led with great feeling by Able Seaman Geronwyn Evans, to the tune of Cwm Rhondda.

When The Bodger saw the milling throng of submarines he felt that he was among friends again. He had had a good exercise, for a new boy (The Bodger was sure that even his most jealous critics in the Staff Office would admit that) and it was good to be home again. The Bodger's heart swelled. He wanted to be hospitable.

"When's the Wash-Up?"

"Tuesday, sir," said Wilfred.

"Tell the wireless office to make to all submarines in company: R.P.C. *Seahorse*, 1900, Monday. We'll have a Wake. If we're going to tell lies we might as well all tell the same one. Who's that just ahead of us?"

"*Terrapin*, sir," said Wilfred.

"Who's driving her now?"

"Lieutenant-Commander Lamm, sir."

Lieutenant-Commander Lamm was one of the keenest captains in the submarine service, so much so that he was known as the Lamm of God. He had reasonably expected to be given the command of *Seahorse* himself.

"Make to *Terrapin*. You're a Blue submarine, I'm a Pink submarine, do we both use the same toothpaste?"

The Bodger was enormously amused by his own joke. Looking at him, Dagwood was reminded of the schoolboy coming home for the holidays.

Meanwhile, the Signalman was occupied with his lamp.

"From *Terrapin*, sir," he said. "Negative. Pepsodent."

The Bodger groaned. "My God, what can you do with a bloke like that? Ask him where the yellow went. . . . No, no forget it. *Now*, what have we here?"

The latest addition to the queue was a huge steel-grey vessel with blunt bows and a swollen body. The short Channel waves were sweeping over her casing. She was as plainly out of her element as a whale in a backwater stream.

"There," said The Bodger, "goes the future. Actually, it's the present now. This mighty vessel of ours is the biggest, fastest and most dangerous submarine we've got but compared with that ugly-looking lump over there we're about

as lethal as a baby's bottle!" The Bodger put up his binoculars. "That monstrosity is the biggest technical break-through
since . . . since the discovery of the wheel. She can stay at
sea as long as Moby Dick, she's faster than a destroyer and
she's got a weapon that can blast across the Arctic Circle and
blot out a whole city. They've pinched a bit of fire from the
sun and put it inside that submarine."

"Cor chase me old Aunt Fanny round the dockyard
clock," said the Signalman to himself, "the Captain's a
bloody poet!"

"Stop *muttering,* Signalman!" said The Bodger.

★ 8 ★

EXERCISE "Lucky Alphonse" had been important enough—
in its own way. It had provided a great many people with
harmless employment and with justification for their
existences. As Exercises went, it had been a fair success.
But "Lucky Alphonse" was only a prelude and insignificant
beside its aftermath, the Post-Exercise Analytical Discussion, known colloquially as The Wash-Up.

"Lucky Alphonse" had been a mock battle. The Wash-Up
was a real and bitter struggle. It was the battleground
of the Staff, the faceless officers who stood behind the
Admirals, the authors of the indecipherable signatures on
the minute sheets. The Wash-Up was not concerned with
the security of nations, nor the exchange of tactical information nor the learning of lessons taught at sea but with
the more urgent and personal matters of furthering reputa-
tions and consummating careers. Those officers who would
have agitated for commands in wartime, in peacetime
angled for staff appointments. Command in peacetime was
too often the prelude to retirement. It was not fashionable
to step on to one's own bridge and take command of events.
It was more profitable to stay ashore and create the events.
A successful exercise was therefore not one which tested
the defences of the nation at sea but one after which the
entire staff were promoted.

There were no Orders for the Wash-Up. Only sham battles needed Orders. Real battles took their cue from a hint, from a judiciously-timed signal, from a face-saving suggestion or a tiny oversight in the opposition planning. The real battles did not take place in the sonar and radar control rooms but in the signal centres and the plotting floors. The sounds of victory were not uttered by gunfire but by the clatter of cryptographic machinery.

The Bodger took Wash-Ups, like everything else, in his stride.

"They're all the same," he said to Gavin, who was hard at work preparing *Seahorse's* track charts and attack narratives. "You never get a word in edgeways anyway. The R.A.F. will be there in force. I sometimes wonder if the R.A.F. don't keep a special Wash-Up *Regiment*. You never see them any other time. The Staff will be there, of course, unto the seventh generation. You can always tell them by their brief-cases and the Japanese binoculars slung round their necks. They're the chappies who always know everything. They tell you all about radio reception conditions over the South Pole and what the correct recognition procedure is when you're challenged by an Abyssinian flying-boat dropping shark repellent but they never tell you anything you really want to *know*, like who that dangerous lunatic was who nearly ran you down the second night out. Then there will be a few blokes like you and me who actually *did* the exercise, and a little man at the back who's waiting to straighten the chairs and empty the ashtrays and get back home to his football pools. And that's about all."

The Wash-Up was held at nine a.m. in the Royal Naval Barracks cinema, the duty R.P.O. having first ejected a class of Upper Yardmen who had been waiting since a quarter to eight to see an instructional film entitled "The Ammeter". The first arrivals were two staff captains of the Indonesian Tank Corps and the last were the Commander-in-Chief, Rockall and Malin Approaches and his staff who included a bewildered young man in a white coat with blue cuffs who had driven a van full of mineral-water bottles up to the Barracks wardroom and had been directed by the hall porter to the cinema along with everybody else.

By nine o'clock the meeting had taken shape. The first three rows bristled with the intelligent faces, clean collars, brief-cases, Japanese binoculars and aiguillettes of the Staff; they formed a barrier of erudition, culture and enthusiasm which it would be difficult to pierce. There was among their ranks much nodding, winking, and secret signs of conspiracy; they were the Magicians who sat pulling strings while their own Petroushkas capered about on the stage.

The next seventeen rows were occupied by R.A.F. officers. They were all moustached, all serious of face, and all holding a sheaf of papers. Behind them sat the hard core of the conference, the captains of *Little Richard*, *Great Christopher* and the guided-missile cruisers, *Black Sebastian* and the other escort captains, the Master of the fleet tanker *Wave Chiropodist* and several rows of ship's officers who, through many sleepless nights, had made the Exercise work.

In the very back row, in an aura of alcohol, sat the submarine captains and their officers. The Bodger's Pre-Wash-Up Wake had been a spectacular success. At midnight, the captain of the Italian submarine *Farfarelli* had executed a variant of the Limbo Dance which had fetched him up under the wardroom table where he lay babbling faintly of the waters of the Po; he was now leaning back in his seat staring at the ceiling, his face drawn in a mask of torment similar to that of Count Ugolino, who was trapped in the lake of eternal ice and condemned to gnaw upon the skull of his murderer for ever. At two o'clock in the morning, two very correctly dressed officers from the biggest technical break-through since the wheel had called on *Seahorse* to collect their captain, whom they knew affectionately as Ole Miss, who had by that time gone critical. Ole Miss was now sitting propped up at the arm-pits by his Navigating Officer and his Exec, beaming round him with a genial, if slightly vacant, smile. At three o'clock in the morning, the Lamm of God had politely taken his leave, steered himself towards his cabin, and solemnly shut himself in the wardrobe where he spent the rest of the night; he was now sitting bolt upright at one end of the row, looking carefully to his front as though he were afraid that any sudden movement would topple his head from his shoulders. The Bodger himself was flanked by Wilfred, Gavin and Dagwood, all four concentrating on preventing their eyelids meeting.

The proceedings were opened by the Commander-in-Chief, Rockall and Malin Approaches, under his abbreviated international title of CincRock, in whose domain a great part of the Exercise had taken place.

CincRock hated international maritime exercises and in particular he hated "Lucky Alphonse" because he had been unable to go to sea for a single day of it. He had, in his own words, been "stuck in a damned beer-cellar gawking at a bloody stupid Monopoly board". CincRock was a plain seaman who had had greatness thrust upon him. He had served almost continuously at sea until he was promoted to Captain when the shortage of ships forced him for the first time in his life into the Admiralty. There, he was an innocent set adrift in a paper jungle and his immediate impulse had been to retire from the Service. But CincRock possessed one of the most priceless assets of a successful naval officer; he was adaptable. In a paper jungle, he became the most ferocious paper tiger of them all. His other qualities, of remembering what was said last week without looking at the minutes, of dealing with papers within twenty-four hours of receipt, and of catching up with the latest scandal in the pubs of Whitehall, made him tolerated, respected, and then feared. The men who sat at desks and administered the Navy began to speak of him with awe, as a naval officer who had civilized the civil servants.

Nobody suspected that CincRock paid only lip service to Whitehall. None of the men who gazed so benignly at him over their committee tables were aware that CincRock was their implacable enemy. It was CincRock who was responsible for the closure of the forty-one stores depots scattered through the United Kingdom which had long since ceased to issue stores and were quietly administering themselves. It was CincRock who obtained a new class of ship for the Navy by unobtrusively crossing out the title "Cruiser" and substituting "Destroyer" as the relevant correspondence passed through his office (the Treasury subsequently decided that the country could afford a new class of destroyers but not cruisers).

More than anything about "Lucky Alphonse", CincRock hated having to make the speech of welcome at the beginning of the Wash-Up. As he said to his Chief of Staff, "I feel like a damned chairman congratulating his damned shareholders on how many damned washing machines he's sold for them."

"My first, and my most pleasant, duty," said CincRock at the Wash-Up, "is to welcome you all here and to congratulate you on your excellent showing during 'Lucky Alphonse'. This year's exercise was more successful than any we've had in previous years. More nations contributed ships. There were more incidents. And the whole thing went with a bang! One or two things cropped up, particularly on the anti-submarine side, which were not quite as successful as we had hoped for. Submarines made a total of ninety-four attacks. Seventy-nine of those were judged successful. That's a very high percentage. Too high. At the same time, only five submarines were judged sunk, one by aircraft and four by surface ships. That was not so good. My Chief of Staff will deal with that in detail in a few moments. My job now is to say how glad I am to see you all here and to hope you have a damned good time while you're here."

CincRock nodded to his Chief of Staff who had been standing, a Svengali-like figure, in the background.

The Chief of Staff made an immediate impression upon Dagwood.

"Augustus was a chubby lad," recited Dagwood irreverently. "Fat chubby cheeks Augustus had. He ate and drank as he was told, and never let his soup get cold."

Augustus was a brilliant officer who had risen to the rank of Rear Admiral on a series of staff appointments. As Staff Commander, Staff Captain, and finally as Chief of Staff he had been the eminence grise behind a number of successful admirals, of whom CincRock was the latest. Analytical discussions were Augustus' forte. He was a master strategist, in terms of counters and symbols, a blackboard Bismarck, a veritable Wellington of the Wash-Ups.

"All yours, Gussie," said CincRock.

Augustus unrolled a map, took up a pointer and began to summarize Exercise "Lucky Alphonse". He described the rapid mobilization which had followed the proclamation of a state of emergency in Western Europe. He outlined the balance of power and the disposition of forces available at the moment the conflict began. He explained the solution of the logistical problems which had made possible the assembly of a vast Task Force of different nations far out in the Atlantic. He traced the progress of the Task Force towards the continent of Europe. Augustus had all the data at his finger-tips. Incidents, times, courses and speeds rolled from his memory. As he expounded, with cross-reference and flash-back, the unfolding of the master exercise plan, every officer present began to understand where his own limited and seemingly unconnected contribution had fitted into the whole. Augustus was like a skilled advocate building, piece by piece, a complicated case in company law and by the time he had completed his summary it was easy to see why he had become a Rear Admiral. His had been the performance of a virtuoso and there was a moment's silence after he had finished speaking, like the momentary hush which precedes the tumultuous applause after a superlative interpretation of a concerto. Indeed, one or two of the more susceptible officers present wondered whether a round of applause might not be in order.

"Well done, Gussie," said CincRock, *sotto voce*.

The audience were given no more time to decide whether or not Augustus should be given a clap. Augustus had hardly put down his pointer when a Squadron Leader with shiny black hair and a toothbrush moustache had stood up and begun to read rapidly from a sheet of paper.

"At fourteen hundred hours on the ninth, Yoke Uncle was on task over the Bay of Biscay. There was seven-eighths cloud at five thousand feet and a force two breeze from the south-west. Some difficulty was experienced in maintaining radio contact with. . . ."

Augustus, who had been about to sign off with a neatly turned phrase which would have thrown the meeting open, remained on the platform, his pointer still poised. He opened and shut his mouth several times without achieving a break through. The Air Show was exactly timed. Yoke Uncle had hardly landed when Mike Zebra was in the air, piloted by a Flight Lieutenant with a ginger bat-handle moustache. Mike Zebra had maintained radio contact successfully but had had other troubles; her starboard wheel had been reluctant to come up and once up, had refused to go down again. Mike Zebra had barely come to rest in a field by the side of the runway when Delta Eskimo, represented by a Squadron Leader in a bushy black moustache, was airborne and suffering damage to her tail-plane. Fox Pepper, with a reduced Salvador Dali and sad spaniel eyes, had been lost in fog. Indian Queen had not taken off at all. ("The ashtrays were full," Black Sebastian said in a resonant stage-whisper.) When at last the Air Show ended the admirals and captains of the greatest Grand Alliance in history had been given a thorough exposition of the trials and hardships attached to anti-submarine flying.

CincRock found his voice. "Did you find any submarines?"

Every flying eye turned towards a pale youth with a faint blond moustache sitting in the back row of the pilots. He was the only pilot who had not yet spoken. The others looked towards him as though to one who had searched for, and found, the Holy Grail. He was their champion, the gentle knight without a blemish. He had seen a submarine.

The gentle knight rose reluctantly to his feet. "Well, actually, the whole thing was rather a bit of joss," he said diffidently. "We were just as surprised to see him as he was to see us. It was very early in the morning. We came suddenly through thick cloud down to about five hundred feet and there he was, lying on the surface. He dived straight away, of course, but we tracked him with sono-buoys until some frigates came up and took over. I believe they got him."

The gentle knight sat thankfully down again, like Sir Galahad after a press conference.

"Well done," CincRock said warmly.

After the Air Show there was some general discussion amongst the Task Force and escort captains about tactics. Of the four submarines judged sunk by surface ships, three were credited to Black Sebastian and the fourth to the Captain who had consulted the Second Book of Kings and Hymns Ancient & Modern.

"I nearly got another," said Black Sebastian, looking balefully at the back row where The Bodger had fallen into a light sleep. "With one more escort in the right place we'd have got him."

This remark touched the Wash-Up audience on its most sensitive spot. The shortage of escorts had hampered everyone. The cry was taken up on all sides. Carrier captains complained of being asked to fly off strikes whilst completely unprotected against submarine attack. The Master of *Wave Chiropodist* complained of being detached from the main body to carry out his own anti-submarine search. "Let me say now, once and for all," he said, "no fleet tanker I ever heard of is equipped to look for submarines. I only hope the Unions don't get to hear of it." One of the guided missile cruiser captains claimed that he personally had made more submarine detections than either of his two escorts. The escort captains retorted that no anti-submarine vessel yet designed could have covered effectively the areas they had been called upon to patrol. The R.A.F. listened curiously, as deep thus called out deep.

The mineral-water bottle vanman had been sitting in enthralled silence. He had followed every word of Augustus' narrative. The Air Show had been meat and drink to him. He had developed a very high respect for Black Sebastian. But now, as the argument gained momentum, the young man in the blue cuffs began to grow impatient. He fully appreciated that he was probably the most junior person present and was not likely to be called upon for an opinion but he could not allow this discussion to pass without putting forward an obvious solution. It was not in his nature to remain silent when the simplest way to solve the argument must surely be staring everybody in the face.

"Why not build more ships, sir?" he called out.

It was the compelling voice of innocence, the voice of the child who pointed out that the Emperor had no clothes on. It cut through the heated atmosphere of the Wash-Up like a cold fresh wind. The escort captain who had been speaking stopped, frowned, and sat down at once. CincRock stood up and searched the rows of faces.

"Who said that?"

The vanman had been dumbfounded by the effect of his remark. He felt like a small boy who, having mischievously pulled at a small insignificant length of chain, discovers that he has stopped the express.

"Me, sir," said the vanman, blushing bashfully.

"Well done," said CincRock. "That's the first sensible thing I've heard today."

Staff Officers who had been bursting to deliver themselves of brilliant logistical suggestions changed their minds and decided to put their ideas on paper. Captains who had been reserving their most telling arguments until last decided that perhaps there was nothing further to add after all. The vanman had killed the Wash-Up stone dead.

Just as he was about to close the meeting, CincRock remembered that there was still one community who had not yet made any contribution to the Wash-Up.

"How about the submariners? Anyone want to say anything back there?"

Like the Traveller, knocking on the moonlit door and asking "Is there anybody there?" CincRock repeated his question.

Dagwood tactfully nudged The Bodger who came awake immediately, stood up and said: "From our point of view it was a *splendid* exercise! It was a good clean fight, no holds barred, and may the best man win!"

So saying, The Bodger relapsed enigmatically into his seat. His place was taken by Ole Miss who was jerked to his feet by a firm hand under each arm-pit. He was a very short man and he was temporarily suspended, his feet pedalling at the floor, like a gnome on gimbals.

"As a career-motivated officer," Ole Miss said, "I can tell you all that Exercise Lucky Alphonse was the goddamned best exercise, logistics-wise and sea-familiarization-wise, we've ever partakelized. The only time we hit trouble was some goddamed *yacht*. He really scared the juice out of me ... !"

Ole Miss stopped, blinked, appeared to have lost the

thread of what he was about to say, and was rapidly lowered out of sight.

The only other submarine contribution was from Count Ugolino who shook off his former mask-like torpor and launched a torrent of Italian, embellished with histrionic gestures, flashing eyes and snapping fingers.

The Bodger stirred uneasily. "Who's that *noisy* bastard?" he inquired irritably. The message was passed along the row to *Farfarelli's* Navigating Officer who spoke softly to his captain. Count Ugolino finished his sentence, bowed low, blew a kiss to CincRock and sat down.

After the Wash-Up CincRock released the normal statement to the press, confirming that "Lucky Alphonse" had been a complete success, having consolidated the maritime defences of Europe and strengthened once more the bonds which united the nations of the free world.

The only flaw in the confident façade was disclosed by CincRock himself. He was button-holed about "Lucky Alphonse" by the Naval Correspondent of the *Daily Disaster* outside the "Keppel's Head" and replied that in his opinion the United Kingdom was no better fitted to defeat a determined submarine attack than it was equipped to beat off a swarm of locusts.

"At least," CincRock shouted, as he was hustled into his car by his Flag Lieutenant and Augustus, "we could *eat* the bloody locusts!"

* 9 *

"THIS week," said The Bodger, "we really *must* get organized. *Work Study* is the latest cry in the Staff Office at the moment. Apparently we've been doing it all wrong all these years. It seems that what was good enough for Nelson is *not* good enough for us after all. Everybody's got time and motion study charts showing that if you hold your glass in your right hand and the bottle in your left you'll have time for twenty per cent more drinks before the bar closes. Or something. Anyway, Captain S/M has told us all to get our Maintenance Weeks organized instead of having the usual shambles."

The rest of the wardroom looked sceptical. The Submarine Service had been trying to organize its Maintenance Weeks since the first of the Holland boats went to sea at the turn of the century.

"*So,*" The Bodger went on, "seeing as how it's Monday morning, I thought we might have a conference and see if we can fix everything to happen at different times instead of in one Godalmighty chaos. It shouldn't be too difficult. Now. . . . What have we got on this week, Number One?"

Looking like a man upon whom great issues hung, Wilfred took out the desk diary which he kept hidden in his drawer. He began to read from it in a hollow voice, as though chanting a rubric for lost souls.

"Paint ship, sir. Twelve bodies overdue for the escape tank. They've got to requalify this week. Five blokes for X-rays. Another six to have a first-aid course. Store ship for six weeks at sea. Survey all emergency stores. Send all the bunk covers and curtains to the cleaners. Get Chippy to mend the cupboards in the Petty Officers' mess. Muster all the attractive items in the permanent loan list. Fix up the ship's company run ashore to Brighton. Captain S/M's rounds of the messdeck inboard."

"Fine, *fine,*" said The Bodger. "I can see you've got a pretty busy week." It was a long time since The Bodger had been First Lieutenant of a running submarine and he had forgotten how many details had to be arranged.

"How about you, Chief?"

Derek opened a huge blue file marked "Engineer Officer —Very Urgent" and found among the papers, drawings and stores notes which overflowed from it a piece of paper covered in figures and squiggly drawings.

"The starboard supercharger was rumbling on the way in, sir. We'll have to strip that down and have a look at it. The main engine lub-oil's due for a change. We'll have to fuel and take on fresh water some time this week. We're docking on Thursday to fit that new echo-sounder for the boffins. And we've got to change the after periscope. . . ."

"Fine, fine, fine," The Bodger said hurriedly. Talking

to technical officers on technical subjects always gave The Bodger a feeling closely resembling vertigo. He nerved himself again.

"How about you, Dagwood?"

"The radar bioscope was on the blink on the way back, sir. And we've got to charge sometime this week. We're fitting a new whip aerial and there's our side of the echo-sounder to fit and test. . . ."

"Rusty?"

"Load three fish on Wednesday, sir. All the sonar ratings are due for another ear test. We need some more smoke candles. *Terrapin* have challenged us at cricket, sir. . . ."

"Pilot?"

"New chart folios, sir, and a new ensign if we can get it. That one's getting a bit crabby. Change binoculars. They're all flooded. We've got to swing compasses again some time before we leave, sir. . . ."

"Have *you* got anything on, Mid?"

"I must get some more films, sir. Everybody's seen the ones we've got. And we need some more squash and lime juice. . . ."

"Well." The Bodger was slightly taken aback by the multitude of requirements *Seahorse* must fulfil before she was ready for sea again.

"Let's not get down-hearted, men. Let's say we do the charge tomorrow, load fish on Wednesday, swing compasses on Thursday. . . ."

"But we're going into dock on Thursday, sir."

"So we are. All right, let's do the charge *today* . . . God." The Bodger stopped, aghast. "I've just remembered. This morning is the only time we can have the Attack Teacher." The Bodger looked at his watch. "And we should have been up there five minutes ago! I'll go and tell them we're still coming. . . ."

The Bodger sprang from his chair.

"Get the Attack Team together as soon as you can," he said to Wilfred over his shoulder as he went.

There was a short silence in the wardroom after The Bodger's passing.

"So much for work-studying our Maintenance Week," said Dagwood, at last.

The wardroom had no more time to ponder upon work study. Messengers from all over the establishment were already queueing up outside. The telephone rang continually.

"First Lieutenant, sir? The Sick Bay say can they have the ratings for X-rays now, sir? It's the only time the Barracks can take them."

"Engineer Officer, sir? The Spare Gear Office inboard says would you send up two hands to collect some gear, sir. . . ."

Each message drained away a little of *Seahorse's* effective force. By ten o'clock, Derek found himself quite alone. The other officers were in the attack team and the ship's company had scattered like autumn leaves. When Derek poked his head out of the wardroom, the control room was empty. The whole submarine, in either direction, was empty.

"Anybody there?"

Derek's voice echoed along the deserted passageway.

"Hello? Anybody there?"

"Sorr?"

A head projected from the door of the stokers' mess.

"Gotobed, it's nice to see you!"

"Want somethin', sorr?"

"No no, Gotobed, it's just nice to hear another human voice, that's all."

Derek sat down again in the wardroom, full of warm thoughts towards Stoker Gotobed. He was enormously cheered to know that there was somebody else there.

Derek's feelings towards Gotobed would have surprised a stranger to *Seahorse*, because Gotobed was not a man of prepossessing appearance. His face, chest and most of his body were covered in a tangle of thick black hair. His arms hung down to his knees. In repose—his favourite position—he looked like a successful mutation of man and ape.

Gotobed was long overdue for a move to another submarine, but Derek had fought off all attempts to have him drafted because Gotobed was the one man in *Seahorse* who was irreplaceable. Other stokers could be relieved.

Derek could be relieved. The Captain himself could be relieved. Gotobed could not. Gotobed was the only man living who could work the Oily Bilge Pump.

Seahorse's Oily Bilge Pump was a piece of machinery which defied the normal principles of mechanical science. On the shop floor it passed all tests imposed upon it, but as soon as it was fitted into the submarine, it became possessed by devils. Dockyard workmen had wept salt tears over it. The maker's representatives had spent sleepless nights by its side. A succession of engineer officers from various submarines and surface ships had tried out every combination of its valves. But the Oily Bilge Pump refused to take a suction for anyone but Gotobed. When anyone else but Gotobed tried to use the pump it not only refused to take a suction but sprayed its compartment with bilge water. Gotobed was therefore as vital to *Seahorse* as her pressure hull.

Derek's pleasant meditations upon Gotobed and his indispensability were suddenly interrupted.

"Excuse me. . . ."

Derek looked up. A young man in clean white overalls, carrying a brief-case, stood in the doorway. He wore two stop-watches slung on lanyards round his neck. In one top pocket he carried a row of pencils and in the other a small slide rule. His eyes burned meanwhile with the fierce fanatic glare of a reformer.

Derek recognized the face at once. This was the keen young scientist in the advertisements for chemical products, the successful business executive advising his less successful colleague to change his brand of tobacco, the wholesome salesman soothing the nervous housewife's fears.

"I'm from the Work Study Team."

"Oh. Well, come in. What can we do for you?"

"We've been asked to do a survey on the way submarines plan their maintenance periods."

"Really? Well, when you find out, let me know, will you? I've been in submarines nine years and I've never managed to plan a maintenance period yet."

The Work Study Man smiled. "That's exactly why we have work study. Frankly, you know, you need it. . . ."

253

"Do we?"

"Yes. Do you know, we did a short survey on *Terrapin* last month and we found that the average time worked by each man per day was *two hours*!"

"Blimey," said Derek. "The Lamm of God must have been cracking the whip! Did she go to sea all right?"

"Yes."

"Did she come back again?"

"Yes, but. . . ."

"Obviously two hours a day was enough then."

The Work Study Man smiled again. Overcoming the subject's prejudices was Lesson One, Line One in the Work Study syllabus.

"Let me show you some of the results we've achieved. . . ."

"Oh no, please don't bother," Derek protested. "You just crack on and do whatever you have to do. Don't mind me. . . ."

But the Work Study Man had already, in two economical movements, unzipped his brief-case and whipped out a large drawing.

"Here are some of the surveys we've done. You can see that in the case of a large shore establishment we cut the pay office staff by fourteen officers and thirty-seven ratings, merely by replanning their office layout. We cut the maintenance time on the potato-peeler in a cruiser by nearly seventy-five per cent! On one air station we cut the rum issue time by a half. . . ."

"Just a minute," said Derek, his argumentative instincts rising, "that may be all right in industry but not in the Navy. What exactly have you achieved?"

"What have we achieved? An enormous saving in . . ."

"Let's take the examples you've given me. You've cut the staff in some wretched pay office by umpteen blokes. But what's happened to those blokes? They haven't gone outside. They're not civilians. The Navy's still paying them. They're probably settled in some *other* pay office right now and when you come to work study *that* pay office you're going to find some familiar faces. And they're going to hate you. And the chaps who save all that time on the spud-peeler. What do you think they're going to do with that extra time? Maintain more spud-peelers? Not likely! I'll tell you what they're going to do. They're going to have time for two cigarettes instead of one. And as for *cutting the time of the rum issue by half*. . . . Do you think the Navy's going to thank you for that? Why, it doesn't bear thinking about! It would be like missing out every other bar of the National Anthem!"

As Derek finished his rhetoric he realized that it had all been wasted. The Work Study Man was still talking.

". . . And so the best thing would be for me to take one of your ratings and plot his daily work."

"You want one of our blokes to work-study?" The idea struck Derek with such force that he blinked.

"Gotobed!"

"Sorr?"

Gotobed's massive face appeared at the wardroom door.

"Gotobed, this gentleman would like to work study you."

"Sorr," said Gotobed blankly.

The Work Study Man was already writing in his notebook "Gotobed," he said briskly. "Right. What's your job, Gotobed?"

"Ah gits a soction on the bliddy bilges with the bliddy pomp, sorr."

The Work Study Man paused. "I *beg* your pardon?"

"He pumps out the engine room and motor room bilges,' said Derek.

"I see. Is that all?"

"It's quite enough."

"I see. Well, this should make a very good subject. A fairly simple operation with clearly defined movements."

Derek kept his face expressionless. "Off you go, Gotobed. Pump out the engine room and motor room bilges. This gentleman will go with you."

Gotobed led the way aft to the small pump space which contained the Oily Bilge Pump. It was Gotobed's own compartment; he was responsible for its cleanliness. It was his shrine. Gotobed climbed down while the Work Study Man started a stop-watch and made symbols in his notebook.

Gotobed's performance was well worth a few symbols.

He primed the air pump with water from a small can, blew some drops of water from the filling hole, replaced the cap and sealed it with two mighty strokes of a hammer. A faint frown appeared on the Work Study Man's brow.

Humming tonelessly between his teeth, Gotobed climbed out of the pump space and shambled along the engine room to the first bilge suction valve which he opened one turn. Returning to the pump, he placed his shoulder against the motor casing and shoved, at the same time turning the starting rheostat one notch.

The Oily Bilge Pump started with an eerie whistling noise which made the hair on the back of the Work Study Man's neck rise involuntarily. The whistling note deepened to a whirring and then to a steady roar. The pump began to give spasmodic shudders which Gotobed met with timed shoulder heaves, crouching by the pump as though assisting a cow in labour.

"Bliddy pomp's got a bliddy wackum!"

"What's that?"

"Bliddy wackum!"

"*Eh?*"

"Wackum wackum wackum!" roared Gotobed over the booming pump. The vacuum gauge quivered wildly, whereupon Gotobed released the pump, hoisted himself out of the compartment, ran to the bilge suction, opened it fully, and dropped down again into the pump space. Once there, he raised a foot, placed it firmly against the pump casing and thrust. The pump gave several more shudders and settled down to a steady contented hum. The Oily Bilge Pump was taking a suction from the bilges.

Derek had strolled aft to watch the show.

"How's it going?" he asked the Work Study Man.

The Work Study Man's face was transfigured with holy rapture.

"It's a classic! This is a natural for the Society! It'll make my reputation! I don't know if you realize it but people will talk about this in years to come!"

"Glad to hear it," said Derek politely.

"I've counted sixty-two separate wasted motions! The whole thing has taken thirteen minutes twenty seconds. I

256

can see at a glance we can get down to five movements and anything over three minutes would be a criminal waste of time!"

"I'd like to see you do it quicker. In fact I'd like to see you get a suction at all."

"You can't be serious!"

"I most certainly *am*!"

"I don't believe it."

"You just have a try. I'll tell you this much. I can't do it."

"But I don't know where the . . . where anything is. . . ."

"You tell us when to do it, and we'll do everything for you."

The Work Study Man climbed down and gingerly started the pump. It started immediately with an ugly howling noise as though the pump casing contained a man-eating animal.

"Open the suction!"

The pump gave a series of seismic palpitations and then exploded. Derek leaned over and looked through the hatch. He could see nothing in the fine oily mist which was rising from the compartment.

"I should stop the pump now," he said. "I've got a towel in the wardroom."

Gotobed stopped the pump. "Too much bliddy wackum," he said disgustedly.

* * *

When The Bodger and the others returned just before lunch The Bodger said: "Before I forget, Chief, we've got a work study man coming down to see us some time today. You'd better look after him."

"He's been, sir. And gone."

"Already? Did he enjoy himself?"

"I think so, sir."

"So much for work study then."

★ 10 ★

THE Submarine Staff Office was, architecturally, an un-distinguished room. Only two chairs were provided, one for Commander S/M and the other for Lieutenant-Commander Barney Lightfoot, resident staff officer; submarine captains, visitors and onlookers all stood. On one wall were bunches of signals and a map of the English Channel; on another, a large board on which were chalked the dates individual submarines were due for various commitments. Above Commander S/M's desk were the two mandatory staff notices "Next Week, We Must Get Organized" and "Haven't You Heard? It's All Been Changed". Above the desk of Barney Lightfoot, an erudite man, was a typewritten notice: "If you can keep your head when all about you are losing theirs, it means you haven't the vaguest idea what's happening."

Nevertheless, the Staff Office was, if the term could be used in its loosest sense, the nerve centre of the squadron. It was simultaneously an operations room, a club-house, and a coffee-bar. There Captain S/M kept his finger on the squadron pulse. There Commander S/M grappled with insoluble logistical problems, and there the squadron technical officers explained to sceptical audiences that their men were only possessed of two arms each and each day contained a maximum of twenty-four hours. There also, the submarine captains attempted to keep up with the latest changes in events.

"Have you met your Boffin yet?" Commander S/M asked The Bodger as he arrived one morning.

"What Boffin?"

"The one you're taking with you. The one you docked *specially* to fit an echo-sounder for."

"He's not coming until tomorrow."

"It's all been changed. He's joining you this morning and he's going to stay with you for about two months, while you amble down to the Equator and take a few readings for him. Don't ask me what sort of readings. I was on the blower to Barwick & Todhunters last night and they say they're sending someone who's been in submarines before. So he should be fairly well house-trained."

Barwick & Todhunter's representative could fairly be described as house-trained. He was at that moment standing at the end of *Seahorse's* gangway, waiting for the stream of sailors carrying bags of potatoes to die down so that he could cross himself. He himself carried a small hold-all bag and a slightly larger black box. He was dressed in a black jacket, striped trousers, an Old Harrovian tie, a white carnation in his button-hole and a black homburg hat. On raising his hat as he stepped on to *Seahorse's* casing he revealed smoothly brushed blond hair, a pink complexion and an air of politely-concealed dismay. He gave Wilfred, who met him on the casing, the impression that he had come expecting to stay for the week-end but had, by some monstrous social mischance, mistaken the time, the date, and the place. He shook hands with Wilfred warmly and produced a card.

"Mr Lancelot Sudbury-Dunne."

"How do you do," said Wilfred. "I'm the First Lieutenant." Wilfred eyed the small hold-all bag and the black box.

"Is that all you've got?"

"Yes," said Mr Sudbury-Dunne. "And it's quite enough, I think, to take in a submarine, don't you?"

"Why yes," said Wilfred. "I'm sorry I sounded surprised. It's just that the last, um. . . ."

"Boffin?" inquired Mr Sudbury-Dunne.

". . . bloke we took to sea arrived twenty minutes before we sailed with seventeen packing cases of stuff. And when we got to sea he announced that he wanted three holes drilled in the pressure hull."

"How trying for you."

"If you just leave your stuff there I'll get a sailor to take it down to the wardroom for you."

"Oh, don't bother," said Mr Sudbury-Dunne and collecting his bag and his box he slid through the fore hatch like an eel. It struck Wilfred that they had been given something extraordinary in the way of boffins.

"I'm afraid the Captain's not here yet," Wilfred said, after he had introduced Mr Sudbury-Dunne to the rest of the officers. "He should be down very shortly."

"Good. I'm anxious to meet him." Mr Sudbury-Dunne was well aware that the Captain's personality was of considerable importance to his experiments. He knew that his own presence had been imposed upon the ship and he would be a guest of the wardroom for two months. A hostile or even an uninterested captain could seriously hamper his work.

The Bodger was just as anxious to meet The Boffin. "I hope to God he's not one of these pale-faced state-scholarship trogs who puke all over the wardroom table and tell me I'm running my ship all wrong." The Bodger knew that he was stuck with this boffin for two months. "If you get up one morning and don't like an officer's face you can tell him to go away and put a turk's head on it and paint it yellow. But with a boffin you've got to be polite, if only for the sake of the Navy Estimates."

In the event, neither need have worried.

"Bodger!"

"Dan!"

Mr Lancelot Sudbury-Dunne was no ordinary boffin. He was an old friend and drinking partner of The Bodger's. They had once suffered together under Black Sebastian. In spite of his faultless social appearance, Mr Lancelot Sudbury-Dunne was a man after The Bodger's own heart, so much so that he had earned the nickname of Dangerous Dan. The wardroom were greatly relieved to hear it. Plainly Dangerous Dan could be told to take his face away and put a turk's head on it and paint it yellow, just like anyone else.

The Bodger was delighted to see his friend again and a little remorseful over his remarks about boffins.

"I take back all I said about boffins, Dan," he said.

"That's all right, Bodger. We're a pretty thick-skinned lot." Dangerous Dan, on his part, was just as pleased to see The Bodger, although he was secretly overawed by The Bodger's present status as the commanding officer of a modern submarine.

"If it wasn't for that dirty laugh, Bodger, I would hardly recognize you," he said. "You're looking so prosperous! Shades of Black Sebastian. He didn't hold out much prospect for the future for either of us, did he?"

"As a submariner," The Bodger quoted, from memory, "this officer is earnestly recommended for duties with the Fleet Air Arm. That's what he wrote about me! But to get back to the main thing Dan, what exactly do you want us to do on this trip?"

"Well, it's like this." Dangerous Dan's manner became precise and business-like. "As you probably know, everybody is looking for the big technical break-through in submarine detection, though nobody knows what form it will take yet. But first of all, we've got to know a lot more about the sea itself. After all, if you were hunting leopard or something you would be a bloody fool if you didn't take the trouble to find out about the sort of country where it lived. And so with submarines. Do you know, most of the earth's surface is covered in water and we know almost damn all about it! Just take the average chart. Have you got a chart handy, Pilot?"

"Any particular chart, sir?" said Gavin.

"Any one will do and I'm Dangerous Dan to you."

"O.K., Dan." Gavin went to his locker and pulled out the first chart which came to his hand. It was a small-scale chart of the Western Approaches.

"Just the job," Dangerous Dan said briskly. "Now, just look at all these soundings here. They look impressive enough and obviously someone in the past has been to a lot of trouble getting them. But as you go more than a hundred miles or so from land the soundings are spread out in lines, each sounding miles from the next one and each line miles from the next line. Anything might be happening between those soundings. It's like trying to find your way through a dark wood using every other eye once every quarter of an hour. Then there's tides. You all know that the tidal streams the average Joe uses on the surface bear no relation at all to the tides at five hundred feet or even at a hundred feet. In the Straits of Gibraltar for example, there are two or three different streams all on top of each other."

"I know just what you mean," said the Bodger. "Do you remember that time with Black Sebastian when we'd been dived for hours and hours and I was trying to make a landfall on the Needles? I can still hear his voice when he looked through the periscope. 'Pass the message to the Navigating Officer, Portland Bill loud and clear dead ahead'!"

Dangerous Dan chuckled. "I believe Black Sebastian was a little shaken himself. It's to try and avoid that sort of thing that we're making this trip. What we're trying to get is a three-D, wide screen, stereophonic picture of the sea. It'll take years to do, of course, and I have a nasty feeling we haven't got years to do it in, but anyway Bodger, *I'll* be doing all the work. Even I haven't got anything to do until we get down to the Equator. It should be a bit of a jolly for you lot."

Seahorse sailed on a calm summer evening, with St. Catherine's light winking in the dusk and the lights of passing ships glowing like jewels. The engines threw out two long trails of vapour which lay on the water without dispersing. Overhead, the stars lit the sky down to the horizon where the red glow of the sun still lingered. It was the weather the sailor knows as "Signing-On Weather".

Gavin read the weather reports and prophesied a falling barometer, high seas and head winds but day after day the miraculous weather persisted. As the reports deteriorated, the weather improved. Each morning the sun rose behind a shining veil of low cloud, shone all day in a cloudless sky, and set in a spectacular display of colour.

"If you saw that on a postcard," Dagwood said of one sunset, "you'd call the artist a liar."

The Bay of Biscay was like a plain of mobile glass, with a long swell running from the Atlantic. *Seahorse* rose and dipped steadily, the water foaming and tumbling off her bows and washing along the ballast tanks. The sea seemed to have a hypnotic effect upon Dangerous Dan. He spent hours at a time studying the water welling up and pouring away again, his eyes fixed on the changing surface of the sea as though he were already trying to penetrate its depths.

The Bodger made his landfall on the Canaries at dawn. The islands appeared magically through the morning mist, their heads wreathed in thin layers of cloud and their bases jutting suddenly from the sea, like the bastions and turrets of a sorcerer's castle. It did not seem possible that such islands could be inhabited by humans; they were more like the homes of fairies who played in the gardens which had once tempted Hercules.

Seahorse fuelled and collected mail at Las Palmas and then set out for the tropical Atlantic. There, it was as though the sea claimed the ship for its own. Dolphins shot up and over in beautiful curves through the wake. The startling water spouts of whales appeared on the beam. Flying fish hopped and scattered at the bows and sea-birds swooped, wailing and watchful, around the bridge. At night *Seahorse* swam through a milky sea of phosphorescence. Fire streamed along the hull leaving sparks which still shone after the wave had receded. The bow wave was an ever-renewing ridge of silver light which flashed and sparkled as it broke and opened out from the ship.

Down below, the ship's company passed the time between watches sleeping, arguing and playing crib, draughts or uckers. The morning rum issue, the afternoon sleep and the evening film-show were the main events of the day. The Petty Officer Telegraphist produced a daily news sheet from the B.B.C. but the items seemed to the men in *Seahorse* to come from another world; it was difficult to relate the events described in them to *Seahorse,* a solitary ship upon a wide sea.

The wardroom grew tired of uckers and tried Monopoly but after the Midshipman had won the first three games The Bodger banned it as bad for discipline.

"I'm not going to have my wardroom's morale undermined by a bloody stupid parlour game," he said. "Besides, Mid, it brings out all your worst instincts."

The wardroom returned to uckers, where The Bodger was on more familiar ground. Uckers bore a family resemblance to ludo but Submarine Uckers, and particularly The Bodger's Uckers, was to ludo as National League baseball is to girls' school rounders. It was a merciless game. It was mandatory to sneer at a losing opponent and to accuse a winner of cheating. The game lent itself to psychological warfare. Innuendo and insult could reduce an opponent to a state where he could barely bring himself to pick up the dice. The Bodger and Dangerous Dan were experts.

Dangerous Dan introduced the wardroom to Chinese Chess. The winner was he who manoeuvred his opponent into taking the last match from three piles of varying size. Dangerous Dan won so consistently that The Bodger insisted on an explanation. The solution, expressed in binary notation, left The Bodger as baffled as before. Dangerous Dan took on the whole wardroom at Fan Tan, selling them the pack for a penny a card and paying tenpence for every card they succeeded in laying out. The wardroom only desisted when they had lost most of the remainder of their month's pay and the ship's welfare fund was beginning to be in jeopardy.

Dangerous Dan was the complete gamesman. Even Dagwood, the wardroom's acknowledged conversationalist, could not outploy him.

"You may be right," said Dangerous Dan, while they were discussing road traffic. "I can only repeat what the Minister of Transport said to me. . . ."

"I've always regretted," he said, when they were discussing Lawrence, "that he didn't sign my copy of *Lady Chatterley* for me. . . ."

When the conversation ranged as far as Freud and Jung, Dangerous Dan clinched the social aspects of psychology with: "I've always been told that an *introvert* marries the first girl who'll sleep with him and an *extrovert* marries the first girl who won't."

Though over-shadowed by Dangerous Dan in the broader issues, Dagwood had one particular game which he had perfected himself. It was called the Needle Game and was played between two players, Dagwood and his victim. The rules were simple. Dagwood won if he succeeded in provoking his opponent into a display of bad-temper or, better still, rage. His opponent won if he kept his temper.

Dagwood often tried Derek, though he was too amiable to make a good opponent. But Derek did have two *bêtes noire* on which he could be relied upon to comment strongly. One was Planned Maintenance, and the other Work Study.

"We don't seem to get much time for maintenance these days, do we, Derek?" Dagwood remarked casually after lunch one day.

Derek raised his head warily from his pillow, like a bull catching the first sight of an intruder far away on the other side of the meadow.

"What do you mean?"

"Well, I mean they never seem to give us any time to. . . ."

264

Derek rose like a game-fish. "We'll never get submarine maintenance periods on a basis until they become a submarine commitment, like an exercise. The date of something like 'Lucky Alphonse' is sacred. Why shouldn't a maintenance period be sacred as well? We should be like the air boys. If an aircraft's routines are not up to date, it just doesn't fly. If the day ever comes when a submarine is not allowed to *dive* because it's routines are not up to date, *then* we'd see a difference! But it won't happen. They arrange the programme first and any gaps they find they give to maintenance. Now shut up Dagwood and let me get some sleep for God's sake. . . ."

Dagwood chalked up the exchange as a draw and lay in wait for his favourite opponent—Wilfred.

Wilfred was almost impregnable as far as the Needle Game was concerned but he had one vulnerable spot. As First Lieutenant, Wilfred was responsible for the sailors' food. In practice the Coxswain ordered, administered and mustered the food but in theory Wilfred was the ship's catering officer and responsible to the Captain. Wilfred took his supervisory duties very seriously.

On the day *Seahorse* crossed the Tropic of Cancer it was unfortunate that the Coxswain provided Olde Englishe pudding for lunch. When Dagwood was given his portion, he held up his hand.

"Anything the matter, sir?" said the Steward.

"Hark," said Dagwood.

Wilfred was still smarting from the previous tea-time when Dagwood had looked at the butter and said "C'est magnifique, mais ce n'est pas le beurre!"

"*Now* what's the matter?" he said sourly.

"What's the matter, Dagwood?" The Bodger asked. The exchanges between Dagwood and Wilfred had often lightened his day.

"I hear the Muse, sir. She's calling to me, in accents soft and low."

"What's she saying?"

"The usual drivel, I expect," said Wilfred.

"She's saying. . . . One moment. . . . Yes, here it is. . . . It's a poem, sir. She's saying,

265

Despite the many moans you hear:
There's one you all forget.
Though Christmas came but once *last* year,
The pudding's with us yet!"

It was a bull's-eye in one shot. Wilfred glowered, while
the rest of the wardroom hooted. Nevertheless The Bodger
thought it a little unfair. In spite of their difficulties in
storing and cooking a variety of food in a confined space
and in a hot climate, The Bodger thought that Wilfred,
the Coxswain and the Chef were doing very well. In the
circumstances, The Bodger was quite satisfied. The Bodger's
main concern was not what the ship's company should eat,
but what they should drink. There would soon be a
shortage of fresh water on board. *Seahorse's* tanks did not
contain enough water for a prolonged passage in the
tropics. There was a distiller but it was fitted in the main
passageway and the noise and heat it generated made the
messes adjacent to it uninhabitable. The only solution was
a compromise, to run the distiller for limited periods and
to ration fresh water. Otherwise, the problem seemed
insoluble without divine intervention.

Unknown to The Bodger, divine intervention was almost
at hand. That evening, soon after tea, *Seahorse* ran into a
tropical rainstorm. The Midshipman was on watch and
knew exactly what to do.

"Close up radar. Tell the Captain."

The messenger found The Bodger with Dangerous Dan
in the petty officers' mess, playing the final of the ship's
uckers tournament against the Chief Stoker and the Second
Coxswain.

"From the bridge sir, he's closing up radar, sir."

"What for?"

"I think it's a rain cloud, sir. . . ."

"Rain!"

The Midshipman pointed out the cloud to The Bodger.

"I'm closing up radar, sir, because of the likelihood of
reduced visibility forrard sir. . . ."

"To hell with radar and to hell with the reduced vis!
It's the rain I'm after!"

The cloud was only four or five miles ahead of the ship. A curtain of rain was lashing the sea over a front of several miles. *Seahorse* was heading directly for the centre of the storm. The Bodger moistened parched lips and rubbed the stubble on his chin.

"It's like an answer to prayer," he whispered. He bent to the voice-pipe. "Pass the message to all compartments, all ratings not on watch muster on the casing with soap for showers."

"Say again, sir!" yelled Ripper, who was on the wheel.

"Clear lower deck! Muster on the casing! Provide Soap!"

"Clear lower deck, muster on the casing, provide soap, aye aye, sir!" shouted Ripper. "The Captain's gone off his rocker," he added to the Radio Electrician, who was petty officer of the watch. The Radio Electrician nodded sombrely.

In a short time over sixty naked men, clutching soap and sponges expectantly, mustered on the casing and gazed at the approaching storm.

Wearing only his soap-bag in one hand, The Bodger conned the ship towards the centre of the storm.

"Starboard five. . . . Steady. . . . Steer that. . . . That should do it. . . ."

With a booming roar of wind the storm was upon them. The rain drummed on the casing and bounced off the sailors' naked bodies. *Seahorse* was enveloped in a grey wall of water. The sailors pounded their chests and shouted songs as they leisurely soaped themselves for their first real wash since the ship left England.

Dangerous Dan joined the crowd on the casing and began to wash himself like a man demented. He scrubbed and rubbed himself as though every second were priceless. His energy amused the sailors who were covering themselves in lather and allowing the blessed rain to wash it off.

But there was method in Dangerous Dan's frenzied washing. The rain storm passed away as quickly as it had come. The rain stopped abruptly. The uncovered sun began to harden the outer layers of lather. The Bodger seized the voice-pipe in a desperate, slippery hand.

"After that cloud! Hard a starboard! Full ahead together!"

Seahorse heeled in a tight turn towards the retreating storm. Her half-lathered officers and ship's company watched her progress anxiously. The artificer on watch in the engine room was advised of the emergency. The engines thundered as they had never thundered before.

Directed by a wild-eyed Bodger, *Seahorse* dodged all over the ocean but the storm eddied this way and that, steadily gaining distance from the pursuing submarine. At last The Bodger was forced to abandon the chase.

Dangerous Dan was conspicuous amongst the throng on the casing. He was as sleek and shining as a seal.

"I must say I admire your soap," he said to Dagwood, whose body and hair were still partly covered in encrusted lather. "What sort is it?"

Dangerous Dan had his own version of the Needle Game.

Dangerous Dan began his survey when *Seahorse* was sixty miles from the Equator. Dangerous Dan working was quite a different man from Dangerous Dan amusing himself with party games on passage. He was up every morning at five o'clock to calibrate his instruments and he did not finish his last calculations on the day's data until after midnight. He had placed the black box on the chart-table but the main part of his equipment including the echo-sounder had been installed in a space between the Coxswain's store and the oilskin locker. Dangerous Dan's working day was spent bobbing and ducking between the control room and the store.

Seahorse dived twice a day for Dangerous Dan's readings, while the Black Box in the control room gave an instantaneous three-dimensional picture of the sea bottom, computed from the echo-sounder transmissions.

The Black Box was the most fascinating side-show any-one in *Seahorse* had ever seen. The ship's company queued up to look at it.

"Roll up, roll up. What The Butler Saw Twenty Thousand Leagues Under The Sea," Leading Seaman Gorbles said.

"Is *that* the bottom of the sea?" exclaimed the Chef. "Blimey, I thought it was flat!"

The Chef spoke for most of the ship's company. If anyone in *Seahorse* had ever thought about the sea bottom at all, they had imagined it sloping downwards from the continents to a flat plain until it sloped upwards again for the next continent—with the odd uncharted pinnacle regularly rammed by submarines off Londonderry. Dangerous Dan's Black Box showed that the sea had a geography of its own. *Seahorse* swam suspended over submarine mountain ranges which would have dwarfed the Alps and over deeps which could easily have contained the Grand Canyon. The Black Box showed a panorama of drowned rivers winding through ancient courses on the sea floor, islands which had been cut off in their growth towards the light, plains as wide as the steppes and foothills which stretched like the folds of a giant's blanket for hundreds of miles. The instrument was also sensitive enough to record objects between *Seahorse* and the sea floor. Strange vast shadows like clouds moved over the screen, marking the passage of a shoal of an unimaginable number of fish. Sometimes the screen picked up speeding images with spiked tails which looked as though sea-dragons on a titanic scale were flying over the landscape below them.

As Dangerous Dan's experiments progressed, every man in *Seahorse* began to have an inkling of the immensity of the ocean. The sea was not a homogeneous mass of water but had currents, like veins, and layers, like muscles. It was always in a state of stress, a shifting, restless, hostile entity. *Seahorse* was an intruder, creeping about on the fringe of a colossal mystery and peering, from an impertinent distance, at the supreme wonder of the earth.

The Bodger maintained the normal sonar listening watch while *Seahorse* was dived for the experimental runs. Although Seahorse was so far off the main shipping routes that there was never any ships' hydrophone effect, the sea itself provided a miscellany of sounds which descended through the whole range of human hearing. There was often a hollow resonant booming, like the pounding of mammoth breakers a thousand miles away, coupled with clicks, thumps, metallic knocking and shrill cat calls. Porpoise wailed near the surface and at every depth there came suddenly a deafening staccato chatter, like the applause of a myriad scaly claws.

"Whoever said this was the silent world needs his head examined," said Leading Seaman Gorbles. "More like Marble Arch on a Sunday."

One morning Leading Seaman Gorbles picked up a new sound. It was a slow eerie beat, accompanied by regular high-pitched squeals. He pointed it out to Rusty, who was officer of the watch. Rusty called The Bodger, who listened himself.

"What do you make of it, Gorbles?"

"Couldn't say, sir. Could be transmissions, though they're nothing like anything I've ever heard before. Sounds like someone having a cheap thrill, sir."

"Put it over the control room broadcast. And don't be facetious."

The control room was filled with the treble squeaks, underlined by the same slow steady beat. The sound had an artificial regularity, without the haphazardness of a sound emitted by a living organism.

Dangerous Dan paused on his way down to the store to listen. Wilfred and Dagwood came out of the wardroom.

"Very slow revs, sir. Not more than twenty a minute. Sometimes not even that, sir."

The Bodger made up his mind.

"Action Stations! Attack team close up!"

★ II ★

THE Admiralty's orders on the action to be taken by a captain on gaining an unidentified and possibly hostile submarine contact were contained in a Top Secret file in the Captain's safe. But The Bodger did not need to consult them. He already knew their general gist almost by heart. Behind the veiled diplomatic language and the ambiguous official wording, they were quite explicit; they could be summed up in the traditional phrase "Engage the enemy more closely".

Although the ship's company had been told nothing of the position, the attack team closed up as quickly as though the Admiral himself were watching them. In *Seahorse,* as in all operational submarines, the step from peace to war was a short one. Leading Seaman Gorbles' reports began to come over the action broadcast with a decisive snap which he had never achieved in fleet exercises.

"Target three two three . . . Moving left. . . ."

The Chef stuck his head out of the galley as the rest of the attack team tumbled by to their action stations.

"Where's the fire?"

"Haven't you heard, Whacker," said the Steward. "We're at war with the whales."

"Less noise," said The Bodger. "Assume quiet state."

It was as though The Bodger had given *Seahorse* the order to die. In a few minutes all inessential fans and motors had been stopped, the telegraph order bells had been muffled, Derek stopped one shaft and the submarine glided on at slow speed. *Seahorse* became as quiet as a hunting cat, ears cocked for the least sound.

Suddenly, with the violence of a thunder-clap, there was a loud clang and an oath from the direction of the engine room. The Bodger jumped in spite of himself.

"Tell that rating to come here!"

A shame-faced stoker appeared in the control room.

"What was that noise?"

"I dropped a spanner, sir."

"You and your chums back in your ivory tower don't seem to realize that there is someone *out there,*" The Bodger pointed dramatically at the bulkhead, "just listening for crumbs like you. Now get out! And take your shoes off!"

". . . Target faded, sir."

"Hah, he's heard us. I'm not surprised. I expect they can hear us back in Pompey with all the noise we're making. Bring all after tubes to the action state."

The Bodger regretted his outburst almost as soon as he had finished it. He remembered that the ship's company had not been told anything yet. He picked up the broadcast

271

microphone and pressed the button. There was no hum from the system. Just as The Bodger was gathering breath to vent his irritation, Dagwood said: "The broadcast system is switched off for quiet state, sir."

The Bodger let out his breath again in a long sigh. "Switch it on again while I talk to the ship's company."

"Aye aye, sir."

"Main broadcast switched on, sir."

"D'you hear there. This is the Captain speaking. We have a visitor. About ten minutes ago we got an unidentified contact on sonar. I don't know what it is yet but I will let you know as soon as I do. The attack team will remain closed up in the meantime. That's all."

"All after tubes in the action state, sir."

"Very good."

"Visitor regained, sir, one five seven. . . ."

"One five seven!" The target had gone round nearly a hundred and eighty degrees, unheard by sonar. The Bodger gritted his teeth, feeling the temper rising in him.

"One five eight, moving right, faint *ecstatic* transmissions. . . ."

"What do you mean 'ecstatic'?"

"Can't describe it any other way, sir," replied Leading Seaman Gorbles apologetically. "Sounds like someone enjoying himself, sir. Can't get a transmission interval or nothing on him, sir."

It was the strangest attack The Bodger had ever carried out. The Visitor appeared to track steadily right, then stop, track back, and shoot suddenly forward again.

"What speed does the plot give?"

"Last speed five knots, sir, mean speed *forty* knots, sir!"

"*Impossible!*"

"That's what the plot says, sir," said the Signalman aggrievedly.

"Check that, Number One."

Wilfred measured the Signalman's angles and made a rough calculation.

"It certainly seems like that, sir."

"It *can't* be!"

". . . Visitor faded, last bearing two one one. . . ."

"Now we'll have to wait, I suppose," The Bodger said. "And see where he pops up again next time."

Dangerous Dan was watching the attack from the tactful safety of the wardroom door. The science of submarine versus submarine attacking had been in its infancy when he left submarines just after the war and he was enthralled by his first privileged view of it. Dangerous Dan knew enough of submarine tactics to appreciate that the procedure he was now watching was as far removed from the normal submarine attack on a surface vessel as higher mathematics was from mental arithmetic. As a submariner himself, Dangerous Dan could guess at the ordeal The Bodger was undergoing. Engaging an unknown submarine was difficult enough; engaging one which behaved so unpredictably was like going out to catch a criminal who was not only waving a meat-axe but fighting drunk.

"... Visitor regained. Zero zero eight. ..."

"Gone through a hundred and eighty degrees again," said The Bodger.

"... Visitor bearing steady. ..."

"Plot suggests target turned towards, sir!" cried Wilfred.

"Full ahead together! *Hard* a port!"

"All round H.E., sir ... *Very loud*. ..."

They all felt the enemy passing very close down the starboard side. There was rushing, sluicing sound and *Seahorse* rocked crazily from side to side.

"Great God Almighty," The Bodger whispered. "The man's mad! Absolutely Harry starkers!"

"... Visitor lost in our own. ..."

"Slow ahead together. Midships."

"... Visitor faded. ..."

There was a profound and thoughtful silence in the control room after the last sonar report. The Bodger became aware that the passageways on either side of the control room were crowded. He noticed the press of faces, all straining to see and hear what was happening.

The last exchange set the pattern for the next two hours. The Visitor circled *Seahorse* at a cautious distance before lunging inwards on a suicidal collision course. Again and again the ship's company clutched at pipes and brackets as the submarine rocked under the assaults. The Bodger was more than ever convinced that he was dealing with a submarine captain who had had a touch of the sun. However, crazy or not, the Visitor possessed a staggering underwater speed and manoeuvreability.

"He's making *rings* round us," The Bodger said. "But that's just about all he *is* doing. How long has the attack team been closed up?"

"Just under three hours, sir," said Wilfred.

"Fall out the attack team. Keep the plot manned. The rest can fall out. Arrange the attack team in two watches."

"Aye aye, sir."

"Let me know whenever sonar picks him up again."

As the hours passed, the Visitor's behaviour began to appear less unpredictable. His movements followed a definite sequence. He disappeared for one hour, circled for an hour and attacked at the end of the hour, only to disappear again. Just as The Bodger was hoping that he had gone for good, he came back. The Bodger came to anticipate the attacks and stood by the officer of the watch as the Visitor hurtled past. The rest of the time The Bodger sat in the wardroom and waited, like a billiard player sweating it out while his opponent ran up a huge break.

At supper time, Dangerous Dan was sitting in the wardroom looking very thoughtful.

"I wonder if I might make a suggestion, Bodger?"

"Of course."

"I've been thinking about that black box of mine. I believe I can fix it to read up to about a thousand feet below us. I can cut out the response from the sea bottom by altering the scale. It won't be very accurate but it might give you a line on him. . . ."

"What a splendid idea, Dan!"

"It'll only be any use while he's below us, of course. . . ."

"That doesn't matter. It's better than nothing. Can you start it now?"

"Surely."

"He's not due back for another half an hour. Will that give you time?"

"Ample. It's all calibrated and warmed up anyway."

"Splendid! What a brilliant idea, Dan!"

Dangerous Dan shrugged modestly. "All done by kindness," he said.

Dangerous Dan climbed down again to his apparatus. Soon, it was clear that something was wrong with the black box. Dangerous Dan passed to and fro, a worried frown on his face.

"Something wrong, Dan?"

"I don't know. There doesn't *seem* to be anything wrong but I can't get any sense out of the thing at all. Something's jamming it. It won't read anything beyond about fifty feet below us."

"Perhaps it didn't like having the scale altered?"

"No, that shouldn't affect it. I do it every day when I'm calibrating it anyway. But it just won't read beyond fifty feet now."

"Perhaps...."

Dangerous Dan started back towards the Coxswain's store, stopped, and clapped a hand to his forehead.

"I've got it! How stupid of me! Of *course* there's nothing the matter with it! It's telling us what we want to know."

"What do you mean?"

"That's where our friend is."

"I still don't get it."

"That's where our little Visitor is right now. He's gliding along.... Fifty feet beneath us...."

The most profound silence of all settled over *Seahorse*. The Bodger ran his fingers through his hair. This was the end of the line. This was where the text-books stopped. The imaginations of those who compiled the Admiralty instructions on submarine tactics had never envisaged an enemy who shadowed his adversary fifty feet below him. The Bodger realized that he was now on his own.

"Let's stir it up! Warn all compartments to expect large angles."

Using full speed, maximum angles and full wheel, The Bodger put *Seahorse* through a series of submarine aquabatics which would have made her designers' hair stand rigid. After each manoeuvre The Bodger slowed down and listened. Leading Seaman Gorbles reported an empty sea. The black box screen was blank.

"That's foxed him," The Bodger said with some satisfaction.

". . . Visitor regained, one one zero, sir. . . ."

"*Damnation!* What's the battery now, Number One?"

"Last reading was thirty per cent left, sir," said Wilfred.

"Take another one."

The electricians' mates scrambled over the pilot cells with their hydrometers and took another reading of the density of the battery fluid.

"Twenty-five per cent, sir," said Wilfred. "On the drop. We had to borrow the Chief Stoker's hydrometer, sir. Ours wouldn't read low enough!"

"It looks as though we'll have to wrap this up very soon whether we like it or not," The Bodger said. "We've tried circus tricks. Now we'll try Grandmother's Footsteps. Can you put on a stop trim, Derek?"

"Yes, sir."

"Carry on then. Mid, you'd better watch this if you want to learn about trimming."

The Midshipman stood at Derek's shoulder while Derek approached the ultimate in trimming, the inner temple of the art. Using the classic method of putting wheel and planes amidships, Derek made a succession of minute adjustments to the trim, transferring only a few gallons at a time. Each time the hydroplanes resumed their functions, they appeared to have less and less to do, until Derek stopped the shafts and the submarine hung in the sea, motionless and level.

"Well done, Chief. Anything on sonar?"

"Negative, sir."

"Anything on the black box, Dan?"

"Nothing Bodger."

"*That'll* give him something to think about," said The Bodger.

The words had hardly left his lips when The Bodger felt *Seahorse's* deck tilt, and slowly right itself again. Just as The Bodger had convinced himself that his sense of balance was playing tricks on him, the deck slowly tilted again. The Bodger felt the hair prickle on his scalp. "Full astern together! Sorry about your trim, Chief. . . ."

The Bodger's order had an immediate and dramatic effect. *Seahorse* heeled violently. Dangerous Dan's black box blew all its fuses. Leading Seaman Gorbles gained contact at once and reeled off a string of bearings.

As the bearings were being plotted, The Bodger noticed that for the first time since the attack began the Visitor's change of bearing suggested a steady course and speed.

"Stand by for a firing set-up! Slow ahead together. Bring all after tubes to the action state. Chop chop with the tubes!"

The Bodger's best estimate of the Visitor's course and speed was set up by the attack team. The firing bearing was computed. The tubes were reported in the action state. Wilfred gripped the handle which would release the first torpedo. The Bodger raised his stop watch.

"Stand by. . . . Stand . . . by. . . ."

At the last moment, when The Bodger's lips were actually framed to give the order to fire, the possible consequences of what he was about to do smote him. *Seahorse's* action might be the crossing of the Rubicon. The torpedo they were about to fire might have the same effect upon the world as the first shot fired at Sarajevo. The Bodger hesitated, but did not dare to give the order to break off. He did not dare to make any sound whatever. The long weeks of training, the weary attack team drills, had led to this moment. At this stage of the attack there could now be no other order than that to fire. If The Bodger so much as coughed, if he did no more than clear his throat, Wilfred would fire.

The Bodger waited while the perspiration gathered in his eyebrows and trickled into his eyes, not even daring to raise his hand to wipe it away. The seconds passed, the firing bearing was reached and overshot. Still The Bodger made no movement nor sound. At last, after a minute, the attack team relaxed. It was obvious that the Captain had changed his mind.

The Bodger swallowed. "Do not fire," he said hoarsely. ". . . Visitor surfaced, sir!"

"Are you certain?"

"Positive, sir," said Leading Seaman Gorbles, scornfully. Think I don't know when a bloody target's surfaced? he said to himself.

"Right. Any other H.E.?"

"Negative, sir."

"Sixty feet. Stand by to surface. Diving stations."

As *Seahorse* rose to periscope depth, The Bodger ordered all the control room lighting switched on. The submarine had been dived for more than twenty hours and he had no wish to be blinded by the daylight.

At sixty feet, The Bodger swung the periscope, tensed to go deep again. When he reached a bearing on the port bow, Wilfred was interested to see a deep blush rise from The Bodger's neck to his forehead.

"Surface."

The Bodger followed Rusty and the Signalman up to the bridge. It was another beautiful day, with a calm sea and a bright sun.

But The Bodger was not interested in the weather. He searched the sea through his binoculars.

"There's our Visitor," he said, pointing.

Two miles off the port bow, a very large grey whale was disporting itself in the sea. As The Bodger watched, it sounded but, before it disappeared, The Bodger swore he saw one huge mammalian eye close in a wink.

Feeling like an old man, The Bodger pressed the button of the bridge action speaker.

"Wireless Office, this is the Captain. Make to Captain S/M: Have broken off navel engagement with amorous whale."

The Signalman's lip curled. "You sex mad *monster*," he said bitterly.

★ 12 ★

THE episode of the Amorous Whale was not mentioned in *Seahorse* again. Nobody on board wished to be reminded of a time when they had all been braced at action stations to fight off the erotic advances of an affectionate marine mammal. Even Dangerous Dan, who could have dined out for months on it, expunged the story from his conversation, realizing that true friendship often demands a true sacrifice. When Captain S/M examined *Seahorse's* log at the end of the quarter and remarked on the day and the night during which H.M.S. *Seahorse* appeared to have been at war, The Bodger shrugged it off, saying that he thought the ship's company had been getting stale and it seemed a good opportunity to liven them up a bit. But privately, in his own wardroom, The Bodger looked back on the episode in a mood of self-reproach.

"I was so *obsessed* by the idea that it was another submarine, when the damned animal was doing everything but *tell* us he was only trying to be friendly. He even came up and nuzzled our ship's side. When I think that I was within an ace of firing. . . . That would have been the most jilted whale this side of the Gosport ferry! But I suppose there's a moral to be drawn from it. We live in such suspicious times that we're apt to fly off the handle for anything. We're like people who're so scared of burglars we shoot the milkman dead."

After the Whale, Dangerous Dan's experiments seemed an anti-climax. Even the Black Box lost its appeal and everyone was glad when the experiments were completed and *Seahorse* headed towards South America.

The nearest representative of the Royal Navy was H.M.S. *Beaufortshire*, flying the flag of the Commodore Amazon & River Plate Estuaries who was on his way to pay an official visit to the Republic of SanGuana d'Annuncion. The Bodger received a signal ordering him to proceed to Cajalcocamara, the capital of the Republic, for fuel, water and mail.

"Cajalcocamara," said The Bodger thoughtfully, when he read the signal. "That rings a bell."

"What's it like, sir?"

"Bloody good run ashore. We quelled a revolution there once, when I was in the Cadet Training Cruiser."

"SanGuana? That rings a bell with me too," said Dangerous Dan. "If I remember rightly, they have a very big motor race there at this time of the year. Let me look in my diary."

Dangerous Dan took out a handsome green leather diary and opened it on the wardroom table. As Dangerous Dan thumbed through the pages, Dagwood could not help noticing that every day in Dangerous Dan's year seemed to be marked by a prominent social or sporting occasion, from the Cheltenham Gold Cup through The Trooping of The Colour to the Chelsea Arts Ball, by way of the Braemar Gathering.

"Here we are. The International Targa Mango da San-Guana. It's one of the big races of the year. It counts towards the World Racing Driver's Championship."

"When is it?" Derek asked.

"Next Sunday."

"When are we due to get there, Gavin?"

"Friday morning. That's if your donks don't give any trouble."

"Don't worry," said Derek. "They won't if there's any danger of me missing the race. I'll speak to them kindly."

"Taking it by and large, it should be a good time to visit the place," The Bodger said.

It was an excellent time to visit Cajalcocamara. The city was already decorated for carnival in honour of the motor race, and the visit of two warships completed the San-Guana's celebrations. The citizens of the young Republic had not forgotten the part the Navy had played in winning them their independence. As *Seahorse* approached her berth she was played in by two brass bands and a native San-Guana orchestra playing on reeds and gourds. The dock buildings were decked with flags and the jetty was a packed mass of beaming faces. On the jetty's edge stood a welcoming committee of the city's most important citizens, including the President of the Republic, Aquila Monterruez himself, his cabinet, the British Consul, the Mayor, the Gieves Representative, the Principal of SanGuana University, the Man from the Prudential and the sporting editor of *The SanGuana*, the official organ of the Republican party.

"I don't see any sign of *Beaufortshire*?" said The Bodger.

"Golly, we've certainly got the first eleven out to meet us. Who would you say that little man in the yachting cap was?"

"The Admiralty Representative, sir," said Wilfred.

"My God, I expect you're right!"

The Bodger marvelled, as he had marvelled many times in the past, at the wideness of the Admiralty's net.

"I bet if you paddled a canoe right up the bloody Amazon you'd find a little man from the Admiralty at the top waiting to come on board and tell you you'd already used up your year's allocation of parrots!"

The Bodger barely had time to get down to the casing before Aquila Monterruez was on board.

"My dear Bodger!" he cried, advancing with hand outstretched. "How very refreshing to see you again! But how are you?"

"Very well indeed, Beaky," said The Bodger. "And you?"

"*Thriving*, me dear fellow! Do you know, this is the first time I have *ever* been on board one of these inventions. Perhaps I'd better make the introductions. I won't introduce my cabinet, they're a very mundane lot. The British Consul, though. . . ."

The British Consul shook hands stiffly. He felt that his position had been usurped by the ebullient Aquila. He was a tall man with weary blue eyes and shaggy eyebrows. He reminded The Bodger of one of those indolent baboons at the zoo which lean up against the bars of their cages and ignore the passing public.

"And this little man who looks as though he's carrying a heavy weight about on his head is one of yours, Bodger. The Admiralty Rep."

Absent-mindedly patting the Admiralty Rep. on the head as he passed, Aquila followed Wilfred down to the wardroom.

"Very cosy," he said when he saw it. The Bodger introduced his officers and Dangerous Dan. "Very cosy indeed. Is there room for a bar?"

Wilfred hesitated, but The Bodger nodded. It was a quarter past nine in the morning but The Bodger was not one to deny hospitality to a President in his own country.

Besides, now that he came to think of it, a drink would go down very well indeed. The Midshipman poured out gins and tonics all round except for the Admiralty Representative who asked for whisky and said unexpectedly: "Salud y pesetas y fors en las brigitas!"

"Hear hear," said Aquila.

The Signalman, who was also the ship's postman, appeared at the wardroom door.

"Mail, sir," he said shortly. He passed The Bodger a bundle of private and official correspondence.

"Hullo?" The Bodger examined one letter. "A letter for the Midshipman postmarked Oozemouth! What's all this, Mid?"

The Midshipman blushed delicately. "There's a girl there who writes to me occasionally, sir," he said.

"Voi che sapete, che cosa e amor?" hummed Dagwood.

". . . And one for Pilot with a pink envelope and. . . ." The Bodger sniffed. "Perfume! You'll be making the Steward jealous, Pilot."

"Her letters are a lot more attractive than she is, sir," said Gavin.

"Come, lad," said The Bodger, sternly. "Think of the lovin' 'ands wot penned this 'ere missive. A man hasn't grown up until he's been embarrassed by a few love letters."

The Signalman reappeared. "Santa Claus has remembered you, sir," he said to Derek.

"Has he?"

"Bloody great package on the casing, sir. They're trying to get it through the fore hatch now."

Aquila clapped his hands. "I'm dying to see what this is! It came a fortnight ago in the diplomatic bag and it's been hanging around the British Consulate ever since."

"How did you know that?" The British Consul inquired sourly.

"My dear Fruity, you're so naïve only the British would employ you. I've been keeping my Chief of Police, a crude man, off it ever since it arrived. He swore it was a time bomb but I reassured him. I told him that the British, like the Americans, only send time bombs to their friends. But open it Derek, do. I'm all agog!"

Just then the Chief Stoker and his store-keeper Ferguson staggered past the wardroom, bent under the weight of a large black wooden packing case. As he passed, the Chief Stoker directed at Derek a glance of such concentrated hatred that Derek hastily finished his drink and hurried out to the control room.

The packing case seemed to fill a good part of the control room. It lay between the periscopes, already surrounded by a crowd of curious sailors.

"What have we got here, Chief Stoker?" Derek asked cheerily and, in the opinion of the Chief Stoker, stupidly.

"Don't know, sir."

"It's a spare Chief Stoker!" called Able Seaman Ripper.

"We already got one spare ——," replied another, anonymous, voice.

"Quiet there," the Chief Stoker growled. "Got that crowbar?"

The top planks were prised off, uncovering strips of foam rubber which themselves enclosed another metal box with a screwed lid.

"Got a screw-driver?"

The lid was unscrewed and a further box wrapped in oiled paper appeared. The Chief Stoker set to work with the crowbar again.

"It's getting smaller and smaller, anyway," Derek said.

The Chief Stoker grunted and wrenched off the lid. A mass of straw spilled over the deck. Parting the straw, the Chief Stoker lifted out a brown paper parcel the size of a shoe box bound with transparent adhesive tape.

"Got a knife?"

Able Seaman Ripper produced a knife. The Chief Stoker slit the tape and, like a conjurer, produced a small cardboard box.

"Abracadabra."

"You'd better open this, sir."

Derek opened the box and took out a small brass gauge with a round dial six inches in diameter. It was a combined pressure and vacuum gauge of the kind used on submarine distillers.

"Was it a time bomb?" Aquila asked.

"No," Derek said brusquely. "It was what is known as Preservation, Identification and Packing."

The rest of the mail was by comparison undistinguished. All the wardroom received tailors' bills which were all thrown into the waste-paper basket.

"Have another drink, Beaky," said The Bodger.

"Thank you, Bodger. Talking of tailors' bills. . . ."

"I remember getting a rude letter from my tailors when I was at Oxford," said the Admiralty Representative, again unexpectedly. "I settled them quite simply. I told them that it was my custom to put all my outstanding bills in a hat at the end of the month, draw one out, and pay it. I told them that if I got another letter like that theirs wouldn't even go into the hat!"

At that moment it occurred to Derek that if he wanted a good view of the motor race, Aquila was just the fellow to ask.

"How's your glass, sir? Let me get you another."

"What a very christian idea, my dear Derek!"

"I hear you have a big motor race on Sunday, sir?"

"Indeed yes. The International Targa Mango da San-Guana. Rather a pretentious, pompous name I've always thought but the press like it. It looks so well on paper. Rolls off the tongue, too. You must all come as my guests, I won't accept any refusal. My Chief of Police, though a very obtuse man in many ways, will arrange seats for you."

"Thank you *very* much, sir!" cried the wardroom in chorus.

"A pleasure. I shall be there myself of course, for political reasons. But I'd just as soon not. The *noise*, and all those impossible *people*! Some of them seem to think that just because they can drive one of those beastly machines at more than a hundred miles an hour I should offer them my own bed and toothbrush! It's too much. I had a go myself one year and some ill-mannered boor rammed into the back of me before I had gone three hundred yards, to say nothing of three hundred miles."

"Can anyone drive then, sir?" Dangerous Dan asked. The Bodger looked suspicious; for a moment he thought he had recognized an undertone in Dangerous Dan's voice which reminded him of the past.

"Of course," said Aquila. "The race used to be open to all comers but the whole thing has grown so much that everyone except the big boys have been squeezed out. I'm told the race is now as important as Le Mans or the Mille Miglia, whatever they may be. There was a rather trying argument one year because the slower drivers were supposed to be getting in the way of the faster ones. I couldn't understand what they were arguing about myself. The whole *thing* seemed equally fraught with peril to me. Anyhow, I stopped it. But there's no reason why I shouldn't start it again. After all, I *am* President. It's *my* race. Why," Aquila said, draining his glass, "do you want a drive?"

"*Would* I?" Driving in a motor race of such magnitude would be, in Dangerous Dan's eyes, second only to opening for England in the Lords Test.

"How's your glass, sir?" Derek said.

"My dear hospitable Derek. . . ." Aquila relinquished his glass.

"Really Monterruez," protested the British Consul. "You're not seriously suggesting. . . ."

"Consul," said Aquila solemnly. He had had just enough alcohol to make him argumentative. "You are forgetting that our host, Commander Badger here, received the Freedom of Cajalcocamara for his valiant part in my revolution. To a Freeman of Cajalcocomara, all things are possible! How about it, Bodger?"

The Bodger caught the British Consul's eye.

"No really, Beaky, it's very kind of you but I'm afraid I must refuse."

"I'm disappointed in you, Bodger."

The shape of the Second Coxswain loomed in the passageway.

"*Beaufortshire* just entering harbour, sir."

"Dear God, that dreadful man," Aquila said wearily. "He visited me last year and bored me almost into an asylum. Do you know that sensation as though someone were drilling steadily into the top of your head? That describes it exactly. He reminds me sometimes of Chief of Police. He has the same inability to think of more than one thing at a time."

"Who's that?"

"Commodore Richard Gilpin."

"Is *he* here?" said The Bodger hoarsely.

"He's Commodore Amazon and River Plate and how's your father. But I must go. Let *him* call on *us*. Come on Fruity," Aquila nudged the British Consul, "down with that one. We must be off."

As he stepped out into the passageway, Aquila collided with an agitated Petty Officer Telegraphist.

"Signal from *Beaufortshire* sir: You are in my berth!"

"Nonsense," said Aquila sharply. "A Freeman of Cajal-cocamara can berth anywhere he likes. Just you send him this message. . . ."

"That's all right, Beaky," The Bodger intervened hastily. "We've got to shift berth anyway. He's going to give us some fuel."

"Oh, very well."

Aquila marched across the gangway to his little car, pushed the British Consul into the passenger's seat, and prepared to drive off. He appeared to have some difficulty in finding the starter but at last the engine fired, the car backed and filled for a time, and then moved off in low gear.

Meanwhile, The Bodger was manœuvring *Seahorse* away from the jetty and out of *Beaufortshire's* way. He was only just in time. *Beaufortshire's* bows slid in behind *Seahorse's* stern as The Bodger backed out.

"What a rude man," said The Bodger quietly.

Seahorse lay off while *Beaufortshire* secured in a flurry of bugle calls, band music and arms drill.

"*Beaufortshire's* flashing us, sir."

"So I see. What's he saying, Signalman?"

"You—May—Salute—My—Flag—At—Noon, sir."

The Bodger blinked. "Has he gone mad? What does he think I'm running here, a Royal Naval Barracks?"

"It's five minutes to twelve now, sir."

"I know."

The Bodger had already been nettled by *Beaufortshire's*

signals. He was well aware that his own ship, with rusty sides and gaps in the casing where plates had been torn bodily away by the sea, compared poorly with *Beaufortshire's* spotless paintwork. He had been goaded almost beyond endurance by *Beaufortshire's* white uniforms and bugle calls, a display of ceremonial which he had hoped to avoid for his own ship's company who were weary after a long sea passage. But the order to fire a gun salute was too much. The last bond of restraint snapped in The Bodger's mind.

"How many guns does a Commodore get?"

"Eleven, sir," said Wilfred.

"Pass the message to the Torpedo Officer to go up to the fore ends and fire eleven white smoke candles from the forrard underwater gun! At the double!"

On the stroke of noon, the first canister curved into the air and dropped into the harbour. A massive plume of white smoke billowed from it. The Torpedo Instructor stood in the fore ends, taking his time from Rusty, and chanting: "If I wasn't a T.I., I wouldn't be here. . . ."

When the salute was finished, Cajalcocamara harbour was enveloped in a dense smoke cloud and a foul smell of carbide.

"From *Beaufortshire*, sir: Are you on fire?"

"Make to *Beaufortshire*: Only with enthusiasm. Intend coming alongside you now."

Seahorse felt her way cautiously alongside *Beaufortshire*, The Bodger sounding the fog-siren in a most ostentatious manner.

Seahorse's officers were invited to take lunch in *Beaufortshire*. The meeting between the two wardrooms did not prosper. *Beaufortshire* had a social wardroom. As a mess, they were the last remaining stanchions of a way of life which vanished from the Royal Navy on September 3rd, 1939. They had a reputation as the most ferocious pride of social lions on either side of South America. The Amazon & River Plate Station might have been designed for their benefit. They rarely met another warship and bore the whole weight of the Navy's official entertaining on both

sides of the continent, a burden under which any other
wardroom would have collapsed. *Beaufortshire's* Navigating
Officer explained the rigours of the commission to Gavin.

"Didn't get any sleep for three nights running in Rio.
And B.A. was beyond a joke. The races were on and
people literally queued up to take us out, old boy. We
were almost glad to get back to sea for a rest. I expect you
find the same?"

"Not exactly."

"Where have you just come from?"

"Portsmouth."

"Take you long?"

"Forty-one days."

Dagwood and Rusty were being entertained by the
Captain of Royal Marines.

"I expect the first things you chaps'll want is a bath,
eh? Wash some of the smell off. Pretty smelly things, submarines, I'm told, eh?"

"Oh not at all," said Dagwood. "All submarines have
baths let into the deck. Black marble ones."

"You're pulling my leg! Black marble! What's that for?"

"Night vision," Dagwood said seriously.

"Great Scott! I never thought of that! I suppose you
have to worry about that sort of thing in submarines,
eh?"

"I should say so. Their Lordships are always telling us
we must take more care over our sailors' health. We get
vitamin tablets, extra orange juice, sun-ray lamps, what
else, Rusty?"

"Masseur," said Rusty, right on cue.

"Oh yes. Masseurs. And pornography."

"Pornography!"

"Oh yes, specially issued to submarines," Dagwood looked
carefully at the Captain of Royal Marines. Reassured, he
went on. "They come in plain wrappers as a special supple-
ment to the Advancement Regulations. People work up
quite a frustration in submarines, you know. It's all that
sea time."

"I can understand that! Have another drink, eh?"

"Thank you," said the frustrated Dagwood. "I will."

Derek was conducting the ritual negotiations between Engineer Officers concerning matters of fuel, lubricating oil and technical assistance. *Beaufortshire's* Engineer Officer was a fat florid Lieutenant-Commander with a hearty laugh and a firm disinclination to be troubled by details.

"How much fuel can you let us have, sir?"

"See my Chief Stoker. He'll fix you up."

"Is it Admiralty fuel?"

"Haven't the faintest idea, dear old chap! Shouldn't think so, for a moment. A little black man came on board somewhere along the coast, forget where it was now, and flogged us some."

"But how about water content and all that?"

"Haven't the *faintest* idea. I expect my Chief Stoker puts a line down and if he catches a fish he knows there's water about, ha ha!"

"Yes," said Derek.

Wilfred was also conducting a tribal pow-wow with *Beaufortshire's* First Lieutenant on such esoteric matters as showers for the ship's company, canteen opening hours, fresh bread, and dress for libertymen. He was finding the going as hard as Derek.

"How about mail, sir? Will your postman collect ours with yours?"

"Tell you what. Why don't you ask your Coxswain to see my Coxswain and let them sort it out for themselves? Do you shoot? We got some very good duck at Recife. We might have a day here, if you're interested."

"I'm afraid I haven't done any for a long time."

"How about you, sir?" *Beaufortshire's* First Lieutenant turned on Dangerous Dan who was staring, with bare-faced horror, at a coloured print of the M.F.H. of the West Rutland Hunt of 1843 which was hanging above the wardroom fireplace.

"I beg your pardon?"

"I said, do you shoot?"

"All our shoots are let."

The First Lieutenant registered immediate interest.

"I didn't catch your name, sir. . . .?"

"Sudbury-Dunne. S.U.D.B. . . ."

"Ah, your mother was a Pye-Gillespie before she married, wasn't she?"

"Correct."

"I believe I had a day at your place once."

"I doubt it. Unless you know the Prime Minister well? Perhaps you do."

In the Commodore's day-cabin, The Bodger himself was having as sticky a time as his wardroom.

"Good to see you again, Badger," Richard Gilpin was saying, coldly.

The Bodger, sitting on the edge of his chair nursing a glass of South African sherry, permitted himself a non-committal grunt.

"We last met when you were my Number One in *Carousel*, is that right?"

"Yes, sir."

"Fine ship. Fine ship. Fine wardroom. Fine ship's company."

"Yes, sir."

Inwardly, The Bodger marvelled at the way Richard Gilpin could contrive to look more like a naval officer than it seemed possible, or permissible, a naval officer should. Standing there by the fender, pouring himself a glass of sherry, his white uniform contrasting pleasantly with his lean tanned face, framed between the portrait of Nelson and the photograph of Admiralty Arch, Richard Gilpin might have been posing for a gin advertisement.

"I noticed several of your ship's company needed haircuts this morning, Badger."

"They've been at sea a month, sir."

"Yes." Richard Gilpin took a seamanlike sip at his sherry. "What was all that smoke this morning as we came in?"

"We had a little trouble with the forrard underwater gun, sir."

"Yes, I suppose we must make allowances for the . . ." Richard Gilpin paused, ". . . illegitimate branches of the service."

When The Bodger reached the safety of *Seahorse's* wardroom again, he said: "Mid. Go ashore now. Find Aquila Monterruez. Tell him, from me, I would be delighted to accept his offer to drive in his motor race!"

The wardroom gave a concerted cheer. Dangerous Dan looked like a pilgrim granted a glimpse of Mecca.

"By the way, sir," said Wilfred. "I'm afraid we've been asked to shift berth forrard of *Beaufortshire* as soon as we've completed fuelling."

"Whatever for?"

The Midshipman went pink. "It was my fault, sir. As we were coming into harbour this morning, Leading Seaman Gorbles said what a good idea it would be to show our films on the upper deck against *Beaufortshire's* ship's side, sir. So I'm afraid I jokingly asked their First Lieutenant if he would mind painting a white square on their side to give us a better picture. . . ."

"That does it! Mid, you can tell Aquila Monterruez that *Seahorse* will be entering a *team* for the International Targa Mango da SanGuana! Number One!"

"Sir!"

"Detail off a ship's motor racing team!"

"Aye aye, sir!"

Snorting with fury, The Bodger retired to his cabin with a bottle of whisky and a copy of the Highway Code.

★ 13 ★

THE news that H.M.S. *Seahorse* was entering an equipe for the Targa Mango was received by the British community in Cajalcocamara with astonishment and delight. Once they had assured themselves that the news was genuine, the British community rallied round. Mr MacTavish, the general manager of SanGuanOil, promised to supply the team's petrol and oil; Mr MacIntosh, executive head of SanGuana Motors (South America) Ltd promised tyres, sparking plugs and accessories; while the Anglican Church Ladies' Scooter Club provided crash helmets for the whole team.

The problem of cars proved to be no problem at all. The British community, except the British Consul, fell over themselves to lend their cars until Scuderia *Seahorse* (as they were christened by the SanGuana motoring press) promised to be, if not the most practised, at least the most varied, team in the race.

The British Consul was sternly against the project from the start but when he saw the response from the rest of the British community he felt obliged to show the way. The Bodger was deeply moved when the British Consul, Aaron-like, offered his own pearl-grey Armstrong-Siddeley. It was an imposing model, with a bonnet as high as a barn roof and doors which shut with a massive clang like the closing of a bank vault.

"Look after the old girl, won't you?" the British Consul said, wiping an unmanly tear from his eye.

The Bodger wrung the British Consul's hand wordlessly, recognizing the magnificence of the gesture.

The planter who turned over his swamp-stained Land Rover to Gotobed and the Chef had a more earthy approach.

"I've filled the tank with petrol and the back with beer. All you've got to do now is get going and keep going. If you do that, you're sure to get a place. Only one in ten finish this race anyway."

Mr MacLean, the managing director of the First National Bank of SanGuana and himself an experienced rally-driver, lent Wilfred and Derek his Sunbeam.

The car was a green saloon with the competent look of all veteran rally cars, being fitted with white-wall tyres, sunvisor, three spotlights, a row of motoring club badges and a large spade strapped to the boot.

On the morning of the race, The Bodger and his co-driver Dangerous Dan went down to have a look at the opposition. They could hear the noise from the square a mile away and if they had needed any convincing of the importance of the Targa Mango, the sight of the square itself provided it. The whole carnival of the international motor racing scene had been set up in the city of Cajalcocamara. Overhead banners advertised tyres, sparking plugs and brake linings. Girls in tight trousers and sun-glasses, shoe-shine boys, lottery ticket sellers, tourists wearing coloured shirts and carrying cameras, short fat men in light tropical suits smoking cigars, and SanGuana policemen in khaki tunics and puttees paraded the square and inspected the cars. The cars were spaced out at intervals along the square and were surrounded by chattering groups of men in overalls, photographers and impatient men with badges in their buttonholes.

The Bodger and Dangerous Dan stopped by one gleaming red car. The engine was warming up with all the authority of high octane fuel, dual-choke carburettors, a trifurcated manifold, a dynamically-balanced crankshaft and twin over-head highlift camshafts. The driver, a dedicated-looking man called Danny Auber, was sitting in the driver's seat, nodding and holding up his thumb.

"Nice drop of motor car!" Dangerous Dan shouted.

The engine noise dropped. The Bodger kicked one of the superb high-hysteresis racing tyres. "Cheap modern tin-ware," he said.

Danny Auber, triple winner of the Nurburgring 1000 Kilometre, hoisted himself out of the bucket seat and approached them. He had heard all about The Bodger and his equipe.

"Do you mind? You may think this is *frightfully* funny. We don't. You see, we *work* here."

The Bodger waved his hands deprecatingly. "But my dear chap. Please don't mind us."

Nonetheless, The Bodger was depressed by the incident. He felt like the captain of a visiting village cricket team who has just arrived at the ground to find his side matched against the Australians.

"Which is just about what we are," said The Bodger despondently.

The race was timed to start at noon but the first car away, Gotobed's Land Rover, mounted the starting ramp at eleven o'clock. This early start, unprecedented in the history of the race, was the outcome of a bitter argument between Aquila and the race officials. The race officials had protested vigorously against Scuderia *Seahorse's* entry.

The race marshals had pointed to relevant definitions in the rule book. The time-keepers had quoted relevant passages in the minutes of meetings of bodies governing international motor racing. The scrutineers had appealed to Aquila's sense of honour. The pit managers had tried bribery.

Aquila remained adamant. Commander Badger was a Freeman of Cajalcocamara and, furthermore, was driving at the personal invitation of the President. Either Scuderia *Seahorse* went to the starting line or there would be no International Targa Mango da SanGuana. The race officials retired and, turning a corner, came suddenly upon the spectacle of Gotobed and the Chef, wearing very fetching lilac crash helmets, sitting in a battered Land Rover. The officials crossed themselves, returned to Aquila, and insisted that Gotobed and the Chef start an hour before the rest. Aquila could not refuse; he himself was secretly conscience-stricken by Gotobed's motor-racing aspect.

Gotobed and the Chef were given a combined send-off by the ship's companies of *Beaufortshire* and *Seahorse* and the citizens of Cajalcocomara which exceeded any ovation given any driver within living memory. The B.B.C. overseas commentator was so moved by the scene that he compared it to the historic occasion when the Flying Mantuan, the incomparable Nuovolari himself, won the race in an Alfa-Romeo at an average speed of sixty-eight miles an hour. (The Midshipman, who had been unanimously voted Duty Officer and was sitting disconsolately by himself in *Seahorse's* wardroom, was strangely cheered by this description and poured himself another very large whisky.)

The Bodger and Dangerous Dan drove on to the starting ramp at one minute to twelve. As the President's personal guest, The Bodger was given the honour of starting the race proper. The SanGuana press had already given him a volume of publicity normally reserved for visiting Presidents of the United States and the reception the crowd gave him reduced the radio commentator to weak repetitions of the word "fabulous".

As the great bell of the Church of the Immaculate Conception across the square tolled noon, amid the "Vivas" of the crowd, and the ominous, predatory growling of the racing engines in the background, The Bodger and Dangerous Dan drove off.

The Targa Mango route lay first through the streets of Cajalcocamara and then out on to the eight-lane motorway which ran beside the sea to the Casino, twenty miles to the south, where the road turned sharply right and up into the mountains.

The motorway had been specially cleared of all other traffic. The lane lines extended to the horizon in a perfect example of perspective. It was not often that the Bodger was given a clear road and urged to drive as fast as he could along it. He pressed the accelerator to the floorboard and watched the speedometer climbing. He had settled in his seat and was beginning to enjoy himself when there was a banshee whine at his elbow, a blast of air and sound, and a low red car hurtled past and dwindled to a blur far ahead, its engine note rising and falling as the driver drew long sonorous chords from the close-ratio gearbox.

The Bodger was so startled that he almost lost control of his car. He had been shocked to discover that fast as he himself was driving he could be passed by another car travelling very much faster.

"He was still changing up, the bastard!" Dangerous Dan yelled in The Bodger's ear.

"Who was it?"

"Harry Boito! Broke the lap record three times running at the Nurburgring last year! Here comes another one! Don't bother about the mirror, Bodger! Just concentrate on driving! I'll tell you when he's coming. Here he comes *now. . . .*"

There was another roar and a blast of air and another car thunderbolted past them.

"Lew Cherubini! Won the Mille Miglia three years ago at an average of a hundred and five! They had to take his navigator Johnnie Dowland away afterwards!"

"Why?"

"He's been in a home ever since!"

The Bodger was driving at just over a hundred miles an

hour but one by one the red, green, blue and silver cars overhauled him and went ahead to the Casino turn where they flicked out of sight. Dangerous Dan supplied biographical notes.

". . . Ted Elgar and Gabby Faure! Only people who've ever won the Monte Carlo, the Tulip and the Safari in one year. . . ."

". . . Charlie Gounod! Won the Indianapolis Five Hundred this year at an average of a hundred and forty. . . ."

". . . Ferdy Herold! Just out of hospital! Turned over and caught fire at Monza two months ago. . . ."

Dangerous Dan's recital of the great names of motor racing lit a fierce fire in The Bodger's blood. He felt the competitive spirit rising in him. When he was overtaken yet again and forced out of line while approaching the Casino turn by a car which was travelling faster than any prevous one, The Bodger swore and trod harder on the accelerator.

". . . Let him *go*, Bodger! That was Jack Ibert! He's won this race twice running. . . ."

The other car slowed, drifted sideways, and accelerated out of the bend like a striking snake.

"Bodger," Dangerous Dan said, in a small voice. "Don't try and do it like that. . . ."

The mighty car heeled over. A group of SanGuanos standing by the straw bales leaped for their lives. Palm trees flickered across the bonnet. The wheel spun through The Bodger's hands. The road swung clear in front. The car came upright. Dangerous Dan opened his eyes again.

"Well done, Bodger," he croaked, weakly.

Derek and Wilfred approached the Casino bend with superb confidence. Derek had once built himself a hot-rod special while he was at college and had competed in hill climbs and sprints. He was the only member of Scuderia *Seahorse* who had ever competed in any sort of motor race before and he swept Mr MacLean's Sunbeam round the bend like a veteran.

"That was neatly done, Derek," said Wilfred.

"I wonder how far ahead the Boss is?"

"I shouldn't try and overtake him, if I were you."

"Why not?"

"That would be the most tactless thing any engineer officer did to his C.O.!"

A mile behind, in the Admiralty Representative's black Mercedes, Rusty and Dagwood (Scuderia *Seahorse* were driving in Navy List order) approached the bend more circumspectly.

"Watch it, Rusty," Dagwood cautioned. "Don't let all this go to your head. This looks like a nasty one."

"Don't worry, I always do cadence braking."

"What's that for God's sake?"

"You put the brakes on and off until you get the front of the car bouncing. You pick up the natural frequency of the suspension and force the tyres harder on to the road. Derek told me about it."

"All right, but just watch it."

As it happened, Rusty was given the opportunity for only one cadence. At the first pressure of the brake pedal the front wheels entered an oil slick. Where Rusty should have swung right, the car slid onwards. Rusty cadence-braked off the track, through the spectators who scattered right and left, down in an elegant cadenza over a flight of steps and on to the Casino lawn where the car pivoted round and dived into a dense bank of hydrangeas. Dagwood's door flew open and he fell out in a praying position amongst the hydrangeas.

"All good things around us," he sang in a hysterical voice, "are sent from heaven above. . . ."

Rusty felt himself all over, got out of the car, walked back to the track and was just in time to see the Chief E.R.A. and the Outside Wrecker negotiating the Casino bend in the Gieves' Representative's red M.G. The Chief E.R.A. was hunched over the wheel, his brows knotted with concentration under his beige crash helmet. The Outside Wrecker, however, had lost his crash helmet and was leaning over the side of the car, retching. Recognizing Rusty, he managed a despairing half-salute before he was whirled away.

Back at the starting ramp, the Coxswain and the Radio

Electrician, two sombre individuals, were giving the race starters a deal of trouble. They had been lent the Chief of Police's cerise and daffodil-coloured Cadillac hard-top and although the car was fitted with servo-assisted brakes, power-assisted steering and automatic two-pedal drive, the Coxswain was having difficulty in driving it up the ramp. At the third attempt the engine stalled.

The Coxswain pressed what he imagined was the starter button, whereupon the car underwent an extraordinary transformation. The wheels locked. Steel shutters rattled down over the windows. Steel blinds rose up to cover the doors. A red light blinked on the roof and a siren wailed on the front bumper. Inside the car, which was now an immobile steel box, articulated arms clamped steel helmets on the heads of the Coxswain and the Radio Electrician. Shutters on the dashboard slid back and revealed a brace of automatic pistols. In the opinion of the knowledgeable SanGuana crowd, it was even better than Gotobed.

There was a delay of several minutes before the Chief of Police's confidential locksmith was fetched from the crowd to free the wheels. The next two competitors, Connie Kreutzer and Leo Janacek, joint holders of the world land speed record for cars up to $1\frac{1}{2}$ litres, waited while the Coxswain and the Radio Electrician, still encased in their steel tomb, were wheeled away. Then, with a derisive exhaust blare and a shake of the fist, they were off.

Seahorse's next entrant was Gavin driving a plum-coloured Maserati, the property of Mr MacDonald, the principal of SanGuana University. He had as co-driver Miss MacDonald who was wearing a very chic pair of white overalls and a white crash helmet with an hibiscus blossom tucked under the rim. It looked as though Gavin was destined for an enjoyable Targa Mango and the crowd cheered him out of sight.

Gavin's place was taken by the Steward, sitting in a British racing green Jaguar lent by the manager of the Casino, a wealthy Levantine. The Casino manager had also lent his daughter, a striking ash-blonde who had been runner-up for the title of Miss SanGuana the previous year (the title being won by the daughter of the Chief of Police).

At this point the B.B.C. commentator lost his voice and was thankful to be relieved by the shipping forecast.

After some fiddling with the radio, Dangerous Dan found a programme of opera excerpts. They reached the mountains and the Te Deum which ended Act One of *Tosca* together.

"Te aeternum Patreus omino terra veneratur!" Dangerous Dan chanted as The Bodger pulled the big car from side to side across the twisting road.

"How're we doing, Dan?"

Dangerous Dan looked at his watch. "I make it we're averaging about fifty miles an hour. That's not nearly good enough for a win, of course, but it's not too bad."

The Bodger's attention was caught by the driving mirror.

"Get back, you peasant," he said.

Dangerous Dan glanced backwards. He had an impression of an infuriated steel animal with glass eyes surmounted by a pair of goggles, breathing down his neck.

"You'd better let them past, Bodger, or they'll burst something."

"All right, but he'll have to wait until we reach a straight bit. I'm not going to stop on these bends. God, what a heavenly view!"

The trees had been cut back from each bend in the road and as the car turned they could see the coastline of SanGuana laid out below. Far away in the blue distance they could pick out the tiny buildings of the city and, on the seaward side, the dockyard and its toy ships.

"Here's a straight bit."

". . . That was Hank Litolff and Jud Meyerbeer! They're the last of the big boys. Did you notice the new rear suspension?"

"Not particularly."

Higher in the mountains, Gotobed and the Chef were still leading the race by a considerable distance, being cheered through every village as they bowled along. They became so used to applause that they were surprised to reach one remote village where there was no cheering. The population was gathered round the only petrol pump in the village, silent, gloomy, as though they had gathered for the announcement of a catastrophe. A catastrophe had indeed occurred. The petrol pump was not working. It was the village's main industry; almost everybody made their livelihood, directly or indirectly, from the trade it brought. A mishap to the petrol pump was as great a disaster to them as the closing of the pit in a mining town. The village elders were congregated round the pump in solemn session. Now and then one of them tried the pump handle, with no success.

Gotobed stopped the Land Rover.

"Bliddy pomp's lost wackum," he said.

The crowd parted to let him through. He examined the pump closely and then, taking up a large stone, began to batter the pump body with it. A rumble of anger passed among the villagers. Gotobed ignored them. He unscrewed a small cap on top of the pump and, placing his lips to the hole, blew.

There was a subterranean rumbling and a heavy odour of petrol. Gotobed replaced the cap and jerked the pump handle. With each jerk a jet of petrol spurted out into the road.

The villagers gasped as though they had been parties to a miracle and gave Gotobed a spontaneous round of applause. The elders took him in their arms and embraced him. The girls threw hibiscus blooms from their hair into the back of the Land Rover.

Blushing like a peony, Gotobed had his tank filled and drove off in a haze of petrol, hibiscus and good wishes.

Just outside the village, the road forked. The Targa Mango took the right-hand road, while the left-hand road led to the wildernesses of the interior, petering out in swamps and jungles. The village elders put their heads together. One good turn deserved another. An adjustment was made to the road barriers.

The elders had just stepped back from the track when the first of Gotobed's pursuers appeared at the bottom of the village street, followed by the rest of the pack in full cry.

One after the other the shining, magnificent cars, the carriers of the flying horse, the three-pronged star and the raised trident, the bearers of the illustrious insignia and the famous initials, swept round to the left. Only Pete Mascagni and Karl Nicolai, fresh from their triumph at Le Mans and experienced Targa Mango drivers, attempted to bear right. The village elders imperiously waved them left.

When the procession of cars seemed to have stopped, the barriers were readjusted. The elders had hardly reached their places again when The Bodger appeared.

"Which way now, Dan?"

"Right."

"Right."

The next car was Gavin, who had been working steadily up through the field, bent on catching The Bodger. He had been driving above his skill and had already forced Leading Seaman Gorbles and the Signalman, in a pea-green Volkswagen provided by Mr MacGregor, the sporting editor of *The SanGuana*, into a ditch.

"In the old days," Leading Seaman Gorbles remarked to the Signalman, as the sound of Gavin's engine died away, "all the bastards were made dukes. Now all the bastards are made naval officers!"

But Gavin's retribution was near. Just as he caught sight of The Bodger, he misjudged the line of a bend and plunged off the road.

The car dropped bodily through some small trees, coasted down a slope and came to rest in a clearing between two bamboo clumps. A cloud of brilliant red butterflies rose into the air.

The trees rustled as they came upright again. An occasional engine droned along the road overhead, its sound filtered by the trees. The clearing looked out over the side of the mountain to the blue Pacific. The spot might have been chosen for a picnic, tête-à-tête.

Gavin turned and looked into the brown eyes, wide and startled as a fawn's. He kissed one shell-like ear under the hibiscus blossom.

"Darling," he whispered. "We've run out of road. . . ."

HIGHER up on the mountain, on the next bend, The
Bodger heard the sound of Gavin's passing.

"Sounds like one of our high-powered friends driving
into the scenery."

"Can't be," Dangerous Dan said. "They've all been
practising for months for this race. They must be miles
ahead by now. I'm afraid that must have been one of ours."

"Well I can't stop now. Let's just hope the Next-of-Kin
Book's up to date."

They overtook Gotobed at the top of the mountain pass
where he had stopped to admire the view and to start
the second crate of beer. Here they changed drivers and
Dangerous Dan took over for the hairpin descent down the
mountainside, humming the chorus of the Grand March
and Chorus from Act Two of *Aida* as he wrenched on the
hand-brake to lock the rear wheels round the curves. The
radio orchestra and chorus were bucking into the Soldier's
Chorus from Act Four of *Faust* as Dangerous Dan drove
out on the long dusty straights of the inland plateau.

"I wonder if the wind-screen washers work?" said
Dangerous Dan.

The Bodger pressed a rubber bulb which might have
been borrowed from a Victorian dentist's surgery. Two jets
of water struck the windscreen with the force of fire-hoses.

"Like opening an artery," The Bodger said.

When the great bell of the Church of the Immaculate
Conception struck half past four, a wave of alarm almost
amounting to panic passed amongst the race officials at
the finishing line. The winner of the Targa Mango could
be expected to average just over seventy-five miles an hour
and was due to finish any time after four and certainly
before a quarter past. It was now after half past four and
the five-mile Avenida d'Aquila, down which the winner
must come, was still empty. Furthermore, it was plain
from reports throughout the afternoon that strange things
had been happening on the track. The true position was
still not clear but officials at check-points along the route

denied any knowledge of Joe Perglosi, or Roger Quilter, or Jan Rameau or indeed any of the favourites. Every check-point relayed the same story. They had seen a pearl-grey Armstrong Siddeley, a green Sunbeam and a red M.G. but nothing else. Later, under pressure, they admitted to a Land Rover, driven fortissimo. But, emphatically, nothing else.

The finishing line control point was besieged by excited pit managers and reporters.

"What's happened to Alec Scriabin?"

"Do you mean to tell me they haven't seen *anything* of Joe Tartini? God, he's just won the Pan-American, he should take this one standing on his head!"

The officials wrung their hands, re-telephoned and returned with the same story, with the addition of a blue Vauxhall.

"That's my girl!" cried the Man from the Prudential. "That's my car!"

"Who's driving that?"

The officials consulted the list.

"Señor C. Stoker and Señor S. Coxswain."

". . . And with that report from Arthur Sullivan, our correspondent in Cajalcocamara, we return listeners to the studio. . . ."

"Damn! I wish I'd got that station before. We might have got some idea of how we're doing, Dan."

"We'll know in another half an hour. Can you get the opera again? I was rather enjoying that. Would you like to drive the last bit, Bodger?"

"That's very generous of you, Dan. I'd love to."

It struck The Bodger that they had not seen another car for some time.

"You sure we're on the right road, Dan? We haven't seen another car for a fair old time."

"We must be. They seem to be expecting us wherever we go. The Navy must be popularity boys round this neck of the woods, judging by the chuck-up we're getting. It's understandable, you know, Bodger. The bright boys can do a hundred and seventy on these stretches. They must be home and dry by now. Our team are all behind us. We're in between."

"Between the sublime and the ridiculous," said The Bodger.

Dangerous Dan looked at his watch. "Still, we're not doing too badly. We're averaging a steady fifty. That's pretty good for beginners. If enough of the lunatics up front pile themselves into brick walls we might even get a place."

The prospect of being placed in a major motor race went straight to The Bodger's head like old wine.

"Steady, old fruit," said Dangerous Dan. "I only said *might*. Ease off a bit. I've got a wife and two kids."

Antonio Vivaldi, the man with the chequered flag, had once been a matador and he had brought his skill with the cape to the track. His cape-work now had more aficionados on the race track than it had ever had in the corrida. The greatest names in motor racing had flashed under his flowing veronicas. The Targa Mango was his favourite race. He had looked forward to it and had even practised a special pass in its honour. But, at five minutes to six, Antonio sadly decided that his services would not now, if ever, be required. Stuffing his flag into a hip-pocket, he retired to the staff cantina.

He had barely tipped the bottle to his lips when there came a great growling roar from the crowd outside. Antonio Vivaldi, of all people, did not need to be told the sound's significance. Such a cheer could only greet the first man home in the Targa Mango.

Spluttering and choking, Antonio Vivaldi was just in time to reach the finishing line, unfurl his flag, and wave it as The Bodger shot past. It was not a graceful movement and would have been hooted out of any bull-ring in Spain, but it was the best he could do with the wine still running down his chin. However, he recovered enough to execute a series of properly elegant passes over the unspeakable Sunbeam, the unmentionable M.G. and the indescribable Vauxhall which followed. Where the other drivers were, Antonio Vivaldi had no idea. He stuffed his flag away again and resumed his bottle, only vaguely conscious that he had played a walking-on part in the twilight of the gods. There were no other finishers except, at midnight, an erratically-driven Land Rover and, at dawn, a Jaguar containing a dreamy Steward and a rapturous ash-blonde.

When the news of The Bodger's winning drive was first flashed round the world, incredulous editors searched their press cuttings and cabled their correspondents to come in out of the sun. It was not until a picture of The Bodger, garlanded, dust-stained, smiling, and being embraced by the Chief of Police's daughter, was radioed to the world's capitals and the headlines appeared "British Cars, 1, 2, 3 in T. Mango!", "New Racing Star!", and "Gentlemen, A Toast—The Bodger!", that the motor racing press and industry awoke to the fact that they had been the victims of what *The Times* later described as "the greatest turn-up for the book since David and Goliath".

The three-legged donkey had won the Derby, slowing up. The tortoise had soundly thrashed the hare. Cartoonists hugged their sides and sharpened fresh pencils. In Modena and Turin and Coventry and Stuttgart men looked at each other in a wild surmise. In Detroit, executives fed the result into computers and said: "Overseas-sales-wise, this is a severe reversalization. It's gonna cost us several mega-bucks, R.J." In Paris, small swarthy men tore their berets into shreds and jumped on them, crying: "Nom d'un poisson, alors qu'est ce que c'est que ça, ce *Bodgaire*?" In London, a bewildered director of the winning firm was shaken from his club armchair and thumped on the back by the committee. All over the United Kingdom, Chief Constables added another name to their lists.

Deep in the unmapped wilderness beyond the mountains of SanGuana, a long line of cars worth over a million pounds had come to a halt because the leading car was axle-deep in a swamp. The magnificent engines were now motionless, gently pinging as they cooled in the shade of a line of mango trees.

The wilderness had already begun the process of assimilation. Ants tentatively probed the superb high-hysteresis racing tyres and wandered questioningly over the mirror-finished engine surfaces. A large green snake dropped with a slithering plop into a bucket seat. The first tendril of a searching vine had completed half a careful revolution around the wire spoke of a wheel.

The drivers had left their cars and were clustered round Wolf-Ferrari who was studying a silver cigarette case on which was engraved a small-scale map of South America.

At half past one the next morning, The Bodger, still wearing his garland, walked back along the jetty towards *Seahorse* alone. The Bodger could not remember a time when he had been more pleased with himself and with life. He and Dangerous Dan had won the Targa Mango (although exactly how, The Bodger was still not sure). Aquila had been very hospitable. They had all been invited to a ball at the British Consulate where they had eaten Crème de Carburettor Soup, Lobster Thermidor au Armstrong Siddeley, Chicken M.G. with slices of orange Sunbeam, followed by café au Vauxhall. The wines had been excellent and plentiful. Afterwards The Bodger had danced with the Chief of Police's daughter who was South American rhumba champion. All sorts of genial people, and even Commodore Richard Gilpin, had come up and shaken him by the hand. He had refused an invitation to drive in the Dutch Grand Prix at Zandvoort the next week. Over the brandy Aquila had decided to form his own navy and offered him the job of Commander-in-Chief. Altogether it had been a memorable evening.

It had all been splendid, but shortly after midnight The Bodger had felt a need for solitude, a craving for that communion with his inner gods which comes upon many men after an evening's drinking. The Bodger's walk through the town led him, with that unerring instinct which leads a naval officer to his bunk like a homing pigeon, back to the jetty.

The Bodger steadied himself on *Beaufortshire's* gangway while he measured the remaining distance to *Seahorse* by eye. His attention was distracted by the row of lights hanging on the gangway rail. The lights fascinated him.

They led his glance towards *Beaufortshire's* quarter-deck. It seemed to The Bodger an inviting sort of place.

Carefully, The Bodger mounted the gangway. The quartermaster at the top regarded him with hostility. The Bodger resented the man's look.

"Where's the Officer of the Day?"

"Turned in."

"Well, get him out then."

The quartermaster hesitated. He had not yet placed The Bodger. He was definitely not one of *Beaufortshire's* officers but he had nevertheless an undefinable, familiar look about him.

"Tell him the Commanding Officer of H.M.S. *Seahorse* wants him."

"Aye aye, sir."

All the quartermaster's doubts were instantly resolved.

"Tell him I want the bar opened. Immediately. Urgently!"

Had the quartermaster then turned back and politely asked The Bodger to leave, all might still have been well. But the quartermaster only hesitated and went to call the Officer of the Day.

The Officer of the Day was the Navigating Officer.

"I'm afraid our bar is closed, sir," he said coldly.

"*Closed!*" The Bodger pondered upon the enormity of the suggestion. "What a ridiculous idea, if I may respectfully say so."

"I'm sorry, sir."

"Very well. Where's your captain?"

"The Captain is ashore, sir."

There comes to every man at some time the sickening certainty that the bartender is not going to give him a drink. The Bodger bowed before the verdict.

"Very well."

The Bodger negotiated the gangway once more. The quartermaster and the Navigating Officer congratulated themselves that they had conducted a tricky interview with tact and finesse, and retired.

With one foot on *Seahorse's* gangway, The Bodger stopped. An idea had just struck him. It was a concept of such imagination, such consummate daring, that The Bodger remained where he was for a moment, quite stunned by his own virtuosity.

Sober, The Bodger could contain his own more outrageous flights of humour; in the cold light of day, he could resist temptation. But under such a starlit night, after such a day, The Bodger resisted only briefly and capitulated.

The Bodger looked cautiously over *Beaufortshire's* upper deck. It was deserted. Stealthily he moved along the jetty, removed *Beaufortshire's* wires from the bollards, and placed them on the jetty. Then he ran to *Seahorse*, crossed the gangway, saluted gravely, and mounted to his own bridge.

"Slow ahead together," he said.

Like a cat The Bodger shinned down the ladders and padded aft to the motor room where he again saluted and said: "Slow ahead together, sir, aye aye, sir."

The Bodger made the switches and set the submarine's main motors turning slowly ahead.

"Both main motors going ahead, sir," he said, in a reasonable imitation of the Signalman's sepulchral voice.

The Bodger ascended to the bridge and said to the voice-pipe: "Very good."

He remained for some time looking aft, watching the water churning from *Seahorse* towards *Beaufortshire*.

"Stop together."

Once more, The Bodger descended to the motor room.

"Stop together, sir. Aye aye, sir."

The Bodger broke the main motor switches, walked forward to his cabin, and stretched himself, still fully clothed and garlanded, upon his bunk.

In the distance, as he fell asleep, The Bodger could hear the sound of voices but they were no more to him than the faraway buzzing of flies around a rubbish heap on a hot summer's day.

★ 15 ★

A SUBMARINE returning from abroad was normally given a very modest press reception—seldom more than a column and a photograph in the local paper and a paragraph in the national press. H.M.S. *Seahorse's* return from SanGuana was given the most complete press coverage the Submarine Service had ever experienced. A helicopter met the ship in the Channel, before she had raised St Catherine's, before even Geronwyn Evans had struck his tuning fork and led off "First the Nab and then the Warner". She was photographed every inch of the way to her berth where Captain S/M and his staff were fighting to keep their feet amongst the television cameras and the clamouring crowd of reporters and families. Photographers swarmed over the jetty and the catamarans, snapping *Seahorse's* ensign, The Bodger's hat, Leading Seaman Gorbles, and in passing, the Naval Correspondent of the *Daily Disaster* who was struck smartly on the head by *Seahorse's* first heaving line.

Some of the press deployed to interview members of the Ship's Company but most of them made for The Bodger. The Bodger was ready for them.

"It was team-work that did it," he said, solemnly. "Team-work all the way."

"Commander Badger," said the Naval Correspondent of the *Daily Disaster*, "do you intend to take up motor racing seriously? Don't misunderstand me, I mean you've won the Targa Mango but. . . ."

"I don't intend to race again."

"Commander Badger, is it true that you drove in this race as publicity for the Royal Navy?"

The Bodger thought very hard, very swiftly; this question had a curly, spiked tail.

"My team and I drove at the personal invitation of the President, as his guests."

"Commander Badger," said the editor of *Woman and Garden* coyly, "there's a rumour of a romance between you and Señorita Alvarez. . . ."

"Who's she?"

"Come, come, Commander. The daughter of the Chief of Police."

"Oh *her*!" A delighted smile spread over The Bodger's face. This was a moment for which he had waited all his adult life.

"No," he said slowly, "we are just good friends."

Whatever the reaction in the national press, The Bodger's return was only a one day sensation in the Submarine Service. The Submarine Service had more important things to think about. The Reunion was due.

The Reunion was the submariners' annual beano. Its date was sacred in every submariner's diary; only death took precedence (and then only after the Mess Secretary had been informed). The Reunion had the same effect on submariners as the Bonnie Prince's fiery cross had upon the clansmen. For it, they abandoned their wives and families. They left their desks at Lloyds, their farms in Dorset, their market gardens in Leicestershire, their bookshops in Winchester, and their garages in Croydon. They left their offices, their sales rooms, their boards, their spades, their benches, their psychologists' couches and converged upon Portsmouth like a mass migration of thirst-crazed lemmings. The first of them began to assemble three days before the event and the last of them were not normally carried away until three days after it and while the Reunion was in progress the foreign exchange market could collapse in ruins, the Middle East flame in insurrection, earthquakes devastate the western hemisphere and the whole of England itself submerge under a tidal wave but all those who had ever been submariners would remain oblivious, gathered under one roof and pouring whisky down their assembled throats just as fast as it would drain away.

When they were all present, the submariners could claim at least one holder of almost every honour, medal and decoration in the Gazette. There were men at the Reunion who had fought a submarine through the nets and mine cables of the Dardanelles into the Sea of Marmara and watched a Turkish cruiser settle on the bottom. There were men there who had patrolled in a submarine in the shallow water, the sudden freshwater layers, and the short summer nights of the Skagerrak. There were men who had run blind through the minefields of the Java Sea with a magnetic compass, a stop-watch and several prayers. There were men who had been depth-charged constantly for a day and a half, who had heard a mine-cable scrape the length of the ship before swinging clear, who had swum seven miles to shore after their ship was mined, who had cleared unexploded bombs from the casing in broad daylight, and who had escaped from three hundred feet with buckets over their heads. They represented a weapon which, in its British guise, had borne the heat and burden of the war from the Atlantic to the Pacific by way of the Mediterranean, and which, in its American counterpart, had crippled the Japanese navy and ripped the bottom out of the Japanese mercantile fleet. It was also a weapon which, used by the enemy, had brought the United Kingdom itself within a few months of starvation.

"All I can say is," said Dangerous Dan, who was already on his fourth whisky, "you wouldn't think it to look at them."

Dangerous Dan had often noticed that the most distinguished submarine officers were also the scruffiest. "There's normally a fly-button missing for every D.S.O.," he said.

Dangerous Dan's eye rested on the Senior Submariner present, a venerable and very distinguished Admiral whose uniform was encrusted with orders and who possessed a row of medals fourteen inches in length and forty years in time. The Senior Submariner was now wearing a very baggy and faded Glen check with scuffed leather elbow-pieces.

"As I see it," the Senior Submariner was saying to a circle of clients, "submarines haven't advanced a bit since I joined 'em. Not one bit!"

The circle of clients clicked their teeth deprecatingly.

"*You* sir," the Senior Submariner said to a very young, fair-haired submarine C.O. with brilliant white teeth who had just taken over his first command. "What's your top underwater speed now?"

"Nine and a half knots, sir."

"What did I tell you! *My* first boat did ten! That was in the first world war!"

"We have advanced a little, sir, in many ways."

"We've fitted *heads* in 'em now, if that's what you mean. When I joined my first boat as Pilot there were no heads. Used to get pretty constipated, I can tell you. The Captain and I, he's dead now poor fellow, used to sit out on either side of the tower in the mornings. One morning off the Scillies, I remember it well, we were sitting there, one on either side, when I heard a bloody great *thump* from the Captain's side. 'Well *done*, sir!' I said. 'Well done be buggered,' he said, 'that was my bloody binoculars!'"

The Reunion agenda had a reassuring permanence. A submariner returning after many years abroad would find the same people observing the same ritual as on his last visit. The programme was simple. It began with drinks, continued with a speech by the Senior Submariner, more drinks, a speech by the Admiral, more drinks, perhaps a speech by a visiting V.I.P. and ended with drinks.

The Senior Submariner made his speech as though he had left a lighted cigarette at the other end of the room and was anxious to get back to it. He welcomed everyone present to the Reunion, expressed his pleasure at seeing them there, hoped they would all enjoy themselves and stood down to a comfortable and thankful volume of applause.

"That's what I like about old Glueballs," Dangerous Dan said to Wilfred irreverently. "He always cuts it short."

"There's something I've wanted to ask you for a long time, Dan. Does the Prime Minister really shoot over your land?"

"Of course not. We live in South Kensington. But I wasn't going to let that young snob get away with it. Good heavens, there's Black Sebastian! He looks more like Old Nick than ever. I wonder what he's doing here?"

Black Sebastian's presence at the Reunion had already caused a great deal of comment; his presence there was almost as incredible as the conversion of St Paul. He himself seemed to be aware of the incongruity and was wearing the artificial smile of a medieval torturer unaccountably forced to mix socially with his victims. He was talking to a man who had joined submarines at the same time but who had long ago left the Navy and taken up insurance.

"I can't think why we don't have far more Shop-Windows," Black Sebastian was saying. "Why tell a sailor to look out for submarines when nine times out of ten he hasn't the faintest idea what he's looking for?"

"Quite," said the insurance man politely.

"Whenever a submarine does a Shop-Window for me I have it raising and lowering periscopes, radar masts, and snort mast until every sailor in my ship's company can tell me exactly which is which as soon as it breaks surface. It takes all day but I do it."

"You always were an unreasonable sort of bastard, Sebastian," said the insurance man, and walked away to get another drink.

Nearby, two very aged submariners were laughing into their whiskies.

". . . Nobby, you've told me that story every year for forty years. I didn't think it funny forty years ago and I don't think it funny now. . . ."

Nobby stiffened.

"That's . . . that's exactly the sort of ill-mannered remark I expect from a man who never commanded anything better than a C-boat. . . ."

"I may tell you, the C-boats were the best submarines God ever gave this earth. No C-boat captain would have had *you* anywhere near him. . . ."

After which unforgivable remark, the two very aged submariners moved sharply apart and cut each other dead for the rest of the Reunion, as they had done every year for the past forty.

The Lamm of God had been cornered by another aged submariner.

". . . Then in 1923 I joined K.67 as Jimmy. God, what a boat! The captain, he died a good few years ago, was as queer as a nine-bob note. He used to read Omar Khayyam to the sailors every Sunday. He once shook Chief in the middle of the night because he'd just tried the whistle and thought it sounded A sharp instead of A flat. . . ."

The Admiral's Chief of Staff was hemmed in by yet another short-sighted and arthritic ancient.

"I'll give you some advice, boy. It was given to me by me first captain before the war, the first war that was, and I never forgot it. It was me first watch and I was as nervous as a virgin. I had the periscope goin' up and down like a whore's drawers. Then I heard water rushing some-

313

where in the control room bilges. When I told the Captain he said 'Go and see what it is you stupid clot.' Always run towards the sound of the water, he said. There you are. Always run towards the water at sea and the whisky in harbour. You're just starting out in life so I pass it on to you. So don't you forget that, heh?"

"Actually, I'm thinking of retiring next year," said the Chief of Staff mildly.

"Heh?"

The Bodger was talking to a man who had the dark, ruddy tan of one who habitually worked out of doors. The Bodger was having a busy Reunion. It was some years since he had attended and he had many friends there who came up to shake hands and demand the full story of the Targa Mango. The Reunion also gave The Bodger some moments of nostalgia; it seemed a long time since his first Reunion, when he and Commander S/M had removed the Admiral's trousers.

"It seems a long time since the first time, Paddy, doesn't it?" The Bodger said.

"Like last century."

Paddy was wearing a shabby Cheviot tweed and black boots. He twisted his neck from side to side occasionally as though it was not often he wore a collar. He had long dark sideburns, a broad fleshy nose, and looked like a poacher. He had been a member of The Bodger's term at Dartmouth and now farmed a hundred acres in Shropshire.

"How's the farm going now?"

Paddy shrugged. "So so. You can never tell with a farm. It takes about twenty years before you can really say. That's if you don't go bust in the first five. One thing *is* certain, I work a damn sight harder now than I ever did in the Service. Do my eyes deceive me, or is that Black Sebastian over there?"

"Yes. I was wondering what he was doing here myself."

"*I* wonder how he ever lived as long as this. If ever there was a candidate for a quick shove over the side on a dark night, it's him. But tell me, Bodger, what's your future now?"

"I don't know. I was all set on retiring but all of a sudden this job in *Seahorse* dropped out of the blue. . . ."

"I heard about that. What actually *did* happen in that motor race. . . ."

Black Sebastian was talking to the Admiral.

". . . I noticed when I was in the Med during the war that submarine losses followed a clear pattern. It was like a ski-ing holiday. You either break your leg on the first day or the last day. When a boat first came out, the first couple of patrols were the anxious ones. They were either so cautious they got thumped without ever knowing what happened or the Captain had been seeing too many Errol Flynn films and got thumped thinking he was God's gift to the war effort. Then they seemed to get into their stride and all was well. After about a year, the losses went up again. The Captain was over-confident or just plain worn out. I can see the same sort of thing happening again. . . ."

"Sir?"

The Chief of Staff appeared at the Admiral's elbow. The Admiral started, as though from a deep trance.

"Oh yes. . . . My speech. . . . Excuse me. . . ."

The Admiral Submarines' speech was the crux of the Reunion. The Admiral himself once described it as "a mixture of a prize-giving speech, a chairman's annual report, and What The Stars Foretell."

"Sssh," said Dagwood to the group round him, "the Speech from the Throne."

"Gentlemen," said the Admiral, "while I was preparing this speech the other day and turning over a few of the things I might say in my mind, I came across some notes left by a predecessor of mine who was Admiral here just after the First World War. What he said then is still true now. The same words still apply. . . ."

"Because we're still using the same submarines," a sardonic voice muttered, from the back.

". . . He said: 'I am convinced that the submarine has a greater future than any other weapon. I prophesy that one day the submarine will occupy the place the battle-ship holds now.' You may think those unbelievably intelligent sentiments for an Admiral. . . ." The Admiral paused for laughter. ". . . But they must have seemed the words of a lunatic thirty years ago. They were said at a time when the Navy was sinking towards its lowest ebb since the reign of Charles II, when there was a strong move in international circles to ban the submarine altogether, as being *unfair*. That particular Admiral's listeners must have thought the old boy was a little touched in the head. He was indeed retired very soon afterwards. But now, those words are coming true. They are no longer the mad pronouncements of a visionary. They are almost a cliché. I believe that the nuclear submarine, which can fire a missile while still submerged, is the supreme strategical weapon. The world has seen nothing like it. The Submarine Service has been handed the instrument of Armageddon. It's a sobering thought to me that the young men we're now training as submariners may one day be in charge of a weapon which might have been measured for St Michael the Archangel. . . ."

Captain S/M leaned over to the Chief of Staff. "You've been letting the Admiral read the newspapers again," he whispered accusingly.

The Chief of Staff blushed and looked guilty.

"The Submarine Service is now approaching a period of great change. It is assuming greater importance every year. You can tell that it is growing in importance because the *Gunnery* Branch are trying to get in on it. Only today I squashed a proposal from Whale Island that our nuclear submarines should each carry a resident gunnery officer! I'm only sorry that I shan't be here to see these changes carried out but I know that my successor feels much as I do. . . ."

The Admiral was a moving speaker. He was a dedicated man, but full of humour. He also had an Admiral's essential quality, of optimism in public. When he had finished, those of his listeners still serving squared their shoulders, confident of good times and more submarines building just around the corner. Those who had retired began to feel that perhaps they had been too hasty.

"With any luck that should be all the speeches," said Paddy.

"No," said Commander S/M. "We've got the visiting V.I.P. to come. Although it doesn't look as though he's turned up yet."

The visiting V.I.P. did not in fact arrive until the company had been drinking for another two hours and had long forgotten all about speeches.

The Parliamentary Secretary to the Ministry of Political Warfare was a political chameleon. Like the Vicar of Bray, he remained whichever government was at Westminster. He had sat for an agricultural constituency in the West of England for more than forty years and had so impressed successive Prime Ministers with his ability that he was even now, at sixty-eight, still spoken of as a coming man. He had been on the fringe of power for so long that he had acquired the mannerisms of power itself. He walked and talked like a cabinet minister. His long years as a politician had given him a touch of absent-mindedness and an ability to speak at any time on any subject. The Chief of Staff had intended to ask the Minister himself but at the last minute had settled for the Parliamentary Secretary because he lived locally.

The Parliamentary Secretary knew exactly what was required of him. Apologizing for his lateness, which he briskly blamed on a late sitting in the House, he brushed through the introductions and edged steadily nearer the dais whence, he knew with the infallible intuition of a born politician, the speeches were made. He was ready to speak long before his audience were ready to listen to him and was actually speaking before half of them were aware that he had arrived.

"Gentlemen," said the Parliamentary Secretary, reading from a sheet of paper, "may I say that I think it a great honour to be asked to speak at your Reunion. . . ."

"Who's that funny little man?" asked Dangerous Dan, who was on his fourteenth whisky.

"Some friend of the Chief of Staff's," said someone, unjustly.

". . . It has always been a pet theory of mine that the Anglo-Saxon races make the finest tank crews of any. If I may roughly paraphrase a favourite saying of the Emperor

Charles V, To God I speak Spanish, to women Italian, to men French, and to my tank—English!"

The submariners raised their heads from their glasses in astonishment. The Bodger caught the Chief of Staff's look of mortal agony and shouted "Hear hear!" in a resonant voice. A few others echoed the sentiment in a bewildered chorus.

"Thank you," said the Parliamentary Secretary, simply. "After all, we *invented* the tank! We perfected it. And we made brilliant use of it, all the way from the poppy-fields of Flanders to the desert sands of El Alamein."

While the Chief of Staff stood wearing the unmistakable look of a Staff Officer when things are going irretrievably, ludicrously, wrong, the Parliamentary Secretary went on to describe a few of the more important technical advances in armoured warfare in recent years, to outline the careers of several outstanding armoured corps commanders, and to express his gratitude once more at being asked to attend the Reunion. It was a carefully composed speech for which someone had plainly done a lot of checking of facts and background and it left the Reunion as well-informed about tanks as any group of submariners had ever been. On reaching the end of his sheet of paper, the Parliamentary Secretary folded it away, stepped down from the dais, accepted a drink, and made general conversation with the Chief of Staff and several other officers.

Anxious not to embarrass their guest, the Chief of Staff racked his brain for tank anecdotes. He saw Captain S/M standing on the outskirts of the circle. "Don't just stand there," he hissed frantically. "Don't you know any Shaggy Tank stories?"

Captain S/M was more than equal to the emergency.

"I well remember taking command of my first Centurion . . ." he began.

The wardroom hall porter touched Commander S/M's sleeve.

"Signal just come, sir."

Commander S/M read the signal, gave a great hoot of jubilation, and showed it to Captain S/M. The signal's contents began to pass rapidly among the crowd. The

Bodger, on the other side of the room, was suddenly aware that he had become the centre of attention.

"Congratulations, Bodger!"

In a moment, The Bodger was surrounded by eager hands competing to clap him on the back. A dozen voices shouted their congratulations. The Bodger himself was quite bewildered.

"But I don't understand it," he kept saying. "I was passed over. I was passed over some time ago."

"Well, there it is, Bodger, in black and white!"

"Let me see that signal again."

"There it is. From Lieutenant-Commander to Commander. Robert Bollinger Badger, H.M.S. *Seahorse*."

"Well, fillip me with a three-man beetle! This calls for a drink! This calls for several drinks! But I still don't understand it. . . ."

"Don't look so baffled, Bodger," said Commander S/M. "You had to be promoted. The Press are already clamouring for it. Your drive in that race was the best piece of world-wide publicity for the Navy in many a year. The Army and the R.A.F. are green with envy, I can tell you. They're already planning their counter-measures, too. I hear the pongos are going in for the America Cup next year and the crab-fats are training a team to climb Everest. . . ."

"I must admit I had my doubts about you in *Seahorse*, Badger," said the Admiral. "I had a lot of doubts, I confess it. But it wasn't only that infernal motor race. You've made a damned good start in that ship. You were worth it on that alone."

"I can't think why you've waited all this time, Bodger," said Dangerous Dan, who was now on his twenty-fourth whisky.

"I'm sorry we're not all here, sir," said Wilfred. "I'm afraid the Midshipman is on a dirty week-end in Ooze-mouth. But for the rest of us, I can sincerely say 'Congratulations,' sir."

"Badger?" said the Parliamentary Secretary. "That's a familiar name."

The Bodger prepared to tell the story of the Targa Mango again.

"Oh yes, I remember. Somebody sent me a docket a year or two ago marked 'New Blood in Submarines'. Well of course *I* don't know anything about submarines. Never have. But I did my best. I got out a list of Lieutenant-Commanders and yours was the first name on the list. So I recommended you. Obviously I knew what I was doing, eh? Now, I must go, Admiral. I have another engagement tonight. I have to speak at the Southern Command Royal Tank Corps Old Comrades Association dinner. So I'll wish you good night. Good-bye, and thank you. Best of luck, Badger!"

Beaming genially to right and left, the Parliamentary Secretary went out to his car and drove off, leaving the Admiral, Captain S/M and The Bodger staring after him.

The Bodger's promotion set the seal on the Reunion. The noise redoubled. The Bodger's health was drunk in a variety of liquids. The atmosphere became charged with the authentic crackle of a successful party.

At three o'clock in the morning, The Bodger suddenly said: "What was that the Admiral said in his speech about his successor? Is he going?"

"Haven't you heard?" said Commander S/M wearily. "It's all been changed. Black Sebastian was promoted Rear Admiral today. He's going to be the next Admiral here."

The Bodger raised his glass. "Ah well," he said. "It's a funny life."